ONE NIGHT WITH A ROGUE

ONE NIGHT WITH A ROGUE

KIMBERLY CATES
CHRISTINA DODD
DEBORAH MARTIN
ANNE STUART

St. Martin's Paperbacks

ONE NIGHT WITH A ROGUE

"Such Wild Enchantment" copyright © 1995 by Kim Ostrom Bush.

"The Lady and the Tiger" copyright © 1995 by Christina Dodd.

"Too Wicked for Heaven" copyright © 1995 by Deborah Martin Gonzales.

"Dangerous Touch" copyright © 1995 by Anne Kristine Stuart Ohlrogge.

Excerpt from *A Glimpse of Heaven* © 1995 by Barbara Dawson Smith.

ISBN: 0-312-95611-8

Printed in the United States of America

St. Martin's Paperbacks edition/October 1995

10 9 8 7 6 5 4 3 2 1

Contents

SUCH WILD ENCHANTMENT

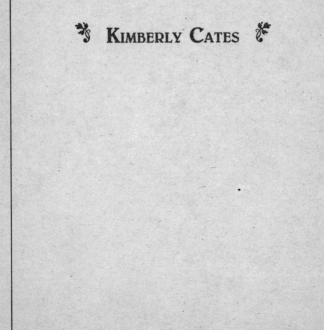

KIMBERLY CATES

ONE

It was a perfect night to go to the devil, but the Honorable Rawdon Wyatt wasn't accustomed to making the journey alone. There had been a time when a half dozen cohorts would have crowded around him, eager for adventure. When flasks of brandy would have been passed about, accompanied by tales far hotter than the burn of the liquor on their tongues.

Yet tonight, there was no one left to share the silver flask at his waist. They had all deserted him one by one, left him, a lone sentinel, in the night.

His gloved hands tightened on the reins of his restive stallion, the night wind tugging at his silver-lined cloak. The black-silk mask bound across his face was glued there with a sheen of sweat he'd tried to cool far too often by the subtler fire of brandy.

Pistols lay heavy on his thighs. A tricorne, its plume red as blood, was perched on the midnight-hued waves of his hair. No Knight of the Road had ever appeared more dangerous, more dashing.

He should have been having a bloody wonderful time, delighting in the feat he was about to pull off upon his dearest friend—no, Rawdon brought himself up short in grim disgust—his most recent betrayer. The man who had broken a blood vow . . .

Rawdon closed his eyes, remembering that long ago

night in the smoky tavern, Percy Davenant grabbing his shirtfront, his brandy-slurred voice almost desperate.

Promise me, Rawdon—a blood vow! Should I ever commit such an abomination, stop me—at gunpoint if you have to . . .

Rawdon's green eyes narrowed as his gaze swept the silvery ribbon of road that shimmered in the moonlight. He was only acting according to Percy's wishes. Wishes laid forth when the man was still sane and reasonable. Before he'd lost his mind.

The clatter of coach wheels in the distance made Rawdon stiffen. His fingers curled around the butt of his pistol, and he drew it out, the barrel gleaming in the light of the moon.

Was the poor bastard attempting to break his own neck already? Rawdon wondered as the equipage hurtled out of the darkness, tipping onto two wheels as it rounded the corner.

Rawdon glimpsed the coachman and the guard beside him, blunderbuss clutched in quaking hands, the whites of his eyes visible in the moonglow. Hell, Rawdon thought, he'd be lucky if the bastard didn't blast him to kingdom come. But even the supreme sacrifice was not too much to demand in this circumstance.

With a whoop, Rawdon spurred his mount into the middle of the road, blocking it. "Stand and deliver!" Rawdon roared in true highwayman fashion.

The coachman sawed back on the reins. The careening vehicle overbalanced, teetering as the horses pawed and reared. The back wheels of the coach slipped over the road edge, then, in an instant, the equipage tipped over with a resounding crash.

The chap with the blunderbuss tumbled head over hindmost off of his perch. Rawdon glimpsed a flash of white face as the man glanced up at him in a heartbeat of indecision. Cowardice won out over courage. The bandy-legged fool raced for the woods. His defection was enough to make the other man bolt.

Rawdon guided his horse to the side of the coach

where the wheels still spun wildly, the coach door pointing skyward. "For God's sake, Percy," he groused in disgust as he wrenched open the door. "It's just like you to get half-drunk coachmen and ruin everything."

He expected swearing, his friend's tousled blond head thrusting out of the coach. And perhaps a bit of sniveling from the female inside, he thought with no little chagrin.

Instead, a pint-sized fury popped out, her face concealed in the folds of a chocolate-dark cloak and hood, a pistol gleaming in her slender hands.

Rawdon gaped at the apparition, astonishment striking him like a fist to the chest. Bloody bulls in Heaven! Could he have robbed the wrong coach?

"Sir, I would much prefer not to shoot you," the moonstruck fairy said in even tones. "I may need the ammunition later, and I don't want to waste it."

"You—you what?"

"I don't have anything for you to steal. I had to run away in the greatest haste and there wasn't time to gather anything of value. I'm very sorry for your trouble, but there should be another coach along soon enough."

She was clambering out of the coach, her eyes flicking with more dread toward the road behind her than the very dastardly figure Rawdon had worked so hard to cut in his highwayman guise.

"Oh, bother!" she said, glancing at the hopelessly tangled horses. She turned her face toward Rawdon, her voice almost pleading. "I don't suppose you would be willing to cut one of these beasts free for me. After all, you *are* the one who got them so hopelessly tangled. I know it's not the usual highwayman task, but I've heard the Knights of the Road can be wonderfully noble at times to ladies in distress, and I assure you, I'm quite desperate."

"Desperate? You must be insane!" Rawdon muttered as the woman slid down the belly of the coach, landing on the ground. She barely reached his shoulder. If he *had* been a brigand, he could have snapped her in two like a bit of dry kindling.

"Blast it, you little fool, don't you have the wits to be afraid of me? I could be itching to cut your throat! Or ravish you!"

There was very real dismay in her voice. "No! You—you couldn't possibly want to . . ." Was it possible for such a petite form to radiate so much indignation? "One man given to such wild hysterics is quite enough," she said in steely tones. "If you start talking about ravishing and locking me in towers until I melt of passion I *will* have to shoot you!"

Rawdon's mouth curved in a grin. The first real grin he'd flashed anyone since the day Percy had given him the dreadful news of his betrayal. "Ah, so you're fleeing a distraught lover, are you, poor angel?"

"Yes. I had to climb out a window to escape him. I nearly broke my elbow climbing to the ground. He's threatening the most outrageous things. And he shot poor Matthew in a duel. Please, if you would help me on my journey, I am certain God would wipe away the most dastardly of the tally of sins upon your soul."

"Would He? I assure you, it's quite a long tally, my dear. Would your guardian angel be too forward to ask to see this treasure of loveliness I'm to snatch away from your poor lover's hands?"

"He's *not* my lover! He's a silly boy who doesn't know the meaning of the word *no!* I've said it to him a hundred thousand times."

Rawdon's grin faded, a dull twist of melancholy wrenching unexpectedly in his chest. "Sometimes it's damn hard for a gentleman to listen to what he has no wish to hear."

He shoved his own pistol into his boot top, then reached one hand toward the rim of her hood. "Don't fear," he soothed as she flinched away. He lowered the veil of velvet, turning her until moonlight melted over gold curls, a heart-shaped face he turned more fully into the light. "I won't hurt you—*sonofabitch! You!*"

If she'd blasted a hole in his chest, he couldn't have been more stunned. He dropped the hood as if it had turned to flame. "Serena! Serena Creighton! What the devil are you doing out after dark? Where the devil is your governess?"

That rosebud mouth dropped open, eyes he knew were violet widening until they seemed the size of the coach wheels still wobbling about. "How did you know my name? I have no acquaintance with any highwayman. At least, not that I know of." She took a stumbling step back, her voice thickening with dismay. "Did Bertrand send you after me? If he did, I vow you'll never take me alive!"

"Bertrand? Ah, so this imaginary lover of yours has a name, does he?" Rawdon snapped. "Never fear, oh fairest of angels. *Bertrand* didn't send me to fetch you. But you might wish he had by the time I'm done with you." Rawdon raised his fingertips to his mask, slipping the knot free. The bit of silk his latest mistress had fashioned slipped from his features.

Serena gaped at him. "Rawdon?"

He expected surprise. Relief—after all, she was a lone woman on the road late at night, completely at the mercy of the denizens of darkness. She should have been elated to see a familiar face. Instead, she looked more dismayed than when she'd believed she was being set upon by a highwayman. "Oh, Rawdon! I had heard the tales of how quickly you were going through your family's fortune, but to have to resort to this!" One hand swept across the folds of his costume. "Highway robbery! You could be hung, for pity's sake!"

"Highway—what?" Irritation shifted to puzzlement. "Oh, Lord! You think that I really am—?"

She was rummaging in a limp, beaded reticule, drawing out a handful of coins. "Rawdon, take this, please," she said, putting her pitiful store of funds into his hand and curling his fingers about it with her own. "Only promise me you won't go about robbing people anymore."

Why was it that her mournful tone made him chafe far more than the scoldings of his uncles, the tears of his mother? It made him shift uneasily. "For God's sake, Rena, I may have degenerated to horrible depths, but I'll be damned if I've gotten low enough to steal money from a mere nursery babe."

"You're not stealing it. I'm giving it to you freely. Please, Rawdon!"

"Serena, I'm no more a highwayman than you are."

"But you were attempting to stop the coach. With a gun."

"I was playing a joke on Percy Davenant. The bloody fool went and fell in love." His lip curled in disgust. "Got himself leg-shackled to a woman this very afternoon. Percy once told me to stop him at gunpoint if he ever married, so I—" The moonlight revealed enough of her expression to make him squirm. "Oh, for God's sake, it was a joke! I wasn't really going to shoot him! Blast, I'd think you'd be relieved I've not resorted to a life of crime!"

"Relieved? You could have been killed. A coachman might have shot you. Or one of the king's soldiers might have stumbled across you. I doubt they would have believed it was a joke. Rawdon, this is the most brainless scheme—"

"No more brainless than a schoolroom child running about the high roads after dark, pretending some passion-crazed lover is hunting her down!"

The shoulders beneath Serena's cloak stiffened the way they had when he'd teased her as a child. "I don't play such mad games! At least not anymore. And if we don't hasten away from here, Bertrand will catch up to us! I hardly want any more bloodshed on my conscience!"

"Bloodshed? My, this is a grisly little fantasy. But then, when you were a grubby little waif, you liked nothing more than playing pirate and feeding prisoners to the sharks."

"This isn't some fantasy!" she said, indignant. "He's been running about challenging half the parish to duels over ridiculous things! The last straw was when he tried to challenge one of our footmen when poor Matthew was only taking a speck of dust out of my eye!"

Despite his irritation Rawdon couldn't stifle a chuckle.

"So you've become a regular Helen of Troy, have you? Starting a war because of your incomparable beauty! Blast you women, anyway. Always stirring up trouble. Any sane man should take the course I have—cast love to the devil and have a blazing good time. That way you wake up in the morning with an aching head instead of an aching heart. Perhaps I should seek out this Bertrand and convince him that the slings and arrows of love aren't worth bothering about."

"Perhaps you should," Serena said with great dignity, turning to struggle with the fastenings of the harness in an effort to free one of the horses. "If you wait here, he'll be along, I'm certain. He has a better nose for finding me than your papa's hunting hounds had for the fox."

Rawdon lounged against the coach. "Serena, Serena. Much as I'm perishing with curiosity to meet this fantasy suitor of yours, I can hardly allow you to go stumbling about the woods alone. My reputation is already in tatters, as you've observed. You wouldn't want to damage it further by adding the desertion of a damsel in distress to my list of sins. What would your papa say?"

"As long as Papa could keep his nose buried in his musty old books, he wouldn't care if the earth crumbled away beyond his library threshold and me along with it." There was a sting of sadness in her voice. "No one need know I ever saw you, Rawdon." She all but landed on her bottom as she jerked a strap free. "I assure you, I won't tell."

"Come now, the least I can do is escort you to your destination. Or had you gotten around to fantasizing where you are running away *to?* One needs a haven to escape from a passion-crazed lover, you know. A castle tower works quite nicely. Or there is always the possibility of a charming gypsy camp."

She turned to him, her chin tipped up, her face still. "If you must know, I do have a destination in mind. I'm going to Claudia's."

Rawdon's grin hardened, his face feeling almost brittle. He blessed the darkness and prayed it would keep Serena from noticing the hot flush spilling along his cheekbones. He'd be damned before he'd let his emotions show on his face. "Ah, Claudia's. That explains why you would prefer to dare the high roads alone rather than accept my aid. Are you afraid I'll play the wild romantic hero? Beating my breast, gnashing my teeth, challenging her husband to a duel?"

"Of course not!"

"No. Knowing you, you've probably come up with a much more creative scheme to get her attention. After all, you were the one who hatched that ridiculous plot where I was supposed to steal her away from the very altar on her wedding day. How many hours did you spend teaching that infernal nag of yours to race up the aisle of the church so I could abduct her?"

"I cannot believe you would bring up something so painful to both of us."

"I cannot believe you actually talked me into it." Rawdon shrugged one cloak-draped shoulder. "However, the incident is not painful to me. Not anymore. I'm quite cured of my bout of lovesickness. Behold me, a new man!" He sketched her an elegant bow.

"I know," Serena said softly. "I scarce recognize my Rawdon in the tales that I hear."

My Rawdon . . . how often had she called him that? Lisped out her ownership of him when she was toddling about? She'd been the world's most determined pest, always underfoot. Why did the memory of her adoring face turned up to his suddenly make him feel wistful? Intensify the memory of the youth he had been, storming away from the village of Wyckham in the wake of Claudia Creighton's wedding, as if the infernal world had been smashed to bits. What a bloody fool he'd made of himself!

"So I'm a grand disappointment to you as well?" he asked, examining the fingertips of his black gloves. "Then it's unanimous. I cannot tell you how relieved I am. All these expectations people chain about you are like blasted shackles weighing you down. I much prefer to be a free man."

It was a most dashing and eloquent bit of speechifying, but at that moment, he could have told Serena that he'd danced with the devil in scarlet stockings and he'd wager she'd not have noticed. Her piquant face was quite still, every fiber of her being seeming to strain to hear whatever lurked on the road behind them.

"Hoofbeats! Oh, Lord, I can't stay here!" She scrabbled to set the horse loose with one desperate tug, but it was hopeless. A harsh laugh tore from Rawdon's throat as she grabbed once again for her pistol.

"What are you going to do? Shoot the poor beast?"

"You have to get me away from here, Rawdon! Please! Can't you hear the hoofbeats? I'm certain it's Bertrand! Listen to that mad pace! No one in their right mind would ride thus on a dark road!"

"Percy and I used to make a game of it, before—oh, blast. All right, midget. I'll haul you off. Better do it fast before someone else sees us, or it'll be you and I blazing up to the altar! I've compromised you, don't you know. The two of us alone, after dark. Damn, but that would be a disaster beyond imagining!"

He mounted up, then grabbed her by the wrist and hauled her up before him. "But once I get you out of here, you owe me an explanation. The truth, by damn."

With that he spurred his mount. The horse reared wildly, then plunged down the road at a pace that would've delighted the readers of any French novels he could name.

Two

The horse lunged into motion, sending Serena slamming back against the hard wall of Rawdon Wyatt's chest. Sinewy arms curved on either side of her waist, the powerful lengths of his thighs cupping her hips. He had taken her riding a hundred times when she'd been a child, trying with boyish arrogance to scare her by leaping fences and plunging down hills. She'd never felt anything but safe in Rawdon's arms.

Yet this ride was nothing like those they had shared in the past. Rawdon was no teasing boy, but a man who smelled of night wind and brandy. He felt hard and strong and oddly dangerous. A stranger after all these years.

And Serena was exhausted, desperate and more than a little heartsick after the madness of the past three weeks. She'd never been able to step on an ant without feeling a twinge of guilt. It was far harder causing Bertrand St. Aubin such pain, especially since it had raked up the glaring memory of Rawdon's broken heart so many years ago. Yet, no matter how gentle she'd attempted to be with Bertrand, he'd pushed and battered at her nerves until she'd had to escape any way she could.

She shuddered, remembering Bertrand's eyes, as wild and desperate as the suitor in a Cheltenham tragedy. Was it really possible that the hoofbeats were those of Bertrand's mount? That he had followed her somehow? A spike of unease plunged deep inside her. If Bertrand did discover her with Rawdon this way, what might happen?

"Rawdon, hurry! Veer off into the woods. That way he'll ride past us."

"Who? Some servant you've offended? The vicar, after you because of one of your pranks? You'd best come clean, Mouse. I was never fooled by your wild tales."

He gigged his mount over a stone fence, the impact when they landed all but cracking Serena's teeth as her jaw banged shut.

"This isn't—"

"Some make-believe game? Some crazed pretending? I have a healthy dread of your plots now. Kept me away from the parish all these years."

He'd been laughing at her most of her life, Serena didn't know why it hurt so badly now.

The hoofbeats behind them drew nearer. "It's probably your papa, chasing after you, poor man," he mused. "We might as well put him out of his misery now. Even if it's a blasted dragon come to devour us, I intend to haul you home by your petticoats."

"You wouldn't dare!"

"Fatal error in strategy, my sweet. You know I never could resist a dare. Besides, if poor Squire Creighton breaks his neck racing about in the dark, it'll be on my conscience." He reined in his mount, spinning it around toward the road. Panic swelled beneath Serena's ribs. She jabbed her elbow back into Rawdon's midsection, scrambling down from the plunging horse, its huge hooves slashing, its head tossing in alarm.

Half-blinded by the tumbling waves of her hair, she scooped up her skirts and bolted away from Rawdon, stumbling through the underbrush. His curses rang in her ears.

She was just rounding a tree when she all but slammed into a form cloaked in midnight—horse and rider. Brawny as a bull the apparition blocked her path, his massive hand holding a pistol, his face masked.

"My, my, what a pretty little partridge lost in my

woods." His salacious words were lost as Rawdon's mount thundered up behind Serena.

"Now look what you've done, you reckless little fool!" Rawdon snarled, sliding from his mount. He stepped in front of her, placing his broad chest between the brigand and Serena.

"Damn you, Rawdon, this isn't my fault. If you'd just listened to me—"

"Make one move toward the pistol, sirrah, and I blast you into eternity!" the brigand snarled.

"Don't tell me Bertrand decided to dress as a highwayman, too." Rawdon's tone was light, yet Serena could feel the tension emanating from him in sizzling waves. "And I thought my idea was so original. Ah, well, I cut much more of a dash than he does, or do you think the scarlet plume a trifle overdone?"

"It's not Bertrand!"

"I'm so relieved," Rawdon muttered. "It's only a highwayman with a pistol pointing at rather vital parts of my anatomy."

Rawdon swept his tricorne from his head and sketched the brigand an elegant bow. "Greetings to a fellow Knight of the Road."

Serena could feel the man's eyes on them, glowing through the slits in his mask.

"This is my stretch of road!" the man bellowed. "Every highwayman from here to Surrey knows it belongs to the Fallen Angel."

"A thousand pardons." Rawdon's voice was cool as iced silk. "I'm rather new to this vocation. You have my word as a gentleman that I will not trespass again."

"A gentleman, eh?" The highwayman snorted, Serena's blood chilling as her gaze stayed pinned on the pistol still clasped with supreme negligence in the thief's hand. "You're a bold 'un. I'll say that for you. Perhaps I'll let your transgression pass, as long as you divide your booty."

Rawdon's voice came hard, diamond bright. "I'm afraid that would be impossible. You see, the woman is the only treasure I found in that coach. Not so much as a bracelet on her wrist."

"So you decided to take her as your tithe? She is lovely. By rights, I could claim her. Perhaps we should let the lady choose?"

Serena glanced from Rawdon to the Fallen Angel. She would have done almost anything to escape Rawdon at that moment, her hurt and anger cut so deep. His threat to return her to her father's estate still hung between them. For a heartbeat she almost considered putting her fate into the hands of this highway robber.

"I-I . . ." she hesitated. Rawdon's eyes slashed to hers, and even in the moonlight they seared her with their intensity, drove the breath from her lungs and any thought of mutiny from her head. "I only wish to be escorted to the nearest inn. I suppose this gentleman will do. Although he's not half as dashing as you are, Mr. Angel."

The highwayman's chest swelled like a banty rooster's. "I could fight him. Give you a demonstration of my prowess. Women love those sorts of theatrics."

"No!" Serena snapped. "If I have one more man fighting over me, I'll—I'll drown him myself! Now, go rob some unsuspecting traveler!"

She caught her breath on a stunned gasp. "Wait! Wait just a moment!" She took a step toward the brigand, only Rawdon's crushing grip on her arm holding her back. "Mr. Fallen Angel, sir, did you happen to see another rider on your way down the road? A big, burly fellow, on a ghost-white horse?"

"If I had, he'd be lighter by the weight of his purse."

"I was just wondering," Serena said in her best wheedling tone. "If you should happen to run across him, could you detain him for me? Take his horse, his money. Maybe hold him prisoner for a while. I don't want him hurt, you understand, just . . ."

"Some children have imaginary friends," Rawdon put in with a conspiratorial wink. "*She* has imaginary lovers. Oof—!" His breath came out in a whoosh as she elbowed him in the midsection. But the insufferable wretch went on in spite of her. "Supposedly his name is Bertrand. If you see him, tell him we'll be at the Red Dog Inn down the road a piece."

"A man would have to be mad to ride the Fallen Angel's road alone at night," the thief boasted.

"Mad or in love," Rawdon scoffed. "But then, it's the same thing."

"You still trespassed on my stretch of road. You owe me a tithe. You may keep the woman if you give me some bauble to satisfy me tonight."

"Blast, I should just fight—" Rawdon muttered, then swore, low. His gaze slashed to Serena. "But what if the wily bastard wins? Devil burn it. What would happen to you?"

He hesitated for a moment, then ripped off one black glove. The moonlight snagged in the facets of a remarkable emerald ring that had been in the Wyatt family since Henry V fought at Agincourt. Serena knew it hadn't left his finger since his grandfather had given it to him fifteen years ago.

"Your ring!" Serena protested, a sick knot in her chest. "You can't—"

"Here," Rawdon snarled, tugging the emerald from his finger. "This is payment for the girl. Believe me, you've got the better end of the bargain."

The highwayman plucked up the bauble, examining it with keen interest. "The lady must be a treasure indeed."

The Fallen Angel swept his hat off in a courtly bow, then placed the ring on his own finger. With a touch of his spurs, the highwayman sent the horse careening into the night.

"What did you do that for? Give him your ring?"

"Because I'll need every blasted tuppence in my purse to get us a room at an inn."

"Rawdon, I'm not spending the night with you in some —some inn! Especially when you all but announced my whereabouts to Bertrand! I'm going to Claudia's! If anyone saw us—they'd, well, they'd . . ."

"Think we were lovers? Think I'd abducted you? It's a little late to be worried about propriety now. You're running wild in the woods, without so much as your maid to attend you."

"Papa would have fired Lettice if I brought her! I didn't want anyone else to suffer."

"How noble. Exactly what some stage heroine would spout. You seem determined to enact some Cheltenham tragedy, I might as well play the role of your pretend lover. Bertrand, wasn't it? Ghastly name."

"I don't need your help! I didn't ask for your help!"

"And you've already gotten yourself into a coach accident and been set upon by a highwayman."

"But we don't need to stop for the night. I'm sure we can reach Claudia before . . ."

He swore low. "You already cost me my ring. The next highwayman we meet might not be in such a charitable mood. We'll travel by day when we're not in quite as much danger of getting our throats slit."

"I should have gone with the Fallen Angel!" she flung back defiantly. "He wouldn't have turned coward at the thought of riding the roads at night! He would've escorted me to Claudia's!"

"Then he and Bertrand could both have fallen in love with you and fought at dawn. Pistols for two, breakfast for one. You grisly little darlings just adore a little bloodshed."

"I don't!" Serena protested, stricken.

"Or, better still, the Fallen Angel could have carried you away on horseback to his demon lair and had his way with you. You could have played out any of a hundred brainless female fantasies stuffed in that blasted head of yours. Too bad you didn't make this decision before I gave the infernal thief my ring!"

"I'll repay you the cost of the ring."

"Oh, of course you will. Doubtless, you've got the key to some wicked troll king's treasure trove hidden away in the trunk where you keep Bertrand's heart. Blast it, Serena, I should've let the highwayman take you. It would have served you both right. Now, I'm going to get a good night's sleep, and then I'm hauling you back to Wyckham and your papa even if I have to tie you up and sling you over the saddle the way we did when we played Cavalier and Roundhead so many years ago."

Serena gritted her teeth. "You just try it, and—"

"Don't tempt me!" Rawdon hissed. His hard hands closed about her waist and he slung her up into the saddle, mounting behind her.

The wind drove Serena's tirade back into her throat as his horse lunged into motion again, its stride eating up the silver ribbon of road that led to the Red Dog Inn.

THREE

The Red Dog Inn was as disreputable as the innkeeper himself, worn down at the gables and listing to one side on its foundation. The only bedchamber that remained was scrubbed, yet shabby, its bed curtains worn and mouse-nibbled in patches, ancient stains worked into the wood floor. But at least the establishment sold brandy. Rawdon needed a stiff belt of the stuff. Badly.

Serena wheeled on him, her violet eyes snapping fire, her cloak rippling as she fairly quivered with indignation. "If you think for one moment I'm going to share a bedchamber with you tonight, Rawdon William Alexander Wyatt, you're out of your mind!"

"I was out of my mind to rescue you in the first place. If I'd had any idea it was you in that coach, I would have ridden the other way! Blast it, Serena, they only have one room left. It's not as if anyone is going to think we were doing anything improper! Besides, no one else will know! We'll sleep a few hours, then be on the road before anyone else is awake."

Her hands clutched the front of her cloak, and Rawdon could see dartings of alarm in her animated features. "Oh, for God's sake, Serena, I'm hardly likely to become overwrought with passion and hurl myself at you!"

"I know." There was something strange in her voice. A touch of . . . wistfulness even through her anger. It made her look small and lost. Rawdon crossed to her.

"Here." He unfastened her cloak as if she were no more than a child. "We're both exhausted. It's been a damned eventful night. You'll feel better after you sleep. And I'll watch over y—what the blazes?" He breathed as the cloak fell away.

In that frozen instant, his gaze locked on a slender figure worlds different from the skinny little waif he remembered. Firm breasts swelled like peaches in the bodice of an amber damask gown, silver lacings cinching about a waist as lithe and graceful as any Fairy Queen's. The skirts flared out, dancing above tiny slippers, while ivory lace cascaded over hands that had become the delicate ones of a woman.

He had laughed at her assertions that she was capable of driving a man to passion. Never had it actually occurred to him that Serena Creighton—little scrape-kneed, tag-along pest—would turn into a veritable goddess.

With great effort, Rawdon managed to get his gaping mouth closed. He tore his gaze away from the white swell of her bosom, his cheekbones stinging, his conscience jabbing him with a dozen pitchforks. This was Serena he'd been ogling like a damn fool, not some bold courtesan. Little Serena Creighton. Even he couldn't call her that anymore.

He fought back the unexpected burn of attraction, and stalked away, flinging the cloak on a chair. Then he downed a swallow of brandy.

"I'll sleep in a chair," Rawdon said, wishing he could get the image of Serena out of his head. He glanced over his shoulder. It was a mistake. She stood in candlelight, her hair polished bright as a child's Christmas guinea, her eyes like pansies, soft and violet, with lashes so long they cast shadows on the cheekbones below. She truly did look pale, Rawdon realized with a start, dark circles under her eyes, the rose-petal bow of her lips bracketed by faint lines of strain. Suddenly, he felt like an ogre for tormenting her so.

His hands suddenly felt over large, his brain scrambled.

No glib Rawdon Wyatt witticisms could be found. She did look as if she were in trouble of some kind, and Rawdon discovered that the prospect riled up the protective beast inside him.

"Rena, what the devil is this all about?" he asked quietly. "Whatever it is, you know I'll try to mend it. Remember all the times I saved you from trouble when you were a runabout little mouse?" He crossed to where she stood, and hooked one long finger beneath her chin. "Tell Rawdon what is amiss."

"I did!" To his dismay, those pansy-dark eyes shimmered with tears. "It's been awful. I never meant to make him love me. I never tried to. I know there are girls who adore that sort of thing, men breaking their hearts over them. They display their list of conquests like the lines on a dance card, laughing over the misery they've caused. But I could never do that after I saw . . ." She stopped, alarm streaking her features.

"After you saw me make a damned fool out of myself over Claudia?" Heat stung Rawdon's cheeks, but his gaze held her anguished one.

"Yes. I always felt responsible somehow. If I hadn't been so insistent, so certain that she had to love you, you wouldn't have gone to the lengths you did to try to wrest her away from that awful Arthur Harbuckle. Only he's not so awful after all. And Claudia . . ." She stopped, and the grief and pain in her eyes wrenched at Rawdon's heart in a way nothing had for years. Maybe not since he'd ridden away from his first heartbreak.

"Claudia loves Arthur," he finished for her.

"How could she? A plodding, complacent . . . well, he was so—so disgustingly *good* and *serious* and there wasn't the tiniest flash of devilishness in his eyes."

"A terrible prospect for a husband," Rawdon agreed, with mock solemnity. "I would have been much better— wild, reckless, without a useful thought in my head." He cupped her cheek with his palm, amazed at the velvety softness of it, and by the wetness of tears.

Serena, who had never cried, even when she'd been

flung from her horse into a bramble patch. Serena, crying over . . . what? A damn fool boy who had battered himself against his first heartbreak until poor Claudia must've been tempted to drop an anvil on his head?

Was it possible that Serena had been blaming herself all these years? Something hot and hard lodged in Rawdon's chest.

"Listen to me, Mouse. Boys have been breaking their hearts in first love since time began. It's—well, it's a little like losing one's milk teeth. A painful necessity. What happened that abominable summer was my fault, and no one else's. In truth, I've always been grateful for your suggestions. If one is determined to make a fool of one's self, it's better to do it with a bit of dash. I'd wager people around Wyckham still reminisce about the pranks I pulled to get Claudia's attention."

"Not around me, they don't!" Serena said fiercely. "They wouldn't dare!"

"And no one will trouble you while I'm here. I promise." Rawdon drew her into his arms. She fit perfectly beneath his chin, her hair soft and rain-scented against his beard-stubbled jaw. He'd wanted only to comfort her. He hadn't bargained for the sweet yielding of her breasts against the wall of his chest, the warmth of her breath dampening his shirtfront, the wistful whispering of her sigh as it rippled from her into his own body.

She had always seemed to belong to him, somehow. And she felt right against him. Too right. He turned his lips until they brushed her hair. She tipped her face up, and his mouth grazed the tender skin of her temple, felt the subtle pulse beat there.

"Rawdon?" She turned those liquid eyes up to his. "Rawdon, please don't take me home. Papa won't listen to me. And Bertrand—I'm afraid he'll do something desperate."

"If he tries it, I'll break his neck," Rawdon growled. His gaze skated down, fascinated, imprisoned by the trembling curve of her lips. He wanted to taste them.

He hovered for a heartbeat, in an agony of indecision.

Saw her lashes grow heavy, drifting down, her mouth moving toward his. Or was he the one closing the space between them? Breath, hot and sweet stirred against his lips, setting his blood raging.

His mouth barely grazed hers, but he felt it burn to the very core of him. He grabbed Serena by the arms and pushed her away from him as if she were afire. She gave a little cry, and stared up at him, a wounded expression on her lovely features.

Anger bubbled up inside him, as hot and fast as the desire that had sliced through him moments before. Anger at Serena for being so damned beautiful she tempted him to madness. Anger at himself for daring to want her.

Want her? This girl who trusted him, who had every right to depend on him to help her in this situation, not imperil her even further? What kind of monster had he become?

Christ's blood, maybe he should bundle her back on a horse, drag her to Wyckham tonight. Highwaymen might not be half so dangerous as the emotions he was feeling at the moment.

"If you looked at Bertrand that way, it's little wonder the man wanted to haul you off to his private dungeon," Rawdon snapped, hating himself for lashing out at her, desperate because he couldn't think of any other way to dash away the emotions jolting him. "Bloody sakes alive, Serena! A man would have to be made of stone."

Rawdon whipped around, all too aware of a part of his anatomy that seemed fashioned of that material at the moment. Heat seared his cheekbones, stark self-disgust overwhelming him. He'd hurt her, and it made him furious. What they both needed was a little distraction.

"Are you hungry?" he demanded. *For what?* God knew, the innocent couldn't be hungry for what he was.

"No." The denial was hard as crystal, and Rawdon remembered a fairy tale he'd once told her of how tears bottled up inside turned to diamonds, cutting their way out of a princess's heart.

"I should bloody well force you to eat. If you faint on

me once we're on the road tomorrow, you won't get a damn bit of sympathy from me! I'll haul you, insensible, into your papa's library and dump you atop his copy of *Paradise Lost.*"

"I won't go back. You can't make me."

He stalked to the chamber door and locked it, then jammed the key into the pocket of his skintight breeches.

Her gaze darted from the door to the window, and Rawdon could almost hear the gears spinning out some crazed scheme.

"Don't even think about it!" he snapped. Grabbing a spindly legged chair, he stationed it before the crude window opening. He grabbed the bottle of brandy, carrying it to the window ledge, then sat down.

"Get into bed, Serena," he said in steely accents, trying to shut out images of her golden hair tossed on a pillow.

There was a stubborn silence, then she crossed to the mattress and curled up on it without so much as loosening her laces or taking off her slippers. Rawdon gazed at the small satin slippers encasing her slender feet, and felt as if it were some sort of omen. He knew Serena well enough to mistrust such easy capitulation.

Then he saw her eyes in the faint light of the candle— wide open and flooded with hot determination. So it was to be a duel after all, Rawdon thought grimly. Who could stay awake the longest. She was pure dying for him to drift off to sleep so she could do God knows what and get herself even deeper in trouble.

He wouldn't dare take his eyes off her all night. His gaze skimmed from her face, all lovely defiance, to womanly curves so fresh and alluring they made him ache.

He should have drawn his pistol in the woods, Rawdon thought grimly. A quick clean bullet, and the highwayman could have put him out of his misery before he'd discovered what a beast he could be.

FOUR

Serena curled up on the bed, seething with outrage, stinging from hurt. Trapped in a bedchamber with Rawdon Wyatt. How many times had she cherished girlish dreams of just such a scenario, yet in her imaginings he'd be tender, not furious; ardent, not harsh.

Thunderation! Why of all the men on earth did Rawdon have to stumble across her tonight when she was neck deep in trouble? Rawdon, with that insufferable note of superiority in his voice. *So you've become a regular Helen of Troy. . . . Where's your governess?* He might as well have said, what are you doing out past your bedtime, little girl?

But then, hadn't Rawdon always seen her as a child? Rawdon, Claudia, everyone. Her clearest memory of the other children was their heels flying, their elbows pumping as they raced away, trying to shake her off as if she were a cocklebur.

And yet, whenever she'd fallen and skinned her knee, or curled up beside a tree, heartbroken, her Rawdon had come back for her. He'd dusted her off and dried her cheeks and even stitched up a rent in her pinafore so she could avoid Nurse's wrath.

She'd dreamed of meeting him again a dozen times— her hair swept up in elegant curls, a breathtaking gown swirling about her. She'd imagined him gasping in astonishment, his eyes filling with that mysterious heat she'd seen whenever he'd gazed at Claudia. Only a heat more intense, more wonderful, more magical . . .

So it only stood to reason she'd crash into Rawdon here, in the midst of the most distressing mess she'd ever been tangled up in. Think how amusing he would find it if Bertrand caught up to them while Rawdon was dragging her home in an ignominious heap. Rawdon would tease and torment and get his head blasted off in a duel!

No. Serena doubted even the pleasure of torturing her would hold much temptation in his current mood. She could see it in every line of his face, the hard arch of cheekbone, the arrogant square of jaw, the aquiline nose, that he was dying to—how had he said it?—dump her atop her father's volume of *Paradise Lost*.

Rawdon couldn't wait to be rid of her. She cringed inwardly, remembering the horror that had flooded those fiery-green eyes when she'd dared to touch her lips to his in the most fleeting of kisses. He'd been stunned, pale beneath the layer of tan buffed into his skin by wind and sunshine and wild rides astride his horse.

Why had she done it? Hadn't she already humiliated herself enough? Or was it that after all that had happened, she no longer had anything to lose? That the one romantic dream she'd ever had was to kiss Rawdon Wyatt just once before she died.

But not this Rawdon—a rakehell, a wastrel who seemed to delight in his own destruction. Who couldn't even be bothered to visit his mother and sister. Who hadn't come near Wyckham for so many years.

Her Rawdon . . . he didn't exist anymore, Serena reminded herself sharply. He was a dream. Maybe he always had been.

There was only one thing to do, wait until the brandy he'd drunk made him sleep, and then escape any way she could.

She feigned sleep, watching him through slitted eyes for what seemed forever. He stood and stretched, stripping off his frock coat. He drank and paced, checking his watch time and again, his eyes regarding her hour after hour with suspicion.

She buried her smirk of triumph in the pillow when he yanked open the front of his shirt and splashed cold water from the washbowl onto his face. But the smirk died as she caught sight of a disturbing spectacle through the veil of her lashes. Water, running in rivulets, to dampen patches on Rawdon's shirt, droplets sparkling on the bronzed wedge of naked chest visible through the shirt's opening.

Heat stung at Serena's cheeks, an odd sizzle of awareness, as if butterfly wings were brushing every inch of her skin beneath her gown. They centered in her stomach, fluttering and hot.

She shut her eyes resolutely, but that only made it worse. The image of Rawdon's chest had burned itself on the inside of her lids, her treacherous imagination allowing her fingers to stray up that opening in his shirt, to touch the hard ridges of his chest. To press her mouth against it, soft and hot and wanting.

Shame and self-disgust made her tempted to pull the quilts over her head. God knew, Rawdon had always possessed an uncanny ability to read her thoughts. If he had the slightest idea what she was thinking now, Serena would die of humiliation.

At last she heard the creak of the chair, and dared a glance at him. He sagged against the chair back, the dark waves of his hair tumbling over his brow. It took bare minutes before a soft snore sounded. Serena opened her eyes. His features were almost boyish in slumber.

Serena watched him, her chest burning. It was as if dream-fairies had wiped away the years of heartache and dissipation, leaving the Rawdon who had always seemed to be her own especial angel.

Serena crept from the bed and stood there, frozen, half-expecting Rawdon to awaken. She eyed the bulge in his breeches pocket where the key was, and knew there was no way she could get it. Better to try the window. She edged toward it, carefully avoiding Rawdon's sprawling legs. Moonlight draped about him in a mystical veil, turning him into an enchanted prince the fairy maid could wake from a dark spell with her kiss. But she'd already tried to kiss him, and it had been a disaster.

It would have been better never to have seen him again than to see him like this, Serena tried to convince herself. Still, her gaze clung to him, her chest constricting with a familiar pain, her fingers burning to sweep back the lock of hair that had always tumbled across his forehead.

No, she had to escape Bertrand, disappear completely until some other lady caught the youth's eye. Odd, to find that the only thing more painful than knowing she'd unwittingly caused Bertrand's pain was looking at what her meddling had done to Rawdon.

Steeling her resolve, she scooted past Rawdon, and leaned out the window to observe her only escape route. A tree twisted a gnarled branch a mere arm's length from the window, leading to the inn yard below, if she had the courage to climb down it. Serena swallowed hard and started to hoist up her skirts when a shadowy figure charged out of the darkness into the pool of light spilled by the lantern beside the inn door.

Bertrand St. Aubin looked as if he'd fought the hounds of hell, his mobile features haggard with fear and anger, hurt and desperation.

"Serena!" he cried out in stark relief as his gaze locked on her. "Thank God I've found you!"

"Damnation!" Serena exclaimed, panic reverberating to the tips of her toes.

She scrambled back from the window, as Bertrand flung himself at the tree, climbing upward like a veritable Romeo.

"Don't fear, beloved, I'm coming!" ·

With a cry, Serena dove for the shutters in an effort to close them, tipping Rawdon over in his chair.

Rawdon swore and scrambled to his feet, grabbing her by the skirts and hauling her into his arms. "Blast it, Serena, do I have to tie you to the bed?"

"The key! Give it to me!" she cried, trying desperately

to cram her hand into his pocket. Rawdon let out a yelp of pain as her fingers gouged deep into a tender bulge of male flesh.

"For God's sake!" He grasped a handful of her sleeve. "You all but unmanned me!"

"Let me go!" Serena shrieked, trying so hard to tear away from him that the cloth in his hand ripped with a sickening sound. A draft chilled the bared flesh of her shoulder, her shift drooping until it barely concealed the swell of her breast. "Let me go!"

The words were lost in a bellow of pure masculine rage as Bertrand burst through the window, red-faced, eyes wild, bits of leaf and twigs sticking in his hair.

"What the devil?" Rawdon gaped as if Hades himself had just popped out of the earth to drag Serena down to hell. His grasp loosened, and Serena scrambled away from him, flinging herself between Rawdon and the youth. But not before Bertrand's face seared into Rawdon's consciousness. It was as if Rawdon were staring at a mirror image of himself so many years ago. Almost unhinged by the first surge of passion, ready to fling himself body-long on the pyre of unrequited love. The insight made Rawdon squirm.

"Please, Bertrand!" Serena begged. "This isn't what it appears!"

Bertrand's sword hissed from its scabbard, gleaming blue-black, reflecting darkness and flame. "I have eyes to hear! This bastard has abducted you! But he will pay for daring to take the woman of St. Aubin! You filthy cur—"

"You must listen!" Serena pleaded. "Please!"

"Listen? Me, I've already heard enough, *n'est-ce pas?* This *poltroon,* he is threatening to tie you to his bed? He is holding you against your will!"

"Who the blazes is this?" Rawdon climbed to his feet.

"Me, I am Bertrand St. Aubin, the man who is going to kill you! You dare to touch her! My angel!"

"He wasn't touching me!" Serena burst out. "I was touching him!"

She realized the tactical error she'd made in the next

heartbeat. Bertrand whitened and lunged at the unarmed Rawdon.

But Rawdon dove out of the way, yanking his own sword from its sheath. "She was grappling for the key to this chamber, St. Aubin. It was in my pocket."

"You lie! The Fallen Angel told me you had taken her captive—dragged her to this inn!"

"The Fallen Angel?" Serena echoed, cursing the abysmal luck that had cast the highwayman across Bertrand's path.

"It cost me my purse, but it was worth the price!" Bertrand snarled at Rawdon. "He told me she was your prisoner! That you dared me to find her here—defiled."

"Defiled!" Rawdon snorted. "Oh, for God's sake!"

"I heard you threatening to tie her to your bed! You do not deserve a death so quick, so clean as a single sword thrust! But I would not horrify my sweet love by carving your flesh away a strip at a time the way you deserve!"

"Bertrand, stop this madness! It's why I ran in the first place! This constant fighting, these wild jealous fits! I'm pure exhausted from them!"

"There is no reason to fight me, St. Aubin."

"Rawdon found me on the road," Serena cried, desperate. "He tried to help me."

"Alone in this bedchamber? With his shirt unbuttoned?" St. Aubin snarled, his blade lashing out, crashing into the parry of Rawdon's own. "You cannot make me believe he didn't plan to steal your virtue!"

"After the episode where she was attempting to dig the key out of my pocket, there's some question I'll ever be able to have such a pleasure with a lady again," Rawdon said, fending off yet another blow with grim humor. The French youth swore.

"Bertrand, there is no need for us to fight. You have my word I had nothing but the most honorable of intentions. I've known Miss Creighton since she was in short skirts—"

"Why would Serena have acquaintance with a highwayman? You think me a fool?" St. Aubin drove his sword forward, the tip catching Rawdon's sleeve. Rawdon dodged to the right, his sword tip nearly snagging in the metal quillon that formed a protective cage around his opponent's hand.

"He's not a highwayman! I have known him forever! And you're being the most insufferable blockhead ever born!"

For a moment, Bertrand's sword drooped, but then he raised it, more fierce than ever. "Still, he meant to abduct you! To steal your innocence! You are in short skirts no longer!" He glared at Rawdon. "You mean to tell me, monsieur, that you have not noticed she is no longer a child? You have eyes, yes? Can any man born look at that face and not want to kiss it?"

"I . . . well . . . ," Rawdon hesitated, and Serena's mouth burned. "What is in question here is the lady's will. I didn't abduct her. I don't want to have my way with her."

"You fiend! I will cut out your lying tongue—" Bertrand slashed at Rawdon, but a flash of steel caught the blade, deflecting it with the teeth-gritting patience of a nursemaid with a particularly stubborn charge.

"The hard fact is that Serena does not want anything to do with you, St. Aubin. She'd rather brave highwaymen and God knows what other beasts racing down the roads at night than to endure any more of your ridiculous scenes."

"R—ridiculous?"

"She was running away from you," Rawdon said, circling his opponent, wary, ready. "I stumbled across her before she got robbed or abducted by some brigand or worse. Truth to tell, I didn't believe her when she told me she had some lunatic lover chasing after her. But I suppose you can hardly blame me. Last time I saw her, she had a dribble from a cherry tart on her chin—not the most alluring picture of romance, I must say. When I found her on the road, she was running away from you, at the risk of her own pretty neck."

He saw Bertrand's dark eyes flicker with doubt, then

burn with stubborness. "A lady—she runs like a mare in season, hungering for a man to chase her! She wants her lover to sweep her into his arms, to bend her to his will. Once I carry Serena away with me, she will be heavenly grateful to let me be her master and her slave."

Rawdon winced. "God, tell me I didn't sound like such a bloody moron," he muttered, then struck like a hunting falcon, his sword tip snagging the quillon, ripping the weapon from Bertrand's hand. It flew across the room, clattering to the floor.

St. Aubin started to dive for it, but Rawdon placed himself and his blade between the youth and his fallen weapon.

Yet it was hardly necessary. Serena grasped the youth by the arm. Bertrand wheeled to face her. "Bertrand, I've told you a hundred times that when I say no I mean it!" Serena raged. "I don't love you! I will never love you!"

The boy looked as if Serena had poised a dagger against his chest and plunged it deep.

"Listen to me, Bertrand," Rawdon said, remembering all too clearly what it had felt like being jilted by the lady you adored. "It's over. Come with me, and we'll drink a keg of brandy. Consign all women to blazes."

But the boy had eyes for no one but Serena. "Why, Serena? Why don't you love me? Am I not dashing enough? Is it my face? The color of my eyes? I will pluck them out if they offend you."

"Don't be absurd! St. Aubin, you're making an idiot of yourself and you're distressing the lady!"

But the most unmanly quiver in the youth's voice drowned out the sparks of frustrated fury from Serena's lovely eyes, gentled her voice with her own pain.

"Bertrand, it's not any fault of yours that I can't give my heart. I . . . I love another man."

Considering Serena's claim, Rawdon expected Bertrand's howl of anguish. He didn't expect the sharp twist in his own chest. She loved someone else? What the devil! Did she have a string of poor besotted fools shattering their hearts over her?

"Who is this man you love?" Bertrand raged. "I will kill him!"

"You could never find him. He . . ." Achingly wistful violet eyes flicked to Rawdon. "He lives only in my imagination." Yet why would a figment of imagination weigh her bell-like voice with so much sadness? Why did the notion of some fool hurting her suddenly fill Rawdon with killing fury. Serena . . . who should always be laughing and mischievous and merry.

He wanted nothing more than to drive Bertrand from the room, and to leave himself before Serena saw . . . saw what? The unfamiliar, raging emotions she managed to set free inside Rawdon himself.

"St. Aubin, get out," Rawdon ordered, sheathing his sword. "And if I ever hear of you tormenting Serena again, you'll answer to me."

The youth's shoulders sagged. Defeat. It was crushing him. And Rawdon knew all too well what the boy was feeling.

"What can you possibly do to me?" Bertrand said. "Kill me? You cannot kill a man whose heart has already been ripped from his chest."

"Your pride will heal, and so will your heart, though I know you won't believe it now," Rawdon said with a sudden sharp-edged compassion that hurt his chest. Rawdon scooped up St. Aubin's sword, and returned it to the lad.

"Come. We'll go to the taproom. It's customary to drown romantic sorrows in brandy. We can toast all women down to the devil."

"I haven't a stomach for drink."

"Maybe not, but there is only one thing to do in your circumstances, St. Aubin."

"What is that?"

"Go riding off like heroes of yore. Do great deeds. Fight great battles. Win the hearts of countless ladies. Make Serena sorry she turned away from you. Show her what a mistake she made in not accepting your suit."

"You think that is the way?"

"I am certain of it. She'll suffer the agonies of the

damned, I assure you. Imagine riding up to her household, with your lady love in your arms—glowingly happy. The world awaits you. And I assure you, the ladies love a man with dark secrets in his past—a brooding heartache they will try to heal."

"Do they? Perhaps if I'd had one before I met Serena . . ." Bertrand mused, heading for the door.

Rawdon dug out the key and tossed it to him, then paused, his gaze snagging on Serena's pale face. He crossed to her, tracing the shadow beneath her eye with his thumb. "Sleep, Mouse. I'll take care of him for you."

"Thank you." Her voice cracked so subtly, Rawdon was certain no one else would have heard it. He forced himself to give her a teasing smile.

Yet in the hours he spent drowning Bertrand St. Aubin's sorrow in brandy, he didn't brood over the misery of the French youth, nor his own shattered dreams from so long ago. Rather, he was haunted by the pulsing sorrow in Serena's eyes, the dark bruising of a heartache left by some shadow of a man who Rawdon already hated.

FIVE

The first rays of dawn were staining the window ledge scarlet when Rawdon crept into the bedchamber where he'd left Serena. He'd expected the brandy he'd drunk and the hours he'd spent away from her to dull the edgy sensation unfurling in his stomach, to shift things back into perspective. He'd hoped the plate of cherry tarts he'd brought would be a peace offering of sorts— not for her, but to help him make peace with himself. Serena would become his Mouse again—a charming memory from childhood, one he'd forever picture as cherry-stained and wide-eyed and untouchable.

But as he stared down at the figure asleep on the rickety inn bed, he knew with jarring certainty that sometime during this endless night things had been altered between them forever.

She looked like an embattled angel, her hair tumbled across the pillow in fairy-gold waves, her lashes dark crescents on her cheeks. Her shoulder, perfect as polished marble, yet temptingly warm, peeped from the tear in her gown, and the laces she had loosened about her waist so she could sleep allowed her feminine figure to blossom above constricting bands of corset and stomacher and bodice.

And he wanted to touch her with a fierce surge that left him reeling. He set the plate of tarts on a wooden table, then crossed to the bed, and sat down on it, careful not to disturb her. One finger stroked a river of golden curl away from the tender bank of her cheek.

"Serena," he said softly, his gut afire with the need to press his mouth to her bare shoulder, to trace kisses down the slope of her breast. "I brought you a treat."

She moaned, a breathless sound that tightened his manhood like a fist. "Rawdon?"

His name—she'd said it a thousand times—bellowed it, laughed it, flung it out in anger. But the sound of it now was liquid chocolate, rich, intoxicating, infinitely sweet.

Her lashes drifted up, and he winced at the redness of her eyes. Had she spent the time he'd been with St. Aubin crying? A thin thread of something like panic pierced Rawdon. God's blood, had she discovered she had feelings for the insolent puppy? Surely not!

She rolled over and levered herself into a sitting position, her shift sagging even more precariously, her face traced with lines pressed into them by the bedclothes.

"You've been crying." The words were the gruff accusation of the boy he had been—never able to bear her tears. The tarts were forgotten. "You're not mooning over that boy, are you?"

Her lips trembled as she gave a nervous laugh. "No. I've no regrets in sending him away. I'm afraid my tears were far more selfish than that."

Fierce tension drained out of Rawdon's shoulders. "Was it that other bastard then? The one who hurt you? I'll kill him for you."

"No." She looked down, toying with a bit of ribbon. Rawdon was damned scared she was lying, but he wasn't sure he had the courage to find out about this paragon fool of a man she'd loved. "I just—well, I know it sounds silly, but I was crying because of—of Claudia."

"Claudia? Be damned if you'd ever cry over her. I distinctly remember you swearing that under a blood oath." He tried to coax a smile from her, stirring up memories of pricked fingers held together by a grubby little girl with worshipful eyes and a damned uncomfortable boy willing to hatch any scheme to see her smile again.

"I was so worried about Bertrand that I hadn't stopped to consider what it will be like facing Claudia in such disgrace. She would do anything to help me, but—well, you know how she'll scold."

"By the time she's done playing the sanctimonious harpy, you might wish Bertrand had locked you in his dungeon."

"Exactly. But there is no point putting off the inevitable. I can't go home to Papa. He'll be too angry that I interrupted his study time by running away. And there's nowhere else to go."

"That may be," Rawdon considered, "but that doesn't mean the two of us can't delay a bit."

She sniffed, but her eyes brightened. "If I could just have a little while to collect myself, I would feel so much better."

It was madness, Rawdon thought, totally improper rummaging about the countryside, alone together. Yet, they'd already spent the night in the inn. Might as well be hung for a sheep as a lamb. "You look as if you could use a little adventure, Mouse. What would you say to racketing about for a day or so with a shameful rogue like me?"

"Oh, Rawdon!" she cried, flinging her arms around him. Rawdon held her, not as he wanted to, not as a lover should. But despite his efforts, her body melted into his, storming his heart, lashing at his pulses, loosing a need that all but overpowered him.

He put her gently away from him, his fingertips accidentally grazing her shoulder—hot satin he longed to touch with his tongue. He stiffened, knowing he should tell her he'd changed his mind. That this was a terrible mistake. But she gave him a dewy smile that slayed him.

"You are an angel!" Serena said, stroking his hair. "*My* angel."

Rawdon gritted his teeth. He'd never been anyone's hero—anyone but Serena's. Surely he could keep the bastard inside himself leashed for a few days for Serena's sake. It wasn't as if he were in love with her. Why did the thought leave an empty place in the hidden reaches of his soul?

SIX

C herry tarts on the sun-kissed shores of a stream, meadows full of blossoms with fat bees buzzing over golden centers. Serena revelled in the adventure Rawdon had promised her, resolving not to waste a moment of precious time in wanting things that were impossible.

He was laughing and attentive, teasing her as he always had, yet with a delicious undertone she'd never experienced before. His green gaze clung to her, misted through with confusion, a heaviness, a heat in those emerald depths that made her heart leap and a forbidden flame of hope shimmer in the most secret reaches of her soul.

He had ridden with her in his arms, held before him as if he were a bold knight, and she was his lady love, as if he were searching for any excuse to touch her. She knew such a fancy was due to her own wild imaginings, and yet she couldn't bear to confront reality now.

No, better to have this little fragment of time to dream on when Rawdon went away.

She leaned back into a fall of flowers like blue stars, the ruins of the feast he'd cajoled from a farm wife decimated before them, and watched Rawdon feed slender blades of grass to his horse. And she found herself far hungrier for the masculine lilt of his voice, the rumble of his laughter, the roguish beauty of his smile than meat pies.

Yet, there was another need even deeper inside her, a need to peel away the layers of cynicism a jaded lifestyle had left on the Rawdon she'd known, to find the man who had somehow lost his way.

"Rawdon"—she began to broach the subject in over-bright tones—"imagine if your friends in London could see you now. Your reputation would be in ruins."

"I suppose."

"They must be desperate for you to join them at those awful places where young noblemen fling away their fortunes."

Rawdon shrugged. "I doubt it. They're tied to home and hearth the lot of them. Traitorous curs. Married off the last of them the night I robbed your carriage."

"I remember. You said that you were playing some sort of joke. Your friends are all wed?"

"Mowed down by Cupid's arrows until there wasn't a man left standing."

"Oh. It must be difficult being a rogue without anyone to—to help you raise mischief."

"I'll find some new rakehells, never fear. London seems to sprout an endless crop of 'em."

She plucked a starflower and contemplated the rich blue cup. "You like being a rakehell then?"

He shrugged one broad shoulder. "Who wouldn't? Endless excitement. Lots of vice. Kegs of brandy."

"It must be amusing."

I remember thinking so, Rawdon thought with a grim knot inside him. Why does it suddenly seem so infernally pointless? *And lonely.*

"I suppose you've taken the advice you gave Bertrand. That you've had adventures and . . . and the ladies . . . I'm certain you have had some of those. Were they very beautiful?"

Rawdon looked patently uncomfortable. "I know you've spent a lifetime wheedling things out of me, Mouse, but nothing on God's earth will convince me to discuss mistresses with you."

"I was just thinking it must be vastly more entertaining

to be with them than, well, say, to visit Wyckham. Your mama and sister are notoriously quiet sorts, after all. Although they do get so excited when they receive one of your letters."

Rawdon leveled her a stern look under a sweep of dark brow. "Are you attempting to apply a willow switch to my conscience, ma'am?"

"Perhaps I'm just imagining how much it would please them if you paid them a visit. It would be such a little thing, really. You could stop by on your way to Lord Boulton's hunting box or Lady Holfield's house party or wherever it is you spend your time. Claudia's off at her husband's home, so she wouldn't trouble you. And there are people who would be so very glad to see you again, Rawdon. People who miss you."

"I'd think everyone would have been damned glad to be rid of me, after the way I turned the whole parish upside down with my nonsense." He peered at her from beneath a thick fan of lashes, yet his gaze was probing, oddly intense. "Did you miss me, Mouse?"

"I cried for weeks after you left. And then"—she stroked a fingertip over the cup of the flower—"then Caesar and I waited for you to come back."

Something squeezed in Rawdon's chest. He could almost see her, hair tumbled and wild, her pinafore askew. She would have stood sentry beside the road with that mangy, ancient dog of hers and balanced one buckled shoe on the bottom rung of the heavy iron gate, shoving off with her other toe to swing herself to and fro in an arc. Poignant as that image was, it wasn't half as appealing as the vision of Serena as she was now, lithe and lovely, and desperately kissable. He deflected the sharp jab of desire with a laugh.

"Well, sweetheart, you hardly look as if you spent the entire time languishing at the gate anticipating my return. You must've had to go inside long enough to get new dresses fitted from time to time. You did a damn lot of growing up in the years I've been away. There was a time I didn't think you could wipe your own tears without me to help you. And look at you. I bet you can even buckle your own shoes if you try terribly hard."

He expected her to laugh, or tease him back. Instead, she flinched as if he'd somehow broken the enchantment of the day. He frowned. "All right, Mouse. If I do my duty and visit Mama and Clarissa, will it please you?"

"Very much."

"And . . . what would you think if I came to see you? After all, somebody needs to beat away these legions of passion-mad suitors you seem to be collecting."

"I do very well myself most of the time. After all, Claudia was always the beauty."

"Was she?" Rawdon said, genuinely bemused. "I know a dozen men in London who would be fighting over you in no time. 'Course, you'd best not ever show your face there, or I'll be spending all my time dueling for your honor or playing father-confessor to your heart-broken beaux."

"Claudia is much lovelier. Everyone always said so."

"Everyone? Like who? Claudia herself?"

"Mama and Mrs. Fitch."

"I'd rely on their opinions, all right. Your mama couldn't see an elephant if it were attached to her nose. Mrs. Fitch had the ugliest batch of daughters in the county."

"You didn't."

"I didn't what?"

"Have a batch of ugly daughters. And I remember you couldn't keep your eyes off of her."

"Claudia did have a certain beauty. But oddly, she's a damn pale copy of you."

"Do you think so?" Serena asked, a trifle breathless.

Rawdon couldn't stop himself from hooking a finger under her chin, turning her face so he could peer down into it. "Claudia's hair is like yours, I suppose, but with all the sunshine washed out of the strands. You're always so busy, dancing around, exploring everything around you that your hair shimmers and curls in a hundred different hues from gold to silvery-blond."

"But her eyes—"

"Her eyes were merely cornflower blue like those of dozens of other ladies. While yours—yours seem to have drunk in all the delicious tints of blue and purple that stain the violets and heather you ran across. They sparkle with all the spirit you showed when you rescued that kitten stuck in the barn rafters, and they burn with intelligence and all the passionate loyalty you showed for a reckless boy who didn't deserve half the adoration you lavished on him. And your mouth . . ." His gaze strayed down to her lips, and need raged through him. "There is something indescribable about it that makes a man want to taste it. Especially when you smile. Must be from all those cherries you eat."

He'd meant to tease her, yet he craved those cherry-red swells with a hunger that stunned him. "Come, now, Mouse. You can't tell me some starry-eyed boy hasn't kissed you at an assembly or in the rose gardens at Creighton House."

"Bertrand tried, but—"

"You've never been kissed?" Rawdon's hunger nudged harder as he watched a delicate rose tint flood her cheekbones. She shook her head, her curls alight with everything warm and bright and inviting.

"Only that one tiny one at the inn, but that scarcely counts." She tugged at the drooping shoulder of her torn gown, and gazed up at him, her eyes soft, her lips trembling. "Maybe you could show me how. To kiss, I mean."

"Serena, I can't." Rawdon was certain that St. Peter must've stricken off a hundred of his sins for this single act of self-denial.

"You taught me to skip stones and play hoodman blind."

"That was different." Everything was different. The pulsing need in the core of his being, the fierce heat that burned in his lips, the only hope of quenching it the sweetness of hers.

Hurt flooded those incredible eyes. "Please, Rawdon. I want you to. So much."

Not half as much as I want to, he thought, stifling a groan.

She touched her lip with her tongue. That tiny gesture undid him.

Rawdon cupped her cheek with one hard palm, and melded his lips with hers. He could taste the tart bite of cherries, the bittersweet tang of his own lost innocence, the poignant memory of those days when he'd believed that anything was possible, that the knight would always win his lady fair. Believed it partly because of the adoration he'd seen every time he'd looked into Serena's face.

Warm, pliant, eager, her lips sought his, her fingers threading through his hair, her thumb skimming the line of his jaw. Never had a kiss curled itself into his very soul. Serena's untutored mouth was sweet intoxication, one Rawdon couldn't resist. He skimmed his tongue along the crease of her mouth, and she gasped with pleasure. Rawdon slipped his tongue into the hot secret place beyond those berry-hued lips.

He groaned, gathering her into his arms, dreaming of tumbling her back into that coverlet of flowers, teaching Serena pleasures her innocent dreams had never imagined.

Even his jaded conscience should be fairly sizzling with guilt at this transgression, but it felt right, so right to kiss Serena, as if her lips had been shaped by an angel's hand to fit his.

He imagined gliding his hand to the front of her bodice, where her breasts swelled, delectable as sweet peaches waiting to be tasted. He could smell the milky warmth of them, the femininity that would be velvety, tempting beneath his tongue.

"Oh, Rawdon," she whimpered into his mouth. "My Rawdon."

The sobriquet jarred him, flooding him with horror. This was Serena. Serena who trusted him even when he didn't deserve it. And the hard bulge at his groin demonstrated all too clearly how little he deserved that trust.

He broke away from her, gently but firmly. "Lesson

complete," he said. "And if any of these suitors wish to forge past what I've taught you, you tell them to go to the blazes. That is, until you find yourself a nice, steady young buck to be your husband."

"I won't. Find a husband, I mean. I'm not going to marry. Ever."

"Don't be ridiculous. Of course you're going to marry."

Her silky brow creased in contemplation. "I don't think it fair to marry when you cannot give your heart."

"Why the blazes can't you give your heart? There's not a blasted thing wrong with it!" Memory dawned. The lover who had left the shadows in her eyes. The faceless rival who had rejected her. Why did the very idea make him thirst for that phantom man's blood. "Blast and damnation, don't even try to tell me some tale of unrequited love. If this mysterious suitor of yours didn't have the brains to fall on his knees and thank God for your affection, he's not worth one of your tears."

"I don't intend to pine away, if that is what you fear. I'll play aunt to Claudia's babies, and take care of Father. I have only one regret."

"What?"

Pink spilled into her cheeks. "I wish that I could experience what a man and woman share. Just once."

"What they share—" Rawdon echoed, perplexed, then suddenly reeled at the realization of what she was hinting at—shared intimacy, shared beds, shared bodies. "Oh, no! Don't look at me that way! Damn it, Serena, this isn't a blasted game."

"You've already taught me how to kiss. I suppose you've done more than your duty. I'm certain I can find someone else to aid me in the rest."

Rawdon's heart nearly slammed out of his chest. "You intend to—to ask some man to bed you?" The notion of any man putting his hands on her made Rawdon seethe with a wild jealousy that made Bertrand's passions seem restrained.

"I've thought about it for a long time. And you know how single-minded I can be once I've made up my mind."

Serena bent over to pluck up a bit of tart that lay on a coarse napkin. She popped it into her mouth. A bit of cherry juice dripped, the sticky sweetness a translucent pink stain on the ivory swell of her breast. It lay there, sweet temptation. "Anyway, it's not your affair, Rawdon," she continued breezily. "I'm certain I'll find someone."

"Have you lost your senses? You can't do such a thing with just anyone! Learning to make love isn't like—like learning to ride a horse, by God, pick an instructor and away you go! Your first lover should be someone you—you trust. Someone who will take care of you. Someone who cares *for* you."

"I know. But it wouldn't be fair to lead someone on, engage his affections when I have no intention of loving him back."

"Serena, for God's sake! I don't want to hear another word of such rubbish from you!"

She sat quiet for a moment, and Rawdon had the oddest urge to scoop her up and lock her in a tower where he could guard her from this mad humor that seemed to possess her. He thought the discussion was over, prayed it was.

Then she spoke, her voice soft. "Rawdon, you know what I wish?" She turned those incredible eyes to his, and there was a world of wistful longing in her face. "The person . . . the man who teaches me . . . the rest. I wish it could be you."

SEVEN

"**M** e?" Rawdon felt as if he were crashing over a precipice, plunging down into a hell of desire and horror.

"I know you would be gentle and kind and—and make it into an adventure. You must be very good at it, with all the practice you've had being a rakehell."

Sweet Jesus, was she driving him insane on purpose? Every inch of his body was raging with the need to take what she was offering, something he wanted more than he'd ever wanted anything in his life. But how could he? He'd told Serena she needed someone to care for her to initiate her into the sweet mysteries of womanhood. But he cared for her far too much to stray into some casual dalliance that would cost them both more than Serena could imagine.

If only that resolute voice of reason could suppress the savage hunger in his loins. He swore, jamming himself up to his feet, snatching the reins of his horse. "It's time we headed for Claudia's," he growled. The sooner he delivered Serena into the safe hands of her sister, the sooner he could drive from his mind these ridiculous fantasies of stripping away the layers of clothing to discover the woman beneath. The woman who had offered herself to him.

I wish it could be you . . .

"Did I upset you?" Serena asked, looking up at him, all

innocence. "I'm sorry if I did. It's just that you always said I could tell you anything."

"That's when your darkest secret was stealing an apple from Robert Picadilly's orchard, or hiding Claudia's favorite ribbon. From now on, there are things you can keep to yourself." Like the fact that you are eager for a man's arms—my arms—my touch, to teach you the ways of passion.

But not because she loves you, wants you, a voice inside Rawdon sneered. *She's just searching for someone to show her pleasure before she casts such dreams away forever.*

Christ, how had things gotten so muddled between them? He'd always adored the scamp in her—the outrageous things she said and did when the rest of the world seemed bland as milksops. She'd made him laugh and warmed secret places in the core of him with her honesty, her sweetness, her keen intuitions. But this—all but asking him to make love to her because of some crazed curiosity . . .

She rose with heart-stopping grace that was old as Eve, yet new as spring's first flower, and Rawdon's chest became a hard knot.

He grabbed her and put her on the back of the horse, then mounted in front of her. If she noticed the new riding arrangements she said nothing, merely clasped her arms around his waist, the tips of her breasts nudging his stiff back, her thighs, half buried in cascades of petticoats, slipping in an intimate curve behind his.

He spurred his horse and rode like a fury, as if he could escape the scent of her, the feel of her, as if he could escape the offer that sent raw desire pooling in his loins. Yet, even as he rode, Rawdon knew it was futile.

If his mount sprouted wings, they'd never reach Claudia's by nightfall. Worse still, if he lived to be a hundred, Rawdon knew he would never forget the blossom-kissed meadow, the sunshine weaving shimmering ribbons through her hair, and an angel offering him a handful of heaven he was almost sinner enough to take.

He cast a baleful eye to the heavens. It would take

another great flood to drown out the fire he was feeling. Maybe he should pray for rain.

"If this is God's idea of a joke, I'm not laughing," Rawdon snarled against the lash of the storm. Bruised clouds clashed in the rising winds, thunder crashing. Serena attempted to make herself small against the shelter of Rawdon's broad shoulders, but it was no use, she was rain-soddened and dejected and certain she'd made the most terrible mistake of her life.

Her cheeks felt white-hot despite the rain. She had all but begged Rawdon to make love to her, there in the meadow. What must he have thought of her? So brazen?

How could she have explained the imp that had goaded her to take a chance—the only chance she would ever have—to make love with the man who had held her heart forever.

From the moment they'd left their sun-drenched meadow behind, Rawdon had been furious, outrage rippling from every sinew in his lean body. She could feel his turmoil as if it were a living thing between them. And most hurtful of all, the mere brush of her against him seemed to screw his anger tighter, until she sensed he wanted nothing more than to dash her away from him altogether.

Serena blinked back tears. She had a lifetime to shed them. She wouldn't make things even worse for Rawdon by inflicting a bout of tears on him.

A jagged spray of lightning slashed the sky, sizzling and crackling as it struck the earth a mile or so away. The horse reared and plunged, every muscle in Rawdon's body straining in an effort to keep it from breaking into a wild run. Serena clutched his waist hard in an effort to keep from tumbling to the ground.

"Why the bloody hell didn't I take you to Claudia's when I had the chance," he ground out.

"Rawdon, I know you're angry, but there's no sense getting us both killed," she cried over the storm.

He swore, long and hard, then angled a glance over his

shoulder. "There's some kind of a building up ahead. We'll stop there for the night."

Within minutes, he'd dumped her inside a deserted stable that stood beside the ruin of a burned-out cottage. By the flickering glow of lightning, Serena pieced together an impression of the interior of the building. Last year's supply of hay had been left behind, along with a pierced tin lantern, the waxy stub of a candle gleaming ghostly white inside it. Rawdon tied off his horse in the nearest stall, then rummaged among his things. In a few moments, the candle flickered to life, setting the stable aglow.

"Get some sleep," he snapped, gesturing to a mound of hay. "I'll wake you when it's over—ah, hellfire!"

"I'll sleep! Blast it, I won't say a word," Serena flung back at him, praying she wouldn't dissolve into tears.

"You're soaked to the goddamn skin!" he accused, glaring at her with an anger so heated her garments should have steamed dry on the spot. "Perfect! You'll catch your death of lung fever if you don't get out of those wet things."

"*I* didn't summon the rain! And I'll try to die quietly so I won't cause you any inconvenience!"

"I don't suppose you brought any change of clothes?"

"I most certainly did. They're strapped to the roof of an overturned coach on the strip of road belonging to the Fallen Angel."

He turned and stalked away, muttering.

"Damn you, Rawdon, this isn't my fault!" she called out as he entered the stall. She hoped his horse would kick him square in the head. Shuffling noises emanated from behind the warped-board barrier, then after a moment, Rawdon stormed back out, something white clutched in his hand.

"Here. Get the devil out of those wet things and put this on." He flung the garment down onto the hay beside her. Serena saw it was a man's shirt iced with Brussels lace at the cuffs and throat. Rawdon's shirt. The idea of putting it on, being haunted by the subtle scent of him, enclosed by the waves of fabric that had draped his broad shoulders was too painful to contemplate.

"I prefer to suffer the consequences of my carelessness in silence, thank you."

"In other words you'd rather freeze? Put it on now, Serena, or by God, I'll make you!" His jaw jutted out with the stubbornness that had made his tutors want to dive in their inkpots.

She met him, glare for glare. "Go to blazes, Rawdon Wyatt!" A racking shiver went through her whole body.

It was as if all the tension, all the anger, all the wild emotion that had been seething inside him burst free in that instant. He pounced on her like a panther, spinning her around. Her cloak was dispatched in a twinkling. His fingers tangled in the laces that caught up her bodice in the back, unfastening them with maddening deftness despite her struggles. He dragged the bodice of her gown down off her shoulders, unfastened the petticoats about her waist. Layer after layer drooped, dragged to the floor by the weight of the water that soaked them.

In a heartbeat, even her heavy boned stays lay on the floor. She was clad in nothing but her sodden shift. She felt Rawdon go deathly still, saw his eyes turn molten, so hot she expected him to burn holes in the fragile fabric that draped her. She glanced down at herself, saw that the soaked fabric clung to her skin, almost transparent in spots, the crests of her breasts rosy kisses in the lantern light, the curls that hid her feminine secrets a dusky shadow at the apex of her thighs.

She raised her gaze to Rawdon's face. Potent male arousal. It hardened his jaw, flushed the aristocratic slash of his cheekbones, simmered beneath his lashes. That mouth that had kissed her to insanity in the meadow was carved with a hunger so fierce he was barely holding it in check.

Serena couldn't breathe, her heart pounding in her chest. He wanted her. That was why he'd been so surly since the kiss in the meadow. That was why he'd wanted to be rid of her. Not because he loathed her or was disgusted by her, but because he wanted her as much as she wanted him.

In that instant, she decided to take the biggest risk of her life. Serena raised her fingers to the delicate ribbon between her breasts, and slipped it free. The bodice of the shift fell open, revealing a creamy slice of breast.

"Rawdon?" she breathed his name, her gaze filled with pleading as she raised it to his. "The cloth—it's sticking to me. Help me. Please?" She took his hand and raised it to the bit of cloth, heard his hissed intake of breath as his knuckles grazed the swell of her breast.

"Damn it, Serena, I'm no saint! This is insane, Serena. We can't—"

She leaned forward, kissing his damp chest, slipping his frock coat from his shoulders. "I don't want you to be a saint. I want you to be Rawdon . . . only Rawdon."

As she drew the sleeve down the arm that was stretched toward her shift, Rawdon held tight to the wet fabric, drawing it lower. He released his grasp for a heartbeat, letting his coat fall onto the stable floor, and Serena knew if he were going to draw away it would be now.

She almost sobbed with relief, when he reached for her again.

"Do you have any idea how beautiful you are, Serena?" he breathed as he stripped away her shift, leaving her bare and glistening with raindrops. "God, you're cold as ice. Let me warm you."

She reveled in the sight of him, stripping away his own clothes, laying her back on the dry silkiness of the shirt he had brought out moments before. He followed her down, his hard, hair-roughened body pressed against her, his mouth seeking hers with a mastery that stole her breath away, a tenderness that probed the depths of her soul.

He warmed every part of her with his hands, with his mouth, licking away raindrops as if they were some mystical nectar of passion, sipping at the fragile skin behind her knees, teasing the slope of her belly, suckling at the crests of her breasts with tender ferocity.

No words breached his lips, only groans of need that

stoked her own, muttered oaths more prayer than blasphemy. And when he mounted her, parting her trembling thighs with his knees, settling the surging male part of him against the place liquid and hot and aching, she thought she would die of pleasure.

"Rawdon! Oh, Rawdon, please—"

"Are you sure, Mouse? Ah, damn!" She drew the curse from him by arching against that hard ridge of flesh, her lips straying to his broad, beguiling chest, and the flat nipple all but hidden in a dusting of dark hair.

When her tongue touched it, he swore, low, and sheathed himself inside her. Her maidenly barrier ripped, and she gave a gasp of pain, but the pain faded at the wondrous weight of Rawdon atop her, Rawdon, a part of her.

"Are you all right?" Rawdon grated against the damp tendrils of her hair. "I'm so damn sorry I hurt you."

"It's the most wonderful pain I've ever known," Serena whispered, unable to keep the tears from searing her eyes.

Rawdon stared down at her, his own throat tight, and drew on every wisp of skill he possessed to bring her the fullness of her woman's pleasure. She was quicksilver in his arms, all inhibitions stripped away. She was hot and eager and tender and brave and when she turned to flame in his arms, crying out as the spasms of fulfillment shook her, Rawdon was filled with wonder.

He thrust deep, his own pleasure shattering, stripping his emotions to the bone, leaving him more raw and painfully open than he'd ever been in his life.

He rolled to one side with Serena in his arms, holding her. This was the time when compliments were expected —glib, pretty phrases cast out to a lover. God knew, Rawdon had always been damned adept at it. But as he felt Serena nuzzle against him, felt the precious weight of her in his arms, he couldn't find any words to tell her what he'd just experienced. A passion so deep he'd never surface from it. A melding of bodies and spirits that might have sprung from one of those ridiculous romances he'd always hated.

He groped for his protective armor of wit and cynicism, but they must've melted in the rain, leaving him only confused and raw and needing. The sensation terrified him.

He'd just made love to Serena. Compromised a girl he'd known from childhood. Broken trust. Now the question was, what the devil was he going to do about it?

"Move over so I can drag out the shirt," he said a little gruffly. "We need to get it on you. It's cold as blazes out."

"I've never been so warm," she said without budging, raising up on one elbow, looking into his face. A tumbled goddess, she smiled up at him, her nakedness as beautiful, as natural as Eve's in the Garden of Eden.

Yet his sin had been far worse than taking a bite of an apple.

Rawdon grabed up his damp breeches, dragging them on. "I'll marry you, of course."

"Excuse me?" Her smile melted away.

"Only thing to be done under the circumstances. I've done a damned fine job of ruining you. The sooner we get the wedding over with the better."

She straightened, groping for the shirt, holding it before her like some sort of shield. Rawdon felt like a bastard. Where the hell were all those glib words he'd used before? Hell, he sounded as if he were handing down a death sentence, not proposing matrimony.

"You're under no obligation to marry me," Serena said. "This was all my idea."

"Damn it, Serena, you *will* marry me! What if I got you with child?"

"Did you get your mistresses with child every time you . . . had relations?"

"Hell, no! But—"

"Then it's highly unlikely that you've done so to me."

"Damn it, Serena, what happened with my mistresses has nothing to do with you! You're damn well going to let me make this right, if I have to drag you to the altar."

"No."

"I'll tell your father what happened. He'll make you see reason."

"Do you love me, Rawdon?" The simple words slashed him, deep.

"Of course I love you! From the time we were children—"

"Do you love me like a man loves a woman, a husband his wife?"

Did he love her? Hell, he'd still imagined her in short skirts three days ago. Nobody could fall in love in the space of two days, could they? Certainly not the rakehell Rawdon Wyatt who'd cursed his friends as betrayers when they'd dared to capitulate to love after months of courtship.

His own humiliation stuck in his throat, and he glared down at Serena. "I will be your husband, Serena, and you'll be my wife."

Something wounded crept into her eyes, her sneering smile brittle. "I wanted someone to make love to me. You were kind enough to oblige. I am grateful."

"Damn your bloody gratitude to hell!"

Her chin tipped up. "I'm grateful, but I would never become the wife of a wastrel like you, Rawdon Wyatt."

He reeled as if she'd struck him.

"Do you think I'd spend a lifetime watching you fling away your fortune? Worse still, waste the talents you've been given? Do you think I'd want my children to look up to a man who would rather play Hazard with his friends at some gaming hell than visit his estates? Or his mother?"

Could anyone else's condemnation have cut him to the bone? "Damn it, Serena, you go too far."

"The subject is closed. I won't be forced into marriage with a man who will likely spend the rest of his life attempting to forget I exist, like he does the rest of his responsibilities." She flung his shirt back onto the ground, and fought her way back into her own wet garments. "Take me to Claudia's. Now. Or I swear, I'll walk every step of the way."

Rawdon glared down at her, knowing damned well she'd do exactly as she threatened. The wonder he'd felt had been ripped from his chest, leaving hurt and self-loathing, the burning knowledge she didn't want him. Rawdon Wyatt, the wastrel, the rakehell. In the end, he'd been good enough to make love to her, but not to wed her. That was reserved for that mutton-headed phantom of a lover Serena still clung to in some corner of her heart.

EIGHT

Claudia's house nested like a plump gray dove at the crest of a hill. Roses, battered by the storm, were bruised and bent, their petals littering the ground. Serena felt a desperate urge to go curl up in their midst, for she felt as embattled as they were.

Grief was a raging beast inside her, hurt a suffocating blanket that made it almost impossible to draw breath. Rawdon had loved her, with his body, his hands, his mouth. Rawdon had opened the doors to every dream she'd dared to have. A lifetime's worth. Then he'd taken that thing of inexpressible beauty and shattered it.

Of course I'll marry you.

He'd cast out the words like a duelist about to be blasted into oblivion, without any thought to the consequences. Reckless Rawdon. Yet this time there was a spark of heartbreaking unselfishness as well. He would marry her, to save her from ruin. He would give her the protection of his name. Chain himself to her forever, even though he didn't love her.

The horse stumbled, and Serena was jarred against the implacable wall of his back. No, not even to realize her own most cherished dream would she trap Rawdon into a marriage he didn't want, saddle him with a wife.

But the price—oh, God, the price for that golden hour of magic that had flowed between them. The pain she'd had to inflict on the raw places, the vulnerable places in

Rawdon Wyatt's heart to save him from his mad notions of honor. She'd devastated him in the places only she knew existed. She wondered if she would ever forgive herself.

Or if Rawdon would.

A groom bolted up to grab the reins of the horse, and Rawdon dismounted. He reached up and swept Serena down from the horse, as impersonally as if she were some parcel he'd been asked to deliver. His face was stone-cold, and Serena knew the effort it was taking him to lock away his anger and pain. Not only had she hurt him, but then, she'd forced him to bring her here, to Claudia's where he would have to face the lover who had scorned him so many years ago. The woman, who for a time, had held the treasure of Rawdon's heart.

"You can just leave me here," Serena said in a desperate effort to spare him. "There's no need for you to—"

"Face the other Creighton sister who told me to go to the devil?" Rawdon shot her a seething glare. "Don't fear. Your gentle refusal has wiped all traces of hers from my memory."

Serena winced.

It seemed forever before they were ensconced in Claudia's drawing room, a chamber the color of blanc mange, with all the spice of gruel. Rawdon, still damp from the rain, his hair wind-tousled against his shoulders, stood at the window, his feet braced apart, his hands clasped behind him, like a prisoner aboard the tumbrel that was to take him to his execution.

Serena couldn't stay still. She paced and fidgeted until the door burst open, and Claudia—a picture of elegance and perfection rushed into the room.

"Serena, what trouble have you gotten yourself into now?" she demanded with sisterly outrage.

"A carriage accident, an encounter with a highwayman, and a half-crazed suitor who would have been happy to flay me into a dozen pieces," Rawdon said, turning to face them.

Claudia gasped, pressing a hand to her heart. "R—Rawdon. Oh, dear."

Serena had expected something sensational, spectacular at this meeting between Rawdon and her sister, but there was nothing of pain and betrayal in his rugged features when he looked down into Claudia's face. No, those emotions were now reserved for her, Serena realized miserably.

"Now that I've delivered the scapegrace to you, I'll be on my way."

"Surely you can stay for tea?"

"I've got fortunes to lose. Wouldn't want to waste any time doing something responsible."

Claudia blinked at him as if he were quite mad. Serena felt his words like the twist of a knife blade in her heart.

He crossed to where she stood, and those green eyes pierced hers, delving down to the part of her that was raw with guilt and grief. "You may expect me to visit you in a month or two, Miss Creighton."

She swallowed hard, knowing that even now Rawdon was guarding her, intent on making certain she wasn't abandoned if she were carrying his child. With a bow that broke Serena's heart, he exited the room.

"Serena, whatever is amiss between the two of you?" Claudia demanded. Serena looked up at her older sister, shattered.

"He's asked me to marry him," Serena choked out.

"That—that's impossible! I can hardly believe— Surely, you didn't accept him!" Claudia blanched. "He's a wastrel! A scoundrel! No fit husband for any woman!"

"That's exactly what I told him," Serena said, more desolate than she'd ever been in her life.

It seemed Serena's sentence for her crime against Rawdon was to die of boredom. Claudia's placid life gave her no room to breathe, no space to run, not a spark of excitement rippling the smooth waters of the Harbuckles' existence. It gave Serena far too much time to think, remember a thousand frozen moments from her time with Rawdon. The wicked curve of his grin, the devilish glint in his eyes, the hunger that had consumed him as his calloused hands explored her body, his mouth melding with her in an intoxicating sweetness that had hurled her into a heaven she'd never imagined.

Her woman's time had come, and she'd been stunned that she'd greeted it not with relief, but with a bout of soul-shattering sobs that had left her drained. It was as if some traitorous part of her actually yearned to feel Rawdon's child beating its way into life beneath her heart.

It was over. She had been willing to risk anything for one night in Rawdon's arms. She just hadn't realized that she'd condemn herself to an eternity of aching emptiness, longing for him to fill her. Not just with the surging power of his body, but with his soul, his reckless laughter, his gruff protectiveness. The light in his eyes that had dared her to be herself, outrageous as such a concept was, the devil with propriety.

She grabbed up her bonnet, heading for the rose gardens, remembering Rawdon's sweet words about how her eyes took on the hues of the blossoms. If that were so, she was certain they must now be the bleakest gray, for she'd never felt so dismal in her life.

She'd nearly gotten to the door when she heard Claudia's cry. "Serena, oh, Serena, you'll never believe what that wretched man has done now! Disgraced his family! Anyone associated with him! I vow, he deserves to hang, so he does!"

"Claudia, what are you babbling about?" Serena turned, aware her sister could mean anyone from the cobbler in the village to the grooms that worked in the Harbuckle stables.

"Look for yourself! Just look!" She jammed the paper she was holding into Serena's hand.

Serena glanced down at the copy of *The Spectator,* the London paper obviously days old.

NOBLEMAN ARRESTED FOR HIGHWAY ROBBERY, THE
HONORABLE RAWDON WYATT CHARGED AS THE DREAD
FALLEN ANGEL.

The floor seemed to pitch beneath Serena's feet. "This is absurd! The Fallen Angel robbed Rawdon! Took his ring!" She scanned the article, outrage blossoming in her chest.

Chumley Varden, Baronet of Fromley, had recognized the Wyatt crest on the ring of the man who had robbed him the very night Rawdon and Serena had spent together, and a certain courtesan had admitted to stitching a highwayman's mask for Rawdon the week before the incident.

Rawdon in prison? Why didn't he just tell them he'd been with her, Serena thought angrily. Why—oh, God. She slumped onto a chair, sick certainty lodging in her stomach.

Would the infernal fool go to the gallows rather than admit that she'd been compromised? Would a man make such a sacrifice for someone he merely had affection for? Or would it take a deeper emotion, one he might not even realize he felt?

Serena cast aside the paper. "There's only one thing to do."

"Serena, you're not going to do anything! Not stirring a foot out of this house! I forbid you to—"

"I'm going to Rawdon, and the Fallen Angel himself couldn't stop me!"

NINE

R awdon leaned against the wall of his cell, his eyes on the block of barred light in his tiny window. His only glimpse of sunshine. One tiny taste. Why was it that it reminded him with such poignant anguish of his night with Serena?

She'd offered her body for his taking, said she trusted him to be kind, but he hadn't been kind, and he hadn't taken care of her the way he had sworn he would. He'd cast his noble principles to the devil, driven by something he couldn't name to mate with her, to claim her in the most primal way possible. He'd hurt her—and if he deserved to be imprisoned in this cell for anything, it was because he'd wounded the woman he loved.

Loved.

God, what a thing to discover. The knowledge had slammed into his chest like a bludgeon as he'd stood before the authorities.

Merely explain to us how this grievous error could have happened, sir. Someone must have been with you that night —perhaps another rogue in a gaming hell? Perhaps a woman?

Rawdon had glared down at them, certain he'd go to the gallows before he'd expose Serena to ridicule and shame, their ugly, knowing stares. Ruination.

He'd held out his wrists to receive the manacles they had attempted to hide discreetly on the floor. And he had refused to see anyone since except for his family's barrister.

Rawdon reached into his pocket, taking out a bit of lace that had torn from Serena's gown during their loving. He'd found it, like a forgotten treasure, in the sleeve of his frock coat. And he'd thanked God for it with every passing day.

He held the bit of lace to his lips, and closed his eyes. It still smelled of her—raindrop-fresh, sunshiny and bright, flowers and mischief. Magic.

Yet, she wasn't his. Could never be his. The knowledge that she loved some other man was a far more devastating blow than anything the courts could deal to him now.

There was a grating sound, a key in the lock, and Rawdon didn't even bother to glance up as the door swung open.

"Pevensy," he addressed the barrister he'd been expecting, "If you're here to try to convince me to change my tale, it's no use. I was alone. In bed that night."

"We both know that is a lie."

He wheeled, staggering to his feet, horror and disbelief and joy surging in a tempest through him as he saw a vision of loveliness silhouetted against bleak stone walls. Serena, garbed in his favorite color—sky blue—her chin resolute, her eyes violet mysteries that made his heart pound.

Behind her stood the barrister and the judge who had been friend to Rawdon's grandfather—an honorable man who had attempted to do all in his power to free Justin Wyatt's wayward grandson.

"Serena, get out," Rawdon ordered, every muscle in his body iron-taut. "This doesn't concern you!"

"You spent that night with me, Rawdon, in a stable halfway between the Red Dog Inn and my sister's house."

"Serena, damn it!"

"You were rescuing me again. I'd gotten in a coach wreck and stumbled across a highwayman. You bought me at the price of the ring your grandfather had given you."

"Don't listen to her," Rawdon begged in desperation, seeing the flush of embarrassment on the barrister's cheeks, the censure in the judge's face as he regarded Serena.

"Maybe he slipped out to commit the robbery," a prison guard sneered.

"No, I was touching him every moment," Serena's soft words lanced Rawdon's heart.

"Then, I believe we shall take steps to release this man at once," the judge growled. "That is, if you would be willing to publicly testify to what you've said here, Miss Creighton."

"I would." Serena was smiling. Damn her, she'd just destroyed her reputation, and she was smiling at him, staring up at him with mysteries in those bewitching eyes.

"Miss Creighton, we've matters to attend to now, if you would be so good as to tell us where to reach you?"

"I'll be at Wyatt House," she said softly, "when Rawdon comes home."

The townhouse had been in the Wyatt family for a hundred years, but never had a Wyatt charged up the stairs with wilder emotions than the Honorable Rawdon did now. It was terror, pure and simple. Terror that Serena had changed her mind, that she wasn't waiting for him there. Mingling with raging uncertainty. What did a man say to a woman who had cast herself to ruin in his name? How did a man convince a woman to marry him when that woman loved someone else?

And how could he ever tell Serena all the things that were in his heart? Emotions so unexpected, so powerful he felt as if his chest would burst with them. Pain and yearning, desire and delight, respect and wonder. And love.

A footman swung open the door, all but oversetting Rawdon in his enthusiasm to welcome his master home. But Rawdon barely heard the youth's greeting.

"Is there a lady here? Miss Serena Creighton?" Rawdon demanded.

The boy broke off somewhere between "ecstatic" and "knew that highwayman rubbish was damned rot." He gaped at his master.

"Miss Creighton? Aye, sir. She's here. Got her ensconced in the Red Room as if she was a bleedin' queen! Old Bumly's been stoppin' by at the back stairs of the barrister's office ever so often on her way to the butcher's beggin' information. When we heard what the little lady did for you, we near kissed the hem o' her gown."

Rawdon shoved past the youth. "The only one who'll be kissing anything of Miss Creighton's is me!"

He stormed up a corridor aglow with the night's first candles, remembering what it had been like to see Serena by that faint glow, naked, needing him.

His chest was a raw hollow only she could fill, his pulse a steady throb of desperation. Her scornful dismissal of his first proposal echoed in his mind, the things she had said, bitter things that were all too true.

He had to find a way to change her mind.

When he reached the Red Room, he hesitated. It took all his courage to shove open the door. He did it so quietly Serena didn't even realize he'd entered.

She sat on the floor in billows of sky-blue satin, feeding the scrumptious banquet of a tea his staff had prepared for her to Rawdon's most disreputable hound. The animal, blind and shaggy and nondescript, was eating from her fingertips in pure canine bliss. Muddy paw prints smudged her dress. The better part of her curls had escaped their pins. But he had never seen anything more beautiful in his life.

"Serena," he grated. Just her name. Because he didn't have a damned idea what he was going to say next.

At his words, the dog hauled himself to his feet, and dragged aching bones to greet his master. He ran a hand over the old animal's head by instinct, his gaze imprisoned by Serena's as she turned her face toward his.

Rawdon's heart turned over. She didn't look ruined. She looked beautiful, bright, her smile dazzling, but tentative.

"Hello, Rawdon."

He stared at her like a raw lad with his first love, his tongue stumbling over words he wished he could say, his hands awkward. "You didn't need to come forward to clear my name," he said at last. "Pevensy would have found some way to get me out. He's gotten me out of scrapes almost as often as I've gotten you out of 'em."

"I was glad to help you. I couldn't bear to think of you in that awful place because of me."

"It wasn't because of you. It was my own damned foolishness that landed me in that predicament."

"One you could have gotten out of easily enough, if I weren't in the middle to complicate everything. Sometimes I feel like I've been doing that your whole life. Complicating things. Muddling them up."

"And I thank God for that every day." Rawdon crossed to her, capturing her hand in his. "Serena, I want you to complicate every day for the rest of my life."

"Wh-what?"

"I know I made a muck of things the first time I proposed to you. And you were right to tell me to go the blazes. But hear me out this time. Please."

Her eyes were shimmering, so earnest, her lips trembled. She nodded.

"I want to marry you, Serena."

"It's not necessary. I told you—"

"It's necessary to me, damn it. I know I'm a wastrel and a scoundrel and a rogue, just like you said. Not a fit husband for any woman. But I'd make myself over into any image you wanted. I'd give up gambling. Hell, I'd live at Wyckham if you wanted to, invite Mama and Clarissa for tea five times a day."

"Rawdon—"

"I'd be so damned steady and responsible no one would recognize me."

"But then I wouldn't either."

"Serena, I know you love that—that mutton-headed bastard who broke your heart. But if you'd give me a chance, I'd do everything in my power to make you happy."

"Rawdon. Oh, Rawdon. I couldn't let you do that for me. Sacrifice yourself."

"It'd be a small sacrifice indeed, if you could . . ." He swallowed hard, all his hopes and dreams in his face. His hands clutched hers so tight he feared he'd bruise them. "I love the way your eyes dance and your lips are full of mischief. I love the way you laugh and the way you tell the world to go to the devil without saying a word.

"I love the spirit that drove you out onto the road that night, and into my arms. The adventurer in you that makes you willing to take risks, to dare to reach out and grasp what you want out of life with so much courage. And I love the tender place inside you that tried so desperately to be gentle to Bertrand. And to me. I'd face any challenge, right any wrong you might name, Serena, just like those knights in the fairy tales you used to adore. If . . . you could love me."

"Rawdon . . ."

"I love you, Serena. There, I said it. You say you don't want to marry where you can't give your heart. Let me give you mine. I pray there's love enough inside it to fill the empty places this paragon of a man left when he cast your love aside."

Serena was peering up at him, her eyes shimmering with tears, and—dare he hope it? Joy? "He was never my suitor," she said, reaching up, cupping his jaw. "He was my hero from the first moment I remember. Gallant and bold, laughing and daring. He helped me bury my kitten under a rose briar, and he taught me how to steal apples and not get caught. I was so certain he was perfection incarnate that I couldn't understand why my sister didn't . . . if he would have loved me, I would have followed him anyplace he might name."

"Serena, you . . ."

"I've loved you for as long as I can remember, Rawdon. That is why I tricked you into kissing me. That is why I . . . in the stable, I—"

"God, Serena!" He crushed her in his arms, his mouth crashing down on hers, hungry, hot with promise. "Marry me! Marry me, or I vow I'll find Bertrand and make him reveal whatever tower he was going to lock you in! Marry me and I'll work to be the man you believe I could be. One who won't disappoint you."

"You've been my hero forever, Rawdon. Now be my love as well."

Rawdon peered down into her eyes, marveling at the miracle that he would be able to do so forever—love her, laugh with her, drag her out of mischief. He prayed for a lifetime of Serena's disasters.

That was what happily-ever-afters were made of.

THE LADY
AND
THE TIGER

 CHRISTINA DODD

ONE

Kent, England, 1813

Miss Laura Haver groped her way toward the ocean cliff, guided only by the sound of the waves and scent of salt water on the breeze. Clouds streamed across the stars, blocking the feeble light, and her foot skidded down the first few inches of cliff before she realized she'd reached her goal.

Sitting down hard, she pulled herself to safety, then scooted back and huddled in the rough sea grass. Pebbles scattered down the steep slope to the beach on the Hamilton estate, and she listened for the shouts that meant she'd been discovered.

There was nothing. Just the endless rocking of the waves on the sandy beach below.

It had been three months. Three months of lonely torment as she pored over her brother's diary and tried to decipher his cryptic scrawls. Three months of futile visits to the London townhouse where Keefe Leighton, the Earl of Hamilton, resided and kept an office. Three months of listening while Leighton assured her the government would avenge Ronald's death.

Three months of knowing that he lied.

A boat crunched on the sand below as it drove onto the beach. Shivering with chill and fear, she pulled the dark hood over her brown hair and scooted back to the edge of the cliff. Although it was a moonless night and so dark she could scarcely see her hand in front of her face, she nevertheless observed as covered lanterns flashed like fireflies. They showed bits of light only as the men deemed necessary, and in their movement she counted at least twenty smugglers—eight unloading the boat, eight receiving on the beach, and three men just standing, apparently supervising the operation.

One tall figure moved back and forth, and from the consideration all the men paid him, it was obvious he was the leader. Ronald's diary mentioned him only as Jean, but Laura feared she knew his identity. She strained her eyes wide and prayed for just one moment of light—and when it came, she stood in indignation.

"He *is* the smuggler."

As if her words caught on the wind and blew to his ears alone, Leighton turned and looked up toward the top of the cliff. She saw the glint of his eyes, and with the instinct of a hunted creature, she crouched behind a rock and froze. She didn't want Leighton to see her here. She couldn't let him find her here. All her ugly suspicions had been proved true, and if he had killed her brother to silence him, she doubted he would hesitate to murder her, too.

Her heart pounded and she wanted to flee with unrestrained panic, but she'd come too far and too much was at stake for her to lose her composure now. Straining to listen, she could hear men's voices above the lap of the waves, but no shout of discovery gave her reason to run. She had to keep her head, get back to the inn, and write her report to give to the authorities. It would be difficult to convince them that a member of the House of Lords was nothing but a common criminal, but with Ronald's diary as corroboration, she'd do it.

She had to, for Ronald's sake.

She crept backwards. Her skirt caught on her heels, rocks ground into the palms of her hands. She stood finally, and leaned to dust off her skirt. When she straightened and squinted toward the horizon, she realized a tall figure blocked out the stars. She stared, pinned by fear, then with a yelp and a start, she whirled and ran.

She could hear the sound of thudding boots behind her. The gorse grabbed at her skirts and the ruts of the mostly untraveled road moved and twisted in snakelike guile. The wind gusted at her back and carried a man's warm breath to touch the nape of her neck. Gooseflesh ran over her skin and she moaned softly, clutching the stitch that started in her side. When she could run no longer, she dared a look behind her.

All she could see was black night. The stars had disappeared completely and the upcoming storm splattered the first raindrops in her face. She'd imagined Leighton when he wasn't there.

With a ragged sigh of relief, she slowed to a walk and trudged toward the inn. How stupid and cowardly she'd been in her precipitous flight! But for weeks she had dreamed about Leighton chasing her. She'd seen his face on every dark-haired man who walked the streets. Something about Leighton convinced her she should flee and never stop.

It hadn't always been that way. When Ronald had been killed, she'd gone to meet Leighton for the first time, confident he would help her. After all, Ronald had been Leighton's first secretary, and he spoke of Leighton in dazzling terms.

Instead, Leighton had been actively and personally repelling her inquiries. According to him, she should remain at home like a proper lady, and the smugglers would be brought to justice when the time arrived. But she couldn't bear to be patronized, especially not by Leighton. She just clenched her teeth and faced up to him, ignoring the breadth of his shoulders, the sculptured perfection of his features, and her own untutored desire to hurl herself into his arms and let him care for her. Early in their relationship, she might have done just that, but from the very beginning some instinct told her that his placid exterior hid something deep, potent and deceptive.

Still apprehensive, she glanced behind her again. Ronald had always said she was too straightforward to sneak around and too blunt for diplomacy, but now that she'd read his diary she'd learned that her brother had led a secret life. He had her convinced he was nothing more than Leighton's secretary, when actually he had worked to uncover this ring of smugglers. A frown puckered her forehead. He hadn't told her because he didn't want her to know and worry. He'd been protecting her, and now she was alone with no one to avenge his death but her.

She'd do it, too. She'd make sure those responsible suffered as she had suffered with his loss.

The rain began to fling itself to the ground with increasing conviction, and she wrapped her redingote, that coat which she'd sewn with her own fingers, tighter around her shoulders.

When she saw the lights of the Bull and Eagle, she fixed on them as if they were her salvation. She knew, of course, that Leighton might seek her, but not tonight. He had brandy to unload and reckless men to pay, and he would never imagine that she'd be on her way at first light, even if she had to walk.

Carefully she crept through the now-muddy inn yard and pushed the outside door open. In the two days she'd stayed here, she'd ascertained that it squeaked if not handled properly, and that brought Ernest bustling out of his quarters to smile and bow and greet her as if she were the salvation of Leighton Village.

And all because of one little lie she'd been driven to tell.

God would forgive her, she was sure, for she'd told it in pursuit of truth and justice, but she didn't know if hearty, bald-headed Ernest ever would.

The hinges didn't make a sound. The taproom was empty, as it had been when she left, and she didn't understand how her luck had held. She didn't want anyone to know she'd been out, yet at the same time during the other evenings she had been here the townsfolk had congregated in the taproom for ale and conversation. Briefly she wondered what kept them away, why the fire burned low and place looked abandoned. Then a burst of angry shouting from the kitchen sent her fleeing up the stairs. At the top she paused and listened.

Ernest's voice she could recognize, and he sounded both agitated and afraid. The other voice was a man's, lower, less distinct, but with a tone that raised the hair on the back of her head.

Who was it? Gripping the rail in both hands, she crept down two steps and listened intently. Why did he sound so menacing? Heedlessly, she stepped on the edge of the third step and it creaked beneath her shoe. The conversation in the kitchen stopped and she froze. Footsteps sounded on the floorboards and Ernest stepped into the common room. She tried to melt into the shadows, and he stared up at her. He saw her; she would have sworn he saw her, but he shrugged and walked back into the kitchen without any indication that he'd noted her presence.

The conversation began again, lower this time, and she sneaked to her room. Silently, she took the key from her reticule and unlocked the door. Slipping inside, she shut the dark oak panels behind her and turned the key again, protecting herself from all comers.

It was just as she'd left it. This was, as Ernest had told her the night she arrived, the best bedchamber in the inn and the one which had served Henry the Eighth when he'd been stranded in a storm. Laura didn't know if she believed that, but certainly a gigantic old-fashioned bed dominated the room. It rested on a dais in the corner, and the canopy was hung with velvet curtains which could be drawn to keep in the warmth. Gargoyles decorated every bedpost and each rail between had been sanded and polished until it shone. Ernest had proudly told her that over two thousand geese had been plucked to stuff that feather mattress. She only knew she'd been lost in it when she slept.

The fire in her fireplace burned, piled high with sweet-smelling logs. On one side was a settle, a bench whose high back protected her from drafts when she sat there. On the other stood a desk and a chair. As she always did, she went to the desk first. The candles had burned down while she was gone, but they still illuminated the papers that were strewn in artful disarray. Beneath them rested a diary. Ronald's diary. His diary was the one reason she knew to be in Leighton Village now, tonight. It was the reason she'd scouted the area earlier in the day and had deducted that the cove would be the landing place.

She reassured herself the diary remained safe, then thoroughly covered it with the papers again. Ronald had taught her that. Always hide things in plain sight, he said. He'd learned that while in service to Leighton, and she'd found it good advice.

Flushed with guilt, she opened the desk drawer and pushed her hand all the way to the back. Her fingertips touched the cold metal, and she drew out a small silver pistol. On this matter, she ignored Ronald and his advice. She couldn't bear to leave the deadly thing out. She'd stressed her need for privacy to Ernest and been careful to lock the door whenever she left, but possession of such a firearm made her nervous. It was Ronald's, and until he'd been killed she'd never imagined she would want to carry one. She knew how to use it, of course. Her father had insisted on her learning self-defense while they lived in India. But back in England, she'd believed herself inviolate. Now, with Ronald's death, her veil of security had been ripped and she trusted no fellow being.

Strange, but her sense of being threatened by Leighton had started long before her suspicions that he was the smuggler congealed into a certainty. Once when she turned suddenly, she caught him contemplating her with a look she'd seen only one other time. When her parents were alive and the whole family lived in India, she'd seen a tiger concealing itself in high grass, waiting for his prey. Leighton's mien betrayed a tiger-like confidence in himself. He was sure he could have her if he wanted, but the time wasn't yet right. It had given her a shiver, but when she tried to verify her impression, all expression had smoothed from his face.

But as the months had worn on, she sometimes thought

she could sense the impatient twitch of his tail and the way he crouched, waiting to pounce.

Shivering, she replaced the pistol. Stripping off her wet redingote, she flung it over the back of the settle, then laid her gloves by the feeble flames. She slipped out of her practical boots, now covered with mud, and placed them neatly by the gloves. Her dark blue walking dress, so suitable for the city and for the occupation of seamstress, was bedraggled from the night's ill-use, and she touched the hem with trembling fingers. She hadn't the money to replace it; every cent she had had gone into this trip to Kent. Still—she firmed her chin—it was worth the loss of a mere gown to bring Ronald's murderer to justice, and she was close to that now. Kneeling, she repaired the fire so it burned brightly again, warming her hands all the while. As her hair dried, the short strands sprang away from her head and curled in wild abandon, but she didn't care tonight, for who would see it?

"She's at the Bull and Eagle." Keefe Leighton, the Earl of Hamilton, gave the boy a push. "Go back and tell the others, then return and wait in the stable. I'll be out when I've got the information."

In the dark and the rain, he couldn't see Franklin leave, but he knew he would be obeyed. Everyone of his men were loyal to him, and only to him, but tonight something had gone wrong. As he kicked the door of the Bull and Eagle, he cursed the woman he'd seen silhouetted against the stars.

Laura. His instincts told him it was Laura Haver, and his instincts were very active where she was concerned. What was she doing here on this precise night? What did she know, and how did she know it? What had her brother told her that he hadn't been able to communicate to Leighton? Leighton needed to know the answers, so he'd abandoned his men as they unloaded casks of brandy and hid them in the caves on the cliffs above the beach. Leighton had to follow the woman.

The taproom was empty. Not even Ernest stood before

the fire that sputtered on the hearth, and Leighton's gaze probed every corner as he scraped mud off his boots. Then the innkeeper bustled out of the kitchen, wiping his hands on his apron. "Hey, what are ye doing out tonight?" he demanded roughly. "Ye know—"

Leighton swept his hat off and Ernest stopped in his tracks. Something that looked like horror flashed briefly across his rotund face, then he wiped his expression clear and allowed a slow grin to build. Hurrying forward, he took Leighton's cloak. "M'lord. How delightful! M'lady assured me ye'd arrive."

"M'lady?"

"M'lady arrived yesterday, but she didn't expect ye for several days."

What was the man babbling about? Leighton kept his face carefully blank. His mother was dead, his grandmother seldom left the manor, and they were the only noblewomen Ernest called "m'lady." In a neutral tone, Leighton asked, "Didn't she?"

Chuckling, Ernest slipped behind the bar and opened the tap on a cask of Leighton's favorite ale. Brown liquid splashed into the mug while Ernest said, "Aye, 'twill be a surprise sure to please her. Almost as pleasant as the surprise ye've given us." He winked and passed Leighton the glass. "Marrying the young lady, and at Gretna Green, too! We'd never have thought it of ye, m'lord, but when love strikes as sudden as all that, a man's got to legshackle the heifer before she's had a chance to think."

"My opinion exactly." Leighton clutched the handle of the mug and wished he could clutch someone by the throat with equal fervor. He'd come in, furious and determined, and been knocked completely awry by Ernest's babblings. Now he found he was supposed to have married—and at Gretna Green. "Who knows about this?"

"Ah . . ." Ernest swabbed the length of the bar with a rag. "Well, to tell ye the truth, m'lord, word seems to have got out in the village."

"Now, how did that happen?"

Ernest scrubbed harder.

Taking a chance, Leighton used her name. "Did . . .
Laura . . . mention this to many people?"

"Nay! She was as discreet as ye instructed, and told
only me."

So it was Laura who awaited him in the bedchamber
above. Of course, she didn't realize her lord would ever
truly arrive, but perhaps these events could be turned to
his favor.

Leaning on his elbows, Ernest smiled at Leighton feebly. "But of course the women wondered, and I gave 'em
just one hint, and before I knew it—" He flung up his
hands in a helpless display. "Ye know women, m'lord.
They're terrible gossips."

"Damn!" Leighton paced away from the bar. The
whole village knew that their lord had supposedly married? Laura Haver had a lot to answer for, and the list
grew with each passing minute. "Gossip can be the cause
of a lot of trouble. Did m'lady happen to tell you why I
wasn't with her or why she didn't go on to Hamilton
Court when it is so close?"

"Aye, m'lord, she told me everything."

Ernest beamed with pride at being trusted with so
many secrets, yet at the same time lines of worry marred
the baby softness of his skin and his dark gaze darted
toward the kitchen as if he perceived danger within.
Leighton had never seen him look so beleaguered, and it
stopped him in his tracks. In his business, he recognized
the signs of a traitor, and he softly paced back to the bar
and leaned on it. "Ernest, have you got a problem you'd
like to discuss?"

Leighton well knew the power of his gaze, and Ernest
cowered, then dropped his rag to the floor and bent down
behind the bar to pick it up. "I'll take ye up there now,
m'lord." He bustled out from behind the bar, his shoulders hunched. "I know ye're anxious for a reunion."

Wanting to see how badly Ernest wanted him gone,
Leighton said, "I ought to eat first."

"No!" Ernest turned on him, then tried to smile. "Not
here. In yer room. I'll bring up a meal to yer room."

"Ernest . . ." Leighton drew out his name in warning.

"Where's yer valet? Is yer horse in the stable?"

Leighton watched Ernest sweat and contemplated the situation. Ernest would have to be dealt with, but Ernest and his family had been the innkeepers at the Bull and Eagle for two hundred years. Ernest would be waiting when Leighton walked down the stairs once more.

Laura Haver was his first priority. She didn't know it yet, but she was going to tell him every bit of information she knew. He would work on her. Hell, he looked forward to working on her. Decision made, Leighton answered Ernest. "I walked over."

"From the manor?" Ernest's eyebrows lifted so high they would have touched his hairline, if he'd had one. "Didn't ye know to look for m'lady here first?"

"We haven't been speaking." It wasn't a lie. He could scarcely talk to m'lady when no m'lady existed.

"A tiff already?" Ernest clucked his tongue and bent down and rummaged under the bar. "But an evening visit such as this will cure that honeymonth uncertainty. Here." He handed Leighton a dusty bottle of wine. "'Tis one of my best. Share it with her tonight."

Leighton took the bottle, looked up the stairs, and for the first time allowed himself to wonder what Laura would do when he knocked on the door. She didn't plan on him arriving to claim his "bride," but . . . his vision blurred in a sudden flush of heat. He'd caught her at last. He'd have to question her about her presence here, and he knew from experience she was stubborn, bad-tempered, and determined.

He might have to question her all night.

He looked at the bottle in his hand. She might need to have her tongue loosened with an application of truth medication, and if that didn't work, he might have to seduce her—for the good of his operation, of course.

He grinned. The little fool had played right into his hands.

TWO

Laura listened as the two men spoke in the taproom below. It was probably nothing, probably the first of the villagers arriving for an ale, but the events of the night had made her wary, and she slipped over to the door and laid her head against the boards while straining to hear.

The knock on the door made her jump backward, stumbling on the thin carpet that covered part of the floor.

"M'lady?"

Only Ernest called her by that title. "What?" she called, and her voice quavered.

"'Tis Ernest, m'lady, with a surprise for ye."

"What kind of surprise?" She feared suspicion colored her tone, but Ernest sounded as cheerful as ever.

"'Tis something to warm yer bones." Metal rattled against metal. "Shall I just unlock the door and pass it through to ye?"

She stared in horror at the metal lock. She'd thought herself inviolate in here, and now Ernest announced he had another key. Should she fling her weight against the door and block it? She looked down at herself and at another time, she would have laughed. "Bird-bones," Ronald had called her, and "Shorty."

Should she start pushing furniture against the door? Her gaze swept the room. No, she wouldn't be able to move big enough things fast enough. And why was she worried, really? As far as she could tell, Ernest had been totally trustworthy, keeping the secret she'd entrusted to him with perfect consideration. Only the events on the cliff colored her suspicions of him.

"I'll open it," she called. She wanted to retain control of access to her room, and not have Ernest thinking he could enter any time. She produced the key and turned it in the lock, then opened the door a crack and peeked through.

Leighton.

She tried to ram the door closed but obviously he anticipated her action, for he shoved and the door sprang open under his weight.

She stumbled back and when he boomed, "Darling!" she almost fell. But he rescued her, swept her into his arms, lifting her until her feet dangled, and kissed her.

For the watching innkeeper, it must have looked like romance personified. For Laura, it was the most frightening experience of her life. Leighton clearly intended to impress her with his size and her lack of it, and he succeeded quite impressively. She jerked her head back, wanting to free her mouth to scream, and found his hand cupping her neck. Where was his other hand? Her mind scrambled to adjust, to discover, and found he held her close with one arm under her posterior. Her posterior! She, who maintained dignity at all costs, had Leighton holding her up by her posterior! Then his mouth invaded hers, and she forgot about dignity and struck at his shoulders. He didn't seem to notice. His smooth lips followed hers with a sure instinct, blocking every little evasive maneuver and countering with some maneuvers of his own. She'd never had a man nibble at her lips and when she opened them, slip his tongue inside. And when she kicked his legs, he chuckled as if he were amused!

So she bit him.

He dropped her to her feet and grabbed at his mouth, and she backed up as fast as she could until the edge of the desk struck her thighs and stopped her. A glance at the door proved it to be shut, and she stammered, "He's gone."

"Quite a while ago."

While Leighton dabbed at his tongue and looked at the blood on his finger, she filled her lungs to scream. He reached her with one giant step, but made no attempt to smother her. He just watched her with a wicked amusement, and her cry for help disintegrated into a whimper.

"Go ahead," he said. "Yell all you want. No one dares interfere between a married couple." He cupped her chin and leaned down to whisper, "And you're my little wife."

Dear God. He knew. She could scarcely speak with dismay. "We're not really married!"

"You told Ernest we were." Leighton straightened and with a swirl of movement swept off his black wool greatcoat. Beneath he wore loose, rough clothes, more fitting to a fisherman—or a smuggler—than to a lord. "Imagine my surprise when I arrived at the inn to be informed my bride awaited me upstairs."

He swung his fist and she ducked, but he did nothing but thrust the papers off the desk and deposit the bottle of wine he held in one fist. Ronald's diary landed on the floor with a thud, but with an effort of will she kept her gaze fixed on Leighton's face.

He didn't seem to notice the precious leather-bound volume, but she could see it out of the corner of her eye, lying with its ruby cover glowing on the otherwise scattered sheets. Leighton seemed to consider her wide-eyed terror nothing but just trepidation of his reprisal, and he said, "I'm not a man to let opportunity slide, especially when I'm long overdue for a wedding night."

She didn't know what to do. Her fingers trembled with the desire to pick up the diary and hide it behind her back, but she didn't want to call it to his attention. At the same time, he was making threats. His voice, always deep and mild, had slipped into a husky whisper, and his eyes gleamed like blue coals from the hottest part of the fire. His black cravat was nothing more than a scarf to warm his neck, tied with true carelessness into a twisted knot.

His dark shirt laid open to the middle of his chest and drops of water clung to the curls that poked forth. The cotton stuck to his shoulders in wet patches, and she could almost see steam rising because of his heat. Her personal fright warred with her fear he would discover what she knew, and it irritated her that she could worry about her own safety when she had a chance to avenge herself on Ronald's murderer.

Moving her hands along the desk top behind her, she crept sideways away from the spilled papers. She had to concentrate on removing his attention away from the betraying diary, and she seemed successful, for Leighton watched her, only her. When she'd reached the edge of the desk, he turned and strode to the settle. Fingering her redingote, he said, "It would seem you've been out tonight."

"Why do you say that?"

"It's damp." He tossed his own heavy wool greatcoat over the top of hers in what Laura thought a most suggestive manner. "And it didn't start raining until a few moments ago."

"I went for a walk."

He nudged at her encrusted boots with his foot. "Through the mud?"

Cocking her head, she replied, "Much like yourself."

"You're a clever minx. Saucy, too." For such a large man, he moved gracefully, and he eased himself down on the settle as if he planned to remain there a long time.

The high back of the seat protected most of him from her sight, but she could see his hands as they came forward to grasp each one of his work boots, and jerk it off.

She stared. What was he doing?

"I'm removing my boots," he answered, although she wasn't aware of asking the question aloud. "I'm wet and I'm cold, and I'd like to spend an evening alone with my new bride—and so I informed Ernest."

She couldn't believe that Leighton spoke to her so frankly and with such provocative intent. Then she remembered the image of the Indian tiger. The lying in wait, the stalking of the victim who, unaware, walked into the trap, the brief race, the tiger's final success. Gulping, she tried to wet her suddenly dry throat. She tried to speak, but knew no words that would sway him. He'd waited, he'd stalked her, now her escape depended on her own speed and dexterity. She paused only long enough to scoop up the diary and thrust it in the pocket of her skirt, then allowed her panic to move her toward the door. Grasping the knob between her sweaty palms, she tried to twist it open, but her grip slipped on the cool metal.

The door was locked from the outside.

Was that part of Leighton's trap? No, more likely Ernest wished to give his lord and new lady privacy. She plunged her hand into her reticule, wanting the key, wanting desperately to escape, but Leighton's next words brought her to a halt.

"Smugglers were plying their trade on the coast tonight. Would you know anything about that?"

The key slithered away from her shaking fingers and fell to the floor with a clink. She dropped to her knees and groped for it, grasped it, stood and tried to insert it into the lock.

"Miss Haver, I asked you a question." Leighton leaned around the high edge of the settle and fixed her in his gaze. "Or should I call you 'my lady'?"

She tried to appear innocent, as if sneaking away from this room was no more than should be expected, and indeed, he didn't seem surprised.

"Are you leaving?"

Show no fear, she told herself. *Stare the tiger down.* "Yes." Her voice squeaked, and she smiled fixedly at him to counteract any cowardly impression.

"You can do that, of course, but it will be quite embarrassing."

Her smile faded. "Why do you say that?"

"Because I'll be forced to chase you down and bring you back. I can't imagine that you'll look your best draped over my shoulder as we go through the taproom."

"I'll scream. Ernest won't let you—"

"Won't he?" She'd always thought Leighton smug, but now he fairly glowed with it. "Ernest would not ever interfere, no matter what he heard."

She looked at him, at the openly tigerous satisfaction on his face, and she didn't care. She wanted to run, she *had* to run, she had to try, and she crammed the key into the lock, turned it, and slammed the door back on its hinges.

He muttered, "Damn!" but she didn't look back. She tore out of the room as if . . . as if a tiger were on her heels.

He was. He caught her before she reached the top of the stairs and lifted her with his arm around the waist. She screamed, loud and shrill, but the sound echoed down the stairs and through the obviously empty taproom. Leighton held her there long enough to confirm his prediction. Ernest wouldn't rescue her. She was his wife, and Ernest would leave her to the man he thought to be her husband.

"Satisfied?" Leighton growled in her ear.

She kicked at him, but her heels bounced on his thighs, and without flinching, he swung her around in the narrow hall and headed back for the bedchamber. She twisted, desperately trying to knock him with an elbow, a fist, anything, but she couldn't get to him, and they swept back into the room. Kicking the door shut with his foot, he carried her writhing form to Henry the Eighth's bed and dropped her into the two-thousand-goose-feather mattress. Its softness billowed up around her, stifling her as she tried to leap back at him. He landed on her. Her foot twisted under her and she gave a yelp of pain.

"Stupid girl," he growled, lifting himself and adjusting her leg.

She rammed her knee into his midsection. He doubled over. She scrambled over him toward freedom. He caught her again and rolled, tucking her under him as he went. "Stupid, stupid girl," he repeated, and she took comfort in the fact that he sounded slightly winded.

Then he kissed her. Last time, she realized, had been playacting. This time, he was angry. He thrust his tongue into her mouth and when she tried to close her teeth on him again, he lifted his head. Looking right into her eyes, he said, "If you bite me, I will retaliate." She flinched and he felt it, lying on top of her as he was, and he smiled using all his white teeth. "And I never make promises I don't keep."

When he put his lips to hers again, she desperately wanted to defy him, but he had made her aware of him and his fury. He was doing it on purpose, she thought, weighing her down with his large body until everywhere she turned, he was there. The scent of fresh air, rain, and heather filled her nostrils, and that was him. The heat of an iron forge covered her, and that was him. The sound of a heartbeat filled her ears, and that was surely him. It couldn't be her own heart that raced so madly, and certainly not because of the way he kissed.

Because she wasn't susceptible to such physical entrapment—at least she never had been before. When he penetrated her mouth with his tongue, she kept her eyes open and her teeth firmly shut.

He didn't seem to mind. He closed his eyes as if she were no threat to him, and it irked her to know it could possibly be true. He explored the inner wetness of her lip, finding untouched places and touching them. His tongue ran the ridges of her teeth and when she tried to shake her head and shake him out, he rapped out one word. "Laura!"

As if she were a child!

Doubling up her fist, she swung at him for his impertinence, but she'd taught him some respect, it seemed, for he caught her wrists in one hand and placed them over her head. She tried to flail away, but the feathers ensnared her and her struggles carried her deeper into the mattress. Her legs churned in useless protest, and panic rose in her. She'd never been so helpless, so out of control, and she didn't want this kiss.

Then he touched her breast, and the kiss seemed innocent in comparison. The wool cloth of her bodice might have been cambric, so little did it protect her from his caress. He explored the lower curve. With each contact, her breath caught. She closed her eyes at last, too embarrassed by such blatant intimacy and the eminent stroke of his fingers against the peak. It must have retained memory of the cold, for it had puckered into that hard little knot. His hand covered it, but not even that warmed it. Then she realized both his hands were busy elsewhere, and she couldn't imagine . . . she ventured a peek *and he had his mouth there.* She froze into immobility. She could scarcely speak, but she managed to choke, "What are you doing?"

He didn't raise his head, but sucked on the cloth until it turned dark and damp. Casually, he said, "I'm making myself happy, and you too, I hope."

"Impertinent!" She took an outraged breath, but that pushed her bosom closer to his face and she hastily tried to make herself as small as possible. Then Leighton, and curiosity, nipped at her, and she asked, "Happy? Why would *this* make me happy?"

Taking the cloth, and the nipple beneath, between his fingers, he rubbed until the friction made her twist to get away, or perhaps to get closer. The lower halves of their bodies pressed together and changes were happening in hers. Changes she didn't want to admit or to have him recognize.

"Can you feel that?" he asked.

"Of course I can," she snapped, pressing her legs together to relieve a sudden, unexplained pressure. "How can I help it when you pinch me?"

"Not here." He cupped her breast in one hand. "But here." And he put his other hand right between her legs! "Doesn't it tingle?"

He pressed his fingers on the mound over her bone, then adjusted them to fit closer. If he weren't careful, he'd have one finger in her slot and she'd have to shake him.

One finger . . . two fingers . . . she reached out to

shake him, but forgot her intention right before execution. She dug her heels into the mattress, she arched her back, and Leighton murmured, "Deep inside, it should be tight, and maybe you're damp."

"Damp?" She sucked in a breath. "Why would I be—"

A mere adjustment of his fingers brought the dampness he spoke of.

"On the curls between your legs. Can you feel it?"

"No."

"Liar."

She was a liar, but she didn't understand what her body was doing or why, and she didn't understand why he remained unaffected.

Or did he? He kept pushing his hips forward in a slow rocking motion, as if he needed to scratch an itch or massage a sore place. She shuddered as some ancient knowledge fought its way up from the depths. She wanted to move like he did, as though she'd danced to that rhythm before, although she never had. When she murmured his name, the way she crooned embarrassed her. "Leighton."

"Keefe," he said.

"What?"

"It's my first name. I freely give my name to you."

Frowning, she tried to understand why his voice resonated with such intention, but he distracted her with those motions. His aggression had modified and her outrage had changed to something softer, and when he put his mouth close to her ear, she shivered.

Gently, he intoned, "Why are you here? Why now? What do you know?"

Her eyes fluttered open, then closed, as she struggled to answer coherently. Then she caught sight of his face. His intelligent gaze was at odds with the passion he simulated, and she realized she'd been duped. He'd been playing her along, and she'd let him. She'd almost betrayed Ronald for a moment's pleasure and a false security.

What was it about this man that made her want to kiss him when all evidence pointed to his guilt? It didn't seem to matter what she knew with her mind, her body still yearned for him. Did she imagine she could find sanctuary in his arms? Did she dream he would protect her from the truth?

Or worse, did she see herself as the tiger's mate? For if she were not careful, she would find herself nothing but a passing meal for that hungry beast.

Venomous as a cobra, she whispered, "I know you killed him. You killed my brother."

He reared back, half off of her, but she didn't make the mistake of trying to run this time. "Are you mad?" he demanded. "Why would I have killed Ronald?"

"You're the leader of the smugglers."

"Is *that* what you think?" Carefully, he lowered himself back down to her and stroked her hair back off her forehead. "Dearest, I'm not the leader of the smugglers. I'm the man who's commissioned to capture them."

She mocked herself for half-believing and said sarcastically, "I would have thought so, once. Brilliant, ambitious, cunning, and brave, Ronald called you."

He half-smiled. "Your brother was an intelligent man."

"Oh, you're all those things Ronald said. When I was notified of Ronald's death, I never doubted you'd help me. He just never realized that you're also wealthy, powerful, well-bred, and"—merciful heavens, she'd almost said handsome—"patronizing."

"I am not"—he struggled, then offered—"patronizing."

"Of course." She mocked him with her tone. "I should have guessed that your campaign to discourage and frighten me was nothing but your way of showing concern for my grief at Ronald's death."

"My campaign to—" He raised himself again and glared. "You've been having delusions."

"Your secretary sneered at me every time I came to you."

His mouth tightened. "Farley sneered at you? I'll reprimand him. What else?"

"When I waited to speak with you, I always saw those young gentlemen going in and out of your office."

"Were they rude to you, too?"

"No, they were most respectful, but sometimes I recognized them skulking about in my neighborhood, and my neighborhood is not a place respectable men visit."

He winced. "You identified them?"

Triumphant, she nodded. "Even in their disguises."

Looking as uncomfortable as she'd ever seen him look, he admitted, "They had instructions to watch over you and make sure nothing occurred which would threaten your safety." He tapped her nose with his forefinger. "You *don't* live in a desirable location, and I intend to change that."

She laughed, her amusement bright and sharp with pain. "Your young men have sold their souls for a cut of the smuggling profits, more likely. Smuggling that takes place on your land."

He struggled with outrage. "Do you credit me with no sense? I'd not be so stupid as to use my own estate."

She stared at him, pressing her lips together and ignoring the tenderness that plagued them. The tenderness he'd caused with his false kisses.

"You don't believe me, do you?" Now he sounded surprised. "What did you think I was going to do to you?"

A vision of Ronald's tortured body flashed through her mind, and she physically felt Leighton wince.

"Kill you? You thought I wanted to kill you?" Cradling her head, he demanded, "Look at me. Really look at me. Do you really think I could ever hurt *you?*"

She saw that the tiger still lurked in his eyes. He wanted to consume her, yes, but for the first time she confronted the fact his meal would be a sensuous one. She swallowed; he watched her throat move and his hunger invoked a like hunger in her.

He wasn't going to kill her. Worse, she no longer believed he killed Ronald. Oh, in her mind she knew he was guilty, but his one flimsy reassurance had lodged in her heart, and she believed in him.

Maybe that explained why she had desired him. She had always believed in him.

He groaned. "Laura." His mouth swooped he placed a necklace of kisses across her throat and placed jeweled kisses on each ear.

He freed her hands and she remained still, horrified by her compliance. Then he kissed her mouth, and it became more than compliance. She kissed him back, opening her mouth willingly. She dared to push her tongue in his mouth and he let her, urging her with his hands as they caressed her shoulders. Her clothing became too tight, then too thick, and when he pushed the sleeves off her arms she helped him.

The cool air of the room struck her overheated skin above her chemise and sanity struck her at the same time. She'd never even been alone with a fully clothed man before, much less one who'd shed his boots and coat, whose scarf had been discarded over the edge of the bed, and whose shirt had miraculously opened all the way to his waistband. "My lord," she whispered.

"My lady." He mocked her.

"This is not proper."

"Most certainly not!" He reared back as if offended. "If it were proper, I would be doing it incorrectly."

She didn't know what to say to that, but when he stripped off his shirt she said, "I will not be a nobleman's toy."

"I never played with toys. I was always too responsible for that." He touched his finger to her bare chest. "But I think I could learn to play with you."

She stopped breathing. How could she allow her chest to rise and fall when his palm hovered just above, waiting to encourage her transgression.

"We are not married. We cannot share this bed."

His mouth curved in a tender smile. "We will be married."

"Do you think I'm bird-witted?" She laughed shortly, bitterly. "I'm far too poor and you're far too noble."

"Darling, didn't you know? I'm rich enough for the both of us." She didn't believe that for an instant, and he seemed to realize it, for he said, "Look at it from a smuggler's point of view. When we're married you won't be able to testify against me. A wife can't testify against her husband."

She didn't know what shocked her more, his blatant assurance or the speed at which he untied her chemise.

"You are the first woman ever to doubt my integrity," he said.

Hopefully, she inquired, "Does that inhibit you?"

Pausing in his assault on her virtue, he thought, then answered, "Not at all. It liberates me."

She held herself stiff as he stripped her chemise down to her waist and looked on her. His lips opened slightly as he viewed her. Totally without her volition, she imagined his mouth there, and her nipples tightened sharply.

He didn't take his gaze away from her breasts. If anything, she more clearly saw the tiger that lurked behind his façade. But he said, "However, I would not like to think you'll put barriers up against me, not even in your mind." In a tone that disguised the significance of his pronouncement, he said, "I'm the Seamaster."

THREE

Laura jumped as if Leighton announced Napoleon fought for England—and indeed, that seemed more likely. Ronald had mentioned the Seamaster over and over again in his diary. The Seamaster directed all the operations in which Ronald had participated. The Seamaster had been bold and daring, intelligent and canny. He was the man Ronald had emulated, the man Ronald had worshipped, and Laura could not imagine that Leighton, with his conservative manner, could possibly be so dashing a figure as the Seamaster.

Then she looked at the man before her. He hadn't been conservative tonight. He'd been as bold as a smuggler, or as the Seamaster himself. The Leighton she'd met in London had been subdued, at least for tonight, by *this* Leighton. This man who used any weapon to get his way. Yes, this Leighton could be the Seamaster—or Jean.

As she finished her contemplations, she realized he now viewed her face with all the interest he had shown her bosom. "You know who the Seamaster is. Your brother wouldn't have told you, so how *do* you know?"

"I'm an eavesdropper." She lied without a hitch, and she was proud of her smooth delivery. But he wouldn't stop staring, using his gaze to scour her mind for guilt. He found it, of course, and she blushed from her waist to the hairs on her head.

Instead of interrogating her, though, he shook his head admiringly. "An eavesdropper. I should have guessed."

"What do you mean by that?" she demanded indignantly. Then she could have groaned. Of course she didn't want him to think her dishonorable, but better he should think that than realize Ronald's diary rested in her pocket close to his hand.

"I mean"—he pressed a kiss on her mouth—"that you're an incredible woman."

"Please." She pushed at him. "I don't want this."

"Don't you?"

"I've changed my mind."

"As you wish."

He moved off her and she covered herself with her hands, watching him warily. He'd given up too easily, this man who claimed to be the Seamaster. The Seamaster, according to Ronald's diary, had much in common with his namesake. Once he sank his teeth into a situation, he never let go.

Ronald's diary. She glanced down at her skirt and saw the red leather peeking out of her dark blue skirt.

He saw it, too. His eyes widened and he lifted an inquiring eyebrow. "What is that?"

His hand reached for it, and she caught his wrist. "Nothing."

"Nothing? It's a book." He pulled a long face. "Laura, what are you hiding from me?"

"What do you mean?"

"That book will tell me all your secrets, won't it?"

"No!"

"Everything I desire to know is there." His fingers twitched closer. "It's a novel, isn't it?"

She was so stunned, she could only parrot his words. "A novel?"

"One of those wicked romances." She couldn't restrain him, and he laid his palm on it, preparing to draw it out. "Let me read it, and perhaps I'll learn enough to seduce you successfully next time."

If he read it, he'd learn enough that he wouldn't have

to seduce her ever again. If he read it, he'd have all his questions answered, and she still didn't dare trust him. Not with Ronald's diary, nor with the information inside.

He brushed off her effort to restrain him like a bear brushing away flies, and pulled it out.

In desperation she gambled, using her virtue as the stakes.

She laid her hand flat on his bare chest.

He paused in the process of opening the diary. His eyes closed, and her hand rose and fell as he took a hard breath. He wasn't as controlled as she had thought; he still wanted her. It was obvious from the tight set of his mouth and the unmoving stoicism with which he awaited her next move.

Inching her palm down his breastbone, she lingered on a ragged white scar right over his ribs. "How did this happen?"

"Occasionally, someone thinks he has reason to resent the Seamaster, and he tries to do him in." Placing his hand over hers, he stopped her restless movement. "The one who cut me there was luckier than most." Plucking her hand off his chest, he examined it, then folded it within his own. "You are, I believe, inexperienced in these matters, so I will tell you—if you wish for us to remain upright, you should keep your hands to yourself." He put her hand back into her lap and patted it, then advised, "It would be wise to pull your bodice up, also."

His focus went back to the book. Again he began to open it—and she returned her hand to his tanned forearm.

He froze. Nothing moved in his face, nothing moved on his body. He wasn't opening the diary, just as she wished, but she couldn't depend on such inactivity, so she slid her palm up over his biceps. The skin there was lighter, with a finer texture, and she rubbed him with her fingertips. The muscles flexed beneath her palm, and, fascinated, she walked her hand up to his shoulder.

With slow deliberation, he put the book down on the mattress. When he looked at her, she clearly saw the hunger of the tiger. Imitating her, he placed his hand on her shoulder, then slowly, slowly he pushed her down until she rested against the pillows. "I gave you a chance to think," he said. "Now think no more while I take my pleasure."

His tiger breath brushed her cheek. A slow pounding began in her veins. Her fingertips tingled with it. Her nose, her ears, her toes, every extremity experienced the force of his influence—and he still touched only her shoulder. It frightened her, his power, and she reconsidered her plan of action. After all, he'd put down the diary . . . "Leighton?"

"Keefe," he corrected.

"I don't think we should—"

"No, no." He pressed his finger to her lips. "You aren't allowed to think. You should only feel." Gathering her into his arms, he pressed their bodies together. "Feel this."

Her curves melted onto the firm structure of his chest, and she trembled. Already he was forming her to his desire, taking her sense of individuality and creating a new creature, one composed of man and woman together.

Yet she couldn't allow that. Not yet. She had a mission. She had a duty, and she couldn't allow him to distract her so completely that she failed. She fought to retain her reason and, moving with a care she hoped would fail to alert him, she knocked Ronald's diary off the bed.

It landed with a muffled thump, and Leighton stopped, suddenly alert. Her voice quavered, but she said bravely, "I think I would like it if you kissed me."

He returned his attention to her as suddenly as he had removed it. "Really?" He almost purred with anticipation, and thrusting his hand into her hair, he held her still and kissed her.

After he kissed her, he no longer had to hold her still. For the luxury of his kisses, she would do anything, be anything he wanted, but her compliance didn't seem to satisfy him. If anything, it drove him to a frenzy of touching. He stroked her jaw to the point of her chin, her neck, and her collarbone. He caressed her arms, then linked their hands and brought them up. "Look," he urged. "See the way our fingers entwine. That's how our bodies will be soon."

As he commanded, she looked. Her fingers rested between each of his, spread wide by the width of his knuckles. Clearly she saw his superior strength, his size, the mastery with which he handled her. The precariousness of her plight broke over her. If she allowed this to happen, would she ever recover herself? If she melded with Leighton, could she return to her former shape, or would she always contain a little bit of Leighton in her soul?

Besides—she looked again at the size of his hand, at the size of hers—this would likely hurt. Physically and mentally, this would change her and she writhed in belated panic. "We can't do this. It won't work."

"It will. I promise it will."

Then she became aware of something else. His palm cradled hers. His hand was moving, pressing and caressing the places where the nerves lay close under the skin. He knew how to make her like it; he alarmed her and made her want more all at the same time.

The man was an expert at whatever he did. If he were the smuggler, he would be the best. If he were the Seamaster, he would catch his man. If he were her lover, she would be satiated when they finished.

"Trust in me," he crooned.

"You'll stop if I tell you?"

"I'll do whatever you wish."

After making her wish for him. Slowly, she agreed, "I will trust you—for now."

"That's a start." Loosening his hands, he used them to strip the gown off her hips. Her white pantalettes tied at her waist, reached below her knees and were so sheer he could see the color between her thighs. She burned when he gazed at her and tried to cover herself with her hands.

"Don't." He took her wrists. "I've fantasized about your body, and it's better than I've dreamed."

Astonished and vaguely offended, she asked, "You thought about this?"

"Of course." He looked right into her eyes. "Didn't you?"

She wanted to refute it. She hadn't thought about it, had she? She'd never imagined what it would feel like if he kissed her. She hadn't thrilled to the thought of his body against her. Yet she couldn't speak the words to tell him so.

His eyes grew brilliant and his nostrils flared like a great cat detecting the eminent collapse of its prey.

The scent of the savage filled her nostrils, and she declared, "I don't think I like you."

"I don't want you to like me. I want no part of such a paltry emotion from you." Her pantalettes loosened under his hands. He stripped them and her stockings from her in one efficient motion.

Her own nudity left her gasping.

His nudity silenced her completely.

In all her life she'd never seen a naked man. Now she knew why. If men like Leighton walked the streets wearing nothing but a smile, women like her would have to join him in the most basic manner. The sight of him made her forget her embarrassment. Fascinated, she touched his chest. Broad, covered with coarse hair that crinkled and rolled, it undulated from the broad, smooth muscles above to the frequent ripple of his ribs. His abdomen rippled, too, strength implicit in the structure beneath the skin.

How did a nobleman build such a body?

She snatched her hand away. By moving barrels of brandy on moonless nights.

He sighed in what sounded like disgust. "You think too much." And he kissed her.

The time for games was over. His intent was clear. He wanted her, wanted her wanting him, wanted her clinging, panting, ecstatic and mindless. He kissed her softly at first, barely lapping at her lips. Then his tongue sought hers while his hands wandered to her breasts, her stomach, and finally between her legs.

This wasn't like before when he touched her and her gown and petticoats remained between them. Now his fingers tugged at her curls, then intruded between the folds of flesh.

Horrified, she pulled her mouth from his. "Stop that," she hissed.

He didn't answer and he didn't stop. He touched her delicately, using little dabs of rapture.

The weight of her eyelids grew too great, and they half closed. "Please."

"Please what?"

She couldn't remember what, so she just repeated it. "Please."

"Stop?"

Her hesitation amazed her. "Yes!"

"As you wish."

He obeyed her so easily, she should have been suspicious. Instead she breathed a sigh of relief—or was it disappointment?—as he took his hand away.

Then he moved his body over hers and pressed his knee between her legs to separate them. That wasn't what she planned, wasn't what she wanted. It was too intimate, too sexual, too soon.

She couldn't believe this was happening to her. She couldn't believe she was doing this. She dared not struggle, yet everything about it was alien.

She tried to clamp her legs shut. He moved his knee up and spread them wider. The hard muscles of his thigh rocked against her, and she woke to an incredible fact. The subtle probe of his finger had aroused her, but she had feared to move. When he touched her so sensitively, it was as if he were the master and she the painting. But this broad thrust of his thigh encouraged her to find her own pleasure. She left delicacy behind and rode his leg, at first hesitantly, then with increasing assurance, and he encouraged her with just the right pressure.

"That's it," he whispered. "Take what you want. Give all you've got."

Self-conscious, she bit off the whimpers before they could escape her throat.

He didn't like that, and opened her mouth with the thrust of his tongue. "Let me hear everything. I want to know what you feel."

How could he know what she felt, when she didn't even know? She was bursting, ripe, wanting more yet not knowing what more she should desire. She moved ever more quickly, and at last the dampness he spoke of moistened his thigh.

"There it is." He sounded satisfied as he moved his thigh away.

She used a word she'd never admitted to knowing.

"I'll take care of it," he promised, easing himself down onto her. "Hold onto me, and I'll take care of you."

Now his pelvis met hers and renewed the pressure. "Better," she moaned.

"Better yet." He arranged himself and when she thrust, she thrust herself on him.

Her breath caught in her throat. That wasn't better. That was odd, intrusive.

"Do it again," he said.

"What?"

"Like you did before. Take all of me. You're ready. Can't you feel it?"

She could feel nothing else. Grabbing his shoulders, she dug her nails in. She had to stop this madness, but at the same time she throbbed all around him. He didn't stir, although little shudders of strain ran through him. He wanted her to do it all. Like the devil himself, he wanted her to take responsibility for her own downfall.

She hovered for one moment between resentment and amazement. Then her body made its demands. She had to finish it. She had to know.

Bracing her heels, she eased her hips off the bed. He pressed down with the same tension. He met something in her; she retreated, but he caught her hips and held her still and her maidenhead tore before his steady advance. She wanted to rail at him, to tell him of the pain, but she was beyond speech now. She could only meet his gaze with a glare of her own, and when he rested fully against her and all of him was inside her, she bit his collarbone, hard.

He jumped and some of the strain which held him faded. "You are a wild one, and you're all mine." He grinned, his teeth white against the tan of his face. "I'm going to make you very happy."

He started slowly, moving his hips back and forth, bringing himself in and out with a deliberate pace that allowed her to accustom herself to the movement. Excitement returned, building low in her belly. She wanted to move like she had before, but he restricted her, maintaining the pace he had set.

She needed more. She'd thought the effort to speak beyond her, but frustration made her beg, "Leighton, please. Move a little . . . just faster . . . Leighton?"

His pace never changed. "Keefe."

He was killing her. Slowly, with great deliberation, he was killing her. He kept the weapon with him always. He could utilize it at any time. If he didn't win all he wished this time, he'd bring it to bear again, and again, and again.

Still defiant, seeking sensation, she twisted beneath him.

He plunged once, hastily, then stopped and held himself so that they touched in only one place. "Keefe," he said.

Her frustration burst its bounds. "Keefe," she shouted.

The rhythm changed, grew. She lifted her hips to his thrust.

"Keefe," he repeated.

She moaned. "Not again."

"Until you know me. Until I know you'll never forget."

She lifted her head and scowled. "Keefe. Keefe, Keefe, Keefe."

With each repetition, he increased the pace. It didn't

help. She only wanted more, seeking relief from the pressure.

"Keep watching me," he said. "Don't look away. I want to see you. I want you to see me."

"Now?"

"Almost."

"Now?"

"Can you feel it?"

The explosive sensation knocked her head back. She arched her spine. She brought her hips up tight against him and fought for every smidgen of pleasure. And when she had finished and rested, panting, against the pillows, he said, "I'm Keefe Leighton. You're my woman now. And I think I'll show you again."

FOUR

L aura woke with a start and knew she was alone in the bed. Her eyes popped open. Where was he, this nobleman who claimed to be the Seamaster? Who was her lover? She didn't see him, and her heart began to pound in a slow and steady rhythm. Had he seduced her, then abandoned her? Worse, had he got what he wanted from her and even now sought the means to dispose of her? Obviously, her faith in him was a flimsy thing, while her distrust blossomed in the dark.

Then she heard someone prod the fire and saw the tongs and the sturdy brown hand which held them. Leighton was there, sitting on the settle wrapped in his greatcoat. The relief she experienced clearly told her the level of her anxiety, and she put her hand to her chest to still the racing of her heart. Slipping from the bed, she pulled on the robe that hung on the bedpost. The cold floor made her toes curl, but she sneaked toward him, ugly misgivings keeping her silent.

Cautiously she peeked around the high back of the settle and saw him leafing through Ronald's diary.

"What are you doing?" she demanded, her voice cracking like a whip.

Leighton turned his head calmly. He'd known she stood there, she realized. The man was aware of everything around him, with senses heightened by the danger he courted. But did the danger exist because the government sought him, or because he sought the smugglers?

"Why did you keep this from me?" He tapped the diary with his large forefinger. "This contains information Ronald acquired before his last fatal trip, and if I had known . . ."

"If you had known, what would you have done?"

"Jean would not have escaped me." His mouth was a tight line, his brow furrowed, and he sounded sincerely distressed. "This Jean has caused England more trouble than any French rat has the right to cause."

"The smuggling, you mean."

"Smuggling, yes, and . . ." He laughed, short and sharp. "Well. The diary says Jean chose this location to land his contraband not because it is my manor and he knew my identity, but because he has an accomplice in the village." Lifting one brow, he asked, "Do you know who it is?"

"How would I know that?"

"By eavesdropping," he shot back at her.

She widened her eyes at him.

"Don't pretend artlessness," he said. "You're not good at it, to start with, and you revealed too much of yourself when you came to me in London and demanded justice for Ronald. I would have known you were his sister if I had never heard your name, for he talked about your intelligence and bravery, and you have proved to have both."

"So you think it was intelligent for me to have come here to help capture Jean?"

"No! Not that." His hands squeezed the leather binding of the book, then relaxed. "But brave."

"I trembled every moment," she answered honestly.

"But you did it anyway. All my best operatives recognize the dangers, then proceed anyway. If you weren't a lady, I would be hard pressed not to recruit you for our forces."

If you weren't a lady . . . Leighton's words made her realize that he did no more than pay lip service to her. He really didn't consider her anything more than an ornament, a thing to be manipulated. He would discard her when he'd depleted her usefulness, of that she had no doubt.

"You have to understand how important this is to me to capture Jean," he said.

"Will you be commended for your willingness to do *anything* to bring the enemy to justice?"

It was an insult, but he took the blow without flinching, only returning it in kind. "Jean killed one of the best and bravest assistants I've ever had, and I'm interested in revenge. I would think you would be, too, and willing to cooperate toward that end."

It struck her then, the thing that had niggled at her earlier. If Leighton was the Seamaster, he'd sent Ronald to his death. Of course it was worse if he were Jean, the man who'd actually ordered Ronald's death, but surely the Seamaster had known the danger Ronald had courted. He had to have recognized that Ronald could be brutally murdered and his sister left alone, desolate, broken-hearted.

And all for a smuggler. All to stop the flow of French brandy into the country. Rage rose in her. Her cheeks flushed, her hands clenched into fists. Somehow, she wanted Leighton to pay. Somehow, she needed to get out of this room and away from him before he stole her indignation and her heart and left her with nothing but dust and memories.

Intelligent. Ronald had told Leighton she was intelligent, and she needed to prove it now. Leighton was a clever man with no visible chinks in his armor . . . but she guessed he had neglected his duty to tarry with her. True, he suspected she was a source of information and he wanted it, but once he'd seen the diary he could have taken it from her by force. If he hadn't been a tiger, hungry for her . . .

Loosening her fists, she smiled at him. Her lips trembled; he'd said she didn't dissemble well, but this time she hoped to distract him with the promise of another sample of her.

Leighton's eyes narrowed and he considered her as if she were a defendant before the court.

So he was wary. What did loose women do when faced with a dangerous customer? She'd seen enough of them on her walks from the small shop where she worked to her even smaller living quarters, so she imitated them and shrugged her shoulders in a rotary motion. The movement loosened the front of her robe and Leighton's gaze followed the light material as it slipped back off her chest and opened a narrow gap around her waist.

He said something; it sounded like, "Geminy." A most fervent exclamation for one so dispassionate.

"Come here." Taking Ronald's diary, he put it to the side and held out his hand. "Sit with me and be warm. I don't know what I was thinking, bringing this up when we just now finished with our wedding night."

She wanted to slap him for patronizing her. Instead she bent her head in a parody of obedience and went to him. He brought his knee—his bare knee—out of his greatcoat and she perched there. The worn wool of her robe didn't protect her from his heat, and she feared to melt like a candle exposed to the flame.

But she wouldn't. This was for Ronald.

Tucking his arm around her, Leighton said, "One of my men should be waiting for me in the stable. I'll tell him about the accomplice, and we'll organize a search, but in truth I doubt we have a chance of finding Jean. He's long gone. He'll not remain in the area with so many of my agents here, so I'll have to seek him another way." Reaching his hand inside her robe, he slid his fingers along her ribs until he'd encircled her with his arm and the robe's protection was but a memory. "You'll be safe here. I'll be back for you in the morning, and we'll finish this thing we've started."

Did he plan to kill her, or take her back to bed and teach her how to be an even more satisfactory mistress?

No matter, she was ruined, and she had no intention of remaining when she could escape.

"Oh, Leighton."

"Keefe."

She didn't want to repeat his name, but she did. "Keefe." The word tasted bitter on her tongue. Flinging her arms around him, she pressed her face into his neck to hide her distaste. "You'll be in danger."

His fingers crept along until they rested over the cleft at the base of her spine. Her motion had exposed even more of her, and when she kissed his ear, then outlined it with her tongue, his body shuddered to life.

Sounding both stifled and pleased, he said, "I'll be fine, my dear. I've performed many of these missions and scarcely received a scratch."

"What about this?" Sitting up straight, she pushed his greatcoat off his shoulder and outlined the bare, white scar by his nipple. "You call this nothing?" Her palm grazed him until goosebumps started on his flesh. "You might have been killed."

"Youthful stupidity," he said. "I'm neither so young nor so stupid anymore."

But he was. He had to be. Her plan depended on it, and when she nudged closer into his lap with her hip, she discovered how his truthful body made a falsehood of his words. She tried to hide her triumph and gaze soulfully into his eyes, but he looked suddenly mistrustful and she remembered his claim she didn't lie well. So she mashed her lips on his. He didn't respond at first, but tried to push her away. Not cruelly or emphatically—that he could have done easily. But like a man who feared to hurt her feelings, yet surmised something was wrong. She didn't let go of his neck, and she opened her mouth on his with as much insistence as he'd shown earlier. The hand that she'd used to caress his nipple she slid down his body, opening his greatcoat as he had opened her robe, until she touched the hollow of his thigh just below his stomach. There her fingers hovered, almost in contact with his shaft.

Did she have the nerve to seduce him coldly, for her own purposes? The plan seemed excellent, but the execution was proving difficult. She'd just learned the rudiments of arousal earlier that night, and she had yet to loose the shyness of innocence. Yet she had to concentrate on titillating him rather than on her scheme to escape, for her acting couldn't stand up under his scrutiny. She had to lose sight of the lie and want him again.

After all, that shouldn't be difficult. She did want him again. She'd always wanted him. She recognized the tiger in him, because it corresponded to the tiger inside her. Even if he were the Seamaster and had sent Ronald to his death, even if he were Jean and ordered Ronald's murder, still she wanted him. She'd let him have his way with her and told herself she had no choice because deep inside herself she acknowledged her mate.

The revelation horrified her.

"What?" Leighton asked.

She found herself sitting back on his lap, staring at him.

"Laura, what is it?" He held her as if he thought she would tumble down without his support. "Why are you looking at me like that?"

"I want you." Her voice sounded little and far away, even to her own ears.

Now he looked as stunned as she felt. "I want you, too. I want . . . all of you. I want to talk to you and . . . make love to you and just . . . be with you." The words seemed to struggle from him, from this composed, restrained, thoughtful man, and one of his hands rose to stroke her face. His fingers were trembling. "It's too early, I've done it all backward, but I want . . . I have to ask . . ."

She grasped his penis with her hand and from his grimace, she thought she'd hurt him. Instead he picked her up and rearranged her so her legs parted over the top of his. He put her back down, and the sensation of her bare bottom against his bare legs shocked her back into good sense. He wanted to do this here, now, and if they did she'd have failed. She had to get him back to the bed, and she pushed against his shoulders. "No!"

"What?"

His eyes were glazed with desire, and her denial didn't break through his daze.

"On the bed. Please." She scooted back and he grappled to keep her close. "Please. Leighton. Keefe. The bed. I want to try something . . . exciting."

"This'll be exciting," he said.

"I can't. Not here." He let her slide off the end of his knees, and the pressure made her aware of her own arousal, of how easily she could succumb to his persuasion. "Please." She stood and tugged at his hand. "Come on."

He stood, too, and looked down at her. "I shouldn't," he muttered.

"This won't take long."

He half-laughed. "No, I don't suppose it will." .

He stumbled over the edge of the rug as she led him to the bed, and that reassured her. He was still off-balance and at her mercy. As she walked, she untied the belt of her robe and placed it beside the pillows when they reached their goal. His hands encircled her waist to boost her onto the bed, but she twisted quickly away. "No, you get on first," she said.

Tilting his head, he studied her. "You're bold for a fledgling."

"A cub," she corrected. Pushing his greatcoat off, she held it in one fist and promised, "You won't need that." She patted the mattress.

Still bemused, he climbed up and stretched out, a broad, large, handsome piece of male flesh that made her mouth water.

"When you look at me like that . . ."

It was obvious what happened when she looked at him like that. It was obvious he expected her to cure him, too. He held out his hand just as she found the end of his coat's belt. Holding it, she dropped the coat to the floor and let the weight of the wool free the leather strap for her use. Then she placed it beside her robe's belt and took his hand.

"You're trembling," he said. "Come up here and let me warm you."

Of course she was trembling. She was scared. Climbing on the bed, she said, "Let *me* warm *you*."

Her voice shook, too, but he smiled at her, all sensuous encouragement. "Have your way with me."

Sprawling on top of him, she threaded her hands through his hair and lowered her lips to his. She pecked at him, then kissed him, then penetrated him with a desperate relish. This would be, after all, the last time he'd want her. If he realized what she plotted, it wouldn't matter whether he were Jean or the Seamaster, he'd extract a terrible revenge. And if she succeeded . . . if she succeeded, she'd have made a fool of him, and no man could bear that.

He responded with quite satisfactory enthusiasm, and she wondered if she might not have a talent for this. Only with Leighton, of course. Leighton was her mate. She ran her hands over his chest, down to his waist, then stroked him as intimately as she knew how. She loved the feel of his skin, the coarse hair over it, the strength of the muscles below it. His arms encircled her, tightened, and he made to roll over to place her beneath him.

"No!" She sat up and pressed her palm into his breastbone. "I want to stay on top."

"Dear heart, I shouldn't even be here on the bed with you. A Leighton never neglects his duty."

"You're not neglecting it, you're postponing it, and besides, haven't you a duty to . . . your wife?" She almost choked on the last two words, and added hastily, "Shut your eyes."

"What?"

"Shut your eyes." Leaning over him, she brushed his eyelids with her lips until they stayed down. "Raise your arms."

His eyes opened again and he directed blue amazement at her. *"What?"*

Taking his muscled forearm in both of her hands, she tugged until his hand was in the vicinity of the headboard. Then she wrapped it around one of the rails. "I want to touch you freely. I want to make you want as fiercely as you made me want." She lifted his other arm and he let her, although he clearly wondered at her. "Is that so strange?"

"I don't understand it," he admitted. "Why would a woman—"

"Give as much as she takes?" Laura lifted a mocking eyebrow at him. "Be generous with her gifts? Seek a sweet revenge?"

His massive arms wrapped around her, hugging her to him, and he held her head while he kissed her fiercely. Letting her go, he raised his hands and grasped a rail in each hand. "Do your worst."

If only he knew!

She didn't demand that he close his eyes again, but instead concentrated on touching him in ways he had touched her. Usually affectionate, occasionally intimate, each caress seemed to effect him more intensely. He waited, almost breathless, for each new contact, and his anticipation built her own. Her body seemed synchronized with his; her muscles tightened when his did, her breath caught with each of his stifled groans.

This was fun. This was fabulous. This was everything she'd promised him, and she had to finish what she'd started. His eyes had closed once in sensual overload, then fluttered open as he struggled to maintain control. She knew she could make him close his eyes. She could make him lose his mind, if only for a moment. She was the female tiger, after all.

She'd used her hands so far, but they formed only part of her arsenal. Now she kissed his body, smoothing the skin of his chest with her lips, then daring to taste his nipple when it came within reach.

He groaned now, right out loud. "Laura." His body shuddered, too, and he twisted on the bed, his eyes tightly shut.

She had him. She'd trapped him. All she had to do was close the trap, but first, she wanted . . . Her mouth wandered to the other side of him while her hands wandered below, and she realized she enjoyed watching him squirm. She liked the power, and she badly wanted to finish the moment.

Not now. Blindly, she reached for the cord of her robe and wrapped it around the rail above his wrists. Not ever. With a quick motion, she used an embroidery knot to secure Leighton to the bed. She was done with love now. She'd never be the Countess of Hamilton again, not in truth or even in her imagination. She wouldn't even dare dream of this.

"Laura?"

His eyes were open now, and he tugged at the knot. She watched the knot tighten, the material stretch, and whipped his leather belt around the other direction to reinforce the restraint. The rail would hold him, even secured as he was to only one. The oak was old and solid, and had no doubt taken greater strains.

"Laura?" He was fully aware now, his gaze shifting between bewilderment to concern. "What are you doing?"

She slid off the bed and looked at him, stretched naked before her. "I'm leaving you."

FIVE

No woman could tie an effective knot. Leighton knew it, and he jerked on the restraint that held him. Nothing gave, and he twisted to look above his head. The knot, complex and unknown, alarmed him. "Laura, this isn't funny."

"Believe me"—Laura picked her clothing off the floor and began to dress rapidly—"I'm not laughing."

He watched hungrily as she lifted her arms to pull the shift over her head, then jerked his attention away. That was the kind of nonsense that had got him into this dilemma, and his body still spoke to him louder than his common sense. She glanced at him, running her gaze down his form, then looked away, and he guessed the constant changes in his body spoke to her, too. Pleased that he had at least that much influence and still convinced he could persuade her to free him, he asked, "Why would you even want to do this?"

From the corner of his eye, he could see as she pulled on petticoats. "Perhaps you are Jean, the leader of the smugglers, as I first suspected."

Damn the woman! She was a tiny thing, her waist so small he almost spanned it in his hands, with direct blue eyes and curly brown hair, and she was as stubborn and opinionated as his grandmother in one of her matriarchal moods. How could Laura not believe him? Pulling himself up the bed by his wrists, he glared at her. "I *am* the Seamaster!"

Laura nodded without a smile and pulled her dress over her head. "If you are, as you claim, the Seamaster, you sent my brother after these smugglers when you knew the danger he courted. Regardless, you are responsible for his death, and I intend to make you pay."

"Pay? How? By humiliating me?"

She had that stubborn thrust to her chin that he'd learned to recognize. "That, if you're the Seamaster. Or by turning you over to the proper authorities if you're Jean."

The flawlessness of her plan left him speechless with admiration. Admiration, and fury, and an unquenched desire that made him determined to teach her a lesson—when he got untied. He tugged at the knots again and frowned when he saw that the strain only tightened them. Perhaps he could have ripped free from the wool band, but she'd been smart enough to use the leather strap from his coat, and that wouldn't fail. "Now, dear." He kept his voice low and soothing. "This isn't a good idea. If you'd just think about it, you'd realize that. You don't *really* believe I'm Jean, the man who killed your brother. You wouldn't have turned to flame in my arms if you believed that."

She glanced up from her buttons to cast him a look composed of equal parts of alarm and disgust.

"You did, you know. This night has been a rogue's fantasy." That wasn't what he'd meant to say. He didn't mean to dwell on the pleasure of the dark, but the memory of her sweet passion still enfolded him. She'd trapped him by recalling that gratification and promising more, but he should have guessed no woman as inexperienced as she had proved to be would be bold enough to attempt a seduction. Indeed, as he looked at her, she folded her generous mouth tightly and her color rose, and he realized he had embarrassed her. He didn't want to embarrass her now; he desperately needed her to stay so he could convince her to free him. Hastily, he steered back toward the logic he hoped would sway her. "If I'm the Seamaster, as you know I am, then Jean is still loose, still capable of murdering more people as he murdered Ronald. Surely there's more satisfaction to catching him than in gaining a petty revenge on me."

"I'm finding there is a great deal of satisfaction in petty revenge." Pulling up her stockings, she tied her garters around her knee, and he strained to see the turn of her ankle. She lowered her skirts with enough haste to tell him she'd noticed, and she said, "You yourself told me you don't think it's possible to catch Jean tonight, that he's escaped from this area."

He'd told her too damned much. He'd been overconfident, treating her like a woman who would be swept away by the scope of his passion. She was completely dressed now, shoving her extra clothes into the carpetbag she'd hauled from under the desk, and he scowled at her. She should have been swept away by the scope of his passion, damn it. Instead, he'd been swept away by hers. He'd never failed to get his way with a woman before; of course, he'd never neglected his duty for a woman before, either, and that made him uneasy. "Surely you know I'm not a man to falter in anything he sets out to do, don't you? I'm determined to capture Jean, and I will. I'm determined to keep you safe, and I will."

"Probably that's why you remained here with me, wasn't it? To keep me safe while your men hunted this infamous Jean."

It was a indication of his perturbation that he wanted to snatch onto the shameful excuse and agree with her. Only her sarcastic tone kept him sane enough to say dryly, "Oh, yes, I'm that noble. Laura, surely you don't imagine I'm going to keep quiet? I know Ernest. He's been the innkeeper at the Bull and Eagle for years. I'll shout and he'll come to my rescue before you've walked across the taproom."

She grinned at him smugly. "I don't think so. We're married, remember? Ernest won't interfere regardless of what he hears."

The phrase sounded familiar. Then he recognized it. He'd said just that to her when she'd threatened to scream. If he hadn't been in such desperate straits, he would have laughed, but damn the woman! She couldn't leave him here. "When I call Ernest, he'll come."

She nodded thoughtfully. "You're probably right."

As she walked toward the bed, Leighton's heart leapt with triumph. "That's a good, reasonable girl," he said. "You'll see. You're doing the right thing."

Stopping short of the dais, she leaned down out of his sight, and when she rose, she had his clothes gathered in her arms. "Yes, I think I'm doing the right thing, too." Walking to the window, she opened it and threw his clothes out.

"Hey!" His incredulous shout came a moment too late. "How could you?"

She shrugged. "I had to do something. Lack of clothing should slow you down even if you do yell for Ernest."

"Of course I'm going to yell for Ernest." As loudly as he could, he bellowed, *"Ernest! Ern—*where the hell did you get that?"

She'd taken a pistol out of the desk drawer and was checking it in a manner that proclaimed her competence. "From my father. He taught me how to use it. I thought it best if I brought it, for I feared I would meet a villain." Her gaze surveyed him coolly. "I did, but I didn't shoot him."

For the first time, Leighton faced an ugly truth. He wasn't going to get his way. She wasn't going to free him. She was going out into the dark and rain to escape him. And Jean was still free and no doubt bent on mischief. Smuggling was a serious crime, but one the government more often than not turned its back on.

Espionage was something else again. England was at war with France, and secrets leaked from this coast to the French command and into the ears of Napoleon himself. Leighton knew all about it, because Leighton was the man in charge of maintaining security in the government.

Ronald Haver had worked for Leighton, not as a secretary as his sister originally believed, but to ferret out the source of the leaked information. The son of a career soldier killed serving in India, Ronald had been totally competent, daring, and courageous—a family trait, Leighton had discovered later—and it was Ronald who'd discovered where the information exchange was made.

Leighton hadn't believed it at first. The smugglers landed on the very beaches of his own manor? Did Jean know his identity and mock him by using his home? Or was it simply serendipity, the fact that his beaches had always been and would always be the best place to land with smuggled goods, with caves in the cliffs above to stash the contraband? Ronald's diary had given him the answer he sought, as well as posing a question—who was Jean's accomplice?

"Laura, don't go," Leighton begged. "I'm not the villain you should fear."

"I can take care of myself." She slipped the pistol into her cloth purse and hung it around her wrist. "I've been doing it for longer than I care to remember."

It was true. Ronald had spoken of his sister in glowing terms. He mentioned her competence, her good sense, and her skills, and before he met her, Leighton had formed a picture in his mind of a brusque, broad, homely woman. Ronald had requested that, in case of his death, Leighton care for his sister, and Leighton had been determined to do just that. He'd give her a pension and keep her in comfort for the rest of her life.

Then Farley had ushered her into his office for the first time, and Leighton had been knocked back on his heels. It wasn't that she was gorgeous or sweet. Quite the opposite. She was too short, too thin, too fierce, too . . . right for him. The wanting had shaken him to the core. He'd always kept his passion well in control. He chose mistresses for their experience and he planned to choose his wife for her suitability.

Laura was not particularly suitable. She dressed well, but that was because she was a seamstress. A seamstress! And poverty obviously hovered close. Her father was the younger son of a baron with not even a knighthood to give his name a title. But for Leighton, these matters were trivial compared to his desires. He planned to find and arrest Ronald's killer and present him to Laura as a nuptial gift. She would have him then. That would vanquish the shadow of suspicion from her gaze.

Instead Jean slipped through the trap set for him, and on entering the inn, Leighton had been hailed as Laura's bridegroom by Ernest.

At that moment, his whole life changed. The calm, rational, duty-bound man he was became an opportunist, and he'd forcefully seduced an innocent.

He grinned. And he still couldn't work up one shred of regret.

After donning her redingote, gloves, and hat, Laura walked to the settle and picked up the diary.

At that reminder of Ronald and his fate, Leighton's smile faded. "Laura, please don't do this. Leave me tied if it makes you feel safer, but don't go out tonight."

Going to the door, she twisted the knob. "It's locked again." She glanced back at him in scorn. "Did you instruct Ernest to make sure I couldn't easily escape?"

Bristling, he said, "I can control you without any man's help."

She inserted the key in the lock and turned it, then looked back at him stretched naked and defenseless. "I can see that."

"I'll find you, Laura," he said, and he meant it.

Six

L eighton's promise echoed in Laura's ears as she walked down the hall. *I'll find you.* Yes, he probably would, but not tonight, and that would give her a much-needed reprieve. She'd take a horse from the stable and go to another inn to catch the stage back to London. She'd wiggled her way through the government bureaucracy until she found someone to listen to her concerns, and if they told her Leighton was the Seamaster, well . . .

Oh, he was the Seamaster. What was the use in fooling herself? He was the Seamaster and he no doubt hunted Jean just as he claimed.

But he couldn't get him tonight, and tonight she needed to get away and try to accept the fact she lusted after the man who'd sent her brother to his death. Oh yes, she lusted after him, but she also wanted him to pay with at least a measure of mortification.

Pausing at the top of the stairs, she listened, but heard nothing. Carefully she crept down, avoiding the squeaking step. The fire had burnt to almost nothing in the tap-room and the complete and eerie silence spooked her. She wanted to run back to her chamber, to the safety that Leighton represented, but she stiffened her spine. She was, after all, a Haver, and worthy to carry the banner of her father and her brother.

Then a burst of shouting from the kitchen made her

stumble backward and she found herself on the top landing again.

Two men. Ernest and . . . another.

"Those are important papers!" the unknown shouted. While Ernest answered, "Ye can't have my lord."

Something crashed, glass broke, there was a hoarse cry, then silence. Laura hastily crept down the stairs, keeping to the wall, listening with all her might.

That unknown voice spoke again, this time lower and with enough menace to make the hair stand up on Laura's head. "I can have anything I choose," he said. "Need I remind you that should your beloved Earl of Hamilton discover what you've been doing with me, he'll tack your ears to the stocks?"

Laura put her hands to her mouth to stifle her gasp. Ernest didn't reply to the man's accusation; he didn't rush to deny it. Then she heard an explosion of sound, like air escaping a clogged passage, and someone gasping in deep breaths. She'd seen enough violence done on the streets of London to recognize this. The unknown man had been choking Ernest.

"They took my cargo, those damned government men, and there are some very important papers which I must recover."

Ernest recovered himself enough to croak, "Ye and yer papers! It's all a cover, isn't it, this smuggling? Ye're spying fer the Frenchies, ye are."

Laura made it across the taproom to the doorway by the kitchen in less time than it took the unknown to laugh.

"What if I am?" he said. "You've been well paid for your assistance."

A spy. A French spy. Jean.

Laura leaned against the casement and listened, her heart pounding, her breath short.

"I'm an honest, God-fearing Englishman, I am, and I never agreed to help a Frenchie."

"Honest?" Jean mocked. "Smuggling's not honest."

"In this part of the world, it is." Ernest sounded firm

and sure of himself. "My father did it, my grandfather did it, and my great-grandfather did it, but we never—"

"Well, you have now."

Laura heard the click of steel and her hand went to her purse where her own pistol rested.

"Hey!" Ernest's voice rose an octave. "There's no need fer that!"

"We're going to go upstairs now, get your lord, and when we're done with him Leighton will get me my information without a qualm."

"He'll never help ye." Ernest sounded as scornful as possible for a man facing a gun. "A Leighton's honor is above all things."

"Normally I would agree with you," the unknown said. "But Leighton has a lady in that room with him. Her name is Laura Haver, and while I doubt they're truly married—"

"They wouldn't lie to me!"

"—I've seen how Leighton looks at her." The unknown chortled until he snorted. "He'll cooperate with me."

Laura stepped back, shocked. She recognized that laugh. Farley. It was that little worm, Sir Farley Malthus, the one who ushered her into Leighton's London office with such obsequious grace and laughed at her desire to find her brother's assassin. He'd taken her aside one day and told her how ludicrous she made herself, pretending that a mere woman could influence the grand workings of English government. She'd hated him for it at the time, hated him even more for his insinuation she only sought an illicit union with Leighton, but she never imagined such a fussy little gossip could be a traitor and a murderer.

Again she touched the pistol in the purse. But no, that wouldn't do. She only had one shot, and assistance waited in the stable. Quickly and quietly, she made her way to the outer door and eased it open. As she stepped outside, she heard voices in the taproom. Swinging the door almost closed, she fled toward the stable. The mud clung to her skirt and sucked at her boots. Ronald's diary hit her knee and the book came flying out of her pocket.

She didn't stop to get it. It was a memento of her brother, but her brother would have told her to rescue the living, and so she ran harder, right into the dark stable. Pausing, she listened, but she heard nothing behind her. She had escaped without being spotted.

She groped her way along the stalls. A man waited within, Leighton said, but how would she know if it was the *right* man? Might not Farley also have stationed someone in here to take care of any unwanted intruders? She sighed, her breath a frightened exhale, when something small and living hit her from the side. She tumbled over, smacking the wall, and small hands reached for her throat. She knocked them aside as a boy's voice demanded, "Where's m'lord? Tell me what happened to m'lord."

When she didn't respond at once, the boy's hands grappled with her again.

"Ye're a woman!" He sounded disgusted, now. "Are ye that woman he saw on the cliffs?"

"Are you the man he left stationed here?" she countered, wondering what to think.

"What's it to ye?"

Of course, a boy to carry messages would be better than using a man, and it would keep him out of harm's way, too. "If you are," she said cautiously, "he might be in need of help."

The boy sprang off her. "What have ye done with m'lord?"

"I haven't done anything with him, but there are two men in the inn who will hurt him if you don't go get assistance."

"I'll save him myself."

She snagged him as he started to run out the door. "Leighton sent me down here with specific instructions that you're to go for help." It was a lie, but she saw no other way to satisfy him. "He wants me to stay."

"Ye?" The boy sounded scornful. "Why would he want a girl when he could have me?"

"Because I have a gun."

The lad paused, then answered, "That's a choice reason. Do ye know how to shoot it?"

"Indeed I do."

"How do I know ye're telling the truth?"

Laura committed herself to Leighton with her next words. "Because I work for the Seamaster."

The boy's indrawn breath told her of his awe, and he answered, "That's good enough fer me."

He was out the open door like a barn owl swooping toward the open air, and when Laura stepped out she couldn't even see his form as he raced across the heath.

Looking up at the inn, she could see the light from the bedchamber where Leighton lay, tied and naked. This wasn't what she'd imagined when she tricked him. Now she would do anything to have him free because for all her knowledge of firearms and for all of her practice with the targets, she'd never shot a man and feared to do so now. She feared it all: going upstairs, confronting two men bent on murder, seeing the accusation in Leighton's eyes. Because of her, Ronald's murderer might go unpunished. Because of her, he might murder again, and this time it would be Leighton—and she couldn't stand to lose both men she loved to such wickedness.

For just a moment, she covered her face with her gloved hand.

What stupidity, to love a lord when she was nothing but a seamstress and a commoner. He'd made it clear he welcomed her into his bed, but she wasn't stupid enough to swallow his talk of marriage. Now she would go up there, and save his life or die trying, and if he wanted her to remain with him as a mistress, she'd do it. She only had the strength to leave him once, and she'd already tried and made it only as far as the stable.

If she didn't save him . . . well, she knew herself well enough to recognize all the signs of rampaging infatuation, and she knew she'd die at his side.

Such resolutions made a mockery of her fears, and she tucked her chin into her chest and marched toward the door of the inn.

Crossing the yard, she swerved at the last moment and looked in the windows. The taproom was empty. The door still stood off the latch, just as she'd left it when she fled, and she stuck her head in. Nothing moved. Stepping inside, she left the door open in case the help she'd sent for arrived and wanted to make a quick entrance.

Light spilled down from upstairs and she listened, straining her ears. Voices sounded up there, and moving like a wraith, she crossed the floor.

Farley's voice rang out. "Untie him!"

Grasping the hand rail, Laura climbed the stairs and moved down the hall.

"I'm trying. I'm trying." Ernest sounded surly. "M'lady's quite a woman. These knots are well done."

"You don't have to tell me that." Leighton sounded cool and almost amused. "I've been struggling to free myself ever since the first time I saw her. I doubt I'll ever get free."

Laura paused just beyond the square of light that marked the floor outside the chamber door.

"Cut the damned things!" Farley snarled. "We haven't got time for this nonsense."

"Haven't got a knife," Ernest said.

There was a troubled silence as Farley thought. Then he said, "Here. Use this one."

Laura heard the clatter as he threw it. Someone cursed. Ernest, she supposed, as he scrambled on the floor.

Farley warned, "Don't imagine you can take me out with a puny thing like that knife."

Moving a step at a time through the shadows in the hall, Laura adjusted her position, trying to see in the door.

"I don't see why you're in such a hurry, Farley," Leighton said. "It's not far to the smuggled goods. I could give you directions . . ."

"You'll take me yourself. That's the only way your men will give me what is mine."

Leighton continued as if Farley hadn't spoken. "And I wish you'd stop waving that gun around. What harm do you think I can do to you? My God, man, I'm naked and trussed like a Christmas goose."

Laura winced at the image, then moved far enough around that she had a view of Farley. He stood with his feet planted firmly, the pistol held in both hands in a manner that bespoke great familiarity with it.

He kept the barrel steady and pointed straight at the bed as he said, "I don't trust you, Leighton. You always have a confederate hidden somewhere or another."

It was her cue. Stepping in the door, Laura said, "So he does."

He reacted almost too quickly. The pistol swung at her. The roar of her pistol mixed with Leighton's anguished shout.

One of Farley's legs collapsed. He fell sideways, but even as he landed he was aiming at her again. Leighton came off the bed, severed shreds of her robe tie clinging to his wrists. Laura threw herself on the floor as Leighton smashed into Farley. The pistol discharged, then flew into the air as Leighton knocked it away.

"Laura!" Leighton's shout left her ears ringing, but his hands turned her over as gently as if she were a fragile china piece.

"I'm fine." She wasn't. She'd hit the floor so hard she'd knocked the breath out of her lungs and bruised her elbows, but the bullet hadn't struck her, and that was all that mattered.

Leighton's sharp eyes observed her, then, satisfied, he rapped, "Ernest, secure that blackguard."

"Got 'em, my lord." Ernest's knee rested on Farley's windpipe until, out of air, Farley stopped clawing at Ernest. Examining the oozing wound Laura's bullet had inflicted in Farley's leg, Ernest added, "Nice shot, m'lady."

Wanting to set matters straight, Laura began, "I'm not—"

Leighton picked her up and cradled her in his arms, muffling her protest with his vigor and the impact of his large, bare body. Then he lifted one finger. "Listen."

Outside, she heard the jingle of horses' tack and the movement of their hooves in the mud of the stable yard. Boots pounded through the taproom and up the stairs, and she realized with a rush of horror their rescuers had arrived. Unfortunately, they'd arrived too late to rescue anyone and they'd arrived too early for Leighton to dress himself in a scant semblance of respectability.

Leighton and Laura were compromised.

"Leighton." She pushed at him. "Let go of me!"

"Keefe," he reminded her, and brushed her hair away from her face. "You banged your forehead."

She touched it and brought her hand away, expecting by his concern to see blood. There was nothing, and it ached only a little. "It's fine. I'm fine. You've got to—"

The pounding boots reached the doorway, and a brisk male voice called, "Sir!" A young man Laura recognized from Leighton's London office skidded into the room, pistol raised. He stopped cold at the sight of the naked Earl of Hamilton crouched on the floor with a woman in his arms. "Sir?" The gun wavered.

"Everything's first rate, Robinson," Leighton said. "Put your firearm away."

Someone bumped Robinson in the back, and he stumbled forward.

A boy of perhaps thirteen looked around, spotted Laura, and pointed. "It's her. She's the one who sent me."

"Did you go get help, Franklin?" Leighton asked.

Franklin clenched his skinny fists and placed them on his hips. "Yes, m'lord, the woman told me to."

"You're a good man."

Leighton's praise made the tall lad flush with pleasure.

Propelled by the crowd behind him, Robinson moved farther into the room. At last half a dozen men with firearms clustered around him. Laura had seen them all at one time or another in Leighton's anterooms. She had despised them, thinking these respectable men had turned to crime for the promise of wealth. Now, she realized, they were part of Leighton's government operation, catching spies to maintain England's integrity during the war. They all stared, first at Leighton and Laura, then at Ernest and Farley, openly betraying their bewilderment.

"What is going on here?" Robinson demanded.

Ernest stood and dragged Farley off the floor. "Here's yer villain. Ye'd best take him before he bleeds to death."

Obviously the man in charge, Robinson didn't seem to be able to grasp the situation. "That's not Jean," he protested, "that's Farley."

"Your scornful tone explains very well how Farley has been successful in his disguise," Leighton said.

The men murmured while Robinson considered. At last, in a tone that pleaded for credence, he asked, *"That's* Jean?"

The men all looked to Leighton for acknowledgment, and Leighton nodded. "That, my friends, is our spy."

"Oafs." Farley lunged for Robinson and succeeded only in falling to one knee.

Examining him with all the fascination of a boy with a frog, Robinson asked, "What's wrong with him?"

Ernest grabbed Farley by the hair and twisted his head back. "M'lady shot him."

"My . . . lady?" Robinson asked.

"The Countess of Hamilton." Ernest pointed. "There."

Laura moaned. When she'd told her little fib, she'd never thought it would spread so far and provide her with such embarrassment.

"That's not the Countess of Hamilton," Franklin said loudly.

Ernest puffed up like a blowfish. "It is too, ye stupid boy."

Leighton said nothing, but when Laura strove to sit up, but Leighton clutched her more tightly and admonished, "You need to be put to bed."

Laura glanced up to see a dozen astonished eyes

turned in her direction, and she stopped struggling and hid her face in Leighton's chest.

No doubt just what he planned, for he said, "As you can see, my lady and I require privacy."

"M'lady?" Franklin's round eyes got rounder. "Tell me it ain't so, m'lord. Tell me ye never got married."

Leighton ignored him. "Robinson, if you and the men would take Farley—"

"Ah." Robinson stood as if paralyzed. "Yes, sir."

"Robinson?"

Leighton's voice sounded polite, but Laura looked up in time to see the faint smile which curled his lips. She wanted to hit him, but his reminder seemed effective, for Robinson leaped toward Farley. The other men surrounded the now-helpless spy.

"Franklin." Leighton winked at the boy and nodded toward the men as they hustled Farley out of the room. "Aren't you going to help them?"

"Yes, m'lord." Franklin back out of the room, his gaze still fixed on Leighton and Laura. Pausing at the door, he shook his head sadly. "I still can't believe ye're married."

Leighton only smiled. "You'll have to imagine the wedding ceremony. *I* did." Raising his voice, he called, "Robinson?"

Robinson popped back into the doorway. "Sir?"

"You know what to do with Farley?"

"We'll do our best to save his wretched life, sir, so he can be questioned. Then"—Robinson's mouth creased with satisfaction—"he'll dance the hemp jig."

"Good man." Leighton dismissed him, and Robinson took the disgusted-looking Franklin by the shoulder and urged him away.

Now Ernest stood alone in the middle of the room and tried to smile. Leighton frowned back at him, and Ernest wilted. "M'lord, I just want to say that I never knew he was anything but a smuggler."

"I know, Ernest." Leighton clutched at Laura as she again struggled to scoot away. He whispered, "You're the only thing keeping me decent."

Bustling over to the fire, Ernest knelt beside it and built it up. "If ye can see yer way clear not to arrest me, I swear I'll not have further dealings with spies."

"Nor smugglers," Leighton said.

Ernest sighed. "Nor smugglers." He brightened. "I've built up my stock of brandy, anyway." Seeing the bottle of wine sitting on the table, he walked to it and, using the corkscrew he kept at his belt, opened it. Taking two cups out of his pockets, he set them beside the bottle, then stepped back with a flourish. "I'll leave ye, then, m'lord and m'lady, to finish yer honeymonth."

With a start, Laura realized she was about to be left alone with a very naked, possibly vengeful Leighton. He wasn't the wicked smuggler or the ruthless murderer, but when she looked closely she still saw the twitch of a tiger's whisker and the gleam of a tiger's sharp tooth.

She needed to get away. She needed to get out *now*. Trying to slide away from the clutch of his paws, she said, "I'll just leave with Ernest so you can dress."

His query jerked her to a halt. "In what?"

A vision of his clothing soaking in the mud ripped through her mind, and she said feebly, "Perhaps Ernest can find something"—she glanced toward the door—"that you can wear." It was closed.

The room was empty except for a tiger and his prey.

SEVEN

"He's gone!" Laura didn't know why she was surprised. Ernest showed a talent for disappearing just when she needed him.

"He probably realized I would want to commend your bravery in private."

Again she tried to ease away from Leighton. This time he let her. Raising a brow, she inquired, "Commend?"

"You did save the life of one of His Majesty's most important agents."

"So I did." Perhaps getting away from Leighton hadn't been such a clever idea. True, it was a relief to escape his embrace, but now she had to look at him. All of him. Especially the part that towered over her when he rose to his feet and stalked toward her.

"You captured a known spy," he said. "I don't even know why my men and I bothered to come to this event."

She backed toward the desk. "I don't think you're being fair."

"Fair? Why should I be fair?" He smiled at her with every evidence of courtesy, but she couldn't relate his society civility with his naked body. It was amazing how large he appeared when stripped of his clothing. Much larger than when his shirt, breeches, and coat gave him bulk. Now she could clearly see the breadth of his shoulders, the ladder of his ribs, the muscles of his thighs.

His legs were longer than hers, too, but he didn't move

more quickly than she did. If anything, he seemed to be enjoying the chase, taking care not to overcome her.

"Of course, you did need me." His mouth twisted. "I served you admirably as bait, did I not?"

"I did not tie you to the bed as bait."

"That's true." He nodded genially. "It was revenge, I think you said?"

The desk bumped her thighs and she grasped the edge with her hands. A sense of déjà vu overcame her—they'd done this before. "Revenge seemed like a good idea at the time."

"Not now?"

"You're not tied, now."

"You are a very astute woman." He loomed over her and took her chin in one hand. "Did it never occur to you I would, one day, be untied?"

"I didn't expect to be here when it happened."

"Bad planning, but I'm grateful." He tried to embrace her, but she shrieked and ducked under his arm.

Skittering toward the door, she tried it and wasn't surprised to find it locked. Ernest had proved himself quite handy with the key.

She turned, expecting to find Leighton behind her. Instead he was pouring wine into the cups and smiling genially. "You're nervous," he said.

"Have I reason to be?" Her tone was a challenge, but she retreated toward the fire.

"A woman as courageous as you should never be nervous. Wine?"

"I don't think—"

"After all, you threw yourself into danger to save my life." He walked toward her, still unashamedly nude, and offered the cup.

At first she didn't want to accept it, but the need for some artificial fortitude overcame her. Taking the cup, she took one sip, then drained it in one long, cleansing swallow. Handing it back to the startled Leighton, she squared her shoulders. "I didn't do it for you, I did it for Ronald. You were just in the way."

"For Ronald only?"

"Anyway, I promise I will never rescue you again."

"I agree." He placed the cups on the floor. "You won't." He efficiently began to strip her of her clothes. "Because I'm going to tie you to the bed until you've learned better."

Now he allowed her to see beyond the cordial smile and play of hospitality. He was, she realized, truly aggravated with her. When she tried to struggle, he treated her like a two-year-old, overcoming her physical objections with plain, overbearing competence.

"This is not acceptable!" she exclaimed, trying to hold the hands that roamed over her so effectively.

"Having my wife step in front of a bullet is not acceptable either." He wrestled her out of her gown, her petticoats, and her shift, and apparently decided he could leave the stockings and garters.

"All right! I'm sorry I told Ernest I was your wife. I didn't know you'd ever find out about it. I certainly didn't know you'd take unfair advantage of a woman traveling alone."

He chuckled. "Why not? You took unfair advantage of me."

"I most certainly did not!"

Swinging her into his arms, he said, "It's quite unlike you not to take responsibility where you should."

She wanted to answer him tartly, but in the place where their flesh met, she experienced a sensation not unlike the one she'd discovered earlier in the evening. Horrified, she muttered, "You've imprinted yourself on me."

"What?"

"I said"—she tried to regain control of herself, at least—"I admit I'm responsible for coming here and trying to find Ronald's killer, and I admit I'm responsible for telling Ernest I was your bride, but of what crime can you accuse me?"

He dropped her on the bed and the feather mattress poufed up around her. Leaning over, he trapped her between his arms. "Of stealing my heart."

"Don't joke about these things."

Coming closer, and closer still, he touched her lips with his. It wasn't a kiss, not really. More of a suggestion, or a promise. With his lips still on hers, he said, "I'm not joking."

She wanted to ask for clarification, but as she told him, she was a coward.

When she didn't speak, he straightened and rubbed his hands together. "I've never done this before, and you took all the ready material the first time. What shall I use to bind you?"

Bouncing up, she said, "Don't be ridiculous."

"Look at this." He lifted his scarf off the floor. "Lucky for me, you must have missed it when you threw my clothes out the window."

"Lucky."

"Now lie back down again." He crawled onto the mattress to enforce his command. "And put your hands up by the railing."

In frustration, she asked, "Are you always reduced to tying your mistresses?"

"Not my mistresses, no." He straddled her. "But I've never had a wife before. It would seem they're a little harder to subdue."

"I'm not your wife."

"You will be."

He looked quite serious as he lifted her hands to the rails over her head, and she realized that it wasn't that she thought he would dishonor her. It was that she objected to being a part of his obligations. "You're doing this for Ronald."

His look of surprise lasted only until he looked her over, naked and waiting. "Believe me, your brother is the last thing on my mind right now."

"I'll not be married out of duty. I'd rather be your mistress."

Throwing back his head, he laughed until she stung with embarrassment and wrestled away. "Whoa." He caught her immediately and tried to regain a respectable amount of gravity. "That is an offer I will treasure. However, I won't marry you out of duty."

He fit the scarf over her wrists and tied them to the rail, and she stared at him in frustration. "Then why?"

"Tug on your hands," he instructed.

She did as she was told. He'd managed to wrap that scarf around securely enough to keep her in place, yet gently enough the circulation still flowed.

He sighed with pleasure. "That's a relief. I'd hate to think you'd shot the spy and tied a better knot than I. It would be such a blow to my ego."

He wasn't going to answer her. He wasn't going to tell her why he proposed marriage when he could have her for so much less, and that made her think that it was duty, or his promise to Ronald, or some other stupid, manly honor thing that reduced her to a obligation and made a mockery of her love. She turned her face away.

He sighed, his breath a faint feather on her skin. "You'll never forgive me, will you?"

"For what?"

"For sending Ronald to his death."

"Oh." She shrugged. "That."

He paused, then complained, "You tie me naked to the bed and leave me for anyone to find in revenge for your brother's death, then you say, 'Oh, that'?"

She could almost have laughed at his disgruntled tone. Almost, if only he weren't pressed so close against her, torturing her with what he offered and withholding so much. "If you'd only told me that Jean was a spy for France, I would have understood. Once Ronald had a chance to work for England, no one could have kept him from it."

"Ahh." He kissed her, a light comforting press of the lips on her cheek. "You knew him well."

"It's the curse of being a loyal soldier's child. We'll all fly into danger for Mother England." She mocked herself and her courage. "It was the thought of Ronald dying for something as trivial as French brandy that made me angry."

"If that was angry, I'd hate to see you furious." He tugged at the scarf. "Not even this would keep me safe, I suspect. So if it's not anger, what is it that keeps you from having me?"

Placing his hands on her wrists, he ran them down her arms. She didn't want to feel anything, but his caress made her squirm. "Laura," he called softly. Never lifting his hands, he smoothed them over her breasts, down her stomach, along her thighs to the garters at her knees. "I should take these off," he said. "But I like them. They remind me of you. You're lying here gloriously nude, exposed, trusting me enough to let me tie you, yet not trusting me enough to tell me your secrets. Yet I can tell you mine." Holding her lips, he laid on her, giving her his warmth. "I love you, Laura Haver."

Startled by his words, his fervency, his need, she turned her face to him and stared.

"You're going to marry me because I'm not going to give you a choice. I've compromised you in front of my men and in front of Ernest."

She wiggled, wanting to grab him by the ears and make him talk. "Never mind the compromising. What about the love?"

"I can't 'never mind' the compromising. My grandmother knows everything that goes on on this estate, and when she hears about this, she'll take a switch to me. You, too, if you won't marry me."

"Love?" she urged.

"You'll learn to love me." He kissed her cheek, then nuzzled the place behind her ear. "You already like to make love with me, I could tell, and that'll just get better and better." His hands stroked a long, slow line from her hips to her throat. "Say you'll marry me, and I'll demonstrate."

Something like a shiver slid up her spine. "If I don't?"

"I'll demonstrate anyway." He kissed one breast, then grinned at her wickedly. "I'll demonstrate to you the same way you demonstrated to me . . . earlier."

He'd make her want him, then leave her unsatisfied.

Her eyes widened as she heard his purr of amusement. No wonder she had seen sparks of the tiger in him. Beneath that placid façade hid a man determined to have his own way and ruthless enough to do anything to get it.

Well, she wanted her own way, too, "I'll marry you," she said.

Taking her nipple between two fingers, he rolled it. "Why?"

Pressure sprang up between her legs, and she pressed her hips toward him to relieve it. But he moved away, still touching her, and she mumbled, "I love you."

His eyelids drooped, then he fixed her with his interrogational gaze. "What?"

Louder, she said, "I love you."

"Truly?"

"I love you truly."

He looked at her carefully, not quite believing her, and she lifted her head and kissed him. Kissed him with her lips and tongue and with the force of her passion.

When she finished, the grave shadow had gone from his eyes and they gleamed with gratification and a wicked touch of elation. "I love you truly, too," he said.

"I believe you." She shifted impatiently. "Now untie me."

Peeling himself off of her, he looked her over from her stockinged feet to her wriggling hands. "No."

Indignant, she struggled to sit up. "You promised—"

Licking his thumb, he circled her navel until the damp brought a chill to her skin. Observing the goosebumps that covered her, he grinned into her face.

He hadn't promised to untie her, she realized. He'd only promised to withhold satisfaction if she *didn't* marry him. Rubbing his cheek on her stomach, he moistened her skin with his tongue.

"Leighton." She used her fiercest voice, but he paid no attention. He only slipped further down her body and wrapped one arm around each one of her thighs. "Leighton!"

He corrected her, "Keefe," and dipped his head between her legs.

She shrieked his name. "Keefe!"

Lifting his head, he said, "You can make as much noise as you wish." Then he nuzzled deep in the cleft between her legs. "No one interferes between a man and his wife."

"I can make a lot of noise," she snapped. Looking down she could see only the forehead and eyebrows. His tongue licked at her in the first sharp, glorious step to gratification. Leaning back, her mouth curled in the anticipation of satisfaction. "But the door is locked, so we won't have to worry."

Too Wicked for Heaven

 Deborah Martin

ONE

London, 1788

"Some ball this turned out to be," Lady Althea Ransome grumbled as she escaped onto the balcony of Lord Farthington's townhouse. She peered back into the ballroom. The pompous fop who'd been bearing down on her was staring about himself in confusion.

Thank heavens she'd lost him. Another encounter with that overly powdered dandy, and she'd have been unconscionably rude. Slowly, she inched back from the doorway, praying he wouldn't think to look out on the balcony.

So much for her fanciful hopes for her first coming-out ball. Contrary to what she'd been told, the balls were not for meeting witty, eligible young men. They were for subjecting unsuspecting young ladies of marriageable age to the largest assortment of simpering coxcombs, aging rakes, and smooth-tongued fortune hunters ever collected in one place. From these, Uncle Winston, her guardian, expected to choose a husband for her? Impossible!

She only hoped Uncle kept his promise to let her approve any suitor he chose, because she'd marry a clerk and live in a garret before she'd marry any of the men who'd ogled her bosom this evening.

But surely Uncle Winston *would* keep his word, even if she refused everyone he chose. She scowled. Then again, he'd only brought her to London so he could find her a husband and be rid of her. The thought brought its usual pang, but she forced it down. She mustn't blame Uncle Winston for his eagerness to have her out of his life. When he'd been made her guardian after her parents' deaths in a boating accident, he'd been only twenty-five. And though he'd always led a singularly sober life, her presence was probably still an encumbrance to him, even if he rarely tolerated it, but kept her isolated at Kensingham Hall with only the servants for company.

She wished he were at her side now, but he was off dancing with his fianceé somewhere, which left her to deal with her troublesome fop. Darting a glance back into the ballroom, she caught sight of the popinjay, still standing guard near the balcony as if expecting her to reappear any moment. Oh, devil take it, would he never leave? Couldn't he take a hint?

Then, to her alarm, he turned and actually peered through the doorway to the balcony. Instinctively, she backed into the shadows, but realized she'd made a drastic error when she felt a rod of cold ceramic hit her calves. All she could do was muffle the cry that sprang to her lips as she tumbled backward over the potted rosebush some idiot had placed in a very annoying spot.

"Blast, blast, and double blast!" she hissed under her breath when she found herself lying ignominiously on the marble floor, her feet thrust in the air, her stockinged legs bared and her hoops making it difficult, if not impossible, for her to rise. A squirm or two only served to confirm that her skirts and her hoop were caught in the thorny branches of the plant.

With a grimace, she laid her head on the cold floor. A fitting end to an abominable night. Hadn't she endured enough? Now she was trapped like a turtle flipped onto its back. She couldn't call for anyone. It would be too mortifying to be found like this, or worse yet, have Uncle Winston brought here, forcing her to explain what she was doing on her back on a balcony.

He wouldn't approve of her creeping about to duck suitors. Not with his keen moral sense and concern for the proprieties. It wasn't proper, and after everything his fiancée Theresa, a young widow who shared his high moral standards, had done to make Althea presentable for society, the least Althea could do was give the appearance of being proper.

But if she didn't call for anyone . . .

As she envisioned lying there until the maids found her tomorrow, tears burned her eyes. She wiped them away with a furious oath. She wouldn't sit here and blubber like a silly girl. She was quite capable of taking care of this without making a fool of herself. Somehow she would get herself out of this fix before she was discovered.

Experimentally she tugged on her skirts, but they held fast. She tugged harder, but they didn't move, and she didn't dare risk tearing them. Torn skirts would be impossible to explain away to her uncle's satisfaction. Even worse, her hoop seemed to have taken root in that infernal pot along with the rosebush. She never wore hoops at Kensingham. She wasn't used to dealing with such preposterous encumbrances.

It was cold on the balcony, especially since she'd come out without her wrap. The spring air chilled her. "Devil take it," she muttered as she rubbed her scantily covered arms.

"Not very ladylike language," rumbled a distinctly male voice somewhere above her.

She closed her eyes. Oh, no. Some blasted man had found her. It wasn't the popinjay she'd been avoiding—this man's voice was deeper—but she was afraid to discover what other leering fop had found her.

Still, she wasn't a coward. Schooling her features to remain even, she lifted her gaze to find a man standing over her, his face in shadow and his arms crossed as he surveyed her.

"Not a very ladylike position either," he added, the amusement in his voice growing more pronounced.

She fought down waves of shame. Though she couldn't make out his features, it was obvious what kind of man he was. And her fears were confirmed when he merely stood there watching her.

Shame was replaced by anger. "You *could* help me up."

A wicked chuckle escaped his lips. "I could." He let his gaze trail to her exposed legs. "But then I'd deprive myself of a truly enticing view."

Blast, she thought as the color rose in her cheeks, how many rakes were in this place anyway? "Excuse me, sir, but I mistook you for a gentleman."

With a laugh, he unfolded his arms and leaned down to clasp her about the waist. "That was indeed a mistake." He lifted her in his arms, carrying her up and over the rosebush. "But be glad I'm not one. A gentleman might have averted his face and gone to summon your family, which I suspect you would *not* have appreciated."

He was right, but she certainly wouldn't let *him* know that. She'd thank him and send him on his way.

Unfortunately, when he set her down, he only tightened his grip on her waist. She lifted her head to give him an acid rebuff, but the words died on her lips when she saw his face.

Him. Oh, merciful heavens, why him?

She hadn't seen him in seven years, ever since she'd gone to live with her uncle, but that made no difference. She'd never forgotten those laughing green eyes or the dimple in only one cheek that gave him an utterly charming lopsided grin.

Nev. Or rather, Neville Blakely, the Marquis of Foxworth. He was the older brother of her best friend Isabella from years ago. The Blakelys' townhouse had been next to her parents' then. During her childhood, she'd spent a great deal of time there and at Foxworth with Isabella Blakely.

How many times as a girl had she worshipped Nev's features, the dark, slashing brows and the mouth full enough to be indecently sensuous? How often had she lain in bed, wondering what it would be like to touch that handsome face?

Now she was close enough to do so. What's more, he was staring at her far differently than he had at the foolish girl whom he'd teased and mostly ignored.

Indeed, he seemed amused by her intense scrutiny. His smile brought forth that fatal dimple once more, making her heart flutter with an ease that disgusted her. "Have I met with your approval, my curious beauty?" he said in a husky voice. "Or must I perform another service to gain your good will?"

His words jerked her from her thoughts. Thank heavens he hadn't recognized her. Of course, he wouldn't have. The last time he'd seen her, she'd been rake-thin and short, with eyes too big for her face. "Please go away before someone comes and finds me in this scandalous situation." *Like my uncle,* she thought.

He tugged on her skirts only to find them still tangled in the thorns of the bushes. "Ah, but you're not free yet. It would be rude to abandon you in your hour of need, madam." With one finger, he traced the line of her jaw. "Besides, I won't go until I at least know your name."

Oh, what a coil. She couldn't tell him her name. If Uncle Winston ever found out she'd been alone on a balcony with the Marquis of Foxworth . . .

It didn't bear thinking on. Uncle thoroughly despised Nev. Ever since Uncle had become her guardian, he'd forbidden her to socialize with either Isabella or Neville.

She wasn't sure why, but it was probably because of Nev's reputation. Nev had a completely opposite character from her uncle. She'd heard a great deal about his exploits, and not only from his sister's clandestine letters. Even before the years when she and Isabella had trailed after him and his dashing friends, he'd cut quite a figure in London. Society called him "The Fox." Like his father before him, he was a notorious blade, the kind of man matrons feared and eligible young virgins sighed after. Not that it did the virgins any good. She'd heard the rhyme that the Prince of Wales himself, one of Foxworth's intimates, had invented to describe him:

The Fox will never take a wife,
He'll be a rakehell all his life.
Though many a woman grace his bed
The Fox will never lose his head.

It was rumored that The Fox had no interest in marrying, preferring to live a life of debauchery unencumbered by a wife. It was said he didn't care who inherited his title. It was also rumored that he'd bedded the most influential women in London.

But more telling for Althea's situation was the rumor that he never touched a woman without stealing her honor. And judging from the way his arm was sliding about her waist, he seemed bent on stealing hers tonight. Or at least tarnishing it.

She tried to wriggle out of his grasp. "I'd thank you to release me, my lord." Her voice was steeled with all the haughty nobility of her upbringing. After he'd seen her sprawled on the floor like an unruly child, she must correct his assumption that she was a foolish chit who'd be flattered by his affections.

Even if it was true.

He raised both eyebrows, though he ignored her request. "'My lord'? How do you know I am titled? Do you know me?"

Her demeanor slipped a notch as she cursed her unthinking tongue. Oh, well, it wasn't as if it mattered that she knew who he was. Everyone did. "I know *of* you. Who doesn't? You're Lord Foxworth, aren't you?"

That one-sided dimple of his appeared once more. "Indeed I am. And now you have the advantage of me, for you know my name, but I don't know yours. Won't you enlighten me?"

"I'm not *that* much of a fool," she quipped.

He merely grinned. "Your distrust pains me to the heart, madam." He lifted his hands to clasp her shoulders, and she could feel the warmth of them even through her gown. "Perhaps my intentions are honorable. This ball is a marriage mart, is it not? Perhaps I merely want your name so I'll know whom to approach with an offer."

Her inelegant snort only seemed to deepen his amusement.

"What? Don't you believe me?" he said with a mock expression of wounded pride. He slid his hands along her shoulders toward her neck.

In a panic, she pressed against his hard chest. To her surprise, he let her put some distance between them, although he kept his hands resting on her shoulders. The touch of his fingers there sent delightful tingling sensations down her spine, and she cursed herself for it.

"Even *if* that were true," she retorted, "and we both know it isn't, I'd have to refuse such an offer."

"Why?" He began to trace light circles along her skin with his thumbs. "I've been told I'm reasonably attractive. I have an adequate income. I'm young and healthy enough to sire a child. What more could you need from a husband?"

She noted that he neglected to mention his title. But then, that was typical of Nev. He'd never been terribly impressed by such things as titles.

As if to prod her to answer his question, he moved his thumbs further in to caress her throat, forcing her to bite her lip to keep from sighing aloud.

"I need a great deal more, I'm afraid," she whispered before he stole all her resolve. "True affection. Honor. Fidelity—"

"What makes you think I wouldn't offer those as well?"

The sarcastic words leapt from her mouth before she could stop them. "Fidelity? An unprincipled rogue like you?"

"Ah, so it's my reputation that gives you pause." There was an edge to his voice now, and he'd stopped his sensuous movements abruptly. "No doubt you've heard of all the women I've debauched in my mere twenty-eight years on this earth."

Merciful heavens, she shouldn't have taunted him like

that. But she had no idea how to deal with a sophisticated
man of his sort. Except for Theresa this past year, there'd
been no women to guide her in the ways of men during
the last seven years, and her mind was so scattered by his
presence, the only advice she could remember Theresa
giving her was, "Stay away from balconies." She'd already
violated *that* stricture.

"You shouldn't listen to nasty rumors, madam," he
went on as he curved his hand behind her neck, "but
since I'm already held rather low in your esteem, I might
as well complete your poor image of me."

And before she could say another word, he gripped her
neck, holding her still as he brought his lips down on
hers. At first, his kiss was as unyielding as the chest she
pushed against in a frantic bid for freedom. But then his
mouth softened, molding hers, teasing her breath from
her, making her forget why she'd been trying to get away.

After all, she'd dreamed of this moment for years. Late
at night in her virginal bed, she'd wondered what it would
be like to have Nev kiss her, and now that the moment
was upon her, she was loath to let it go.

He must have felt her acquiescence, for he released his
hold on her neck. With one of his hands he clasped her
waist while the other slid along her jaw in a caress as soft
and tempting as the velvet lining of a winter cloak. He
rubbed her lips apart to run his tongue over her clenched
teeth. Then his fingers tightened on her jaw, the gentle
pressure urging her mouth open.

She scarcely realized she'd opened her mouth until he
slid his tongue inside, shocking her, intriguing her. Something leapt in her belly when he touched his rough tongue
to hers and then swept the inside of her mouth with a
sensuous stroke that sent sheer pleasure gathering inside
her.

The sensation of having his tongue fill her mouth was
intense . . . . hot and sweet and wholly unfamiliar. Her
childish imaginings hadn't prepared her for this heady
experience. While he drew her closer, his tongue probed
relentlessly until she lost her balance and swayed against

him, her breasts crushed to his chest as he steadied her with surprisingly strong arms.

He shifted restlessly against her, and with a shock, she felt him slide a hand between their bodies and up to cup her breast. It jolted her out of her dazed state.

"No," she whispered as she tore her mouth from his. She pushed his hand away as her eyes widened. He was looking at her with a satisfied expression on his face that only mortified her more. He reached for her, but she backed away, only to come up against the rosebush once more. Blast the man, he had her trapped and he knew it.

"Please, my lord," she heard herself saying, all her haughty façade gone. "Please, no more. You've chastened me suitably for my hasty words. Now leave me be."

"You admit that you enjoyed that, do you?"

She knew he was laughing at her for her earlier moral stance, but she didn't care. She only knew she must escape him before he went any further. "I'm not a liar. I . . . I enjoyed it very much. Then again," she added dryly, "I suppose I'd have to be dead not to enjoy it."

Something flickered deep in his eyes before he lifted his hand to clasp her chin. "After a compliment like that, surely you don't think I shall simply walk away."

He started to lower his head to hers once more, and a feeling of despair washed over her. If she let him kiss her again, she wouldn't be able to resist any of his seductions. "Please don't," she begged. "Please, Nev . . ."

She broke off when he paused inches from her, surprise passing over his face. "Only my sister calls me that," he whispered. "How did you—"

He broke off as someone gasped behind him.

Lord Foxworth jerked back from her, giving Althea a sudden glimpse of who'd seen them. Oh, dear, it was her uncle's fiancée, Theresa.

"Is that you, Althea?" Theresa whispered. As the marquis unwittingly moved to get a better look at the woman, light flooded Althea's face. "It *is* you! Lord have mercy!"

And before Althea could make any kind of protest, Theresa whirled and fled back into the ballroom.

"Wonderful," Althea muttered with heavy sarcasm. "Now she'll tell my uncle. Please, you must leave at once!"

She swung her gaze back to the marquis, but his expression had changed, and he was staring at her intently. "Althea? Isabella's little friend? And Kensingham's niece?" He lifted his hand to stroke her hair. "God help me, I should have realized. You always had that honey hair . . . those expressive eyes—" He broke off as she dropped her gaze, embarrassed but absurdly pleased to discover that he remembered her.

When he continued, amusement threaded his tone. "You've certainly filled out nicely since the last time I saw you." His voice lowered to a rumble. "Yes, quite nicely indeed. Kensingham must be fighting off the suitors with a stick."

The blood rushed to her face as his mention of her uncle reminded her of their situation. "He'll be fighting *you* off with a stick if you don't get out of here. Didn't you hear what I said? Theresa will bring him here, and that wouldn't do at all."

"I suppose it wouldn't." He released her, but to her surprise, bent down on one knee. With steady fingers, he began to work her satin skirts free from the rose brambles. "But it will take time for her to find him in this crush, and I can't leave you trapped here for some other rakehell to find, can I? I can have you free in a moment—"

"No!" she hissed. "If Uncle Winston should find us together, I'll be in a peck of trouble!"

He ignored her. "Your hoops are caught fast, and there's no time to work them loose, so you'll have to get out of them." She felt him lift her skirts and petticoat in back. She gasped, but he was already undoing the hoop ribbons. In desperation, she grasped his shoulders, trying to push him away.

Then everything happened at once. The ribbons came loose. Her hoop slipped down, leaving the marquis with her skirts draped over his left shoulder.

And her uncle burst onto the balcony.

She groaned as Uncle Winston roared with anger. She could only imagine what a sight they made, with Lord Foxworth kneeling half beneath her skirts and her hands clutching his shoulders as if for support. The marquis quickly rose to his feet and she stepped out of her cursed hoop. But it hardly mattered that he'd freed her, since her uncle was striding forward in a fury as Theresa rushed in behind him, wringing her hands.

"You bastard!" Uncle Winston spat. "You damned lecher!"

Nev's features were calm as he brushed dirt from his breeches with a casual nonchalance that only seemed to infuriate her uncle more. "Good evening, Kensingham."

How could he stand there so coolly? Didn't he know what trouble he was in? She forced herself between the two men, alarmed by the murderous glint in her uncle's eyes. "Please, Uncle Winston, this isn't what it appears."

"The hell it isn't!"

"It was clumsy of me, I know," she went on, her voice rising stridently in her effort to convince him, "but I fell over that rosebush and caught my hoops in it. Lord Foxworth was merely helping me to get free. That's all it was."

Her uncle's jaw tightened. "So Theresa only imagined that she saw him kissing you, did she?"

A blush rose over her face before she could stop it, and her uncle swore. Then he glowered over her shoulder at the marquis. "I should have expected this of you, Foxworth. Seducing a young woman and getting her to cover your tracks is typical of you."

"Uncle Winston!" Althea protested, hurt by his characteristic lack of faith in her. "I would never let him—"

"I'm not speaking to you, Althea," her uncle bit out. "Go back in that ballroom and stay there until Foxworth and I are through."

Her uncle had often spoken to her in such imperious tones. But this time was different. She'd never seen him this furious, his black eyes aflame and every muscle tight with anger. She could only imagine what would happen if she left the two men alone together.

"Your uncle's right, my lady," Foxworth interjected through gritted teeth. "This has nothing to do with you. You and I both know you're innocent of any wrongdoing, so 'tis best you leave him and me to sort out our differences."

She whirled to look at him. Innocent of wrongdoing? She was certainly not that. And if he was her uncle's enemy, why wasn't he using this as a weapon against Uncle Winston, boasting of the kiss she'd given him?

His eyes glittered as he looked at her, but his words were gentle. "Go on, Lady Althea. I'm glad I could assist you, and I hope you won't hold my . . . ah . . . impertinence against me."

"I'm not leaving." She faced her uncle. "Lord Foxworth has been a perfect gentleman, Uncle Winston. I won't allow you to—"

"A perfect gentleman? Really? Accosting a young woman on a balcony without a chaperone in sight?" Her uncle's eyes narrowed as he fixed them on the marquis. "Let's see how much of a gentleman you are tomorrow at dawn, Foxworth."

Althea and Theresa gasped in unison. Both women knew exactly what her uncle meant.

Lord Foxworth knew as well. But though his eyes flickered dangerously, he merely said with nonchalance, "Don't be absurd, Kensingham. There's no need to be foolish about this—"

"Foolish!" Uncle Winston took a menacing step forward. "It isn't foolish to defend my niece's honor. I know you well, Foxworth. If I don't do this, you'll boast to your friends about how you took advantage of my niece almost before my very eyes!"

"That's ridiculous!" the marquis retorted hotly.

"No, it isn't. Which is why I demand you meet me at dawn and give me the satisfaction I require!"

The two men stared at each other, locked in a battle of wills, the one a dark avenging angel and the other a carefree rogue who'd been jerked up short by an overly moral uncle. Thanks to her.

The marquis's features evened out into a forced nonchalance. "You've been itching to do this all these years, and you won't rest until you've had your shot at me, will you, Kensingham? Very well. Dawn it is."

"No!" Althea cried out.

At the same time, Theresa stepped forward to clutch Uncle Winston's arm. "Surely there's another way to settle this—"

He thrust her aside. "This isn't your concern, Theresa."

Althea took Theresa's place. "But it is *my* concern." Althea felt caught up in a maelstrom that she'd never known existed until this minute. "Uncle Winston, you can't do this—"

Her uncle paid her no mind as he turned back to Lord Foxworth. "Where shall we meet? Leicester Fields?"

"Nay," the marquis said in deadpan tones. "My estate. It's not far, and it's more secluded." A bitter sarcasm crept into his voice. "That is, if you trust me to behave honorably on my property."

"I'll be there," her uncle answered through gritted teeth.

She clasped Uncle Winston's arm. "Don't do this. 'Tis absurd! Nothing happened! You cannot . . . you mustn't—"

"Come along, Althea," he retorted as he planted his hand in the small of her back and propelled her toward the ballroom. Theresa cast a backward glance at the hoop still caught in the rosebush, but apparently realized that it would be worse to carry it through the ballroom, for she shrugged and left it there.

The maids will speculate on that tomorrow, Althea thought bitterly as she glanced back at the marquis, who was standing stiff and silent beside the hapless piece of female vanity.

Her uncle paused in the door just long enough to snap at the marquis, "Send word to me of your seconds." Then he was pushing her into the crowded ballroom, with Theresa trailing on behind.

Althea blinked in the bright lights, stunned to find that not a soul appeared to have heard the interchange on the balcony. In truth, it had probably only taken a few seconds, instead of the lifetime it seemed.

So this would be a private duel. No one would know of it. Until, of course, one of the blasted fools was killed and the other forced to flee England. And all because of her.

Wasn't there something she could do to stop it? But one look at her uncle's implacable features as he dragged her toward the entrance told her he was beyond reason. He wouldn't even look at her.

She choked back a sob. Now he must be absolutely convinced of her poor character, if he hadn't been before. She could never live up to his standards of morality. Any other man would have noted the ensnared hoop and seen that her story was sound, but not Uncle Winston. No, he was terribly fastidious about such things as women's virtue and such, and he would die before he'd let her honor be besmirched.

And it was all her fault for being weak enough to let Nev kiss her.

As soon as they'd reached the entranceway, Uncle Winston said, "I'm going to call the carriage. I'm sending you home—"

"Please, Uncle Winston, you must believe me." She grabbed his arm. "The marquis did nothing more than kiss me out there. Plenty of other men have attempted that tonight without your demanding that they fight you."

He looked at her, eyes dark with remorse. "You don't have to lie for him, Althea. I know his kind. He's a blight on society. But after tomorrow, he won't bother you any more. I've failed you this evening, but I won't fail you then."

His words confused her. "You? You haven't done anything wrong—"

"That's enough. You're going home now." He extricated himself from her grasp. "Theresa and I will leave as soon as I find my seconds for tomorrow."

He turned to Theresa. "Keep an eye on her while I get the carriage." Then he was gone.

The moment he was out of sight, Theresa turned on Althea. "You've got to stop him from fighting this duel! They say Lord Foxworth is a crack shot and an expert fencer! And you know . . . well . . ."

Theresa didn't have to say more. Uncle Winston was a dreadful shot and had never won a fencing match in his life. Althea's heart sank. If he fought the duel—

"Oh, Theresa, what can I do?" Fear made Althea's heart race. "He won't listen to reason!"

"I know. I would never have told him about seeing you on the balcony if I'd thought he would—" The young widow took a shuddering breath. "'Tis all my fault, isn't it?"

Althea shook her head. "Nay. There's more to it than what happened on the balcony. I think Lord Foxworth would have refused to fight the duel entirely if it had been just that."

Then Althea's eyes narrowed. The marquis had indeed been hesitant to fight. Obviously, he'd known he was the better duelist and hadn't wanted to hurt Uncle Winston, despite all the nasty things Uncle Winston had said to him.

Perhaps . . .

She spotted her uncle coming toward them. Before he could reach them, she bent to whisper in Theresa's ear. "Don't worry about tomorrow, all right? I have a plan."

Theresa eyed her with suspicion. "What are you plotting?"

"Do you want to see your fiancé live through tomorrow?" Althea hissed.

Theresa's eyes flitted to Uncle Winston, who was nearly upon them. She hesitated only a fraction of a second. "Yes."

"Then trust me. I promise I won't get into trouble and everything will be fine."

Please, let it be fine, she added in a silent prayer to the Deity she'd neglected of late. She had to make it fine. Because after losing her parents, she couldn't bear to lose Uncle, too.

Two

Neville stood on the balcony long after he'd watched Kensingham march off. Good God, had it come to this? A duel, and over Althea Ransome, no less.

A bitter smile tipped up his lips as he thought about the irony of it. Little Althea. Hard to believe he'd kissed Kensingham's niece and not even recognized in her the ungainly eleven-year-old who'd been Isabella's friend. The two girls had enjoyed traipsing after him and his companions, bedeviling them with incessant questions and sulking when told to go play with dolls. He'd never have guessed that the young slip of a girl who'd often stuck her tongue out at him would grow up so well. So very well.

Desire knotted in his loins, reminding him of how that slip of a girl had felt in his arms tonight. And how wonderful she looked. By Judas, what a beauty she'd turned into. Her thin form had sprouted lovely curves and her lips were full and pouting. She'd grown tall in the intervening years, and although it was unfashionable for a woman to be so tall, she carried it well. Once he'd rescued her from that rosebush, she'd stood straight and regal, comfortable with her height as most women her age were not. No slouching for Althea. No, she'd stared him right in the eye.

He smiled, remembering how she'd scoffed at his hints about marriage. Other young girls would have flattered themselves that he was about to choose *them*. A more experienced woman would have played verbal games laced with coy innuendos. Yet coyness didn't seem to be in her nature. Nor was she very good at flirting. In a world where every young woman was taught to flirt, her candor was refreshing. She'd been straightforward and self-assured and not the least cowed by him.

Except when he'd kissed her. His smile deepened. Then she'd become as flustered as any young virgin, blushing to the roots of her honeyed hair. It had emphasized even more the changes in her from when she was eleven, for she'd rarely blushed back then. But she'd often watched him with those ingenuous amber eyes, and if he hadn't been so caught up in his own youthful importance at that age, he might have noticed her more. Instead, he'd treated her as he'd treated Isabella, as all men in their early twenties treat their younger sisters, with impatience and mocking indulgence.

He snorted aloud. He couldn't treat her as a sister now if his life depended on it. By Judas, who'd have ever guessed he'd be lusting after Kensingham's niece like a dog in heat? Althea. Cheeky, sullen, inquisitive Althea. Now beautiful, quick-witted, compassionate Althea. She was something, wasn't she?

And after tomorrow, she'd never speak to him again. He rubbed his eyes wearily. What to do about Kensingham's determination to duel? The bloody idiot couldn't hit the side of the proverbial barn, and wasn't all that adept at swordplay either. Neville's only choice was to aim to wound and hope that satisfied the man's foolish notions of honor.

Then again, there *was* a more attractive alternative. Since tonight's contretemps had come about ostensibly because Neville had manhandled Kensingham's niece, an offer of marriage might solve the problem.

He let that thought sink in a moment as a faint smile touched his lips. Marriage. To Althea. What an enticing thought. It would solve two of his problems at once, for despite what Althea believed about him, he'd come to this absurd ball in the first place because he was seeking a wife. He'd been seeking a wife for weeks now, attending all the balls in search of a woman who would suit.

The rumors about his desire never to marry had been started by his father as a joke. The late marquis had said it was as good a way as any of protecting Neville from doting matrons while he sowed his wild oats.

It was the kind of thing Neville's father had been wont to do in his later years. The marquis had only become a rakehell after Neville's mother had died birthing Isabella, but once he'd immersed himself in the life, he'd loved it. He'd introduced Neville to London's delights when Neville was only fifteen. But Neville had fast rivaled his father in the enjoyment of sensory pleasures.

Eventually, however, Neville discovered that he differed from his father, who'd remained a charming rogue until his death six years ago. Neville grew tired of having mistresses, of dallying with married women and grasping widows.

He'd been old enough to remember the pleasant home his mother had created before her death, a home his father had found tedious even then. More and more lately, Neville wanted that kind of home for himself, especially now that his sister was gone, leaving him alone at Foxworth. He wanted a wife, children . . . a son to carry on the title. He wanted it very badly.

Until now, however, he'd found no one who appealed to him, no one with whom he could endure more than a few minutes' conversation. Until Althea, he'd despaired of ever finding someone who suited him.

Althea would be the perfect wife. Daughter to the late Earl of Kensingham and niece to the new earl, she certainly had the breeding to be his wife. Although money was of no concern to him, she probably had that too. She was young and beautiful and—

And he wanted her. God, how he wanted her. One kiss had made him want her with a fierceness that surprised him.

He sighed. But Kensingham would never allow her to

marry him. Never. Not after what had happened between Neville and Kensingham eight years ago. Neville slammed his fist against the balcony rail. It was all so bloody unfair. He'd assumed that Kensingham's anger would fade with time, but obviously that hadn't happened. And there wasn't a damned thing Neville could do about it. Kensingham was itching to find some vengeance for Neville's youthful error. The fool.

With a groan, Neville turned away from the balcony rail. It did no good to think on it. The duel was set. He'd best find his seconds, then get a good night's sleep, so his aim was true enough tomorrow to make sure he only clipped Kensingham's wings.

He maneuvered his way through the crush in the ballroom, easily finding two friends willing to second him. Then he headed for the door. He had no more stomach for society tonight, for the coy glances of women and the double entendres of the men who courted them. He was tired of all of it. Especially now that he'd had a few moments with a woman unlike any of them, a woman with the courage to speak her mind.

Once he'd fought his way through to the entrance hall, it took him only moments to have his coach summoned. As soon as it drew up, he told his coachman, "To Foxworth!"

"Yes, my lord. But I think you should know there's a woman waiting for you inside."

Neville scowled. "A woman?"

"Aye. Said she wanted to talk with you."

He groaned. This was the last thing he needed now, some overly forward woman with a penchant to see if "The Fox" was as good in bed as his reputation said.

Opening the door, he tried to keep his temper in check. The woman's face was in shadow, so he couldn't tell who she was.

"I believe you've stumbled into the wrong carriage, madam," he said through gritted teeth.

"No, my lord. I haven't the wrong carriage."

Her voice was low and hesitant, almost fearful, but he recognized it instantly. And couldn't believe his ears.

"Lady Althea?"

"Aye. I had to speak with you alone, and this was the only way I could manage it. I knew you could send your carriage to take me home when we are done."

He made a quick decision. Climbing into the carriage, he knocked on the roof to tell the coachman to drive on. The carriage shuddered into a start.

As he stared at his unexpected guest, her face shielded from him by the darkness, he murmured, "Where is your angry uncle?"

"He sent me home, but I persuaded our coachman to let me out at the corner and keep silent about it."

"Your coachman must be a fool."

"Nay. He merely thinks it wise to placate me since one word to my uncle about his dalliance with my maid would lose him his position. He'll keep silent. And if Uncle Winston asks for me, my maid will make my excuses."

The sudden steely tone in her voice reminded him that Althea was no ordinary eighteen-year-old. This was a woman who'd lost her parents at the age of eleven, then been entrusted to a young bachelor who'd doubtless been unhappy to be saddled with a child to raise. By all accounts, Kensingham's method of child-rearing had been to stash Althea at his newly inherited country estate and then go on about his business as if she didn't exist. She'd been forced to take charge of her life far earlier than most.

Still, it was a wonder Kensingham didn't fight duels over his niece's honor every day. "Now that you've gone to all this trouble, why don't you tell me why you're here?"

He could almost see her shift her posture, straightening her spine against the cushioned seat of the carriage. "I'm here to ask you not to duel with my uncle."

Her answer didn't surprise him. He settled back, crossing his arms over his chest. "I see. I suppose it was too much to hope you were here to give me a kiss for good luck."

Although he couldn't see her face, he knew his words had probably made her blush, which pleased him inordinately.

"I care for Uncle Winston, Lord Foxworth. I don't want to see him die."

Stung by her concern for a hothead like Kensingham, he quipped, "What makes you think *he'd* be the one to die?"

Her tone grew bitter. "Don't toy with me. You know quite well my uncle is no match for you. He's a poor shot and a terrible swordsman. If you fight him, he'll lose."

That had been Neville's own assessment, but it surprised him coming from her. Few women of her age were so objective about the men they cared for. "Losing and dying aren't the same."

"You know as well as I do that duels are unpredictable. Even a crack shot like you can't determine the outcome." When he remained silent, she went on, "I know I'm asking a great deal. Refusing Uncle Winston's challenge would brand you a coward—"

"Yes, it would."

"But if you don't refuse, he could die, and I wouldn't wish to have that on my conscience. I-I'm afraid I've been enough of a trial to my uncle without adding that to my account." They passed a lighted manor, which lit her face, long enough for him to glimpse her pain before darkness shielded her once more.

Suddenly the full implications of the situation hit him. Lady Althea was alone with him in his carriage. The two of them had the same dilemma—how to keep Kensingham from getting hurt. And there was a logical solution. A quick word to the coachman, and they would be off to Gretna Green, where he could make her his wife and solve all their problems. No one could stop him.

Except her. Her words came back to him—that she would never marry him. And while he thought she'd more readily accept the idea once she got used to it, if he carried her off against her will, she'd dig in her heels and be determined to fight him.

He thought of how she'd melted in his arms, how sweetly she'd whispered his nickname. Obviously her memories of him weren't as bad as the rumors she'd heard. Obviously she was more kindly disposed to him than she would admit.

His eyes narrowed. She seemed convinced that if he fought her uncle, the man would die. The idea was spurious at best, but her misconception could work in Neville's favor. She wanted something of him—her uncle's life. And he wanted something of her—her hand in marriage.

Unfortunately, only her uncle could agree to give that to him, unless Neville could convince her to elope, which was doubtful. Then an idea hit him that was so perfect, he nearly laughed aloud. There was a way to soften her toward him while at the same time ensuring that Kensingham accepted Neville's suit.

"If I am to refuse this duel," he said, wishing he could see her face, "I'll expect something from you in return for the blow to my honor and reputation."

Her entire body went rigid. "Something from me," she echoed woodenly. "I suppose I should have expected that."

"Yes. You should have know better than to think an 'unprincipled rake' like myself would commit such a noble act with no hope of gain at all."

Her fingers curled into fists.

He leaned forward to cover her fists with his hands, ignoring the way she tensed at his touch. "Spend the night with me, Althea. One night. Stay with me tonight, and I swear I'll cry off on the morrow."

She snatched her hands from his and crossed her arms over her chest. "Only *you* would make such an abominable suggestion."

"Probably. Does that mean you refuse to do it?"

Her breathing grew labored, as if she were struggling to hold back tears. "What a choice you give me. Either sacrifice my reputation for my uncle's life or let him sacrifice his life for my reputation."

"You need not sacrifice either. No one need know that you've been with me. You've already arranged for this meeting to be secret. In the morning, you can return home before anyone awakens in your house." But he would do his dead level best to be sure she was there when her uncle came at dawn. At the sight of his niece eating breakfast at Neville's table, her uncle would be forced to let Althea marry Neville.

"You are no gentleman to ask this of me, Nev," she whispered in an aching voice.

Her use of his nickname tweaked his conscience, but he squelched the feeling. What he was doing was best for all concerned, he told himself.

He leaned back against the carriage seat. "We established earlier that I am no gentleman. And you knew that when you came to my carriage alone to plead for your uncle."

"You were a gentleman years ago."

"I was young and foolish years ago," he replied.

The carriage stopped suddenly, and he looked out to find that they'd reached his estate. Light from the outside lamps flooded her face, revealing a heartbreaking loveliness that made his breath catch in his throat.

And if you'd been then what you are now, he thought, *I'd never have been a gentleman. I'd have acted ruthlessly to get you, my beauty.*

He could almost see her weighing his proposition, her quick mind trying to find some way out of it even while she acknowledged that there was none. He waited, wondering if he'd gone too far. If she refused, what would he do?

When next she spoke, her voice sounded brittle and somehow older. "I suppose that when you say 'one night,' you mean that night to be spent in your bed."

Something in her fearful tone of voice kept him from confirming her assumption. He had to play this carefully, if he were to win. He didn't need to bed her to compromise her, and if it made her more willing to accept his proposition, he could easily promise not to do so.

And pray he could keep the promise. "No. That's not what I meant at all."

Surprise was plain on her face. "No?"

"Although I'd like nothing better than to have you in my bed, forcing you to go there would be tantamount to rape, and I've never stooped that low."

"Then I don't understand," she said in a confused voice. "What could you possibly gain from spending one night with me if not my virtue?"

She had him there. He couldn't exactly tell her the truth—that he hoped to force her uncle into marrying her to him. She wouldn't understand. He didn't quite understand himself why he'd hit upon this course of action or how she'd gotten under his skin so quickly. All he knew was that if he had to have a wife, he wanted it to be her.

But he didn't tell her that. Instead he gave her an answer as close to the truth as he could manage. "After tonight, no matter what happens on the morrow, your uncle will do his damnedest to keep you away from me. Yet I find myself loath to part with you just yet. So if you'll give me a few hours to enjoy your company, I'll accept my fate tomorrow and refuse to fight your uncle."

She eyed him suspiciously. " 'A few hours to enjoy my company'? Truly?"

"Truly. I swear I'll not press my attentions on you without your permission, although I can't promise I won't spend the entire evening shamelessly attempting to get that permission. And you must agree to stay in my presence the entire time." He flashed her a look of mock solemnity. "Also, I'd prefer it if you'd stay awake for at least part of the evening."

For the first time since she'd entered the carriage, she smiled. "My, but you have rigid conditions."

"I do indeed." He leaned forward. "Come now, what have you got to lose? You spend an enjoyable evening chatting with an old friend about whatever amuses you, and in return, I publicly proclaim myself a coward. What more could you want?"

"You could proclaim yourself a coward *without* my staying the night with you," she said hopefully.

Crossing his arms over his chest, he shook his head. "The bargain is on the table, my lady. Take it or leave it."

She sighed. "No one will ever know? You can keep your servants from talking about it, and you swear not to tell anyone of my presence here?"

"My servants won't recognize you, I assure you. And I swear I won't say a word to a soul." That was true, wasn't it? He wouldn't have to say a word. All he had to do was make sure Kensingham found her at Foxworth at the wrong hour.

"Oh, very well," she snapped. "You don't give me much choice, do you? I'll spend the night. But you'll regret forcing me to do so when you find out how tedious I am."

He laughed. Infuriating? Perhaps. Maddening? Most assuredly. But one thing he knew she could never be, and that was tedious.

Thank God.

THREE

As she entered Foxworth Manor, Althea realized why she'd agreed to Nev's preposterous proposal. It hadn't been his charming but highly suspicious promises not to seduce her. Nor had it been solely to ensure that he called off the duel.

No, it had been her perverse curiosity to see whether the teasing, protective young man she'd been infatuated with as a girl had truly become a callous rake or if the accounts of his character had been wildly exaggerated. And walking into the familiar surroundings of a place she'd visited as a child, she felt sure in her heart that the latter was the case.

For some reason, she trusted him. She was probably a fool to do so, but she did. After all, he could have demanded her virtue of her. He could have forced himself on her in the carriage. No one could—or would—have stopped him.

Instead he'd asked for her company for the evening, and what woman in her right mind could resist an appeal like that? Especially a woman who'd never had someone ask for something as mundane as her company nor go to such lengths to get it.

"Are you hungry?" he asked.

She smiled at the warm solicitude behind the request. "No. I was so nervous about the ball that I didn't eat all day. Then when I got there, I was so famished, I ate everything in sight."

He laughed. "You know, you're the only woman I've ever met who'd admit something like that."

"You're right," she said mournfully as the footman took her cloak, and Nev led her down the hall. "I'm always doing and saying improper things. But I can't help it. I don't know how to make small talk, and I can't pretend to like things I don't. I'm afraid I have a bad habit of speaking my mind."

"I've noticed."

"The thing is . . . I don't know how to behave in polite society. My uncle's fiancée did her best this past year to teach me how to act, but after seven years in a bachelor household, I was too woefully ignorant even for her tutelage."

He opened a door and ushered her through it. "I don't know about that. You handled yourself well on that balcony when any other woman your age would have been blubbering and screaming and making a general fool of herself."

"Oh, *that*. Well, that's different. I can deal with that sort of thing . . . most of the time. I do try to keep my wits about me." She shrugged. "It's people I don't know how to deal with. I didn't handle *you* very well, did I? That's why I ended up in this mess."

"By 'mess,' I hope you're referring to the awkward situation with your uncle and *not* to the condition of my study," he quipped.

She looked up, startled to find that she'd followed him into his study without a thought. A twinge of unease hit her when he closed the door behind her. Then she relaxed. At least he'd brought her to his study and not his bedroom. If anything convinced her of his sincerity, that did.

She surveyed the room, then gave a laugh. "Believe me, your study is the picture of neatness compared to Uncle Winston's. You have nothing to be ashamed of."

Nothing indeed, she thought as he walked to the

brandy decanter that sat on a writing table and poured himself a glass. The study was tastefully decorated with mahogany furniture, and the other furnishings—drapes, rugs, overstuffed sofa, were just rumpled enough to make the room look comfortably male. To her surprise, there were estate ledgers scattered across the desk and other obvious signs that he used the room for more than just a male retreat.

Then again, if memory served her correctly, the marquis had been showing interest in his father's business affairs even before the old marquis had died and left the running of the estates to his son. Lord Foxworth might be a rake, but that obviously wasn't the only facet of his character. And somehow it only enhanced his trustworthiness in her eyes.

Then he began to untie his cravat, renewing all her unease. "Wh-what are you doing?" she blurted out as he slipped off the strip of silk and loosened the neck of his shirt, then tossed the cravat across a chair and began to unbutton his coat.

He smiled wide enough to bring out his dimple. "I'm getting comfortable. Surely you've seen your uncle do the same."

She stared in horrified silence, unwilling to tell him that her uncle never so much as unbuttoned his coat in her presence, though he occasionally did it when he was alone with his friends and thought she couldn't see.

"I'd say that you should get comfortable, too," he went on. "Loosen your stays. Let down your hair. But since you'd construe that as an attempt at seduction—and you'd be right—I'll refrain from making that scandalous suggestion."

When she opened her mouth to retort, he held up a hand. "Look here. I shan't sit here all night with my neck in a vise. Nor shall I wear my coat and suffer through the suffocating heat that will be necessary to keep you warm in that . . . ah . . . less than adequate gown."

She turned a rosy pink when he let his gaze trail down to her low-cut bodice, which bared an alarming amount of her skin to the air, even if it was fashionable. She had to admit her satin gown was no match for his clothing in warmth.

As if to emphasize his point, he removed his coat and hung it over the back of a chair. But when he removed no more clothing and only rolled up his sleeves, she let out a sigh.

He grinned and held up his hands. "You see? Nothing to be alarmed about."

Not true, she thought as he turned around and bent to stoke up the fire. His coat had shielded certain parts of his anatomy from her eyes, but with it off, she couldn't help noticing for the first time the sleekly muscled thighs outlined by his tight breeches and the taut, firm shape of his buttocks.

Oh, dear, she thought, ducking her head with a low groan. What on earth was she thinking about, looking at a man's behind? Women were not supposed to notice such things. Theresa had been very adamant about that.

Then why did she feel a rabid curiosity to see more of him unveiled? Why did the very sight of his bared forearms make her remember the excitement of being held by him on the balcony?

"Now we'll be nice and cozy," he announced in a cheery voice once he'd finished with the fire.

Nice and cozy, she thought. She could never feel "nice and cozy" with him. Agitated and hot was more descriptive of how he made her feel. Very unladylike feelings, she had to admit, but she felt them all the same.

He seemed to know it, too, for he flashed her the very devil of a grin before he gestured her toward a chair.

She moved to it and sat gingerly on the edge, wondering how she'd ever make it through this night without doing something to disgrace herself. "What now?" she asked, needing to get her mind off the unsettling feelings he stirred in her.

Picking up his brandy glass, he shrugged. "Why don't you tell me what *you* want to do? Consider this your stolen night. No one will ever know what you do during these hours, so why not do something you've always wanted? Whatever you choose will be our secret. You're free to engage in any activity your heart desires . . . within the confines of this house, of course."

She stared at him blankly. Then she realized he was absolutely right. This *was* a stolen night. There was no Uncle Winston or Theresa to please, no crowd of earls and duchesses to impress. There was only Nev. And nothing she did seemed to shock him.

"Would you like to drink a brandy?" he offered as a suggestion, his eyes twinkling. "Or perhaps some port?"

She wrinkled her nose. "I've already had my share of champagne tonight, and too much liquor gives me a headache."

"Then I suppose cigars are out," he quipped, eliciting a giggle from her. "What then? What would you like to do that you've never been allowed to do before?"

With a frown, she thought of all the many restrictions that had been placed on her through the past seven years . . . nay, through her whole life. There were mountains and mountains of them, yet absurd as it seemed, all she could think of was—

"I should like to slide down the bannister in the hall."

He sputtered, nearly choking on his brandy. "You'd like to do what?"

"Slide down the bannister." When he continued to look at her as if she were mad, she explained. "When I used to visit here, Isabella and I would watch you and your friends slide down that lovely long bannister. It looked like such fun and we were green with envy. Yet the only time we attempted it, we were caught before we could go down, and then soundly chastised by your father, who said girls shouldn't do such things, for it might ruin them."

He snorted. "That sounds like something Father would have said."

"At the time I wondered what he meant. How could it possibly ruin us to slide down a bannister?" She tossed her head back. "Anyway, I think he only said it to keep us from doing something he thought was too dangerous for girls but perfectly safe for boys."

"Sliding down a bannister isn't perfectly safe for anyone," he muttered.

"*You* did it. I should like to try it, too."

He cast her a look of pure exasperation.

She met his gaze with an angelic smile. "You said I could do anything. Are you going to renege?"

He drained his glass, then set it down on the table with a sigh. "No, of course not. If you want to break your bloody neck on the bannister, then by all means, have at it."

Her smile widening to a grin, she leapt to her feet. Maybe this night wouldn't be so bad after all, she thought. It might even be fun.

She changed her mind about that minutes later when she was standing at the top of the staircase staring down the smooth, hard length of oak bannister. She hadn't remembered it being quite so long . . . or so high above the ground. Suddenly she wasn't at all sure she wanted to slide down a bannister. Nev was right. It didn't look at all safe.

Glancing down at Nev, who stood at the bottom of the stairs, she caught his smug glance and knew he'd noticed her sudden reluctance. Blast him! If she didn't do it now, he'd tease her about it the rest of the evening.

She absolutely would *not* give him the satisfaction.

With a look that was pure defiance, she set herself up on the even stretch of bannister that came before the drop.

"You don't have to do this," Nev called up from the bottom.

"I know," she muttered, but before she could think any more about it, she pushed off from the top.

The slide down was a heart-stopping blur as her satin skirts sent her sailing along the well-polished wood. The air whipped her hair back, tugging some of it loose from the pins and making her gasp. Her pulse raced and the speed made her delightfully giddy.

All too soon it was ending. She thought she saw Nev's face register surprise as he moved into a position right below the bannister as if to catch her. But before she could look again, she'd reached the bottom and had vaulted right into him. He staggered back, but she'd gained too much momentum, and they both went crashing to the floor.

For a second, she lay atop him, stunned into silence by the impact. Then realizing that he was perfectly still beneath her, she pushed up onto her elbows and peered into his face.

"Nev?" she whispered. He didn't so much as blink.

Her heart raced in a panic. Surely she hadn't killed him. Then again, he'd fallen awfully hard. What if she'd hurt him? "Oh, merciful heavens, Nev . . . speak to me!" She cupped his face in her hands and peered into his eyes. "I'm so sorry . . . I didn't mean to . . . Oh, Nev, I'll just die if I've hurt you—"

That's when she felt his arms clamp her waist. He opened his eyes and grinned up at her. "You were saying?"

She scowled, then pushed against his chest. "You wretched pretender! I thought I'd killed you, and here you are, perfectly well—"

"Not perfectly well," he corrected. Without warning, he rolled over, putting her beneath him. "I'll probably have bruises upon bruises tomorrow, but I'm not dead." He shifted until he lay half on her, half off, supporting his weight on one elbow as he rested his free hand on her waist. "No, I'm not at all dead," he added as his gaze drifted over her face, then lower, to her breasts, which were near to bursting out of her dress, thanks to her corset and her awkward position.

A blush stole over her cheeks. One of his legs lay cradled between hers and he pressed it along the length of her thigh in a sensuous movement that made her suck in her breath.

That seemed to delight him. "Or perhaps I *am* dead,"

he murmured as he bent to nuzzle her forehead. "Dead and gone to heaven."

"I doubt that's where you'd go," she retorted, trying to stem the tide of emotions surging in her at his touch.

"Probably not." He flashed her a seductive smile, staring down at her through eyelids heavy with desire. "I'm much too wicked for heaven."

And to prove it, he ran his fingers through her already half-fallen hair until it was completely free of pins. Lazily he scattered the strands of hair through his fingers before stroking them away from her face.

Oh, dear, she thought as her pulse quickened, this wasn't wise at all. She should tell him to move. She should push him away. But their bodies fit so well together. And it was exciting to have his weight on her.

That was her last conscious thought before he lowered his head. Then he was covering her mouth with lips so warm she thought they would melt her. They caressed and stroked with light, teasing touches until her breathing grew heavy and her heart raced.

Then he touched his tongue lightly to her lips. This time he didn't need to prod her to open her mouth, for it seemed to open of its own accord, letting him plunge his tongue into the very depths and sweep the inside with a stroke that was at once soothing and thrilling.

But he didn't stop there. His mouth slanted over hers more demandingly as his tongue began a driving rhythm that turned her to jelly. In a daze, she brought her arms around his waist, holding him to her. The dear torment of his kiss so captivated her that she hardly noticed when his hand traveled down to rest on her breast or when he parted her legs even more with one muscular thigh. She was too caught up in tasting the brandy on his breath and smelling the musky male scent of him to push him away.

He kneaded her breast through the satin of her gown, and she sighed low in her throat. She felt warm and full to bursting, like a ripe peach threatening to split its skin.

Her own skin tingled all over, alive with delicious new sensations. She seemed to be thinking on a level below consciousness, where her body acted on its own instincts, pressing against him wantonly and arching into his hand in a desperate attempt to soothe the ache he roused in her breast.

And still the kiss went on, deeper and more drugging until she was practically insensible. Only then did he drag his mouth from hers, but just to move it lower, scattering kisses over her throat, the sloping curve of her neck, and then the half-moons of her breasts showing above her bodice. He kissed the swells of flesh, his whiskers scraping the tender skin.

Then his fingers stopped their caressing motions to pull down the bodice and shift of her gown, freeing one of her breasts for his perusal. The chill air against her warm skin brought her briefly to her senses and she pressed her hands against his shoulders, but when he lowered his mouth to cover one pink nipple, her fingers curled into his shirt as she gasped.

It was so . . . so hot and exciting and daring. It seemed right to let him do this scandalous thing to her on this night, her stolen night. And he did it so very well, sucking the nipple until it grew hard as a pebble, then swirling his tongue around it, over and over . . . and over.

"You like that, don't you, my beauty?" he murmured, his eyes glittering as he stared at her. With a mischievous smile, he blew a breath across the wet, puckered skin, making her clutch him to her. "Oh, yes, you definitely like it."

"I'm very bad, aren't I?" she whispered with regret. Was this where she should tell him to stop? Could she?

Amusement danced in his emerald eyes. "Not at all. I think you're very good." He tugged at her nipple with his teeth, then closed his eyes. "Ah, yes, very good indeed."

Before she could retort, he began to draw on her breast more roughly than before, making her cling to him. Her head fell back and she closed her eyes with a moan.

What heaven he was creating with his mouth! Now she

knew how he'd gotten his reputation and why "many a woman" would "grace his bed." He knew how to make a woman quiver and tremble and ache. And she couldn't bear to make him stop.

She hardly noticed when he moved his hand down to the hem of her skirts, then pushed them up until her thighs were exposed. But when he slid his hand between her legs to cup her most secret place and rub it with the heel of his palm, her eyes shot open. What he was doing was outrageous. Scandalous!

She loved it.

Oh, I really should make him stop, she told herself.

Yet she didn't, even when his fingers parted her thatch of hair and stroked a tight little nub there, sending fire shooting through her veins. She squirmed against his hand, her fingers digging into the flesh of his shoulder as he fondled her more and more boldly.

But when his finger delved inside her, she went stiff all over. The intimacy of it, the shock of the caress jolted her from her inexplicable acceptance of what he was doing.

This wasn't right. No matter how good it felt to have him touch her like this, she mustn't let him. Not if she wanted to keep her virtue.

"Nev?" she whispered, closing her fingers around his wrist and trying to force it back from her.

He let her pull his hand away, but lifted his head from her breast, his eyes blazing. "Yes?"

"I-I think we should stop this now."

For a moment, she didn't know if he'd understood a word she said. There was a wild light in his face, and his breath was coming hard as a stallion's after a race.

"I said—"

"I heard you."

She swallowed at the hard note in his voice. "Then . . . then could you please get off of me?"

He closed his eyes, as if seeking for mastery in the depths of his mind. Then he bit out, "Yes. Of course."

With a great shuddering breath, he rolled off to lie

beside her on the floor. Blindly he stared up at the ceiling, his jaw rigid.

She felt momentarily bereft, shut off from him and his thoughts. And the wonderful comfort of his arms. But she forcibly squelched her brief regret, tugging her bodice back into place and jerking down her skirts. It didn't matter how pleasurable he'd made her feel or how angry he was now. If she gave in tonight, she'd hate herself on the morrow.

Still, she felt guilty for letting him touch her so intimately, then making him stop. Turning onto her side, she stared over at him. "I'm sorry."

His words were clipped. "You've nothing to feel sorry about."

"But I shouldn't have let you—"

"There's one thing you should learn right now, Althea." He shifted to face her. Desire flared briefly in his eyes as he let his gaze trail over her prone form. Then he seemed to master it, and with it, his anger.

When he continued, his voice was lower, huskier. "Never apologize to a man for giving him an inch. In the first place, any man is happy to have that inch. In the second place, if you apologize for giving an inch, the man will use your apology to take a mile. You are perfectly in your rights to stop a man from taking your virtue. At any point."

She couldn't believe he was giving her such candid advice. As he'd no doubt intended, his words made her smile. "Even you?" she teased.

"Especially me." He gave a mock scowl. "Though you can't expect me to like it."

Thinking of how he'd just warned her away from himself, she burst into laughter. "You know what, Lord Foxworth?"

"What?"

"You are a complete hypocrite."

He stared at her with raised eyebrows. "Oh?"

"No self-respecting rake would give his intended victim advice on how to rebuff him." She stabbed a finger at his chest. "You're a fraud. You're not nearly as self-serving as you pretend."

He grinned as he caught her hand, then kissed the inside of her wrist. "On the other hand, perhaps being straightforward is simply one more weapon a rake uses to seduce his 'victim.'"

She snatched her hand back with a gasp. "Oh, I hadn't thought of that. Such deviousness is beyond the realm of even *my* imagination."

With a laugh, he propped himself up on his hand. "Actually, Isabella sometimes also accuses me of being a hypocrite. She says I'm not nearly as bad as I pretend to be, and that I'm not sure myself what I am."

"Is she right?"

His eyes twinkled. "You'll have to decide that for yourself." He took his finger and ran it along the curve of her jaw. Before she knew it, he'd clasped her chin with an intimate grip, and she knew he was going to kiss her again.

She knew, too, that she mustn't allow it. With a quick motion, she drew back, then sat up, trying to think of something to say that would destroy the spell he had cast on her.

"You mentioned Isabella," she said a bit too quickly. "How is she? I would so love to see her, although I don't imagine that's likely now that she has moved to France. But I miss her."

With a sigh, he sat up opposite her. His hair, loosed from its ribbon when she'd crashed into him, now fell about his shoulders like a lion's rumpled mane. She wanted to touch it, but she resisted the impulse.

"Isabella misses you, too," he said.

"I doubt she misses me much. Not with her handsome French count hovering about."

He scowled. "The bloody bastard. It took ten years off my life when they eloped."

"I don't know why. They're perfect for each other." She tucked her legs beneath her. "After two years of marriage, she still writes about him in glowing terms, and he seems to dote on her."

"I suppose he turned out all right," he grumbled, "but I still say he's not good enough for her."

She laughed. "You mustn't begrudge them their happiness. I know you didn't think she was ready for marriage, but obviously she—and the count—didn't agree. And just because marriage isn't your choice for yourself doesn't mean it can't be good for someone else."

He planted his hands on the floor and leaned back as he stared at her. "What makes you think it isn't my choice?"

His sudden scrutiny embarrassed her. She dropped her gaze to her lap. "Well . . . I . . . everyone says—"

"You've heard the Prince's ditty, I suppose. The one about The Fox never taking a wife."

She nodded, confused by the brittle note in his voice. "Isabella told me about it. She found it amusing that the heir to the throne had immortalized her very own brother in verse."

Turning his face from her, he sighed. "Yes, I'm sure she did."

She looked at him. His face was rigid and closed as he stared up at the bannister.

"Are you saying it's not true?" she asked.

His gaze shot back to her. For a long moment, he simply watched her. Then he leaned forward and lifted his hand to stroke her cheek. "Would it make a difference if I said it wasn't?"

The dark emotion flickering in his eyes sent a thrill throughout her body. Then she chastised herself for letting his words affect her so. This was undoubtedly another technique he'd perfected for seducing women. She must be careful not to act like a henwit and take him seriously. "We both know you wouldn't mean it. Rakes don't marry. Or if they do, it's for money or to get heirs. And since you don't need money and apparently don't want heirs, why bother with a wife? This is obviously another of those . . . er . . . 'tricks' a rake uses to seduce his 'victim.' You know, pretending that he's eligible, when he knows he'd never marry the woman he seduces."

His expression altered subtly, growing somehow more cold, though he continued to caress her cheek. "What if I vowed my sincerity? What if I went counter to all the rumors and asked you to marry me? Would you?"

She chewed on her lower lip, unnerved as much by his touch as by his words. This was some sort of game he was playing. It had to be. Theresa had warned that some men said anything, including promising marriage, to get what they wanted. That didn't mean they'd keep their promises, however. So if she took the bait and said she'd marry him, what would he do? Laugh at her? Seduce her, then abandon her? She didn't want to find out.

At her silence, his voice hardened and he caught her chin in an iron grip. "Would you marry me if I offered for you, Althea?"

"Of course not." She forced her tone to be light. "I'm not fool enough to marry a rake." Intending to sound sophisticated, she added, "Even *if* you were sincere and this wasn't a trick to get me into your bed."

He dropped his hand from her face, a mocking smile flitting over his lips. "I've trained you too well, I see. You won't fall for my tricks, will you?"

"If I were another woman who didn't know so much about your reputation, perhaps I would be fooled, but I know too well that The Fox . . . well, everyone knows—"

"The Fox will never marry," he finished for her, speaking the words in a strained tone that confused her. He cast her a forced smile, then suddenly stood, holding out a hand for her. "I think we've exhausted this tedious subject. So, how would you like a little refreshment?" He glanced at the hall clock. "It's nearly two A.M., and you've a few more hours to endure my company. Do you want some tea?"

Confused by his abrupt change of subject, she mumbled, "Tea would be lovely," and stood up.

But as she followed him down the hall to the kitchen,

she couldn't help wondering about his words and his peculiar reaction to what she'd said. Was it possible he really *did* want to marry?

No indeed, she told herself. Not by all accounts.

And yet . . .

The very thought roused too many confusing emotions in her, so she put it out of her mind at once.

FOUR

I'm a bloody coward, Neville thought as he sat at the kitchen table with Althea, watching her polish off three rolls spread with butter, then wash them down with half a pot of tea.

When she'd spoken of marriage, he should have asked her if she'd marry him. He should have simply told her what he wanted.

Why hadn't he?

Because she'd made it quite clear she wouldn't marry him if her life depended on it. She might not have meant it . . . but he couldn't take the chance that she did.

It was easier to deceive her and play on her trust until he could get her uncle's consent. In essence, it was easier to force her into marriage.

I'm worse than a coward, he thought. *I'm a bloody bastard.*

Yet he couldn't bring himself even now to tell her what he wanted. The thought of watching her stiffen in disgust, then walk out of his house, taking all his hopes with him, was unbearable. Especially now that he'd had a taste of her.

Yes, he was being unscrupulous. But what else could he do? Leave the choice to her? She didn't know her own mind. She didn't really know *him,* for God's sake, so any decision she made based on the gossip about him wouldn't be wise.

No, he must go on as planned. Once they were married, he'd make it up to her. He'd shower her with everything she deserved.

Unfortunately, that thought didn't ease his conscience.

"Don't you want anything to eat?" she asked.

"What?" he said, jerking himself from his unpleasant thoughts.

"Food. The thing I am presently gorging myself on. Don't you want any?"

Her expression, teasing and a little flirtatious, made him forget all his doubts, all his uncertainties. It made him salivate, and not for food either.

He reached across the table and caught her hand. Before she could stop him, he lifted it to his mouth, swirling his tongue around the tip of one of her buttery fingers. "I *am* hungry, now that you mention it." He sucked another fingertip, watching as her eyes turned a molten amber. Then he added wickedly, "But what I want isn't food."

She yanked her hand away, her breath coming in staccato gasps as she stared at him. "You're very bad, you know."

He leaned back in his chair. "I thought you said I was a hypocrite and quite honorable."

Frowning, she wiped her fingers on a kitchen cloth. "I don't know *what* to make of you. But I wish you would stop . . . you know . . ."

"Trying to seduce you?"

She nodded and stood up, flashing him an impudent look. "You told me this was *my* stolen night, to do what *I* wanted, but we always end up doing what *you* want."

He laughed as he stood and offered her his arm. "I plead guilty to the charge, my lady. I shall try to behave from now on. So, what else would you like to do on your night? Climb a tree? Shoot a pistol?"

He could feel her relax as she took his arm, then let him lead her toward the door. Unfortunately, she appeared to be seriously considering his proposals as they walked to his study. What in God's name would he do if she said she wanted to learn to shoot? It was too dark for that, and the last thing he wanted to put in her hand was a gun. It had been bad enough watching her nearly kill herself on that bannister.

"I detest firearms," she said after a moment, flooding him with relief. "And believe it or not, I did climb a tree or two in my youth. Besides, after my experience with the bannister, I don't fancy braving any more heights tonight."

"You didn't enjoy sliding down the bannister?" he teased.

"I suppose I did. Until I fell on you, that is."

He led her through the door into his study. "That had its moments, too. The part on the floor was quite enjoyable."

Her instant blush delighted him, even when she followed it by snatching her hand from his arm. "You simply can't get off that subject, can you?"

"I'm trying. But *you* keep bringing it up again."

"I do not!" She faced him, putting on an expression so prim it would have impressed the strictest governess. "We were talking about what I want to do. And I've made my decision."

"That sounds ominous. What is it now? Swing from the chandelier? Learn to fence? I swear, if I didn't know better, I'd think this was all a plot to break my neck before morning so I *can't* duel with your uncle."

She chuckled. "That's a thought."

"And not a very pleasant one," he said dryly. "Out with it. What daring trick would you like to perform now?"

"I'd like to talk."

He cast her a wary glance. "Talk?"

"Yes." Moving to the sofa, she settled herself on the edge of it, her spine stiff as she smoothed her skirts. "You see, I have so many questions that no one will ever answer, and I want you to answer them."

"You may not believe this, Althea," he remarked as he went to pour himself a brandy, "but I don't know everything. I might not know the answers to your questions."

"These aren't questions about facts. These are questions about . . . well, about things people say that make no sense. Everyone talks in riddles, and no one will tell me what they're talking about. Especially my uncle's friends."

Neville arched one eyebrow. "For example?"

"The first night we were in London, as we were leaving a dinner party, several of my uncle's friends congratulated him about his engagement. Just then, the butler brought my uncle his hat and gloves. One of his friends snatched up the gloves and said, 'Judging from the size of these, we should congratulate the bride-to-be instead of the groom.' Then all the men burst into laughter, except for Uncle, who scowled at them and hurried Theresa and me out the door. I asked him what the men meant, but he wouldn't explain. And for the life of me, I can't imagine how gloves could possibly affect a marriage."

Turning to hide his smile, Neville drank deeply of his brandy. He suspected he'd need it for this discussion. "They weren't commenting on the gloves, but the size of them, and thus the size of your uncle's hands. I gather he has large hands?" He shot her a glance.

Her face filled with confusion. "Why, yes. How did you know?"

"There's an old wives' tale," he said, swirling the brandy in his glass, "that says the size of a man's . . . ah . . . most private part is directly related to the size of his hands. Or the size of his feet or thumbs, depending on whom you talk to. Thus a man with large hands, for example, is assumed to have a large—" He cleared his throat. "Need I be more explicit?"

Her eyes had gone very round, and she was blushing furiously. "No." She chewed her lower lip, looking a bit uncertain. Then she straightened her shoulders and said, "Well, yes. I mean, I know what you're talking about. The housekeeper at Kensingham Hall was good enough to explain to me how children are made, so I know what a man . . . does with his most private part. But she didn't mention . . . er . . . you see . . ." She drew a deep breath, then blurted out, "Is it considered good if a man is large there?"

Only with great effort did he keep a straight face. "Since I'm not a woman, I can't say for certain. But I've been told women prefer it."

"Oh." She grew silent, and he wondered if she were working out the logistics in her mind or were simply appalled by what he'd said.

After a moment, he realized she was staring at *his* hands. The hands themselves were average, but he had long fingers, and he wondered what she'd make of that. The very thought of her mulling it over made him grow hard.

He swigged his brandy so fast, he almost choked on it. Keeping his eyes carefully averted from her curious gaze, he dropped into the chair opposite her. "Is that the only thing you wanted to ask?" he said in a strained voice.

"I don't know." She had finally torn her gaze from his hands. "I mean, I've heard or overheard so many things Uncle wouldn't explain. I assumed he was merely too busy to bother with my silly questions. But now I wonder if . . . I mean . . . is it possible that everything I heard referred to something indecent, and that's why he wouldn't explain?"

Neville fought to look serious. "It's possible."

She considered that, then shook her head. "That can't be true. For example, I overheard one of my uncle's friends say he'd love to view Miss Merryweather's garden, but when I pointed out that Miss Merryweather had no garden, all the men burst into laughter, except Uncle." Crossing her arms over her chest, she settled back against the sofa. "Now what could they possibly have found to laugh about in that? Gardens aren't indecent."

"Most of the time, no." Swirling his brandy, Neville stared into it, wishing he hadn't agreed so readily to answer Althea's questions. Every one of them was making him more heated by the moment. "But 'garden' is also a euphemism for a woman's private parts. Obviously your uncle's friend was interested in seeing Miss Merryweather without her clothes on." He took a great sip of the fiery liquor, lifting his gaze to see how Althea took that.

This time Althea's blush wasn't so marked. In fact, she was stiff with outrage. "Do you mean to tell me someone has taken a perfectly innocent word and turned it into . . . into . . ." She gave a snort of disgust. "No wonder that horrible man laughed even louder when I volunteered to show him *my* garden."

Neville nearly choked on his brandy. "What in God's name was your uncle's reaction to that?"

She shot him an irate glance. "He told them my garden was inaccessible, then sent me off to find Theresa. At the time, I couldn't imagine why he was making such a fuss over our gardens."

"Now you know why."

She was silent a moment. Then her face clouded. "I hesitate to ask this, but what is a House of Civil Reception?"

He shot her a keen glance. "A brothel." When she winced, he asked gently, "What did you think it was?"

"Something like the House of Commons, I suppose. I wasn't quite sure."

"I'm sure most of the House of Commons would prefer to meet at a House of Civil Reception," he muttered.

She ignored that and leaned forward, her expression worried. "What is a cockloft?" When he spewed brandy into his glass, she looked sadly at him and added, "It's not the place where chickens are kept, is it?"

Coughing violently, he shook his head. When he had control of himself, he said, "The word meant that once. But now it's used . . . well, it means the same thing as 'garden.'"

A look of distress crossed her face. "Oh, merciful heavens, then I'm afraid I've said an awful thing."

He held his breath. "What did you say? And to whom?"

"I . . . you see . . . I was trying to pay Lady Paxton

a compliment. And so I . . . I told her that one of Uncle's friends said she had a fine cockloft."

This time he couldn't stifle the amusement in his voice. "Lady Paxton? You said that to Lady Paxton? My God, she's as prudish in public as she is promiscuous in private! I hope you didn't say it in front of anyone."

"Only her husband," she said in a small voice.

He couldn't keep back the laughter that bubbled out of him. "Her husband? Her bloody husband?"

"It's not funny!" She looked close to tears. "I-I had no idea what I was saying, don't you see? It's so hard to make polite conversation when you don't know anything and you're never out in society."

One look at her face and his laughter faded. "I know, I know. But I swear I'm beginning to feel sorry for your uncle. How on earth have you acquired this colorful vocabulary when, as you say, you've never been out in society?"

With a sigh, she dropped her gaze from his. "Until recently, I rarely left Kensingham Hall, but Uncle sometimes came home and brought his friends. And I trailed after them all. You know, as Isabella and I did with you and your friends."

She toyed with the braided trim on her gown. "Anyway, whenever Uncle's friends knew I was around, they made small talk, but . . . well, it was so dull at Kensingham that when they stayed up late to play cards, I often sat on the stairs and listened to their conversations. They never knew."

She met his gaze with a worried one. "Still, if I'd had any idea how . . . shockingly improper his friends were, I'd never have repeated anything I heard them say. But Uncle Winston is such a moral man himself, so careful of the proprieties and so prudish, that I never dreamed his friends were saying such—"

"Kensingham?" Neville interrupted with a laugh. "Prudish? A moral man? By Judas, your uncle certainly kept you in the dark, didn't he?"

She crossed her arms over her chest. "And what's that supposed to mean?"

"Your uncle is anything but prudish, my dear. In fact, many in this town consider him as much of a rake as I."

"You jest!" she said in disbelief.

"Nay. Ask anyone." He settled back against the chair, surprised that she'd had no idea of her uncle's true character. "When Kensingham isn't with you, he's as randy and hot-blooded as the next bachelor. He's so charming with the ladies that they call him 'Winsome Winston.' Now that he's planning to marry, I'm sure he's curbed his activities. But before that, I assure you, he visited the House of Civil Reception often enough to have a passing acquaintance with its inhabitants."

Pure shock filled her face. "How can that be? If he were as disreputable as all that himself, he wouldn't be risking his life to save my reputation—"

"For God's sake, Althea, this duel isn't about your reputation. Not really. Kensingham is merely furious with himself for not watching over you better, and he's taking it out on me."

She shook her head. "It's more than that. He hates you. It was *you* he objected to more than anything."

"That's true. He's furious at me because of—" He broke off, realizing he'd said too much.

She straightened in her seat, her eyes narrowing. "Because of what? What happened between you two to make him hate you all these years?"

Damn it, his petty urge to let her know the truth about her precious uncle had blown up in his face. He hadn't meant to mention that fiasco. Not at all. He didn't want her to know. It would only reinforce her poor image of him. With a groan, he set his brandy down and rose to pace the room. "What happened between us is none of your business."

"Oh, yes, it is!" Her tone was controlled but he could tell from her set chin that she was very disturbed by all he'd told her. "I'm risking my future because of this duel, so I have a right to know why it's happening!"

She had a point. She *did* have a right to know.

He turned to stare into the fire, his hands folded behind his back. Then he sighed. "Eight years ago, your uncle's mistress left him for me. Nan was his third mistress, but he was very attached to her. So he decided that I'd used unscrupulous methods to get her, when in truth, Nan had come to me herself. She was a greedy woman, and she fancied me because she thought I might be more extravagant with my gifts. She only lasted with me a few months, before I found her trying to make some extra money by . . . er . . . being friendly with yet another man while under my protection."

His voice grew taut as he faced her. "Nan was a low opportunist not worthy of Kensingham's anger. But he didn't see it that way. She'd humiliated him by leaving him for a youth barely old enough to have a mistress. And I'd humiliated him by taking her. He's never forgiven me for that."

For a moment, she looked stunned as she stared at him, mouth gaping open. Then she closed her mouth with a prim little expression of disbelief. "So you expect me to believe that this whole thing is the result of some . . . some woman I didn't know existed? You expect me to believe that my uncle, who is the soul of virtue, is a . . . a loose-living debaucher who would fight a duel out of peevishness?"

Her tone of disbelief cut at him. She was so convinced of her uncle's good character that she'd rather believe in it than accept the truth. Neville gave a weary shrug. "I don't expect you to believe anything. I shouldn't have brought it up, since your thirst for truth obviously doesn't extend to your uncle."

"Truth? That's not truth! It's lies!" She crossed her arms over her chest, her body trembling. "Y-you're only saying these awful things to blacken him in my eyes. You want me to believe everyone is as wicked as you. You can't accept that there are a few men who are decent and upstanding and—"

"I'm saying it because it's true, whether you like it or

not," he bit out, angered by her blind defense of her uncle. He couldn't resist echoing her earlier words. *"Everyone* says your uncle is a rakehell, everyone in the whole bloody city." Her lower lip began to quiver, but he went on relentlessly. "Why do you think he spends so much time in London? Without you?"

"He comes here on business," she protested, but her voice was shaky.

"Aye. And to see his current mistress and to go to one or two gaming hells before getting drunk at his club."

"But he's always been so strict with me! He's always chastising me for things I say . . . and do . . . and . . ." She broke off with a sob that she muffled with her fist.

Her distress hit him hard. Too late he realized the source of it. Her uncle had obviously made her believe she had to be a perfect example of womanly virtues while he was off being a perfect example of manly vices. The bastard.

Neville forced his voice to be more gentle. Maligning her uncle further wouldn't comfort her. "Of course he's strict with you. You're his ward. He probably feels it's his responsibility to keep you from doing anything that would attract the wrong kind of men . . . men like him. Most men are like your uncle. My father was. He had very different expectations for my mother and Isabella than for his mistresses."

At the mention of his father, sympathy flickered in her eyes. "Y-you're saying that men like my uncle and your father are two-faced deceivers."

He shoved his hands in his pockets. "I suppose you could look at it that way. Or you could see it as their way of protecting their women. Your uncle is a normal young male with the same penchant for wenching and gaming as most of his friends. He simply doesn't want you exposed to that."

Her pretty throat tightened convulsively. "It's so hard to believe he could be so . . . so . . . I-I can't even imagine him as a rake."

He moved to sit beside her on the sofa. "Come now, Althea, surely you've overheard *him* use some of those terms you asked me about."

She paled, then gave a hesitant nod.

"You see? He has probably worked very hard all these years to keep his bachelor role separate from his role as guardian. And apparently, he's been relatively successful." He glanced away. "Until tonight, that is, when I foolishly opened my mouth."

She placed her hand on his arm as if to reassure him. "Don't feel bad about telling me." Her voice shook. "I'm *glad* you told me."

"So you *do* believe me."

Ducking her head, she sighed. "How can I not? As you say, all I have to do is ask someone, and I'm sure they'll tell me with pleasure. It's a wonder no one has told me before now. But then, no one else is honest with me the way you are."

Guilt stabbed at him. He wasn't being entirely honest, was he? "Yes, but my honesty has hurt you, hasn't it?"

She stared up at him. "Still, I would rather know the truth." Then her eyes blazed as she dug her fingers into his arm. "It infuriates me the way he . . . he pretended he was too perfect for words, and everyone upheld the image. All this time, he's been telling me I must be more proper if I want to find the right kind of husband, while he's been as improper as can be!"

"It's difficult to be a bachelor raising a girl alone. If anyone knows, I do. I had the devil of a time keeping Isabella out of trouble."

"Yes, but you didn't send Isabella off to live alone in the country. You kept her with you in London. You didn't shield her from the real world. Or pretend you were some . . . some saint who never had a bad thought!"

"And she ran off with a French count at the age of seventeen," he put in dryly as he took her hands in his. "I wouldn't say that's an argument in favor of my competence as a guardian."

She gave a wan smile. "Her French count is wealthy

and titled. You know quite well she made a good match. She just made it sooner than you wanted." Her expression grew earnest. "The fact is, you brought her to London where she could experience society, at its worst and at its best. You gave her your support, no matter what, and you gave her choices. That's a good thing, not a bad thing."

She stared down at their joined hands. "But my uncle kept me closeted and ignorant, giving me nothing on which to base a choice. He made me think that he didn't want me around, that he was ashamed of me, when it was himself he was ashamed of."

"You thought he was ashamed of you?" he asked incredulously.

"What else was I to think?" Her voice was laced with bitterness. "Whenever his friends came, he kept me away from them as much as possible. He never took me to London with him or introduced me to anyone. He was always admonishing me to be more of a lady. I-I thought he disapproved of me. I thought he hated me." A tear escaped her eye. Then another and another.

His heart lurched within him as he rubbed her tears away with his thumb. "By Judas, don't cry. Please don't cry." He pulled her into his arms, and she went into them with a muffled sob. He stroked her back and her hair, murmuring comforting words as she cried on his shoulder.

His poor darling. All this time she had thought she was a disgrace to her uncle, when in truth it was the other way around.

He rubbed his chin against her forehead. "Strange, isn't it? The bloody fool probably thought he was saving you from the poor influence of him and his lecherous friends." He gave a harsh laugh. "Yet despite all his attempts, you've ended up in a scandalous situation with a notorious rake."

"A notorious rake who's been more honest with me in one night than my uncle has in seven years." Her voice was muffled against his chest. "You're the first man to answer my questions honestly, the first man who hasn't treated me either as an annoying child or a beautiful woman without a brain. You can't know what that means to me."

Guilt raged through him, reminding him that he hadn't been honest with her about everything. Ruthlessly he squelched the call of his conscience. Having her in his arms and speaking well of him felt too good. He couldn't give that up just yet.

She toyed with the buttons on his shirt. "*You* would never leave me sequestered on a country estate like my uncle, would you?"

He tightened his arms about her fiercely. "Never. If you were in my care, I'd spend every free moment with you. I'd want to hear you laugh. I'd want to stroll with you through those gardens you spoke of—the real ones. I'd want to know everything that was in your inquisitive mind."

She was silent so long, and her body felt so good against him that he couldn't resist. He nuzzled the top of her head, then began planting kisses in her hair, drinking in the scent of rosewater that clung to it. And when she didn't pull away, he moved his lips lower, to brush her temples and her wide, smooth brow.

After a moment, she whispered, "Nev?"

"Yes, darling."

The endearment made her tremble in his arms. "Are . . . are you trying to seduce me again?"

He held his breath as she lifted her face to his. He let his gaze trail over her beautiful features, her lips slightly parted and her creamy skin glowing in the candlelight. If he said yes, would she bolt?

The truth was he would seduce her at once if he thought she would let him. It was more than lust, though he certainly felt that. It was the urge to let her know what she was worth to him. Seducing her hadn't been part of his plan, but now it seemed essential. Completely essential.

"Perhaps I am," he murmured, lifting his thumb and rubbing it along her lower lip, feeling her breath warm it.

She dropped her eyes, a pretty flush spreading over her cheeks. "Then perhaps you . . . you should stop."

He dragged the back of his thumb down to her chin, then along the curve of her throat. "You don't want me to stop."

"No." She caught his hand, then lifted it to her lips and kissed it. "Heaven help me, I don't. But I should."

The throaty words made his loins tighten with an urgency at once painful and pleasurable. "Why? This is your stolen night, remember? You can do whatever you wish."

A small smile graced her lips. She flattened her hand against his chest as if uncertain whether to push him away or caress him. "The idea of a stolen night is lovely, but we both know there's no such thing. There are always consequences. If I let you make love to me, what will happen tomorrow?"

Her words came back to him—*I'm not fool enough to marry a rake.* Perhaps they were just words. But not sure of her yet, he bit back the impulse to answer her with the truth.

Instead he used what he thought was a compelling argument for seduction. "And if you *don't* let me make love to you? Will you be content to leave, knowing you won't see me again . . . except at those few parties and balls where our paths cross?" He drew his hand from hers and slid it along her collarbone, then beneath her gown to caress her bare shoulder. "Will you be content never to have me kiss you, caress you?"

Then he tipped up her chin, forcing her to look into his eyes. "After tonight, you'll marry whomever your uncle chooses, won't you? And judging from his hopes for you, his choice will be the kind of man to make love timidly in the dark. Your husband will no doubt burn for you as much as I, but he'll control his impulses because it would be ungentlemanly to show passion to his lady wife. Instead, he'll find a mistress with whom he can express his 'improper' desires."

He could tell his words wounded her. She tried to turn her face from him, but he wouldn't let her, tightening his grip on her chin as he went on fiercely, "All the while, you'll have those same passionate urges, but you'll suppress them for fear that he'll think you a wanton. After a time, you won't be able to bear it anymore. Then, like Lady Paxton, you'll play the proper woman while finding your pleasures anywhere but in your husband's bed."

"I'd never do that!" she protested, her lips quivering. But he could see the awareness in her eyes. She knew truth when she heard it, even if she couldn't bring herself to admit it.

"After tonight," he went on relentlessly, "do you think you could live in the kind of marriage your uncle would arrange for you?" He reached behind her back to undo the top buttons of her gown, then slipped her gown off her shoulders to below her breasts. She still wore her shift, but the cloth was so sheer, she might as well have been naked, for he could see the swells of flesh with their sweet rosy crowns beneath it.

His eyes locked with hers as he filled his hand with one soft, cloth-draped breast, kneading it and stroking her nipple until her eyes grew wild and dark with what he knew was desire.

"Could you forget what it's like to have a man give you pleasure?" he said huskily. "Could you live your whole life wondering what it would be like to make love to someone of your own choice, to feel him stroke and caress your whole body?"

He drew her gown down to her waist. Her corset pressed her breasts up high and proud beneath the thin muslin of her shift. He sucked in a breath. "Could you relinquish this?" he murmured as he fondled them both, thumbing the nipples and watching as her face flushed and she arched back to give him better access. "And this?" He bent his head to cover one nipple with his mouth, sucking the hard pebble through the cloth until she gasped.

Her fingers against his chest curled into his lawn shirt, clutching it as if for support. "'Tis no wonder they spin tales about you, my lord," she choked out as he flicked his tongue over her nipple. "You could seduce a nun."

The words stung. She thought him a seducer, nothing more. She thought this was one more conquest to him. He enfolded her in his arms, his heart beating fiercely with the desire to let her know it wasn't. "Perhaps I could, but I only want you." He gave her a long kiss, burying his tongue in the velvety warmth of her mouth over and over before murmuring hoarsely against her lips, "You want me, too. Don't deny it."

"I-I can't deny it. I want to. But I can't."

The reluctance in her voice sent guilt spiraling through him. Angry at himself for it, he lowered his head to her neck where he kissed the fragile pale skin, the sloping hollow of her throat. "Then let me make love to you, Althea. Please. Just this once forget all you've been told about what a lady should and shouldn't do." He kissed his way to her ear and ran his tongue around the outside curve, eliciting another moan from her. "Do what your heart tells you, and it will all come right."

He pressed forward, forcing her to lie back on the sofa. She made a defeated little sound in the back of her throat, part gasp and part sigh, but when he lowered his mouth to hers once more, she slid her arms about his neck and gave herself up to his kiss, her body relaxing beneath his.

He knew then that he'd won, just as he'd won before, with other less reluctant women. He knew he could take her, and she wouldn't protest. And yet . . .

What happened next made no sense to him. As if in a trance, he lifted himself off her and stood beside the sofa, fighting the overwhelming desire that surged through him at the sight of her lying there half-clad, her face flushed with pleasure.

"I can't do this," he bit out.

Then he turned away.

FIVE

Still half-dazed by the force of her own desire, Althea stared at Nev's rigid back, at the hands he held clenched at his sides. What had happened? What had she done? One minute he was stealing her will from her and the next . . .

Dragging her gown up to cover her breasts, she sat up. "Wh-what do you mean, you can't do this?"

When he answered, his voice was tight. "I want you. God knows how much. But I want you to want me, too. To care for me as I do for you. You think this is merely another seduction for me . . . one more woman to add to my string of 'victims.' So tomorrow you'll hate yourself for giving in."

There was no mistaking the pain in his voice. Or that he meant what he said. It touched her deeply, for this wasn't the protest of a rake, but the heartfelt need of a man who wanted more than lovemaking. She could never understand the rake . . . but she understood the man very well. No matter what she'd heard about him or the façade he wore, she knew Nev needed something more in his life.

Was she that something more? She didn't know. But she couldn't finish the evening without finding out, and for her that meant giving herself to him.

Without stopping to think, she rose from the sofa to

stand before him. He stared past her at the wall, a muscle in his jaw twitching.

Reaching out, she took his hand and put it on her waist. "I do want you, Nev. I've always wanted you, ever since I was eleven and you were the handsomest, most charming boy I knew. I've wanted you each time Isabella told me of her fine, hard-working brother, who spent as much time tending his estates as in wild living."

She reached up to stroke his square jaw. "I wanted you even when Uncle Winston said you were a blight on society."

His gaze shot to hers, uncertain, perhaps even angry. "He said that?"

"Aye. But we both know he lies, don't we? And I shan't let his lies keep me from doing what you suggested for my stolen night. You were right. Seduction is the perfect choice."

Every muscle in his body tightened as his eyes blazed. "Seduction? You weren't so sure of that earlier. Or is this merely a way to strike back at your uncle for lying to you? Are you trying to act like him to punish him?"

She flinched from his angry words. She shouldn't have mentioned her uncle at all, but it didn't change anything. "Nay. You know I'm not foolish enough to relinquish my virtue in a petty act of rebellion. You said yourself that I want you, so you know it's true." Her voice shook a little. "And . . . And what you said about my future husband. That's true, too. You're right. I can't bear never having a man of my own choice make love to me. I can't bear never having *you* make love to me."

She could tell her words had affected him, for he gave a great shudder and tensed all over. But he did nothing, said nothing, obviously fighting her for reasons of his own.

She added in a soft, taunting voice, "Perhaps you lied when you said you wanted me. Perhaps you were merely toying with me, trying to see how far I'd go."

With an oath, he grabbed her hand and forced it to his breeches, pressing it against the hard ridge there. "This, my beauty, is how much I want you. I ache with wanting you. But once I have you naked beneath me, I don't want you drawing back as you did by the bannister. Once we've begun, I don't think I can stop for your virginal protests. Not this time."

She knew he was deliberately being crude to scare her, to make her reconsider what she was doing. But she'd come this far, and she couldn't go back. She didn't even want to. Her eyes locked with his as she curved her hand around his aroused member. "I thought we'd already begun," she whispered as she leaned up to press a kiss to his mouth. "Was I wrong?"

That was all it took. He hauled her into his arms, a groan erupting from his throat as he brought his mouth down on hers, possessing it, stabbing his tongue over and over inside it.

After that, all consideration of past and future was gone. There was only the present . . . and the man who was devouring her mouth like a starving animal, his hand roaming freely over her body to unclasp her gown and petticoats. It briefly occurred to her that he knew quite well how to undress a woman, but he drove that thought right from her mind with his soul-deep kisses.

Suddenly, she felt him shove her gown and petticoats down over her hips, leaving her wearing only her corset and shift. And feeling strangely naked.

With a shyness she couldn't help, she stepped backward, out of her clothes and away from him. He kicked them aside, then halted, his eyes hot on her, as if he waited for her to back further away and prove that all her passionate words were lies.

As she met his uncertain gaze, she forced herself to speak boldly and move back to him. "Shouldn't you take off some of your clothes, too? I-I want to see you in the flesh."

Surprise briefly flickered over his face before he relaxed and gave a low, wicked chuckle. "Do you now? And which part of me do you wish to see first?"

With trembling hands, she took hold of his shirt, undoing the ties. At first, she could barely manage them, but as she bared more and more of his chest, a hunger built in her to see the body she'd only envisioned in her dreams. His breathing grew heavy as she pushed the shirt off his wide shoulders, then trailed her hands over his naked chest with its sprigs of dark hair sprinkled generously over an expanse of taut, well-knit sinews. Smoothing her hands down his magnificent chest, she felt her heart pound with excitement.

She'd never seen a man's nude body before. And all her half-formed, innocent imaginings hadn't prepared her for the pleasures of it. She'd never dreamed it could be so thrilling to touch the skin raspy with hair or to feel every tightening and undulation of muscle beneath it. But when she reached the waistband of his breeches, she paused, her throat going dry as a sudden embarrassment assailed her.

"Don't stop there," he said hoarsely as he took her hands and pressed them to his buttons. "Don't you want to see for yourself if the old wives' tale is true?"

It took her a moment to remember what he was talking about. Then she blushed furiously. But she couldn't deny that she'd wondered about him, about that part of him, even before he'd told her the ridiculous tale about a man's size. And even before she'd noticed how long his fingers were.

The very thought of it made her tremble. With shaky hands, she worked the first buttons loose, but it took her so long that he brushed her hands aside before undoing the rest and yanking his breeches and his drawers down, then stepping out of them.

To her utter mortification, all she could do was gawk at him, her curiosity getting the better of her. He seemed to grow before her eyes, the sleek member thickening in a way that fascinated her.

She reached out to touch him, but he caught her hand. "If you touch me there, I fear you'll find yourself still a virgin in the morning."

"What do you mean?"

"Never mind. Turn around."

She did as he asked, thinking that he was embarrassed to be seen by her. Then she felt his hands at her corset, loosening her laces, and she knew that wasn't it at all.

He dragged the corset off with a new urgency, burying his face in her neck with a groan. Slowly he swept his hands up from behind to clasp her muslin-covered breasts, to rub them with the heels of his palms, making a pleasurable ache erupt in her belly and radiate outward in ever warmer circles.

"You're not like any other woman I've ever known," he whispered in her ear. "Did you know that?"

"Is that good? Would you rather I was more . . . sophisticated or—"

"God, no." He swept her hair aside to plant kisses over the place where her neck joined her shoulders. "You're perfect as you are." He lifted his hands to draw her shift off her shoulders, sliding it down over her body with sensuous slowness and dropping soft kisses on every inch of skin he bared.

When he'd moved her shift past her hips, he let it slither to the floor in a whisper. She could feel his breath move down her body, and when he turned her to face him, she found him on one knee, looking up at her with that crooked dimple as he added, "Absolutely perfect."

With a shy smile, she rested her hands on his shoulders. Swiftly he untied her garter and slid the stocking down. It unnerved her, having him kneel at her feet, his face so close to a part of her that no man had ever seen. And when he drew her stocking off, only to plant a warm kiss on her inner thigh, she dug her fingers reflexively into his shoulder.

"Nev?"

"Yes, darling?" he whispered as he removed the other stocking.

"This is . . . very embarrassing."

He kissed her other thigh, much higher up and closer to the thatch of hair between her legs. "Is it?" he murmured. Then his fingers actually parted the hair down there.

Her ability to breathe seemed to have disappeared entirely. "V-very much s-so," she stammered, but anything further she might have said was cut off by a gasp when his tongue darted out to caress her in the most intimate way she could imagine.

"Neville!" she exclaimed, meaning it for a protest. Instead it came out like an enticement to go further.

And he took it as such. He buried his face between her legs, kissing the delicate folds that his fingers had unveiled. His hands gripped her hips and held her against his hot mouth as his kisses grew more bold.

She melted. If he hadn't been clasping her so tightly, she would have collapsed right there. His tongue found the little bud nestled in her petals of skin and flicked over it like the licking flames of the hearth fire. With a cry, she squirmed against him, wanting more, wanting less, wanting it all and not knowing how to get it. The longer his mouth caressed her, the more heat pulsed through her, sparking wanton fires.

She could feel the heat everywhere, in her breasts, her belly, even in her throat. The heat drove out the chill of the night air until she felt like a bundle of coals being stoked higher and higher, coming nearer with each moment to bursting into flames. And when he suddenly drove his tongue inside her, she clutched his head tight as the urge to be engulfed by the blaze grew stronger.

"Oh, Nev . . . yes . . . yes . . ."

He groaned and increased his caresses until she felt on the very brink of exploding. Then he sucked hard at her aching bud and the explosion came, a white-hot surge of energy that poured light and heat through all the empty, cold places inside her.

"Nev!" she cried out. She convulsed against him, holding onto his shoulders for support. "Merciful heavens, Nev!"

"Yes, darling," he whispered. He slowed his caresses as she went limp in his arms. "For you, all for you."

A languid warmth spread through her . . . a mix of pleasure and delight as she came to her senses gradually and saw that the room was not ablaze and she was not held captive in some spell of magical fires. In wonder, she stared down to where Nev was clutching her against his cheek as if afraid to let go of her.

"I've never . . . oh, that was glorious," she whispered, reaching down to stroke his thick hair.

He flashed her a dark smile, then rose to engulf her in his arms. "There's more," he whispered as he kissed her hair, her cheeks, her eyebrows. She could feel his arousal press against her thigh. To her surprise, it excited rather than frightened her. She found she craved the "more" he offered.

He caught her up in his arms, carrying her swiftly to the sofa. As he laid her down on the soft, cushioned cloth, he covered her body with his. Nudging his knee between her legs, he spread her thighs so he could settle himself between them, and a thrill of anticipation coursed through her.

Even when she felt his shaft press between her legs, felt him find the place his mouth had just been, then ease himself into her, she lifted her hips to welcome him.

"Slowly, darling," he whispered against her ear. "You're not used to this. It will hurt at first, though I'll try not to let it hurt too much."

She didn't care if it hurt. She wanted to have him inside her, soothing the bone-deep craving he'd aroused. Although there was a feeling of invasion, of impossible stretching as he inched his way in, there was also excitement.

This was Nev, after all, the dream lover of her childhood and the only man who'd spoken the truth to her. She suddenly wanted him fiercely. Longing to feel him deeper, she arched her back until her breasts were crushed to his and her hips were opened even more to receive him.

He groaned and halted his movements abruptly.

Twisting her body beneath him, she met his gaze in alarm. "I haven't hurt you, have I?"

His face did indeed wear a look of torment, but his eyes glittered with desire. "Nay, but I must be careful with you, and your innocent movements are making it next to impossible."

She smiled a soft, dreamy smile, then arched deliberately against him once more. "Good."

"By Judas, you're a witch!" he growled. Then he drove into her fully.

She cried out, and with a moan, he covered her mouth, plundering it with bold strokes of his tongue. He'd been right about the pain, she realized as he held still, letting her adjust to him. But when he began to move inside her, slowly, insistently, pushing deeper and less hesitantly with each thrust, the pain lessened.

The feeling of having him joined to her so intimately was utterly indescribable. And the closer they were joined, the more she lost herself. She moaned and writhed beneath him as if another creature possessed her, making her into a wanton. But she didn't care. She wanted more, ever more.

His breathing grew labored. "I've caught you now, Althea," he said hoarsely. "You're mine. Say it!"

She curved her arms about his back and shifted her hips up, searching for an even greater closeness to him. She gasped when he thrust hard into her as if to coerce the words from her.

But there was no need for that. "I'm yours," she admitted gladly. It was true. No matter what came of this reckless act, she was indeed his. If not legally, then in her heart.

His answer was to clutch her to him and fall into a rhythmic motion that was no longer checked or careful. It was like her ride on the bannister, wild and unexpected, thrilling but frightening, too. This time, however, she knew when she reached the bottom he'd be there to catch her.

So she gave herself up gladly, craving the piercing pleasure of his thrusts and the heat that swept through her with each one. She no longer saw the ceiling above her or heard the crackling of the fire in the hearth. There was only his face with its undiluted passion, his voice murmuring endearments, his slick body meeting hers in a quickening cadence. And around them rushed a wild swirl of color and lights like the world rushing past her on the bannister until she felt herself hurtling off the end, bucking against Nev with a cry of guttural abandonment as the searing pleasure overtook her once more.

"Oh, God, yes! Yes!" he cried out against her mouth as he too found his release, plunging to the hilt before spilling himself inside her with a series of jerky thrusts.

Then he collapsed atop her. He lay there several moments as they both settled to earth. His weight on her gave her an odd comfort, reminding her that he was human and not some strange god who'd brought her to heaven and back.

"Would you like me to get up?" he whispered after a while, his breath brushing her ear. "There's not much room on this sofa, I'm afraid."

Wordlessly, she shook her head and clasped him close, uttering a sigh when he acquiesced and buried his face in her neck.

Now that it was all over, she didn't want to face the reality of what she'd done. She didn't want to see the clothes scattered across the floor or the blood that she'd been told would be staining the sofa beneath her.

She wanted to pretend this was her haven, her safe harbor. She wanted to pretend she hadn't just given her virginity with heedless unconcern to an infamous, though lovable scoundrel, who'd no doubt break her heart now that he had what he wanted.

But after a few more moments passed, she knew she couldn't pretend any longer. The hour must be late. Soon she'd have to leave, before her reputation was compromised forever.

"What time is it?" she whispered.

He shifted to his side, barely able to stay on the sofa as he stared down at her with surprise. "Why?"

"You said I could leave before dawn, before anyone even knew I was here."

A shuttered look passed over his face as he dragged one finger over her breast, watching the nipple pucker beneath his touch. "Do you want to leave?"

Alarm bells sounded in her head. "Of course. I can't stay here until my uncle comes. You know that."

With a sigh, he pressed a kiss to her forehead. "Yes, I know." He left the sofa and looked past it at the clock on the opposite wall. "It's only three-thirty. You're safe yet."

She sat up on the sofa, suddenly very conscious of her nakedness, especially since he was so heedless of his and she was having trouble keeping her eyes off his un-ashamedly male body. Without looking at him, she reached down and found her shift among the tangle of clothing, then drew it over her head.

As she turned, she caught sight of the blood staining the upholstery. She glanced at him. "I fear I've ruined your sofa."

He cast her a wry smile as he pulled on his drawers. "'Tis a small price to pay, I assure you, for what you just gave me."

Somehow his talk of payments didn't make her feel any better. If anything, it made her want to be away as swiftly as possible, to be done with the untidy awkwardness of their leave-taking, so she could nurse her remembrance of their night together.

She swallowed. "I really must be going, you know. It will take me at least half an hour to get home, and I—"

"Don't go yet," he said quickly, moving to sit beside her on the sofa. He lifted her hand to his lips for a quick kiss, then kept hold of it when she would have drawn it away. "You said you'd stay the whole night and only leave right before dawn. There's still two hours or more before you must leave."

"Yes, but you've had what you want of me."

He clasped her chin, turning her face to his. "It would

take many more hours than that to have what I want of you, darling. And this may be the last time we're ever together like this."

Her mouth went dry. Really, he was too logical. And far too good at speaking endearments. It frightened her that he knew so well how to make her heart leap and her will weaken. "I-I don't know—"

But he cut off her words with a kiss, a tender one that grew more persistent when she went limp beneath it. His hand slipped under her shift to fondle her breasts, making her moan.

"Two more hours," he whispered as he slid his other hand between her legs to caress her with soft, sweet touches that dissolved all her determination. "Please?"

She gave him the barest nod, knowing that what she was doing was insanity, yet not ready to leave him yet. To her surprise, he withdrew from her. But it was only to stand and sweep her up into his arms before turning toward a door in a corner of the room.

"Where are you taking me?" she whispered as she clung to his neck.

"To the room that adjoins this one." He gave a sensuous smile, his eyes alight with the force of renewed desire. "'Tis my bedchamber. This time we shall be comfortable, my beauty."

As if I care about comfort right now, she thought, then hid her face in his broad chest, feeling the blush steal over her cheeks as her blood raced once more. *Oh, I've become very wicked, haven't I?*

And she didn't care a whit.

Six

Neville paced his study, fully dressed for the confrontation at hand. Thank God Althea had let him convince her to "rest" a moment after the second time they'd made love or she'd already be racing out of here to evade her uncle.

He moved to the open door to his room and glanced inside. Guilt surged in him again at the sight of her curled up in his bed, asleep and totally unaware of his plans. He should have told her. After the first time they'd made love, when he could see her remorse for what she'd lost, he should have asked her to marry him. But she'd been so damned eager to get away from him that he'd been afraid to ask.

Then he'd been too caught up in seducing her again, in exploring the absolutely delectable body now shielded from his gaze by the counterpane. Fortunately, the cover didn't hide her flushed face or her tangle of hair or her soft, reddened lips—

"By Judas!" he swore under his breath as his loins grew heavy once more. It wouldn't do to greet Kensingham in such a state. The entire situation was delicate enough without that.

A knock came at the door, and he winced, hurrying to open it. "Yes?" he murmured to the footman outside.

"There are six men awaiting your lordship's pleasure in the drawing room."

Six men. Damn, he'd forgotten all about the seconds. And of course, Kensingham had brought a doctor. How should he handle this?

He thought a moment, then told the footman, "Ask the Earl of Kensingham to come to my study. Alone."

The footman raised one eyebrow, but left to convey the message. Neville ran his fingers through his hair, his gaze darting automatically to the open door to his bedchamber. The time had come to put his plan into action. And yet . . .

And yet this wasn't what he wanted. He didn't want to spring this on Althea while she wasn't even awake. Until now he hadn't considered what would happen to *her* when her uncle caught sight of her. But now he knew it would shame her. He couldn't bear to shame her, especially in front of the uncle she felt so ambivalent about.

Surely there was a better way to bring Kensingham around. There must be. And he would find it.

By time the second knock came at the door, he'd made up his mind. He moved quickly to the adjoining door and closed it, after checking to be certain that Althea was still asleep. Then he strode to the outer door to his study, opened it, and beckoned the earl in.

Kensingham was dressed soberly, his face a pale hue as he entered. Neville was vaguely conscious of his own unkempt hair and mussed clothing, but didn't worry about it. The only important thing was to get this settled, so he could have Althea forever.

"What is this about?" Kensingham snapped. "Why weren't you waiting out front? Are you planning to cry off?"

Nev shook his head, meeting the man's gaze unwaveringly. "Not exactly. But as I said last night, I have no wish to fight you. I'd prefer to settle this more amicably. And I think I've found a way to do so. I'd like to offer for your niece."

For a moment, Kensingham merely stared at him, mouth agape. Then his eyes narrowed. "Is this some trick? The Fox? Marry? Why, everyone knows that—"

"Everyone is wrong," Nev said through gritted teeth. He was getting tired of having his reputation flung in his face. "I have always intended to marry at some time or another. Why do you think I was at a marriage mart last night? I want a wife. And I'd like it to be Althea."

Kensingham gave a harsh laugh, his hands balling into fists. "What in the name of God makes you think I'd let her marry a scoundrel like you?"

It was the answer he'd expected. Still, he pressed on, forcing down the anger boiling up in him. "Don't let what happened between us eight years ago stand in the way of your niece's future. You know quite well I'm a perfectly suitable candidate. My exploits in the past have been no more outrageous than yours. You're marrying a respectable woman. Why can't I?"

"Because even if I did approve—and I don't—she won't have you," Kensingham retorted. "I promised to let her have the final say on any suitor I choose, and she'll never approve of you."

"She will approve," Neville insisted. "I know she will. If you don't believe me, why don't you go home and ask her?" He didn't know how he'd get Althea home before her uncle, but somehow he'd manage it.

"How can you be so damned sure—" Kensingham began, but broke off at the sound of the door opening at the other end of the room, and a female voice saying, "You promised to awaken me before dawn, Neville. Why didn't—"

Neville groaned as he turned to see Althea standing in the doorway to his bedchamber, her face still flushed from sleep and the counterpane draped around her, barely covering her breasts. No man with an ounce of perception could mistake what she'd been doing for the past few hours. And certainly not Kensingham.

As her color turned to ash, Kensingham let out a roar. "What the bloody hell— Althea, what in God's name are you doing here?"

"I-I . . ." Her eyes went wide as she clutched the

counterpane to her chest with a groan. "Oh, merciful heavens, Uncle Winston, what are *you* doing here?"

"It appears I am interrupting something abominable!" He turned to Neville, his face contorted with rage. "You bastard! You lecherous, deceitful—"

"He's done nothing worse than you've done to other women in the past, Uncle," Althea cried out in defense of Neville. Her face filled with outrage as she stepped toward him. "You have no right to chastise him for sins you commit regularly."

It was Kensingham's turn to blanch. He stared at Neville, his eyes black with horror. "What did you tell her about me? Oh, God, how much did you tell her?"

Neville felt a sudden pity for the man who stood trembling before him. "Everything, I'm afraid. She wanted to know the truth, and I gave it to her."

Kensingham looked as if he'd been struck. "The truth? Why? So you could use it to seduce her? Did you say, 'Look at what a lecher your uncle is. You might as well behave as wantonly as he'? Is that it? Is that how you got her into your bed?"

"He didn't seduce me, Uncle," Althea interjected. "I went willingly. What he told me had nothing to do with it. It was my choice."

Kensingham's face grew bleak. "Your choice? You had no choice. Don't you see? When a man like Foxworth decides to have a woman, he does what it takes to succeed." Kensingham looked from Althea to Neville, then went pale again. "In your case, he had to have you in his bed so he could force you to marry him. He wanted to marry you, he knew I wouldn't approve, and this is how he made sure it would happen."

Neville's heart sank. Somehow Kensingham had managed to ascertain Neville's intentions exactly, and Neville doubted that Althea would appreciate those intentions.

"Don't be absurd," Althea glanced at Neville, dropping her voice to a shaky whisper. "Neville doesn't want to marry anyone. Everyone says—"

"He just offered for you," Kensingham broke in. "Ask the man himself."

Althea faced him with an incredulous expression. "Did you offer for me?"

"I never said I didn't want to marry," Neville told her, praying she would understand. "Not once, if you'll recall. You believed the rumors, but they weren't true. I simply never wanted to marry until now."

Kensingham stepped forward, his voice growing bitter. "Apparently, last night this damned scoundrel decided he wanted you for a wife. That's why he seduced you—to force me into accepting his suit."

Her face was ashen, and she wouldn't look at him. "D-did you really plan all this just to make sure I married you?"

"It's not the way he makes it sound," Neville protested, feeling his hold over her slipping. "I did want to marry you, 'tis true. From the moment I met you on that balcony, I knew you were the only wife I wanted. And I knew your uncle wouldn't let me marry you, so when you came to me last night—"

"You lied to me." She clutched the coverlet more tightly to her chest. "You . . . you told me all you wanted was one night with me, that you'd let me go before anyone could ever know." The pain in her voice tore at him. "You told me it was my stolen night. But you never intended it to be that, did you? That's why you didn't wake me before Uncle came. What did you plan to do? Give him a glimpse of me in your bed? Describe in detail all the ways you . . . you—"

"Please, Althea, it's not like that," he said, his gut clenching inside him.

But it was very near to that, and he knew it. He'd never once considered her wants during his little campaign. He'd convinced himself that she would want what he wanted.

"You could have asked me, you know," she whispered. "All you had to do was ask me to marry you, and I—"

"Your uncle would never have allowed it."

A sudden change came over her face. Anger suffused it until her eyes blazed. "That had nothing to do with it! If you had told me what you wanted, I could have helped you. Somehow we could have made him listen to us both. But you didn't even ask me!"

"If you'll recall," he snapped, "the subject of marriage came up a few times, and you weren't at all amenable to the possibility."

The instant he said it, he realized he'd made a major blunder.

Her face went stony. "Yes, I do remember. I was very clear on the subject of marrying you, wasn't I? I believe I said I wouldn't marry you even if you offered."

"That's because you didn't believe I would offer!" he protested, feeling like a drowning man just before his head disappears beneath the water for the last time. "You were so convinced I would never marry anyone—"

"You're saying if I'd meant what I'd said, if I truly hadn't wanted to marry you, you would have made sure I did so anyway?"

Neville's eyes went wide. "If? *If* you'd meant what you said? That means you *do* want to marry me, doesn't it?"

She lifted her head, her face etched with hurt. "I wouldn't marry you now if you were the last person on earth."

Neville felt his heart twist inside him. "Don't say that! I understand why you're angry, but—"

"You don't understand a thing about me," she interrupted in a broken voice. "I-I thought you were an honest man, the only honest man in the kingdom. A rake, to be sure, but honest. Yet all along you were lying to me just as Uncle did." A great shudder went through her. "Except it was worse, much worse, because you made me . . . care about you. You, a heartless deceiver who played on my trust!"

She turned away, and he stepped forward to catch her arm. "I want to marry you, Althea. Why is that so awful?"

Tears were streaming down her cheeks, and she wiped them away with the back of her hand. "Because you gave me no choice in the matter." She looked at him, her lips tightening. "But I do have a choice now. And I'm not going to marry you."

Her uncle, who'd been watching the exchange with increasing bewilderment, exploded then. "What? But you *must* marry him! I'll admit his methods are reprehensible, but the deed is done now, and you're fully compromised. You *have* to marry him!"

Wrenching her arm from Neville, she faced her uncle. "You promised I would have the final say on any man you chose."

Kensingham tugged at his shirt collar, looking extremely uncomfortable. "Well, yes, but—"

"Was that a lie like all your other lies?"

There was a long silence. At last Kensingham sighed. "Devil take you, no. If you refuse to marry him, I won't force it." Then he leveled an angry gaze on Neville. "But I can still fight him. I can still gain justice for you. The seconds are waiting and—"

"No!" she said firmly. "No duels!"

Her uncle drew himself up. "You won't change my mind on this, Althea."

She turned a steadfast gaze to Neville. "And you, Lord Foxworth? Have you nothing to say about that?"

Neville winced at her use of his title. But her appeal reminded him that she'd fulfilled her part of the unholy bargain they'd made. She'd more than fulfilled it. Now it was time to fulfill his part, something he'd never expected to have to do. And she knew it.

With his eyes fixed on hers, he said, "There will be no duel, Kensingham. Proclaim me a coward if you wish, but I won't fight you. I'm crying off."

"The hell you say!" Kensingham protested, but knew he could do nothing about it if Neville refused to fight.

Althea stared at Neville a long moment. Then she whispered, "Thank you, Nev," and began to move about the room, picking up her clothes. "Now, if you gentlemen will excuse me, I'm going to get dressed. Then I wish to go home."

She was really leaving. She was really planning to refuse his suit. "Althea, please don't go," Neville whispered. He hadn't realized how much it would hurt to watch her leave. He'd been so bloody confident in his plan that it had never occurred to him she might choose not to marry him anyway. "I only did this because I wanted so desperately to have you marry me. Doesn't that mean anything to you? You know I've never wanted that from any other woman!"

She paused on her way to the door of his bedroom. When she turned her face to his, she was wearing a grim smile. "Yes, I know. But sometimes you have to ask for what you want, Neville, instead of just taking it." Then she moved into his bedroom, shut the door, and locked it.

Neville stared at the closed door, a gut-wrenching pain assailing him. What a fool he'd been. What a bloody, stupid fool! All she'd ever wanted was for someone to tell her the truth. Yet knowing that, he'd still lied to her. He deserved to lose her. He knew that. But he didn't think he could bear it.

"I don't understand this," Kensingham said in a strained voice behind him. "This isn't how it's supposed to happen. She should be ecstatic that you'll marry her, and you should be trying to get out of it. None of this makes sense."

Neville gritted his teeth. "Not everyone behaves according to society's expectations, Kensingham. And if anyone goes against type, it's your niece."

"She's not the only one," Kensingham muttered. "You bedded her. You could have abandoned her without a thought. Of course, I would have fought you for it, but you'd have won. We both know that." He paused. "Instead you offered for her, before I even knew she was here. And then, when she turned you down, you refused to fight me. You'd rather be branded a coward than go against her wishes?"

His tone was so incredulous that Neville shot him a sad smile. "Yes."

"But why?"

Neville uttered a ragged sigh. "Why? Because I've fallen in love with your niece." It was true. He knew it was true. He stared at the solemn-faced earl. "You couldn't have asked a better revenge for what happened eight years ago, you know. I love Althea, and she'll have none of me. Given the way Nan treated you, it's most fitting, wouldn't you say?"

Kensingham shook his head. "I don't know. Perhaps. But Althea is a better woman than Nan ever was, as you know. And I never loved Nan as you apparently love my niece."

"Still, I've lost her as you lost Nan." Neville glanced at the closed door, his throat constricting. "The fact that she's a better woman only makes it worse."

Kensingham was silent for a long time, watching as Neville stood motionless, his eyes fixed on the door that shut him out from what he'd hoped to gain.

After a while, the earl's expression grew thoughtful. "You know, you're not what I thought, Foxworth. Not at all. I can almost believe you *do* care for my niece."

Neville laughed harshly. "Your approval comes a little late, don't you think?"

"Perhaps not." Kensingham gestured toward the closed door. "Give her time to soothe her wounded pride. Come back in a few weeks. By then, she may be more willing to listen to your suit."

"What?" Neville flashed the earl a suspicious glance. "You're advising me to offer for her again? Why?"

"You want her, don't you?"

"Yes, but—"

"You were right when you said we shouldn't let something that happened eight years ago stand in the way of Althea's future." He drew himself up. "No matter what you think of me, I've always wanted only what was best for Althea." He shrugged. "If I read my niece correctly, she cares for you. Otherwise, she'd never have compromised herself. So that leaves me only one choice. To assure her future happiness. And if it is with you, then so be it. I'll do what I can to ensure it."

"You're forgetting one thing," Neville ground out. "She detests me now."

"You'll find a way to fix that, won't you?" His voice tightened. "You've always had a way with women."

Neville sighed. "Ah, but your niece is no ordinary woman."

For the first time that morning, Kensingham smiled. "That's true. But then, you're no ordinary man. Perhaps you can make her happy. You may be just what she needs."

Neville hoped Kensingham was right. But he feared that he wasn't. Althea's uncle hadn't been terribly good at recognizing his niece's wants and needs heretofore, and there was no reason to believe the man could do so now.

No, it was far more likely that Neville had lost her. And now that he'd tasted her wit, her loyalty to those she loved, her enthusiasm for living, he didn't know how he could stand life without her.

How the Prince will laugh, Neville thought. *The Fox has finally lost his head. The pity is, no one wants it. Not even me.*

SEVEN

Althea stared blindly out over the gardens of Kensingham Hall. The night was cold, and she shivered, drawing her wrap more tightly about her.

Inside, the orchestra was playing a minuet, and her uncle's guests were dancing themselves into oblivion. She could scarcely believe Uncle Winston had decided to have a full-fledged ball at the estate. He'd never done such a thing before.

Then again, he'd changed a great deal since that awful night three weeks ago. For one thing, he'd talked to her. He'd told her why he'd been so circumspect about his activities, why he'd been so cold and aloof, so solemn. And it had been exactly as Neville had said—he'd merely been trying to protect her.

So Neville had been right about that, too.

At the thought of Neville, she bit her lip, stifling the urge to cry. She'd cried far too much these past three weeks.

At first, her tears had been for the heartless way he'd betrayed her. But after some time had passed, she'd begun to reconsider everything that had happened that night. She'd remembered all she'd said about marriage, and suddenly she understood why he'd been uncertain of her. After all, she'd told him more than once that she'd never marry a rake like him.

And yet . . . She clenched her hands on the marble

railing. And yet, he should have asked her. He should have been honest about his feelings.

But she hadn't been entirely honest with him either. She'd protected her heart every way possible. She'd been as unwilling as he to chance rejection. It was true that she hadn't gone so far as to put him in a situation where he *had* to marry her. Still, when she'd given herself to him, a secret hope had been in her heart that he'd marry her once he'd compromised her. So she wasn't that different from him, was she?

Besides, he'd suffered for what he'd done. She knew that much. She could tell it in the heartfelt apologetic notes, accompanied by flowers and gifts, that he'd sent her the first three days after she'd left his house. And when she'd written to say that she didn't want to hear from him again, she could hear his suffering in the silence that said he'd obeyed her request.

Then there was Isabella's letter. Isabella had expressed surprise over a whirlwind visit her brother had made to France, in which he'd begged her forgiveness for having been so stubborn about refusing the count's suit.

"He's gone soft all of a sudden," Isabella had written. "He was such a dear. One curious thing, though. He asked all sorts of questions about you. I can't imagine why."

Althea knew why, just as she knew why Nev hadn't been seen at any balls or parties for the past three weeks. She knew why there'd been nothing but silence from the Foxworth estate, to the point that even the Prince had commented on The Fox's uncharacteristic withdrawal from the world.

Yes, after three weeks of thinking, she knew a great deal. For one thing, she knew he wasn't the wretch she'd painted him to be in those first few days after their night together. He'd deceived her, true, but he'd also given her so much that night. He'd shown her the pleasures of passion and had never made her feel ashamed for enjoying them. He'd taught her she wasn't the measure of what others thought of her, but was only herself. And he'd demonstrated amply that being herself had its own rewards.

She couldn't help but remember that when she'd been willing to let him seduce her, he'd hesitated, not wanting her to do it for the wrong reasons. Too late she remembered that the door to his bedroom had been shut when Uncle arrived, that if she hadn't come out herself, Uncle might never have known she was there.

No matter how much she tried to attribute all of that to some devious intent on Nev's part, she couldn't. She knew better. Because despite his deception, he'd been the only man she'd ever been able to talk to honestly. He'd been the only one to accept her for what she was.

Now she regretted her hasty words that night. She regretted never telling him she loved him. Oh, yes, she loved him. She probably always had. But she didn't know how to turn back time, to set things right again. She'd wounded his pride sorely. And he'd wounded hers. So how to move past all that?

"I see you keep the potted plants to a minimum on your balconies," came a voice behind her. "A wise decision indeed."

She froze at the sound of that painfully familiar voice. It was a dream. It had to be. He couldn't be here, for Uncle Winston would never invite him. Would he?

She didn't move an inch, afraid that if she did, he would disappear. "What are you doing here?" she whispered, holding her breath.

There was a long pause, and then he said in a stiff voice, "Your uncle invited me to attend. I assumed it was at your request, but I see I was wrong." He hesitated, and when he continued, his voice was achingly soft. "I'm sorry. I won't trouble you further."

She whirled around as he turned toward the balcony entrance. "Wait!"

He stopped. Slowly he faced her, and she feasted her eyes on him, on the broad shoulders he'd let her cry on three weeks ago . . . on the cheek that held his lone dimple, now hidden, and the unsmiling mouth so taut and grim. He didn't look well at all. His face had a hollow sharpness to it, as if he hadn't been eating, and his beautiful green eyes were glittering too brightly.

"I need to know one thing from you, Nev," she whispered. "On that night at your estate . . . did you intend for my uncle to find me in your bed? Is that how you planned to make sure I married you?"

Although his face filled with guilt, his gaze held hers steadily. "No. I'll admit that at first I had some vague idea of having him find you at my breakfast table. But once it came to the test, and the choice was either to make the offer without revealing your presence there or to show him that I'd compromised you, I . . . I found I couldn't embarrass you. If you hadn't come out when you did, I would have brought you home without his knowing. And I would have repeated my offer, to you as well as him."

Relief coursed through her. She didn't think she could forgive him if he'd chosen in the end to use her in such a despicable manner, shaming her before her uncle.

"Althea," he added, "I know what I did was callous, and I *am* sorry for it, more sorry than you can imagine. You were right. I should have asked you to marry me. I shouldn't have taken the coward's path and tried to force you into a situation where you *had* to marry me."

His apology was like balm to her already healing wound. He looked so remorseful, so devastated that she couldn't help wanting to comfort him. "I suppose I shouldn't have made it so hard for you to ask either," she said, taking a step toward him.

He went very still, his eyes glimmering in the light from the ballroom. The faintest hope lit his face. "No, you shouldn't have." He moved toward her, his hands clenched at his sides as if he fought to keep from reaching for her. "But you were in your rights to protect yourself, given what you knew about me and my reputation."

"I've been thinking about that reputation, my lord," she said softly. "It seems to me I might have been more right when I said you weren't nearly as self-serving as you pretended than when I called you a heartless deceiver."

He dragged in a heavy breath. "You're too generous by far. I thought I had taught you better how to recognize the tricks of a rake."

"Oh, you taught me a great many things. You taught me that men, especially rakes, can act like fools when they want something."

"And when they're in love," he added, his voice husky with emotion.

Her eyes went wide. "Are you in love?"

He lifted one eyebrow, his gaze searching hers. "Are *you?*"

She took another step toward him, reaching up to stroke his face. Her heart leapt when his breathing quickened. "That's how we went wrong in the first place, remember? Asking questions of each other that we both were afraid to answer honestly. Don't you think it's time we stopped playing that game, Neville? Don't you think it's time to say what we feel and forget our pride?"

"You're a wiser person than I am, darling." He covered her hand with his. "I love you, Althea. I know you probably find it hard to believe that I could have fallen in love with you in only one night, but it's true."

"I don't find it hard to believe at all," she whispered, her heart soaring, "since I did exactly the same thing."

He gripped her hand. "Does that mean you'll forgive me for the wretched way I treated you?"

After three weeks without him, forgiveness came easily to her. "Yes."

A relieved smile broke over his face. "And you'll marry me? You'll take on the project of reforming a wicked rogue?" His voice lowered. "You'll have my children?"

The very thought of it warmed her through and through. "Yes. Oh, yes, my love."

He caught her about the waist, clutching her so tightly to him that she could scarcely breathe. "Now that's a decidedly better answer than the one you gave me three weeks ago," he whispered against her neck, then covered it with kisses.

"It was a decidedly better way of asking the question," she retorted.

He laughed. "Oh, I don't know. I rather enjoyed our stolen night." He pressed her back against the balcony until she could feel the hardness in his breeches. "Indeed, I wouldn't mind repeating it."

She muffled her own laugh, flashing him a look of mock disapproval. "Are you trying to seduce me again, Nev?"

"Always, my beauty." He grinned as he lowered his mouth to within an inch of hers. "You wouldn't want me to reform *that* much, would you?"

No indeed, she thought as his lips claimed hers, as sweet and demanding as she remembered.

There were definitely some advantages to marrying a rogue. Most definitely.

DANGEROUS TOUCH

❦ ANNE STUART ❦

ONE

Johnson County, Wyoming, 1889

Caldwell's Mercantile and Saloon was busy that Thursday afternoon. With the long harsh winter over and spring arriving, there was too much work for folks to be spending the better part of the day in town. But Jacob Elder had come into the house and ordered his young wife to put on her bonnet and shawl and get out to the wagon. They had business in town.

That was odd in itself, Sara had thought as she climbed into the old buckboard. Jacob was just as likely to leave her at the homestead, out of the gaze of men. He didn't believe in womenfolk getting fancy ideas, and even a small town like Cedar Bluffs had too much temptation for the likes of Jacob Elder.

But Sara wasn't about to put up an argument, nor was she about to ask any questions. She'd been married to Jacob for almost seven years, and she'd learned early on not to question him. He always took it amiss, using it as an excuse to correct her behavior. Such corrections were usually painful.

He wasn't a man for strong liquor either, but the moment they arrived in town he left her with no more than a mumbled admonition to keep her head covered and her eyes down, heading into the saloon section of Caldwell's.

Sara followed him up the steps, obediently moving into the store. It was crowded as well—Marijane Wilks was busy poring over some ribbons while she gossiped with

Abigail McKinley. They looked up when Sara entered, and she steeled herself for their usual greeting—the uneasy look of pity in their eyes.

"Good afternoon, ladies," she greeted them, holding her homespun skirts like they were fine silk. Not that she'd ever worn silk in her life, but she'd read stories, long ago, before Jacob had caught her and confiscated the sinful books. He couldn't read and she could. That knowledge rankled.

"Afternoon, Sara," Marijane said kindly. She was an older woman with a handful of daughters and she tended to treat Sara like one of them. "Looks like the men are getting all riled up again."

"Looks like," Abigail echoed. "I can't say as I blame them, though. Did your husband tell you what's happened?"

Sara didn't want to admit that Jacob never told her anything. Never spoke to her, except to give her orders or chastise her. "No," she said in a low voice, her hand reaching out to touch the lilac-flowered calico that lay on the counter with a reverent caress.

"That bastard Harrison Stark is bringing in a hired gun," Marijane said flatly. "Excuse my language, Sara, but there's no other word for him. He's hired a professional killer from out of Cheyenne. Stark's own gang of hooligan cowboys haven't been able to drive us off our land, so now he's going one step further."

"How do you know?" She pulled her hand away from the calico. It was the prettiest thing she'd ever seen, and she wanted it. The wanting it, and the knowing she'd never have it, made it all the worse.

"He arrived last night. My husband got word from his cousin down in Cheyenne that Stark had planned to hire a couple of gunslingers to try to drive us homesteaders out, and the first one's already here. The men are in the bar trying to decide what to do about it."

"What can they do about it?" She turned her back on the calico resolutely, advancing on the abandoned counter. Obviously Mr. Caldwell was in the bar with the other loud customers, arguing the fate of the world and leaving the store side of Cedar Bluff's only business unattended.

"Well," said Abigail in a low voice, "some of the men are for hiring their own gunslinger, to fight back."

"No!" Sara said, horrified.

"Yeah, that seems to be the opinion of most of them. Besides the fact that after the winter no one's got any money to spare."

Jacob's voice filtered through the door along with the smoke and the stench of whiskey, deep and somber. "We won't fight him. It'll be that simple. He can't make us fight, and he ain't going to shoot us in the back. If we just keep our tempers . . ."

"You're the one with the temper, Jacob," a man's voice said with a laugh.

"We'll call on Almighty God to guide us," Jacob intoned. "To grant us deliverance from unjust anger. Let us pray, brothers."

"Hell, no. Let's have a drink," an already drunken voice shouted out.

"Sounds like your husband's showing more sense than the rest of those hotheads," Marijane confided to Sara. "Most of the men listen to him. As long as they've got him to follow, we've got a chance."

Sara managed a faint smile. "My husband is a very good man," she said. The noise in the bar grew louder, and she turned back to the lilac-sprigged calico, drawn like a magnet.

"They'll be in there all afternoon and half the night as well," Marijane said with a sniff. "And come home stinking like a brewery, and expecting . . ." She glanced at Sara, faltering. "Well, you know what they're expecting," she added in a lowered voice. "We're all married women here."

"Exactly," Abigail said. "And I for one am not going to wait around any longer. I'm going over to the hotel for a cup of tea. Why don't you join us, Sara?"

She had no money. And she knew it was sinful pride,

but she couldn't stand those hidden looks of pity a moment longer. Besides, there was the simple fact that Jacob had told her to stay put. If she disobeyed, he'd punish her. And she was still aching from his last effort to instruct her in what was most becoming in the frailer sex.

"No, thank you, Abigail," she said. "I believe I'll wait for my husband."

Marijane looked at her for a long moment. "You know, I believe I envy you, Sara. There's something about an older man that makes things a little more orderly."

"Yes," said Sara, her arms wrapped tightly around her middle as she summoned forth a tight smile. "I'm a very lucky woman."

She watched them go, and suddenly she was alone in the store. On the other side of the swinging doors she could hear the angry shouts of the men, the laughter and the clink of glasses. The town elders were turning this latest disaster into an occasion for a drunken party. Jacob wouldn't approve.

Sara was good at shutting things out. She closed her eyes, and the voices disappeared. She could feel the smoothness of the lilac-sprigged calico beneath her fingertips, smell the richness of cinnamon and tobacco that filled the store, mixed with fresh sawn lumber and the mud and manure out on the street. If she took a deep breath she could imagine other smells, leather, and rum, and she could feel him watching her.

Her eyes flew open as she realized the dimly lit store was no longer deserted. A man stood silhouetted in the outer doorway, motionless, his eyes on her.

She stared back at him, mesmerized. She had never in her life seen anyone who looked like him.

He was tall, taller even than her husband, though not nearly so broad. This wasn't a man who made his living off the land. He was whipcord lean, not burly, and he was dressed in black leather, with silver spurs that jangled as he moved.

And he moved. Into the empty store, with a feral kind of grace, and as he emerged from the shadows she could see the guns at his side. And she looked up and saw his face.

He looked like an angel. Beneath the brim of his black hat she could see a face of almost eerie beauty. His eyes were shielded by the brim of the hat, but she could feel their force, their strange, chilling heat. He wore his hair western style, long and flowing, and it was almost white blond, adding to the strange impression of almost other-worldly beauty.

And then he pushed his hat back on his head to get a closer look at her in the dimly lit store. "That would look real pretty on you, ma'am."

His voice was low, and mesmerizing, and it took Sara a moment to recognize the import of his words. To realize she was still stroking the lilac-sprigged calico.

She snatched her hand away as if she were caught doing something shameful, as indeed, Jacob would have told her she was. Covetousness was a sin, so was vanity. And her need for that calico was a direct result of both.

She lowered her head. Being alone in the presence of another man was an even greater sin, one Jacob wouldn't forgive lightly. "If you're looking for the storekeeper he's in the saloon," she said in a hushed voice.

He was going to come closer, she knew it with every fiber of her being. There was no sound, but when she looked up he was standing directly in front of her, his hat pushed back so that for a moment her skittering gaze caught his eyes.

They were a very pale blue, almost silver in color. Very cold as well, despite the lazy grin on his mouth, as they swept over her body with an assessing gaze that might have been insulting if she didn't know full well what he would see.

A quiet young woman. A good woman. A plain woman. And though she'd never seen anyone like him before, she knew instinctively that he would have no use for women who were good or plain or quiet. The knowledge made her braver, and she lifted her eyes again.

"That's better, sugar," he murmured in a voice that

was almost seductive. "Just because your man dresses you in sackcloth and ashes doesn't mean you aren't alive."

"Mr. Caldwell's in the saloon," she said again, trying to keep her voice steady.

"So is half the town," the stranger said. "I think I'd rather stay here with you, ma'am."

"My husband's in there."

"Is that a warning? Or encouragement?" The man reached out a hand and touched her face. She was so shocked she couldn't move, couldn't say a word. She could only stand there, frozen, as one long finger traced the curve of her jaw beneath the shielding bonnet.

And then he smiled, and that smile was a revelation. Just as she was coming close to hating him, his mouth curved up in a grin of self-mockery and despair that just about broke her wary heart. She stared up at him in shock, and from somewhere deep inside she found she wanted to touch him back. To pull that angel face against her breast and soothe him.

And then she heard Jacob's voice, louder than the rest. "If we stand together we don't have to be afraid of Stark's hired killer. I don't care what they call him. Mad Billy Maddox, or the Angel of Death. He's not going to drive me off my land."

The stranger stepped back from her, and where his hand had touched her skin it felt strangely hot and cold. It took all her wavering self-control not to reach up and caress her face where he had, not to smooth the fiery path his touch had taken.

"I believe that's my cue, ma'am," he said with that same, mocking courtesy. "I'd rather stay here with you, and see if I could get you to say something more than 'the men are in the saloon.' Do you have a name?"

She shook her head.

"No name?" he murmured, a faint thread of humor in his bleak, charming voice. "I'll have to have words with that husband of yours. Which one is he?"

She shook her head again. "Can't even answer me that

one? I'll find out soon enough. And if he won't buy you that lilac calico, I will."

A moment later he was gone, into the smoke-filled saloon, leaving Sara stunned and silent, staring after him. Wondering if she'd imagined him.

And then she realized the silence extended beyond the empty mercantile. The bar was now equally silent, ominously so. And if she'd had any doubts before, she knew exactly who it was who'd walked into Caldwell's Mercantile and stroked her face.

The voices started again, low and dangerous, and Sara knew what she should do. There was a bench over by the potbellied stove—she should go sit there, eyes modestly downcast, waiting for her husband to come and claim her.

And she knew she wasn't going to. She crossed the rough plank flooring of the store to the swinging doors of the saloon and carefully, surreptitiously peered inside.

The stranger stood at the bar, his long, black-clad body seemingly at ease in the crowd of hostile strangers. He was leaning back against the railing, surveying the homesteaders with a cool, amused gaze that was bound to put men like Jacob and the others into a fury.

She should have known it would be Jacob who'd confront him. Jacob and his temper would bluster up to the dark stranger as he lounged against the brass railing Mr. Caldwell tended so lovingly, his thick body radiating hostility.

"We know who you are," he said.

The stranger smiled faintly. "Then you have the advantage of me, sir."

If there was gentle mockery in that phrase it went directly over Jacob's head, but then, he'd never been a man for subtlety. "You're that killer Stark brought him from Cheyenne. Maddox, ain't you? Mad Billy Maddox, they call you."

"Now do I look like a Billy to you, old man?" the stranger countered.

"You look mad," Jacob shot back. "And you sure ain't no Angel of Death, for all you've got those fancy clothes and that pretty face. You're the spawn of the devil, but you're no match against the righteous."

"That you, old man?"

"Jacob Elder. Duly elected head of the Homesteaders' Vigilante Protection Forces."

"Fancy that. Then maybe you're the man I should be dealing with." He straightened, slowly, sinuously, every move spare and controlled. His hands came nowhere near the guns that sat low on his hips, and yet Sara knew that Jacob's life was hanging by a thread.

Jacob seemed oblivious. He moved closer, and his rounded belly pressed closer to the dark stranger. "You think I'm scared of you, Maddox?"

"No," the man said. "I don't think you're smart enough to be scared." He let his arms hang loose, casual, and even through the smoky distance she could see the elegance of his long-fingered hands. The hands that had stroked her face. The hands that could kill her husband.

"You yellow . . . ," Jacob began. And the Angel of Death would have finished it, and him, if Sara hadn't flung herself through the louvered doors separating the saloon from the store, stumbling forward into a place where no decent woman ever set foot.

"Jacob," she cried breathless, refusing to even look at the dangerous man who now leaned back against the bar once more, seemingly at ease. "We have to go now."

Her husband looked at her as if she'd suddenly grown two heads. In their years of married life she had never dared make even so much as a public suggestion, much less what might almost amount to an ultimatum. He would chastise her for it when they got back to the homestead, chastise her severely. But at least he'd be alive.

"Go back to the store, Sara," he said heavily. "This is no place for womenfolk."

"We need to go, Jacob," she said stubbornly, she who never insisted on anything. "Now."

For a moment no one moved. And then the dark stranger, Maddox, they called him, turned back to the bar, and the eerie promise of death had lifted.

"We'll finish this later, old man," he said lazily. "Looks like your daughter wants to go home."

"My wife," Jacob corrected fiercely.

Maddox looked back, at him, at her, his silver-blue eyes shaded by the hat he'd replaced on his mane of bright hair. Jacob was an old man—he'd been past fifty when he married her, and she'd been fifteen. Seven years later he looked like her grandfather.

"Come along, Sara," he said, taking her elbow in a punishing grip, so tightly she would have made a moan of protest if she hadn't been expecting it. "This is no place for a decent woman." He herded her toward the door, his thick fingers digging cruelly into the tender flesh above her elbow, but she didn't say a word.

They were at the door, almost safely out of there, when the stranger spoke. "Old man," he called after him. "Your woman has a hankering for a new dress. You shouldn't make such a pretty young thing wear rags."

Sara could feel Jacob grow rigid with fury, and if she hadn't had the temerity to tug at him, all her efforts might have been for nothing. It didn't matter how mad she got him now—her punishment was already assured. But she wouldn't have his death on her conscience.

"I can take care of my own woman," Jacob said fiercely. "You keep your eyes off her."

"Doesn't hurt to look, old man," Maddox said softly.

The saloon was still and silent in the afternoon, the stench of sweat and whiskey and smoke rising around them, as every man in town watched the confrontation.

"Come, Jacob," she whispered in an urgent voice.

And Jacob came, after casting one final threatening glance at the silent, dangerous stranger.

Maddox turned back to the bar and picked up his glass of whiskey. Slowly the men of this pretty little piece of no-where began to talk again, in low, worried voices, and if he'd bothered to listen he could have picked up what they were saying.

He didn't bother. It didn't matter what they said, he

knew what they were thinking. There was a rattler in their midst, and sooner or later he was going to strike.

He knew it as well as they did. It was what he did, how he earned his living. Sometimes he did it in the name of the law, with a tin badge on his chest. Sometimes he did it for the money, for whoever could pay his price. And sometimes he did it because he had no choice.

He had a choice this time. Harrison Stark had hired him to break the spirit of these homesteaders and send them running for cover. Stark needed all the grazing land for his cattle, and he was sick and tired of more and more sodbusters coming in and putting up fences.

Maddox didn't give a damn about fences, about cattle, or about homesteaders. At this point all he cared about was money, and Stark was paying him a tidy sum. He was also willing to give him anything else he wanted, up to and including whichever homestead took his fancy.

He wanted a home. He wanted a place to settle, a place where he could stop and rest and put down his guns. And he was more than ready to kill one more time to get that place.

Pick off the leader, and you demoralized the troops. It was simple military strategy, dating all the way back to Julius Caesar. Maddox was a man who knew his classics.

He was going to enjoy this one. That mean old man with the shy, pretty wife, who blustered and bullied, had already outlived his time. He'd choose the occasion carefully—there was no particular hurry. It wouldn't take much to goad the old man into a fight. And it wouldn't take much to put a bullet through his brain.

She wouldn't thank him for it, that shy little mouse of a girl. She'd probably weep and mourn and hate him. It made little difference to him. He'd be rich, and she'd be a hell of a lot better off. Maybe she'd choose better for her next husband.

Hell, maybe he'd buy her that lilac-sprigged calico before she left town and went back to her family.

"You really Mad Billy Maddox?" A young voice said behind him. He'd heard him approach, and known with an instinct honed over the years that he was no threat. Yet.

He turned, slowly, to eye the eager young man who stood before him. Wearing shiny six-shooters that hadn't seen much use. Maddox hoped, with a kind of weary desperation, that he didn't want to try them out on him.

"The name's William Maddox," he said slowly.

"You're the man who killed Doc Bentsen over in Tucson, aren't you?" he demanded eagerly. "The one who shot the Waco Kid down in Abilene? The man they call the Angel of Death?"

"I don't take much to fancy names."

The boy was a fool. Maybe as big a fool as the gun-mad sixteen-year-old who'd called him out two months ago on the streets of Cheyenne. He hadn't known how young the boy was when he'd killed him, and he told himself he had no choice, and he didn't give a rat's ass. Any more than he'd mind putting a bullet through this young cub either.

"I sure do admire you, mister," the boy said. "They say you're the fastest gun alive today."

"You want to prove you're faster?" His voice was cool, almost idle, and it took a moment for the boy to comprehend. When he did, his ruddy complexion turned a deathly pale, and he backed away.

"No, sir," he said, and there was no missing the utter panic in his voice. "I just wanted to tell you . . ."

"That you admire me. Yeah, you said that." Maddox started to turn back to the bar, but the kid couldn't seem to learn his lesson.

"Why are you here, mister?" he persisted. "What made you come to Cedar Bluffs?"

He could feel the tension in the room. They all knew, everyone but this green kid with more hair than brains. He turned back, plastering a cool, lazy smile on his face.

"To kill someone, kid," he said. "What else?"

And there was dead silence in smoke-filled saloon.

Two

S ara lay, still and silent, in the small alcove bed just off the main room of the cabin. She could hear Jacob snoring, a fact which gave her only a little comfort. He'd sent her from their bed two years ago when she'd lost the baby, telling her that it had to be her sinful nature that had brought her only pregnancy to such an abrupt and early end. After all, she'd been young and healthy. It could only be a message from God, that she was tainted. It couldn't have had anything to do with the fact that he'd taken his belt to her with righteous enthusiasm just before the cramps started.

Since then he'd barely touched her. Only to punish her, for Jacob was a man who believed that physical pain brought spiritual purity. But he'd taken her miscarriage as a judgment against himself as well. And they'd never shared a bed since.

It wasn't that Sara particularly minded. She wanted babies, wanted them with all her heart. But she didn't want to risk the pain and grief of losing another. And she was glad to dispense with the wifely duties Jacob had expected of her since she was fifteen.

But in the week since the stranger came to town, things had changed. She dreamed about him. The Angel of Death. Bad, wicked dreams, where he touched her face once more. Where he spoke to her in that slow, southern voice that made her bones melt, and draped her sinfully naked body in lilac-sprigged calico.

Her guilt and shame were such that she almost welcomed Jacob's "lessons." For the first time she could believe she deserved them.

She'd half hoped his anger with her would keep them home from the town dance. Jacob was not a particularly social man, but he believed in presenting a good example for the neighbors. Besides, with the latest trouble in town, he wasn't about to relax his vigilance.

As far as Sara could tell, William Maddox had done nothing but play cards in Caldwell's Saloon. He didn't drink too much, he didn't make conversation, he simply sat there, playing poker with those who were brave enough or fool enough to join him in a game. He always won.

She wanted him to go away. She'd accepted her life. It was a hard one, but then she'd never expected anything better. Jacob was a good man. Sooner or later he'd forgive her for losing the baby and this time when she got pregnant she'd carry it to term. She'd have children to love, to sing to and read to.

If Jacob ever let books back in the house. If she only sang hymns.

She liked to sing. Jacob was a deep sleeper, and he was snoring so loudly he wouldn't hear her humming softly beneath her breath. A song she had heard long ago, before her family died and she'd been left with nowhere to turn but to the kindness of Jacob Elder. "Drink to me only with thine eyes, and I will pledge with mine. Just leave a kiss within the cup and I'll not ask for wine."

It had always sounded so exotic to her. Leaving a kiss inside a silver goblet, all the while eyes met, looking, longing, promising. And suddenly all she could see was Mad Billy Maddox's silver-blue eyes, staring down into hers.

Jacob's snores halted abruptly, as if he could read her mind. "What's that noise, Sara?" he demanded, his voice thick with sleep.

She considered ignoring him, then thought better of it.
If he could see her sinfulness even in his sleep she would
be no match for him when he was awake. "Just a hymn,
Jacob. I was singing Rock of Ages."

"You don't need no music," Jacob snapped. "You just
say the words in your head, and let me sleep."

"Yes, Jacob," she said meekly. And closing her eyes,
she let the words drift through her mind. And she could
see the stranger's firm, mocking mouth touching the silver goblet in her dreams.

The town of Cedar Bluffs held two public buildings. Caldwell's Mercantile and Saloon, and the brand-new Town
Hall. Next would come a church, and a school. If Stark
didn't manage to drive them out first.

The Town Hall was festooned with streamers and paper flowers, the food tables were set up along one side,
and on stage the band played. It wasn't much of a band.
The piano player was half drunk, Reb Johnson sawed
away on the fiddle, and Elmer Perkins made a mighty
effort with the harmonica. But it was more than most of
the homesteaders usually got, and the floor was filled
with dancing couples.

"Aren't you going to dance, Sara?" Marijane came up
beside her. "It's one thing for an old lady like me to sit on
the side. You should be out there enjoying yourself."

"My husband doesn't care for dancing, Marijane," she
said quietly.

"Well, there are other men here, even a few of the
better behaved cowboys. Surely Jacob wouldn't object . . ." The words trailed off, as Marijane thought
about it a moment longer. "That's a very pretty dress,"
she added lamely.

"It was my wedding dress." It was the only decent dress
she owned. It was made of muddy brown satin, and it had
fit her when she was fifteen. Seven years later it squashed
her breasts and pinched her waist and barely made it to
her ankles, and she felt like she'd always felt. Poor and
conspicuous.

"It's very nice," Marijane said again, and Sara smiled at her, grateful for the lie. Marijane cast a worried glance toward the door. "We're just hoping there won't be any kind of trouble tonight. Stark's cowboys seem sober, but if that hired killer of his shows up I don't know what we'll do."

It was a lucky thing the room was dimly lit. "He wouldn't do that, would he? This is a peaceful gathering."

"Seems to me that's exactly the kind of thing they'd want to disrupt. I expect the menfolk think so too," she added tartly, glancing over at the men surrounding Jacob. There was a distant thunder of voices beneath the scrape of the music, and Sara could see the angry faces, the abrupt gestures.

"Maybe if we get them to eat they'll stop thinking about fighting," she murmured.

"Maybe," said Marijane. "But it's not the menfolk who started all this, or who want the fight. It's Stark." A sudden hush fell over the room. "Speak of the devil," she added tartly.

It was Stark all right, standing in the wide doorway of the Town Hall, gussied up for a party. And he wasn't alone.

The stranger stood next to him. Mad Billy Maddox, the Angel of Death, moved into the room at his employer's side. He hadn't bothered with dressing for the party. He still wore black leather, and a black shirt, though this time the silver guns were gone from his lean hips.

He glanced around the crowded room, slowly, casually, and his eyes slid over her without pausing. Sara released her pent-up breath in unconscious relief. "They're not looking for trouble, Marijane," she said. "They're not even armed."

"Trust me, Sara, trouble's all Stark has in mind. They may not be planning on killing tonight, but this is just one more battle in the war. If you're not going to dance, why don't you see if you can get Jacob to take you home? He's got one of the quickest tempers I know, and it would be better if he kept away from Stark and his hired killer."

"He wouldn't go," Sara said, moving back against the wall, out of the light. Maddox hadn't seemed to notice her before, and even if he did, he probably had no particular interest in Jacob's plain little wife. But she still felt better, safer in the shadows.

"Well," Marijane said briskly, "then I s'pose we'd just better make the best of it. You sure you don't want to dance? My husband's not pretty to look at but he sure likes to waltz."

Sara shook her head. "I'll just stay here."

Slowly the noise in the hall returned to normal, covered by the sounds of the small band playing away with tuneless diligence. Alone in the shadows, Sara gave in to temptation. She watched the stranger move through the room, watched the men move out of his way, Stark's cowboys as well as the homesteaders. She watched the assessing look in the women's eyes, part fear, part flirtation, and she wondered if her own plain brown eyes looked the same.

She couldn't help it. His lean, elegant body drew her like a magnet. He was the most exotic, mysterious thing she had ever known in her short, painful life, and she couldn't resist drinking in the sight of him.

At least he seemed to have forgotten her existence, a definite blessing. For all his seeming indolence he was the most alert man in the place, and Sara had no doubt he was intently aware of everything around him. Even her.

But when his eyes happened to glance her way they slid over her without recognition.

Suzanna Forrester was fast, the despair of her mother. A born flirt, she tossed her blond ringlets as she sashayed up toward Maddox, and the entire town watched, wondering what would happen next.

No one could hear what she said over the noise of the band. But they saw Maddox throw his head back and laugh. And a moment later they saw him take her in his arms and swing her onto the dance floor.

His hand on Suzanna's tiny, cinched waist was tanned and strong, his long, elegant fingers splayed against her back. He danced the way he walked, with a deliberate grace that seemed almost lethal. Sara touched her own waist beneath the too tight dress, an unconscious caress. And then she turned and ducked out the side door, into the clear Wyoming night.

There was a pile of wooden crates by the little-used door, and she sank down on one of them, taking in deep breaths of air. She'd been a vain fool to try to squeeze herself into a dress that had been altered and enlarged too many times. She could barely breathe in it; it was no wonder she felt dizzy. That and the noisy, smoke-filled room would be enough to give any woman the vapors.

She leaned back, staring at the starry sky, looking for answers. Her head ached, her chest was tight, and part of her, that dark, wicked part that Jacob tried so hard to beat out of her, just wanted to take off at a run, across the high prairie, towards the spiky mountains. Take off, and never come back.

She wouldn't do that, of course. She'd do her duty, as she'd been taught by her parents before they died of cholera, as Jacob taught her.

The music changed, and the ache inside her tightened. It was a cowboy waltz, "Red River Valley," and she wondered what it would be like to wear a pretty dress like Suzanna Forrester, to flirt, and to be held in a man's arms while he swung her around the dance floor to the sad refrain. To be held in that dangerous man's arms.

Almost without thought she rose. There was no one to see her, just the quarter moon and the bright stars, and she swayed in time to the melody, closing her eyes and humming beneath her breath.

She smelled the cigarette smoke first. She froze, opening her eyes, and she saw him there, watching her, the cigarette drooping from his mouth.

"Care to dance, Mrs. Elder?" said Mad Billy Maddox, tossing his cigarette to the ground and advancing toward her like a predator.

She shook her head, panicked, backing away from him.

"Didn't that stern old man teach you that lying is a sin,

Mrs. Elder?" He kept advancing. "You wouldn't be out here, all alone, dancing in the moonlight if you didn't like to dance. Unless you're meeting your lover. Maybe one of Stark's cowboys?"

"No!"

"At least I got you to talk. So what have you got against dancing, Mrs. Elder? It's a beautiful night, a sad, pretty song, and there's no one to watch you, no one to see you."

She should have kept silent, kept running. But she didn't. "You're here," she said.

"So I am. Dance with me, Sara." His voice was low, seductive, irresistible.

She shook her head. "I can't."

"Sure you can. There's nothing to be afraid of. The old man you married is too busy figuring out how he can kill me without risking himself. He's not going to worry about his pretty little wife."

No one had ever called her pretty. Not since her mother had died. He was mocking her, and she told herself she hated him more than ever. But she didn't run. "I mean I can't dance," she said. "I never learned how."

She must have imagined the expression that crossed his face in the darkness. Tenderness had no place on a man like that. "Then it's about time you learned," he said, putting his hands on her.

He was a strong man, with strong hands. Not the beefy, bullying fists of Jacob Elder, but narrow, tensile strength that clasped her waist with a touch that seemed to burn through the layers of too-tight clothing. "Relax, Sara," he murmured, "and do what I do."

She resisted for a moment, trying to keep herself still and awkward. But he wasn't a man who paid the slightest heed to resistance, and she found herself moving over the rough ground, only inches away from his tall, lean body, one hand held in his grip, the other resting against his shoulder.

She'd never touched a man's shoulders. She'd never touched a man—when Jacob had done his marital duty he'd instructed her to lie quietly, arms at her side, and pray.

She could feel the heat of William Maddox. Through the skin of his hands as they held her, through the linen of his black shirt, from the body that was closer to hers than any young man's had ever been.

He smelled like soap, and cigarettes, and whiskey. And she wanted to move closer.

"You're a fast learner, Sara," he whispered, moving her in time with the music, and the words danced in her head: "Just remember the Red River Valley, and the cowboy who loved you so true."

But there was no cowboy to love her. And the man who held her in his arms was more dangerous than a sidewinder, and prettier than the Tetons in the moonlight. She halted suddenly, trying to break away from him.

But just as quickly his grip tightened, capturing her. Pulling her toward him, closer, so that she could see the heat in the cold, silver-blue eyes, the inexorable purpose.

"You ever been kissed in the moonlight, Mrs. Elder?" he whispered, his voice barely a thread of sound.

The question was like a cramp in her stomach. She shook her head, mesmerized. "You're about to be," he warned her.

There was no way she could escape, she told herself. His arm slid all the way around her waist, bringing her body up close against his. He was so tall he had to arch her body up towards his, so that she stood on her toes, her head tilted back, staring at him in shock and defiance. "Don't worry, Sara," he whispered. "It's even better than dancing." And he settled his mouth against her.

It was hot. It was wet. It was open against her tightly closed lips, and the shock of it sent a shudder racing through her body.

His hand moved from her waist, down to her hips, pulling her up against him, and she realized he was aroused. Wanting. She opened her mouth to protest, and he put his other arm around her head, holding her there, as he pushed his tongue into her mouth.

She should have screamed in protest. She should have bitten his tongue, she should have swooned. Instead, her hand clutched his shoulder and she closed her eyes, letting him kiss her, caught, captured, entranced by the slow, raw wonder of it.

She didn't want him to stop. She didn't want to think, she only wanted to feel. She heard the tearing of her old satin dress, and the cool of the night air hit her skin. When he pulled his mouth from hers she made a soft cry of protest, and when he put her away from him it was all she could do not to cling. To reach for him again, to see if she'd imagined the dark magic of his kiss.

He wasn't looking at her. He'd let go of her, his hands at his sides, and he was looking past her, over her shoulder, a faintly amused expression on his beautiful, deadly face.

She didn't want to look. Shame flooded her pale cheeks, and as she turned she pulled her torn dress around her.

"Get out to the wagon, Sara," Jacob said in a cold, harsh voice.

"I was just dancing with your wife, old man," Maddox drawled. "Seems to me her education is sorely lacking. I thought I could teach her a few things."

Jacob lunged for him with a bellow of rage, his thick fists ready to wrap around his neck. There were others, standing behind him, who tried to stop him, but Jacob was like a hornet-maddened bull, charging in fury.

No sooner had he reached Maddox, however, than he halted, frozen. And everyone stared at the tiny silver derringer that Maddox held directly in the center of Jacob's reddened forehead.

"Now it's against my policy to kill an unarmed man," Maddox drawled. "But I could be persuaded to change my mind if you don't take a step back, real easy like."

Sara held her breath, waiting. And then Jacob retreated, uttering a foul word underneath his breath.

"That's right," Maddox murmured, pocketing the deadly little gun. "I guess you have some brains after all. I trust you have enough to know that this wasn't your wife's fault. I took advantage of her innocence and her sweet nature."

"Women are weak," Jacob said. "Helpless in the face of the devil's temptation. It's up to the menfolk to wipe out that temptation, and instruct the frailer sex in decency."

"I'm not sure that I think women are the frailer sex, or particularly helpless. They scare the hell out of me," Maddox said lazily. "And how do you intend to wipe out the devil's temptation?"

"The next time I see you anywhere near my wife, I'll kill you."

Maddox smiled. A slow, mocking grin that would have goaded a saint. Jacob Elder was no saint.

Sara saw her husband pull the knife from his belt before anyone else did, and her cry of horror was instinctive. She tried to move between the two men, to shield one of them, she wasn't sure which, but she wasn't fast enough. Mad Billy Maddox may have put his gun away, but it took only a second before he brought it out again.

Jacob stopped his furious advance, and his huge body shuddered. A fraction of a second later she heard the sound of the gunshot. One shot, one bullet, and time ground to a halt, as they all stood there, motionless, horrified.

Jacob crumpled, his sturdy legs collapsing beneath him. By the time he reached the ground Sara was there to catch him, but it was too late. He was already dead.

She knelt beside him in the dust, in the growing pool of blood, numb with shock and horror. In the distance she could hear screams and sobs, but she knew they didn't come from her, did they? She looked up, at the man who'd shot her husband to death. He was leaning back against a tree, casually lighting a cigarette, and his eyes met hers over the curl of smoke.

And they were bleak and empty.

* * *

The night smelled like death. Maddox should have gotten used to it by now. In fact, he'd gotten used to it years ago. It was only recently that it had started to bother him again.

He cupped his hand around the match to keep it from shaking. She was kneeling by that old bastard, staring at Maddox as if he were a monster.

And he was. He pushed away from the tree, just as Harrison Stark came toward him. "Fair fight," Harrison announced loudly. "Me and my boys were witnesses. Jacob pulled a knife on him. He was just protecting himself, weren't you, Maddox?"

Maddox tossed the spent match onto the ground. It landed in the ever-growing pool of blood. "If you say so, Stark," he drawled.

One of those stout, older women had her arms around Sara, trying to draw her away from her husband's body. She didn't weep, but he didn't make the mistake of thinking she didn't mourn. She was too deep in shock. When she started to come out of it she'd hate him, and she'd mourn that mean old bastard she'd married. She wouldn't realize he'd done her a favor.

Stark moved closer, arrogantly oblivious to the settlers who crowded around Sara Elder. "You're as fast and as good as they said you were, Maddox. There'll be a bonus for you."

Maddox just looked at him. The derringer held two bullets—he could put another right between Harrison Stark's dark, piggy eyes. But then there'd be nothing left for him, and Maddox was a man who always liked to prepare for eventualities.

"No need," he said shortly.

But Stark wasn't listening. Stark wasn't noticing that as they pulled Sara away from her husband, her ugly satin dress torn and blood-stained, she looked toward him with strange comprehension in her eyes.

"I've never seen anyone move so fast. And he jumped to the bait, just like a hungry salmon. All you had to do was lay a hand on his woman and he was yours. Damn, you're good."

She heard every word. He didn't know whether it sank in or not, whether she'd remember when she came out of her shock. He didn't know why it should matter.

"Come on, love," one of the women murmured to her, pulling her away.

She let them take her. She didn't look back, and he knew he'd never see her again. Never look into those wide, vulnerable eyes, never taste that mouth.

The taste of death had superseded her softness. He wanted to kiss her again, to wipe out flavor of violence.

But she was gone, and the only way to rinse the smell and the taste and the feel of death, of Sara, was to drink as much of Caldwell's godawful whiskey as he could force down his throat.

He moved through the crowds, and they parted in horror, staring at him. He didn't mind—he was used to it. They had the right to be afraid. The good sense.

Stark and his men walked with him, in high good spirits, and Maddox kept his face cool and unreadable. He'd get good and drunk, and then tomorrow he'd collect on what Stark had promised him. Two hundred dollars and a homestead where he could run his own cattle.

And he wouldn't think about Sara Elder. And the fact that he'd never see her wearing lilac-sprigged calico.

THREE

Jacob Elder was buried two days later in the tiny, wind-swept cemetery just outside of town. Maddox sat on the front porch of Caldwell's Mercantile and Saloon and looked out toward the hill with its clump of dark-clothed mourners. He couldn't see the widow, hadn't seen her since that night. It was better that way.

"Pig farmers," Harrison Stark snorted, following his gaze. "This oughta be enough to break any last resistance. They looked up to Elder like he was some sort of voice of God or something. With him gone there'll be no one to lead 'em. They'll go quietly enough. Hell, I'll even pay 'em for their land, even though they stole it from me in the first place."

"I'm not too sure the courts would agree with you on that one," Maddox said lazily, rolling a cigarette. She must be somewhere in the middle of that crowd of women, all dressed in black like a bunch of crows. He could hear the wails and lamentations drifting over the hills, caught on a cool spring breeze. He'd heard that sound too often in his life.

Stark glared at him. "You siding with them sodbusters, Maddox?"

"No. I don't side with anyone who doesn't pay my fee," he said lazily enough.

Stark laughed. "You're a cool bastard, Maddox, I'll say that for you. You sure you don't want to help me finish this up right now? I got protection from the law—no one would come after you if a few people got killed."

"No, thanks," Maddox murmured.

"Suit yourself. You want to see the place I got picked out for you? Sweetest little bit of acreage around here, if I do say so. You just keep those fences down and let my cattle run through and we should get along real neighborly."

"And if I don't like it?"

"Hell, you can have your pick of any of these sodbusters' claims, once we drive 'em out. Or I'll pay you for the land and you can find a place somewhere else. I might almost prefer that."

"You got your choice, Stark. Have thousands of acres to yourself, or have a hired gun as a neighbor to help you keep your thousands of acres."

"I think you'll make a mighty fine neighbor," Stark said abruptly.

"I thought you'd feel that way."

Sara had no more tears left. They buried Jacob in the cold, hard ground, with prayers and hymns, and then it was over. The womenfolk kept their arms tightly around her, Marijane's face grim and determined as they herded her back to the wagon. She went with Marijane, heading out into the countryside. The men stayed behind to fill in the grave.

"I don't want you going back to that place by yourself," Marijane said. "Your homestead's one of the most remote, and with no man around to take care of you, I know I wouldn't rest easy."

"I've got to go back sooner or later," Sara said in the dull, quiet voice that had become second nature to her. "I can't keep having your menfolk go out and take care of the livestock. It's not right. I have to get on with life."

"You've always got a home with us, and you know it," Marijane said. "One more daughter won't make any difference to Web and me. What kind of life do you have, way out there? It's too big a place for you to manage."

"Then I'll cut back. Sell off some of the livestock."

"It's no place for a woman alone."

A woman alone. That phrase had haunted her for the last three days, the dire words of warning, the sympathy, the grieving glances. A woman alone. She should have been terrified.

But she wasn't. There'd be no one to help get the wood in for the long winter. No one to help with the chores, to plough the ground under, to feed and then slaughter the pigs. No one to talk to, no one to cook for, no one to give her children.

No one to force her to her knees for hours on end, praying forgiveness for an evil she didn't believe she possessed. No one to instruct her, to punish her with that wide leather belt he'd been buried with. No one to force his body into hers, and hurt her, and then call her a whore for letting him do it.

A woman alone.

If she froze to death this winter, alone, she'd die a happy woman.

"Take me home, Marijane," she said urgently. "I need to get back. To get on with my life."

Marijane looked at her, her plain, elderly face troubled. And then she sighed, turning the horses toward the Elder homestead. "I hope you know what you're doing, Sara. You're a stubborn little thing beneath your quiet ways."

"Stubborn can be good," she replied, keeping her head down, her gloved hands pleating the dusty black of her newly dyed skirt. It wasn't even her dress. Marijane had given her this one, and if it was too big in the waist, too short, the black dye covered most of those imperfections.

"Stubborn can be a sin."

"So Jacob told me," Sara said.

There was a long pause. "I'm going to say something that I probably shouldn't," Marijane said. "We're just two women, alone, and even though I'm old enough to be your ma I think we're friends. I don't want you feeling guilty about Jacob. It wasn't your fault."

"Wasn't it?" She kept pleating the material.

"That hired killer would have found one way or another to get to Jacob. He used you, but he would have found another way if that hadn't worked. Jacob had no call to go after him with a knife."

"He goaded him."

"Well, Jacob was a good, godly man, but he always had one hell of a temper," Marijane said flatly. "Frankly, Sara, you're better off without him."

Sara dropped the skirt, turning to stare at her old friend in shock. "He was my husband," she whispered.

"He was a mean old man who was far too holy for this life," Marijane shot back. "Once you accept that fact you'll do just fine. You'll get married again, this time to someone closer to your own age. This time to someone who won't hit you all the time."

"He had his reasons," Sara said quietly.

"Maybe. But he ought to have damned good reasons." Marijane snapped the reins, and the old farm horse quickened his pace. "I think we're due for a spring storm. You sure you won't come back and stay with us for a while longer? You know my man would be happy to have you."

"I want to go home, Marijane."

Marijane nodded. "Stubborn," she said again. "God protect you."

The house was as spotless as she had left it that evening, a lifetime ago. Jacob's clothes still lay folded in the bedroom, his cup and plate on the bureau in the kitchen, his guns on the rack by the door.

His bible was gone: they'd buried it with him. And his hard, judging spirit was gone as well.

She waited until Marijane had left, and then she opened all the windows, letting in the cool spring breeze flowing through the tiny house. Jacob hadn't liked the windows opened. He said it brought disease inside.

Her hair was braided tightly at the back of her neck,

and her head hurt. She was just beginning to unpin it when she heard the horses.

She pulled Jacob's rifle off the wall, praying she looked like she knew what she was doing, and edged her way out the plank door. For a moment they didn't seem to notice her in the late afternoon shadows—Harrison Stark was too busy talking to the man beside him.

But the stranger wasn't a man who missed a thing. She'd hoped she'd never have to see him again, but there he was, astride a huge, black horse, staring down at her.

"You know how to use that thing, Mrs. Elder?" he drawled, interrupting Stark as he rambled on about *her* homestead.

Stark turned to stare at her. "I hadn't realized you were here, Sara," he said, all oily sympathy as he slid down from his horse. "Allow me to offer my condolences on the loss of your husband. Jacob was a fine . . ."

"Don't come any closer," she said, pointing the gun directly at Stark's ample middle.

Stark halted. She didn't dare take her gaze from him, but she sensed that Maddox had dismounted as well. The gun was heavier than she expected, and it wobbled slightly until she strengthened her grip.

"Of course not, Sara," Stark said easily.

"What are you doing here, Mr. Stark? And why did you bring *Him?*" She let the anger and contempt flow in her voice.

"If you'll put that gun down I can explain . . . ," Stark began, when a dark figure walked directly between them.

Maddox simply grabbed the end of the rifle and pulled it from her unresisting hands. "She doesn't know how to use a gun, Stark," he said, breaking it open and letting the bullets drop onto the dusty ground.

"Jesus Christ!" Stark exploded. "That thing was loaded?"

"Yeah," Maddox said, holding it out to her. She made no effort to take it.

"Did you know that?" Stark persisted.

"I figured it was."

"You must have balls of steel, Maddox," Stark said admiringly. "Begging your pardon, Sara."

She simply stood there, blocking the doorway to her house. The wind had picked up, tossing her heavy black skirts against her legs, but she wasn't about to move. "You still haven't told me what you're doing on my land, Mr. Stark."

"I'm afraid it's not your land, Sara," he said, all oily regret. She wished she'd taken the gun back from Maddox. She could have hit him with it. "Your husband was a bit shy of money the last few years. The Blizzard of '86 hit all of us hard, and some of us didn't have the resources. He borrowed heavily from the bank."

She didn't move. She couldn't very well call him a liar —she doubted life would be that simple or that forgiving.

"Then I'll pay the bank off," she said.

"Now, honey, you know I own the bank," Harrison said in his sweetest voice. "And I'm afraid I've already foreclosed."

"Don't call me honey," she said, her voice fierce with anger.

"I filed the papers yesterday. I own this place, lock, stock, and barrel. Now I'm a reasonable man, Sara. I'll be more than happy to pay you for what you've put into this place, though you gotta realize I'm under no obligation to do so. But I'm a generous man. I'll settle enough on you so that you can make a new start. New clothes, a stagecoach ticket out of here, and enough money to keep you until you find your feet. You can't ask for more."

"I want you to get off my land," she said.

Stark turned a knowing grin toward the dark figure standing just behind him. "If I'd a known she'd be here I would have come prepared," he said plaintively. "Now, Miss Sara, you know you can't run this place by yourself, even if your husband hadn't lost it due to unwise investments. I'm offering you a life of ease, a life of absolute luxury. You can go to San Francisco, start a new life . . ."

"I'm not leaving. You don't need this place, Stark, and

you know it. There are other homesteads that are more important to your cattle operation."

"Smart girl," he said approvingly. "As a matter of fact, I've already deeded it over to Mr. Maddox here. It's his."

She'd been very careful not to look at him. She'd had no choice, when he'd yanked the gun out of her hand, but then he'd retreated into the shadows, and she'd told herself he didn't exist.

But he did. He was there. Tall, dark, and dangerous. Looking at her out of icy blue eyes. The Angel of Death.

"No," she said, her voice just a thread of sound.

"'Fraid so," Stark said, and she couldn't miss the undertone of malicious pleasure in his voice. "Part payment for a little matter he took care of for me. I'm a generous man, like I told you."

"Over my dead body." That lifeless sound was gone from her voice now.

Stark cast a smirking glance back at his hired gun, then at her. "I don't know as someone like the Angel of Death would be too particular. I'm sure he's killed women before, and he'll do so again. I wouldn't cross him if I were you."

She looked past Stark. Directly into Maddox's chilly eyes, daring him. The afternoon had grown stormy dark, the wind blew his silver blond hair away from his fine-boned face, and there was no expression at all as he watched her.

"Now as I said, I'm a reasonable, generous man. You have a couple of fine horses here, Sara, and by rights they belong to me. But I'm perfectly willing for you to take one with you. Go on back to Marijane Wilks—she'll see you safely taken care of. This place is your past. You gotta look ahead to the future."

"I'm not going anywhere. Get off my land, Harrison Stark," she said fiercely. "And take your hired murderer with you."

"I'll take it from here." Maddox's voice, when he spoke, was low and mocking.

Stark glanced at him. "I'll send someone out to get her . . ."

"I said I'll take it from here. You can go now, Stark. Our business is at an end."

For a moment Stark didn't move. And then he chuckled, a low, evil sound. "Yeah, I guess you can handle things after all. This is your last chance, Miss Sara. You want to come with me, or stay here with my hired killer?"

"I want you both off my land."

"Stubborn little thing, ain't she? She don't have much else to say," Stark murmured, mounting his horse. "Good luck with her, Maddox. Lemme know if you need any help. I can send some of the boys around to take her away."

Maddox didn't say a word. Didn't move. He simply stood there, dark and silent, in the stormy corral of Jacob Elder's homestead, and watched Harrison Stark ride away.

And then he turned and glanced at Sara.

Full knowledge of her foolishness hit her then. She was alone, in the middle of nowhere, with a murderer. The man who killed her husband, a creature with no moral sense, no decency. A man who had taken her husband and now planned to take everything else as well.

She would die before she let him.

She turned, walked back into the cabin, and slammed the door behind her.

Maddox was still holding the shotgun she'd pulled on him. There weren't many people who held a loaded gun on him and then lived to tell the tale. But Stark was wrong. He'd never killed a woman. And he never intended to.

Though he had the suspicion that sweet, shy Sara Elder might come close to tempting him.

That wasn't all she tempted him with. He led Bosco toward the stable, carrying the gun with him. He hadn't really expected to see her again—like Stark, he thought she'd stay with friends, maybe go back to her family when things settled down again. She was crazy to think she could run a spread like this on her own. Even her bullying husband hadn't been able to make a go of it.

But then, she wasn't acting on common sense right now. She was still half-crazy from grief and guilt, and it was his own damn fault. He never should have gone after her. Certainly never should have kissed her. It wouldn't have taken much to goad Elder into a fight—by using his vulnerable wife he'd made the whole situation a lot more complicated. Particularly since that vulnerable creature seemed a lot more capable than she had before.

He unsaddled his horse, brushed him down, and gave him some fresh feed. There were two other horses there, both of them old but in good condition. Not a bad start for a small operation. He could make a life here. If people just left him alone.

First things first, though. He had to get rid of Sara Elder, and fast. She had a bad habit of distracting him, and a man in his line of work couldn't afford to be distracted. He expected she was busy packing her things once she'd slammed that door on him, and he'd do his best not to taunt her when she came out, dressed and ready to go.

Hell, he might even be a gentleman and hitch up the wagon for her.

There was a crack of thunder, loud enough to shake the barn, and Bosco, always high-strung, danced backwards in his stall, whinnying nervously. "Whoa, boy," Maddox murmured, reaching out a hand to stroke him. And then he realized there was a shadow in the barn door.

His gun was out and cocked by the time he whirled around. If his reactions weren't so lightning fast she would have been dead, but he managed to take in the sweep of her skirts, the faint scent of her on the storm-laden air.

He straightened, uncocking the gun slowly and tucking it back in his gunbelt, despite the fact that she held an old-fashioned Colt pistol on him. "I should warn you,

Miss Sara," he said in a cool voice, "that I don't like having people hold guns on me. It makes me irritable. And you don't want to see me irritable."

"I don't give a damn."

He doubted she'd ever said that word out loud in her life. She seemed half shocked that it popped out, and if she weren't using both hands to keep the gun from shaking she probably would have slapped one over her mouth.

Which reminded him. He was partial to that mouth of hers. She looked like holy hell—pale, dressed like a crow in another old gown that didn't fit her, her hair so tight around her head that she must be in pain. "I don't care how grumpy you get," she said fiercely. "The bad temper of men no longer has the power to disturb me. I want you to saddle your horse, climb back on, and ride away from here. And I want you to do it now."

The gun was wavering slightly. An amateur with a loaded gun was more of a danger to him than a professional. And she was a very angry amateur. "We're due for a hell of a storm, Sara," he said, not moving.

"You won't melt. Saddle your horse."

She might shoot him. It was a definite possibility, and he was a man who considered all possibilities. He wouldn't actually mind if she managed to kill him. He lived with death every day—it was bound to claim him sooner or later, and he couldn't argue that she didn't have the right to do it.

But chances were she'd simply blow off his kneecap and let him bleed to death, and that didn't seem so appealing.

"Put the gun down, Sara," he said.

"No."

Her grip on the pistol was iron-tight—he could see her knuckles whiten. Damn, he was tired. Hungry, too.

His other needs could wait. "Put the gun down, Sara," he said again. "Or I'll take it from you."

"Try it," she snapped.

She didn't know how fast he could move. He wasn't just fast with a gun, he was fast with his whole body, his reflexes. The lightning flashed, an electric crackle that filled the air, followed by a clap of thunder so loud it shook the ground. Maddox threw himself at her, grabbing the gun, and a moment later she was flat on her back in the fragrant hay, with him on top of her, covering her with his body.

He'd already managed to pluck the gun out of her hands and toss it away. And then he took her flailing hands as they tried to slap and hit at him, shoving them down in the straw beside her head. He straddled her, and the more she fought and squirmed between his legs the more he thought about pulling up those dusty black skirts of hers.

He leaned over her, his mouth close to her face as she thrashed about, and he kept his voice low and dangerous. "If you don't stop rolling around beneath me, Sara, I'm going to figure out a way to hold you still. Don't push me."

She became motionless, rigid, and there was no missing the real fear in her eyes. It had a distinctly unmanning effect on him.

"Shit," he muttered beneath his breath, releasing her and climbing to his feet.

To his astonishment she turned over and threw herself toward the gun he'd tossed in the straw. He caught her in time, shoving her face first in the straw and holding her there, imprisoning her hands with one of his, as he kicked the gun into Bosco's stall. No way in hell she could get it there.

And then he rose, dragging up her with him, keeping her tight against her body despite her struggles. "I wouldn't put it past you to try for one of my guns," he said in a low voice, "but I'd think twice about it if I were you. I might break your arm."

"I don't care," she shot back, struggling. She wasn't much a match for him, and she was weary, weepy, worn out. It took only a minute to subdue her, till she sagged against him, the fight gone.

"That's better," he murmured approvingly. "So I take it you aren't about to leave me to my new home?"

She managed to stir herself enough to snarl at him. "No."

"Then we might as well get back to the house before the storm hits. I'm hungry."

"What's that got to do with me?"

"It's my house. You won't leave. Looks like I got myself a cook."

"You have a taste for rat poison?" she said.

"You have a taste for lead, lady?" he murmured in return. He released her, and she staggered back away from him, casting a furtive glance toward the stall. "I wouldn't even consider it, if I were you. Bosco doesn't like anyone near him except me. He's particularly distrustful of females. You go for that gun and he might be likely to trample you."

She might be madder than spit but she was no fool. "I'm not cooking for you."

"Suit yourself."

"And I'm not leaving."

He grinned at her. Slow and steady, just to watch the color rise in her cheeks. "It's up to you, Sara. I'm sure I can always find a use for you."

She turned and ran from him, out into the gathering storm, heading back toward the house. Starting after her, he wondered wearily how many guns he'd have to hide from her.

He'd been hoping for a peaceful life, where he wouldn't have to watch his back every spare second. It looked like he'd moved in with someone determined to kill him.

Fate certainly had a sense of humor at times.

FOUR

She didn't want him in her house. He was too big, too male, too foreign. The cabin was small—just the main room with the kitchen, work table and alcove bed, and the adjoining bedroom, and there was no way she could get away from his presence. Particularly since the storm hit moments after she ran in the front door.

She resisted the impulse to slam the door behind her and lock it. Locks wouldn't keep a man like Maddox out. And instinct told her there was a limit to how far she could push him.

She ignored him as she moved through the house, closing the windows against the driving rain. He stood inside the door, watching her out of those unnerving eyes of his, and it took all her newfound willfulness to ignore him, ignore the feel of his gaze burning into her narrow back as she walked into Jacob's bedroom.

He didn't follow her, a profound relief. She closed the window, then surveyed the tiny room with its wide bed. She had once shared that bed with Jacob. Never again would she have to share a bed with any man.

When she came back into the keeping room Maddox was fiddling with the stove. Her stove. "What are you doing?" she demanded in an admirably cool voice.

"Starting a fire. It's cold in here—some fool left the windows open."

He said it deliberately, to goad her. If she had any

sense she wouldn't let it annoy her. But where Maddox was concerned she had no sense. Seven years of married life and subservient behavior seemed to have flown out those open windows. "It's my house. I can leave the windows open if I want."

"Not any more," he said mildly enough, moving out of her way as she quickly, efficiently started a fire going. "Didn't your husband ever let you open the windows?"

"I'm not going to discuss my husband with you," she snapped. "You murdered him in cold blood . . ."

"I killed him in self-defense," Maddox interrupted her calmly. "And you know it."

"You goaded him. You were looking for an excuse to kill him."

"Hell, Miss Sara, anybody with any sense would have wanted to shoot that cantankerous, self-righteous jackass. You included. If you expect me to repent my sins you're going to have a long wait."

"I don't expect anything from you," she said furiously, blotting out the memory of those long nights when she lay in her bed, hurting, wishing Jacob were dead. "Except to leave me alone."

He cocked his head sideways, his long, silver blond hair drifting over his black-clad shoulders as he seemed to consider the notion, and for the first time Sara knew real misgivings.

He might have read her mind. "Are you certain you're doing the right thing, Miss Sara? Staying out here, all alone, with a dangerous man like me? Who says I won't decide to use you for target practice?"

"I don't think you need any practice."

She managed to surprise a laugh out of him. "What happened to that shy little mouse I saw scurrying around the mercantile? You've got a tongue like a whip, lady."

She could feel the color drain from her face, and she could only thank God that men weren't observant. He wouldn't notice her reaction to his casual words.

"Being widowed has a strengthening effect," she snapped, turning away from him.

"What do you think those kindly neighbors of yours are going to think?" he continued, moving over toward the fieldstone fireplace and leaning against the mantel. "Won't they mind that the young widow has taken up with her husband's killer?"

"I haven't taken up with you!" she said furiously.

"They're not going to know that. They overlooked the fact that Jacob caught me kissing you. They figured it was my fault. But if you stay here you'll be branded a whore, Miss Sara. They'll turn their backs on you, and you'll have no one."

His voice was cool, insinuating, far too clever. She looked out at the storm-laden afternoon. It would take her the better part of an hour to get to Marijane's house, but she could do it. She could let go of the only home she'd ever known, the place she'd suffered for, leaving it in the hands of a conscienceless murderer.

And she could will her heart to stop beating, pigs could fly, and the man taking up far too much space in that small room could turn out to be a decent, godly man. Jacob had taught her the foolishness of believing in the impossible. Of dreaming.

"The settlers know me better than that," she said. "If they believe such shameful things of me then their opinion shouldn't matter."

"But it will, Miss Sara," he said heavily. "It will. You just say the word and I'll saddle up one of the horses for you. Hell, I'll even drive you in the wagon."

"You can't get rid of me."

She didn't like the smile on his face. It wasn't a pleasant smile, a warming smile. It chilled her to the bone. "Don't count on it, Miss Sara. I can do anything I set my mind to."

She made him supper. She told herself it was easier than to keep arguing, and it kept her busy. She didn't have to watch him as he brought his saddlebags in and dumped them in the corner. Didn't have to watch him move around the tiny cabin with a feral grace, his long, pale hair catching the firelight as he built a blaze to warm the cabin. She filled the tin plate, Jacob's plate, with biscuits and bacon and eggs from her chickens, dumping it noisily on the table before serving herself a smaller portion. And then she started toward her alcove bed.

He caught her arm, and she almost dropped her food. She hadn't realized he was so close. "There's room at the table, Sara," he said.

"I'll cook for you, since I'm cooking for myself," she said, trying to pull away, "but that doesn't mean I have to sit with you and be pleasant."

"You don't have to be pleasant, but you have to sit with me. I don't feel like eating alone." He glanced over at the alcove. "Where were you heading?"

He'd already managed to drag her to the table and push her down into the other chair. She didn't like being manhandled, yet she had to admit those long, elegant hands of his weren't nearly so painful as Jacob's had been. In fact, they weren't painful at all.

"That's where I sleep," she said, staring down at her plate of food. She began eating, slowly, mechanically, avoiding his gaze.

"Wouldn't share a bed with old Jacob, eh?" he murmured. "I can't say as I blame you. How did he take to that? Most husbands wouldn't let their wives get away with refusing to share a bed."

Outside the thunder rumbled. She should have ignored him, but her temper had already frayed. "Where my husband and I chose to sleep is none of your business." The biscuits tasted like sawdust, but Maddox didn't seem to notice. He ate steadily, watching her.

"Maybe not. Where you're sleeping now certainly is."

Again there was the hint of a threat. Of a danger she didn't recognize. She glanced up at him, at his distant, ironic expression, and she felt the need to shock him. To embarrass him, as he was trying to embarrass her. "My husband put me from his bed two years ago, Mr. Maddox. I was going to have a baby, and then something happened. I lost it, and he decided it was a judgment from God. We wouldn't have children until sin was purged from this household. So he built me that bed in the alcove there, and that's where I intend to stay. Alone."

His smile was slow, taunting, and she steeled herself, waiting for his next comment, his next goading remark. "Then you have no objections if I take the bedroom," he said mildly enough.

"I don't want you in my house."

"My house," he corrected. "And if I'm kindly enough to give you a roof over your head you might consider thanking me."

The guns were gone. It was sheer, unadulterated rage that made her glance toward the gun rack, but the two that were left had disappeared while she was cooking dinner.

"No," he said, reading her mind. "You can't shoot me, Sara. You can't get rid of me, you can't reform me, you can't make me repent of my sins. Your best bet is to get the hell away from me and this place and start a new life. Stark will stake you to it."

"I won't take blood money from that man," she said furiously.

He shrugged. In the flickering firelight his eyes were almost silver, and the pale hair flowed down his back. "Suit yourself, Sara. You'll have to give in sooner or later. Don't say I didn't warn you."

"Give in to what?"

His smile was cool, brief, and oddly, shockingly sexual. "What you're fighting so strongly," he said.

She pushed away from the table and he made no move to stop her. She noticed with surprise that her plate was empty—since Jacob's death she'd barely eaten a thing. For some reason that seemed one more strike against Maddox, and she took the plate and stalked to the sink, slamming it down noisily. "I'm going to bed," she snapped. "Unless you have any objections."

"None at all, Sara. I'll even do the dishes."

It was quite the most provocative thing he'd said so far. "Of course you will," she shot back derisively.

She climbed into the narrow bed, pulling the quilt up

over her as she turned her back on him. She closed her eyes tightly, trying to shut out the sound of him as he moved around the cabin. Not that he made much noise. The hiss and crackle of the fire was louder than the soft tread of his booted footsteps, yet she knew where he was, what he was doing. Awareness was overwhelming and disturbing, and when he came to stand over her she held her breath, listening to her heart slam against her rib cage.

"You're going to sleep in your shoes, Miss Sara? The clothes are bad enough, but the shoes seem a little extreme."

She hated that soft, ironic voice. "I'm quite comfortable," she said. In truth, her tightly pinned hair made her head ache, and even the ill-fitting clothes were binding. She wanted to wash her face and brush her teeth, she wanted to throw off her clothes and sleep in her shift. She didn't move.

"Suit yourself," he said.

Slowly, inevitably the cabin dissolved into silence. It all felt so different, and yet the same. Once more she lay, tense and sleepless, alone in her alcove, listening to a man move around the cabin, readying himself for bed. And yet not for one moment could she pretend that everything was still the same, that it was all a nightmare, that in the morning she would awake to find Jacob snoring noisily in his bed.

She must have drifted to sleep. When she heard his voice it almost seemed part of a dream.

"How old were you when you married Jacob, Sara?"

She knew she should refuse to answer. He was already in bed—his voice drifted toward her from the far room, and for some reason that made it safe. "Old enough," she said, without any real rancor.

"How old?"

"Fifteen. My parents died of cholera on the way west. Jacob was a godly man and a bachelor. He decided marrying me was his Christian duty."

"And what did you think of that?"

"I didn't really have much choice," she said, more to

herself than to him. She didn't want to remember those years. The helpless grief. The need for comfort that no one, least of all her gruff, elderly husband, would provide.

For a moment he didn't say anything. "You have a choice now, Sara. I'll take you to your friends in the morning."

"If I have a choice, I'm not going," she said.

It was odd, two voices in the darkness, talking, separated only by the small cabin. Jacob never spoke to her once they were in bed. There was something unnerving, intimate about it, so that when Maddox spoke again in his deep, slow, disturbing voice, she ignored it, pretending to be asleep. Even though the words lingered in her mind, sneaking into her dreams when she finally did relax enough to sleep.

"You're going," he'd said, and it had been more to himself than to her. "If not for your peace of mind, then for mine."

Will Maddox, alternatively known as Mad Billy Maddox, the Angel of Death, lawman, gunslinger, lapsed son of a bible-thumping preacher man, lay back in the wide bed and stared at the ceiling, listening to the rain outside. It almost drowned out the quiet sound of Sara Elder's breathing, but he was tuned to the quieter sounds of humanity. The ability to hear a heartbeat over a thunderstorm had saved his life countless times, and it would again.

Not that Sara would kill him. She pulled on a gun on him twice today, and that was twice more than anyone else had and lived to talk about it. But she wasn't a killing sort of person.

He shook his head, half grinning to himself. She'd changed. When he first saw her, alone in that general store, lusting over a piece of purple-flowered material, she'd been shy and sweet and scared to death of him.

She'd developed a backbone and a sharp tongue in the last couple of days. Whether she'd ever admit it or not, the death of that old bastard who'd married her was the best thing that could have happened to her. Maddox knew she was still scared to death of him—he could see it in the depths of her blue eyes. But she was strong enough to fight him now.

If he had any sense he'd simply tie her up, throw her over the back of a horse, and take her to the nearest farmhouse. If she came back, he could shoot her. There was no room in his life for a woman, particularly a good woman like Sara. She might make the best biscuits he'd ever had in his life, the taste of her mouth and the feel of her body might linger in his dreams as no one else's had, but he still didn't need or want her around. She was a distraction, and every distraction made him vulnerable. He simply couldn't afford that.

He could get up, cross that small section of cabin, and climb in bed with her. For the life of him, he couldn't figure out why he didn't. No one would be surprised, except maybe the oddly innocent Mrs. Elder. He could strip her body of those crow-black clothes, loosen her hair and lose himself in it. In her hair, in her mouth, in her soft, sweet flesh. He'd almost forgotten what it was like to bed anything that wasn't a whore.

Whores were professionals—they knew how to please a man, he reminded himself. Even her righteous husband had found Sara Elder a disappointment—surely bedding her would be a boring waste of time.

So why couldn't he get it out of his mind? Why couldn't he just do it; take her, or forget about her?

He sat up in bed, kicking away the heavy covers. It was a cold night, the fire had died down, and Sara Elder might welcome a little body heat. She wouldn't be in much of a position to stop him.

He was halfway across the room when he heard the noise. She was sound asleep, there was no doubt about it. She made a quiet little noise in her sleep, a sigh that was more than a sigh. It caught on her breath in a strangled sob that was buried so deep inside her she probably didn't know it existed.

Maddox stopped. She'd turned to face the fire, and the

quilts were bundled up to her chin. He hadn't realized quite how young she was. Jacob Elder had married and bedded a child. She wasn't a child any longer, but there was still a stubborn innocence about her that ate through all his resolve.

He'd never been a man to despoil innocence. He killed when he had to, but only in the line of duty, private or public. He left widows and children and orphans alone. This woman was all three.

He turned away from her then, cursing his unexpected noble streak beneath his breath. It was time to get out of the business. His best and maybe only friend, Ike Walters, told him that once you start developing a conscience you were doomed.

And as he stretched back out on that big bed, he could see his doom. Curled up beneath a pile of covers, a fist under her chin. Grief in her heart.

When she woke up the next morning she was alone. The sun was shining through the small windows, sending a pool of light on the rough plank flooring, and it was shockingly late. There was a pot of coffee on the stove, still warm, the dishes were washed and put away, and there was a note on the table.

Jacob could barely write his own name, and his handwriting was rough and ill-formed. Maddox's script was flowing and elegant, like his mane of pale hair. Like the man himself.

"If you have any sense at all you'll be gone by the time I return from town. Take anything you wish, and I won't grudge you."

She stared at the black, graceful script. And then she crumpled the paper and threw it onto the coals in the fireplace.

FIVE

Maddox had one simple, basic reason for taking the buckboard into town, and that was to get as far away from Sara Elder as he could. She didn't stir when he rose and made coffee, and he didn't doubt she was in the middle of a deep, exhausted sleep. He sat there at the table, watching her while she slept, and wishing he could lie next to her.

Hell, he'd been at this too long, he told himself in disgust, draining his coffee and resisting the impulse to slam it down on the table. If he wanted to lie next to her he damned well could. And even if she put up a fight at first, he knew full well she wouldn't fight for long. He recognized that curious, dreamy look that came into her eyes. He knew the other signs. He expected she didn't.

She wouldn't know that she wanted to lie naked in bed with him. If she even thought about it, the sinfulness of the notion would shock her rigid. But underneath her proper, godly upbringing lurked a curious longing. A longing he'd already tasted on her mouth. A longing he wanted to taste on the rest of her.

Which was why he was getting the hell away from her before he made any big mistakes. If she had any sense at all she'd be gone by the time he returned. He'd given her free rein—she could take all the livestock for all he cared. Just so long as she left that damnably small house.

He was halfway to town before he finally realized his

problem. Sara Elder reminded him of someone, and he was a man who never forgot a living soul. Yet he'd be unable to place her resemblance. Every time he looked into her sad, pretty face he felt a familiar/unfamiliar reaction, one he couldn't define, and it made him edgy and irritable. If he could just figure out who she reminded him of, or where he'd seen her before, then maybe she wouldn't get under his skin like a burr under a saddle.

But he couldn't have seen her before. He wouldn't have forgotten her, not those fierce, brave eyes nor her stubborn, vulnerable mouth. If he'd seen her before, he'd know her now.

So she must remind him of someone he knew, long ago. He cast his mind back, way back, to his childhood in Missouri, in the river town where his daddy preached hell and damnation and his mama preached love thy neighbor far too literally. Until his father caught her in bed with a boy not much older than he was, and it ended up a haze of blood that time had been unable to erase from Maddox's mind.

She wasn't like his mother, feckless and pretty and loving and the hell with the consequences. She wasn't like his little sister, who died of a fever when she was twelve; she wasn't like the good women in the town where he grew up.

It hit him with the force of a blow. He couldn't remember where he'd seen her, or someone like her, before, because he hadn't. He'd dreamed her, long ago, when he was young and half-crazed with grief and anger. He'd run from that small town in Missouri, not even waiting to see his parents buried side by side, partners in death as they hadn't been in life. He hadn't heard the words spoken over them, uniting them throughout eternity. He'd been seventeen and he'd run, and during that first endless year he'd dreamed of a safe life, of a small, tidy house, a family, and a woman who looked at him with love and kindness in her eyes.

That dream woman had been the image of Sara Elder. Not that she looked at him with love and kindness, nor ever would. And not that he wanted it anymore. It had been a boy's crazy dream, relinquished long ago. He still wanted that house, a place of his own. But he had no use for family. For another living soul.

She was a smart enough woman—she'd be gone by the time he got back. She was a stubborn woman—she'd be there waiting for him.

Caldwell's Mercantile and Saloon were quiet and almost deserted when he stepped inside that morning. Caldwell stood behind the counter, eyeing him warily. He was used to that look in men's eyes. He'd done what he could to cultivate it, but suddenly, this morning, it was a burden.

"Mr. Stark's in the saloon," Caldwell said, concentrating on wiping down the counter. "He said as I was to tell you if you happen to come in. Says there are some people he'd like you to meet."

Maddox considered ignoring him. His business with Stark was finished—he'd done his job and received his pay. If it were up to Stark he'd wipe out the entire population of homesteaders in Cedar Bluffs, but Maddox had flat out refused. He had enough blood on his hands.

"Where's Sara?"

There was no missing the quavering fear in Caldwell's voice when he asked that question. Maddox turned to look at him, long and slow, and he noticed the old man's knees were shaking. "What?" he said mildly enough, giving Caldwell a chance to think better of his question.

But Caldwell was a braver man than he seemed. "I said, where's Sara? People around here care about that girl. They're not going to take too kindly to you doing her any more damage."

Maddox just looked at him. "And what are the brave people of Cedar Bluffs aiming to do about it?"

Caldwell had a prominent Adam's apple, and it bobbed vigorously as he struggled for a coherent response. "They won't like it," he said finally.

"Life's full of things we don't like," Maddox murmured. And it wasn't until he walked through the swinging doors into the saloon that the full irony of that statement hit him.

The bar was empty, with the exception of three men. Harrison Stark sat at a table, his short legs stretched out comfortably in front of him, his rounded belly relaxed. Beside him sat two men Maddox had hoped never to see again.

"There you are, Maddox. I thought you might be in this morning, though I would have laid odds you were still busy between Mrs. Elder's legs. Where is she?"

He let the doors swing shut behind him, strolling into the saloon with a casual stride that fooled no one. Particularly not the two newcomers. "Still in bed, Stark," he said.

"Well, you probably put her through more than that old man did in his entire life. No wonder she's worn out."

"I'd watch my mouth if I were you, Harrison," the younger man next to Stark murmured. "Maddox doesn't like it when you talk disrespectful about women. He once near-kilt a man just for taking a knife to a whore."

"But I didn't, Johnny," Maddox said smoothly. "I let you go."

"That's coz Ike wouldn't have taken kindly to having his only brother split open, would you, Ike?"

The older man met Maddox's gaze. "No," he said heavily, "I wouldn't have."

Maddox took a chair, turned it around, and straddled it casually. He poured himself a shot of whiskey and tossed it back, then looked across the table. His best friend, and his worst enemy. The Walters Brothers. Johnny Walters, who'd killed seventeen men by the time he was twenty-five, who killed for the fun of it, and Ike, his much older brother, who was a gunman of the old school, who killed when he needed to, or when the price was right, but never for the sheer pleasure of it.

If it hadn't been for Ike, Johnny would have been dead years ago. But with Ike looking out for him, Johnny had lived a charmed life.

"Long time since I've seen you, Will," Ike said. He

looked like holy hell, Maddox thought. He was only a few years older than he was—maybe forty, and he looked sixty. Thin to the point of gauntness, with sunken eyes and a yellow cast to his skin, Ike Walters was staring death in the face. And it was coming hard and painful.

"Not long enough," Johnny muttered, tipping back another shot of Caldwell's best and only whiskey.

"What brings you to Cedar Bluffs?" Maddox ignored Johnny's jibe. "Or do I need to ask?"

"I brought 'em," Stark said. "You seemed to have developed an inconvenient case of scruples, Maddox. I still got me a little problem here. I'm just not convinced that one dead man is enough to teach these sodbusters a lesson."

"And you know how good I am at teaching people a lesson, don't you, Angel?" Johnny mocked him.

"Don't call him that," Ike snapped.

"Hell, he don't mind. He's used to it, ain't you, Angel?"

"From you, Johnny, I'm used to anything," Maddox said.

"We could use another gun," Ike said, breaking in. "Stark here has offered a bounty. Five hundred dollars for each family we get to clear out, a hundred dollars for each man we have to kill. I don't mind sharing."

"No, thanks, Ike," Maddox said in a gentler tone he used with anyone. "My killing days are over."

"That's what you think," Johnny muttered.

Maddox looked at him, long and slow. He'd always known it was going to come to this. Johnny Walters wouldn't rest until he killed Will Maddox. Or Maddox killed him.

Maddox had hoped it wouldn't have to happen. He loved Ike as much as he hated Johnny, but when it came to his crazy little brother Ike had a blind spot.

Maddox turned to Stark, ignoring Johnny. "I told you I was through. I did what you hired me for, and that's enough. I won't interfere in your plans if you won't inter-

fere in mine. Elder's place is far enough out that we don't
have to get in each other's way."

"What about the widow?" Johnny murmured. "I hear
she's right purty, and you know I got a weakness for
brown eyes. That whore I cut down in Abilene—she had
brown eyes, didn't she? 'Course, she's not very pretty any
more."

Maddox didn't move. If he killed Johnny now he'd be
dead in the next moment. Ike might be at death's door
but he was still one of the fastest men Maddox had ever
seen.

"You come anywhere near her and I'll cut your balls
off," Maddox said pleasantly, pouring himself another
shot of whiskey.

"Now, boys," Stark said, his gruff voice nervous. "I
didn't bring the Walterses here for you to fight amongst
yourselves. I got some pig farmers to get rid of. Concentrate on that, Johnny."

"Oh, I intend to take care of all the garbage around
here," Johnny murmured, his clear eyes alight with mal-
ice and something close to madness. "And then I'll par-
take of what's left over."

Maddox let his hand relax, ready to draw. And then his
eyes met Ike's. Ike, who knew every thought that was
going through his head.

"Ignore the kid, Will," he said lazily, rising. He swayed
a little on his feet for a moment. "Guess I drank a bit too
much this early in the morning," he said, before he
straightened. "Let's go for a walk, Will. We can catch up
on old times."

Maddox cast a glance at Johnny's smirking counte-
nance before following his old friend out into the morning sunshine. They started along the plank walkway,
Maddox slowing his pace to accommodate Ike's slower
walk.

"If it were any other man I'd think you were setting me
up for Johnny to shoot me in the back," he said easily.

"And if you were any other man I'd kill you for saying
such a thing," Ike said, unoffended. "We'll never see eye

to eye on my kid brother. I know he's rotten, but he's all I got. I promised my ma I'd look out for him, and a promise is a promise."

"You really going to do Harrison Stark's dirty work?" Maddox asked him.

"Why not?" Ike paused to lean against a railing, pretending to admire the view. He was trying to catch his breath. "The pay's good, and I'm going to hell anyway. Why should it matter? You were working for him."

"It was a fair fight."

"There's no such thing as a fair fight where you're concerned, Will. You're too damned fast. No one stands a chance against you. You must have egged the old man on, then moved in on his wife. She must be even prettier than Stark said."

That nagging trickle of unease began to build. "Why was Stark talking about her?"

"He seemed to think Johnny might be interested. Assuming, of course, that you got tired of her. Or she got tired of you."

Maddox looked at him, as the pieces fell into place. "He's offered you a hundred for each person you kill. How much did he offer for me?"

Ike didn't even hesitate. "Seven hundred. If I were you I'd be insulted. Years ago, when we both had a price on our head, they were offering five thousand bucks for you."

"Times change. You going to kill me, Ike?"

Ike laughed. The sound was eerie, hollow, like a man already dead. "You think I could still take you, Will? Look at me. I'm eaten up by this damned sickness, and we both know it. But Johnny'd pay for the privilege. He's never forgiven you for Abilene."

"He can try."

"He's fast, Will. Maybe even faster'n you. And when he's finished with you he'll take that pretty little widow and make her wish she'd never been born. He's real bad when it comes to women, Will. There's something twisted inside of him that makes him want to hurt them."

Maddox drew out his pouch of tobacco and proceeded to roll a cigarette, taking his time. His hands didn't shake, and nothing betrayed the storm of rage that swept over him. Not that he fooled Ike. The two of them had roamed Colorado and New Mexico during the '70s and '80s. They'd been lawmen together, they'd been in jail together. And it looked like they were going to die together.

"Why are you telling me this, Ike?" he said finally when he'd lit the cigarette.

Ike laughed that same cold, hollow sound. "You're looking at a dead man, Will. And when I go, there'll be no one to look after Johnny. To keep him out of trouble. Without me to keep an eye on him he's out of control."

"There's only one way I can keep Johnny out of trouble, Ike," he said in a measured voice, drawing on the cigarette.

"I know."

The two of them smoked in silence for a bit, as the future spilled out in front of them. Blood red, Maddox thought.

And then Ike straightened, and there was a ghost of a grin on his emaciated face. "I need you to take care of it. Take care of Johnny, so he can't hurt anyone anymore. And take care of me. I'm sick of hurting."

"No."

Ike ignored his protest. "I heard you were here, Will, and I knew I could count on you to do the right thing. You're the toughest man I know. And one of the best."

Maddox just looked at him. "And if I won't?" he asked, tossing his cigarette into the mud-caked street.

"Then you're a dead man. And the little lady too."

There was nothing he could do. No choice, but the bloody one. "Damn you to hell, Ike Walters."

"There's no doubt about that, old friend," Ike said with a wheezing laugh. "I just hope I don't see you there any time soon."

* * *

Borrowed time. He was living on borrowed time. Hell, they all were, most of all Ike Walters. And they were all running around, trying to take care of business before that time ran out.

Johnny Walters was stupid and mean, and crazy enough to enjoy hurting people. Particularly women. If Maddox had had any sense he would have failed to react when Stark brought up Sara's name. In the fifteen years he'd known Johnny, since he was a vicious child of twelve, he'd never shown any weakness, any partiality to a woman.

Johnny Walters hated just about everybody, but he hated Maddox most of all. If he recognized Maddox had a weak spot, he'd use it. Twist it. Destroy it.

Johnny was stupid all right, except where it counted. He wouldn't have missed Maddox's reaction. And that would have signed Sara's death warrant.

He had to get her the hell away from Cedar Bluffs. Away from him wasn't good enough—he was the only man who could protect her if Johnny got his hands on her. Ike was too sick to be any good at all.

It was early afternoon, and a thin plume of smoke curled out of the chimney in the brisk spring weather. He took care of Bosco, then headed toward the cabin, knowing with a mixture of regret and relief that she was still there.

The door was open to the cabin, letting in the cool air. He could hear her singing in a high, clear voice "Red River Valley." Was she dreaming about a cowboy to love her?

And then he recognized the other sound. The splash of water. And he knew she wasn't washing dishes.

He stepped up to the door, silent, watching, unable to help himself. She had dragged the hip bath in front of the fire, and she was sitting in it, scrubbing herself, singing, totally unaware of her watcher.

He backed away, into the shadows, far enough that she wouldn't see him. Close enough so that he could watch

her. He didn't give a damn whether it was honorable or
not. For the moment he was transfixed, watching her.

She rose, and he realized she was wearing a thin cotton
shift that clung to her wet body. For a moment he was
distracted by the thrust of her pebbled, firm breasts, the
way the material hugged her body.

And then he saw the welts.

They stood out clearly across her back beneath the almost transparent white material. Someone had beaten
Sara Elder with a piece of leather, most likely a belt, and
he had no doubt at all just who had done it. Some of the
bruises were darker than others, attesting to the fact that
this had gone on a long time. And he found himself wishing he'd taken a little longer to kill Jacob Elder. And
made it hurt more.

He moved into the doorway, his tall frame blocking out
the sun, and she threw her arms around her body, as if to
protect it from his gaze.

"Honey," he said lazily, "you're still fully dressed,
though for the life of me I can't imagine why. Do you
always take a bath in your shift or is this in my honor?"

She didn't move. He could see the color mount her
face. She'd washed her long hair, and it hung in damp
ringlets around her face. She shook her head, and it covered the marks on her back. He wondered if she even
knew she'd been branded by her righteous brute of a
husband.

"I always bathe in my shift," she said in a low voice.
She glanced toward her bed. There was a thick linen
towel lying there, just out of her reach.

He crossed the room, allowing himself to get close to
her. Close enough to breathe in the soap and water on
her skin. Almost close enough to touch, as he reached
and caught the towel. "Did your husband teach you that
nakedness is a sin?" He asked in a relatively tranquil
voice. She didn't move as he draped the towel around her
shoulders. Covering her narrow, bruised back.

She pulled it around her. "Everyone knows that, Mr.
Maddox," she said tightly.

He moved back, and she stepped out of the tub, the calf-length shift dripping water on the rough flooring. "I guess someone forgot to tell me," he said. He began unfastening his holster. "If you're finished with that bath then maybe I'll use it."

"The water's dirty," she protested.

"Now how dirty could it get from a good woman like you, Miss Sara?" he drawled, dropping the gunbelt on the table. Still in reach. He began unfastening his black pearl buttons, slowly, and she stared at him in shock.

"You aren't going to take off your clothes," she said in a horrified whisper.

"I sure the hell am. Why don't you sit and keep me company while I bathe? You can wash my back for me."

She was already heading for the door, her waist-length hair flowing behind her, the wet shift leaving a trail of water. "Running away?" he taunted her as she headed out the door, barefoot.

She didn't bother to answer. She was almost out of hearing when he called one more time. "I thought this would give us a chance to know each other better. I could tell you about my good friend Johnny Walters, and why you should be scared out of your drawers at the thought of him.

"And you could tell me why your husband took a belt to you."

It was cold outside, but Sara didn't care. Inside, with the fire blazing, she'd welcomed the fresh spring breeze. Outside, with nothing but a wet, icy shift, a damp towel, and no shoes, she was ready to run back inside.

She wouldn't do it though. He was probably trying to give her pneumonia—he might say he'd never killed a woman but there was no doubt her death would make things a lot easier for him. Particularly since she refused to vacate her home.

The sun was bright overhead, but the warmth it imparted was minimal. There was a breeze as well, and Sara made it as far as the barn, sheltering behind the wall as she fought to control a sneeze.

There was a horse blanket out there, but that would negate the effects of the bath, and heaven only knew when she'd have a chance to bathe again. She certainly couldn't imagine risking it as long as William Maddox lurked around.

She leaned against the rough wood wall, shivering. Pneumonia might not be a bad idea. At least then she wouldn't have to worry about how she was going to make a go of this place. She'd be dead, they'd place her in the ground next to Jacob and say prayers over them.

She didn't want to spend eternity lying next to Jacob Elder. The more time passed, the more she relished her guilty freedom. She'd already spent too many years as his faithful helpmate. She'd given him enough.

How had Maddox known Jacob used his belt on her? Were those silver-blue eyes of his gifted with the sight? She'd managed to cover up any sign of pain over the years—for one thing it gave Jacob a righteous satisfaction she wanted to deny him. For another, she didn't want the pity of the other settlers.

But Maddox had seen through the polite coverups. Through to her soul. The very thought unnerved her. He seemed to know her secrets, her thoughts, her guilty longings. Did he know the most shameful longing of all?

That as her husband lay dead, all she could think about was the way William Maddox had kissed her. And whether anyone would ever kiss her like that again.

SIX

Maddox was lying stretched out across the bed when he heard her come in. He didn't move. She'd feel better if she thought he was sleeping. She didn't realize that even in his sleep he was more alert than most people were at noon.

He could see her from his vantage point on the bed. Her long hair was still damp, curling slightly down the length of her bruised back. The shift was dry now, and annoyingly opaque. With his luck she'd simply pull the rest of her clothes on over it.

Which was exactly what she did. He watched with fascination as she fastened the tiny buttons up the back of her plain black dress. He wanted to see her pull up those skirts and put on her stockings. He wanted to see her bare legs, so that he could imagine them better during the long, empty nights.

He watched and waited, silently, until she reached for her hair and began to twist it into a tight, painful knot. And then he rose from the bed.

"Don't do that."

He managed to startle her. She dropped her brush, and her hair fell like a waterfall of silk over her shoulders. He stood in the doorway, watching her, but her own gaze was somewhere beyond his left shoulder. He hadn't bothered to put on a shirt, and the sight of his naked chest seemed to send the shy widow into a panic.

"It gets in my way," she said, starting to twist it up again.

He was in a contrary mood. He crossed the room so swiftly she panicked, backing away from him, dropping her hair. She came up against the edge of her alcove bed, and she stared at him in panic.

"If you pin it up," he said, "I'll have to take it down for you. And you'd rather not have me put my hands on you, would you?"

"No," she said in a strangled voice.

"You want me to put my hands on you?" he mocked.

"I want you to keep away from me," she said hoarsely.

She smelled utterly irresistible. Of soap and water and fresh air and sunlight. He wanted to take her narrow shoulders and pull her against him. He wanted to bury his face in her long, silky hair. He wanted to touch her, and keep on touching her, until he found some kind of peace that he knew no longer existed. Not in this world, not for him.

He turned away from her. "Pack your clothes," he said mildly enough.

"I told you, I'm not leaving," she said, summoning up her lost courage. "You can beat me, you can kill me, but you can't make me leave."

"You're used to being beaten," he said. "I don't imagine that would frighten you much. And killing you wouldn't get me anywhere. I'm not in the mood to dig a grave, and if I just left your body lying out it would draw predators. After a while it would begin to stink."

He glanced back at her, to check her reaction. She was looking at him in utter horror, a fact which pleased him. It still wasn't a good enough argument.

"Suit yourself," she said, tossing her head, and the hair shimmered down her back. "If you want to kill me I can't stop you."

"Sure you can. You can get the hell out of here."

"I'm not going."

Maddox was not a patient man. He wasn't used to people saying **no** to him, particularly women. He was used to fear, and respect, and instant obedience. He had no doubt that Sara Elder feared him. She just didn't fear him enough.

"No wonder your husband beat you," he said bitterly. "If you were this stubborn with him I'm surprised he didn't strangle you."

"I wasn't this stubborn with him."

Her words were so soft most men wouldn't have heard them. But Maddox wasn't most men. He turned back to look at her—a major mistake. Her mouth was pale and stubborn, but her brown eyes were filled with a longing that ate at his heart. And he knew if he didn't do something about her, and fast, she would be the death of him.

"Sara," he said in a softer voice. "This is too dangerous. For me, and most especially for you. Whether I'm here or not, there's no way Stark's going to leave you alone. He doesn't want me to have this place either—he wants to own everything in this valley and he's not going to stop until he does."

"Then why did he give the place to you?"

"I think he figured I'd lose interest sooner or later. A gunfighter isn't the kind of man to settle down."

"Then why are you here?"

It was a simple question, one that cut him to the heart. "Because I was young once," he said wearily. "I had dreams once. And every now and then I'm fool enough to remember them." He turned away from her. The late afternoon was growing cooler, and he missed his guns far more than he missed his shirt. "There's going to be another storm," he murmured. "If we leave now we can miss it."

She said nothing, and suddenly he wasn't in the mood to argue. "Suit yourself," he said. "We can wait till later. But rain or no rain, you're getting out of this house tonight."

Sara didn't pin up her hair. She felt strange, almost sinful with it hanging down her back. Jacob had always cautioned her about a woman's vanity, and Sara knew she had pretty hair. It might be an ordinary brown, but it was long and thick and wavy. A wild, willful part of her reveled in the weight of it, covering her shoulders. And she knew Mad Billy Maddox was watching it. Watching her, as she made dinner for the two of them.

At least he'd put his shirt back on, though he hadn't buttoned it. She could still see his chest and stomach if she didn't remember to avert her eyes, and the sight unnerved her, did strange things to her own chest and her stomach and lower still.

It wasn't as if she hadn't seen a man's chest before. But Maddox looked so different. Jacob never tanned—his burly, thickly muscled torso simply turned bright red in the sun. And Jacob had been covered with curly gray hair, on his shoulders, on his back, on his thick biceps.

Her surreptitious glances at Maddox were a revelation. His skin was smooth, dark bronze, with a flat stomach and lean, muscled chest. Every time she looked at him she could feel a tightness in her stomach, and she did her best to concentrate on a point somewhere past his left shoulder.

He sat at the table, cleaning his guns, while she made supper. His pale hair was tied back with a piece of leather, and his light eyes concentrated on his work, ignoring her as she moved back and forth between the stove and sink. She might have thought he didn't even remember she was there, except she suspected that Maddox was aware of everything.

She found she was feeding him well, a fact which disturbed her. There were biscuits left over from the night before, but she baked fresh ones anyway. She found the last of her dried-up winter apples and made a pie for him. She'd even managed to kill an old chicken and stew it for hours on the back of the cookstove.

"It won't work," he said.

"What do you mean?" She looked up at him from across the table, startled.

"I don't give a damn how good a cook you are. I don't

care how sweet you're pretending to be. You're leaving here tonight."

"You can't make me."

"Yes, I can. I'm dropping you off at the nearest neighbor, and then I'm heading out of town."

For a moment she couldn't believe her ears. "You're leaving?"

"That's right."

"But why? I thought you wanted a place of your own."

"You trying to change my mind, Miss Sara?" he murmured. "Let's just say I'm old enough to know who and what I am. I'm a gunfighter, not a rancher."

She didn't move. The weight of her hair down her back had a strange effect on her. It made her feel curiously free, different. And oddly troubled by the thought of his leaving.

Ridiculous, she told herself. "If you're leaving then there's no reason for me to go. I'm glad you've decided to be reasonable, though you might want to wait till after the storm . . ."

"Haven't you been listening to me, woman?" he said wearily. "I said we're both leaving. You can't stay out here, unprotected. You don't even know how to use a gun, and Stark wants this piece of land along with everything else. I'm your only hope, and I'm leaving."

"My only hope," she echoed, hoping to sound ironic. Instead her voice was painfully wistful. "What made you change your mind about staying?"

"I wish I could say it was your grudging hospitality, but I'm afraid it has nothing to do with you. An old friend showed up."

"I would have thought . . ."

"He wants me to kill him." Maddox's voice was harsh. "And his crazy kid brother besides. And I can't do it."

Sara just looked at him. "I think you are mad," she said softly, defiantly.

"In your world that's crazy," he said. "Not in mine. Ike Walters is dying. He wants me to take care of it for him. And I'll be damned if I'll kill the only friend I've got just to put him out of his misery." He tipped back in the chair, looking at her. "Stark brought him and his brother here to finish up what I started. They're going to kill or drive out every homesteader in Cedar Bluffs. If I know Johnny, it'll be killing. And they'll be coming after you first."

"Why? My husband's already dead. I wouldn't think I'd matter much."

"Sure you do. They know it's a way to get to me."

In the silence that followed the rain seemed to increase in intensity. Sara didn't know what to say. She was afraid to ask, afraid to ignore what he said. She simply sat there, silent, confused, wary.

And then he pushed back from the table. "Someone's coming," he said harshly, reaching for his rifle.

"Don't be silly," she protested. "I've got excellent hearing and all I can hear is the rain and the fire."

He caught her arm, dragging her out of the chair, and his grip was painful. "Get in the bedroom."

"There's no one . . ."

He didn't listen. He simply shoved her into the bedroom and closed the door on her, shutting her in. She reached for the door handle, but it wouldn't budge.

"If you poke your head out of there I'll shoot you myself," he said in a bitter voice. "Stay put and be quiet."

He was crazy, Sara decided. Mad Billy Maddox indeed. There probably wasn't any old friend in town either.

She looked at the bed. The covers were rumpled, the pillow dented from where he'd put his head. It was Jacob's bed, and yet it no longer seemed like it. Maddox had lain there, and it was his.

She could picture him, stretched out, shirtless. She reached a hand out to smooth the rumpled quilt, and it took her a moment to realize she wasn't straightening the bed. She was caressing it.

She snatched her hand back in horror. She couldn't hear a sound from the room beyond, and she was half tempted to open the door.

The other half told her to do as she was told for once.

She wandered around the room that she'd once known so well.

She sat down on the edge of the bed, gingerly. It was much more comfortable than her pallet, and she scudded back a bit. She hadn't slept much the night before, or any night since Jacob had died, and suddenly she felt unutterably weary. If he was going to keep her prisoner in the bedroom, then he'd have to put up with her using the bed, she thought, climbing all the way up onto it.

She put her head down on the pillow where his head had lain. She stretched out her legs, reveling in having the bed all to herself. She had no idea how long Maddox would sit in the front room, waiting for someone who wasn't coming. But at least she could steal a tiny nap while she waited.

She didn't know how long she slept. When she awoke she was disoriented, dizzy, filled with a sense that something was terribly wrong.

She tiptoed to the door, listening for the sound of voices. "Maddox?" she whispered. There was no answer. She tried again. "Will?"

Still no answer. She reached for the latch, opening it slowly, but the main room of the cabin was shrouded in darkness. There was no sign of Maddox in the place. His guns and saddlebags were gone.

The panic that swept over her was unreasonable and infuriating. She should be rejoicing that the man who murdered her husband had thought better of his determination to take her away from her home. He'd left her, and she'd never see him again. She needed to celebrate, not fight back the clawing anxiety that filled her belly.

The dishes were still on the table, the remnants of food scattered across the scarred surface. One chair was kicked over, as if he'd left in a hurry.

"I'm glad," she said out loud. "Damned glad." The profanity came out sounding forlorn and defiant. She looked out the window, but the darkness was impenetrable, and the rain was coming down in torrents. Was he out there somewhere, riding away from her?

From her? The phrase was absurd. He was nothing to her but the man who'd destroyed everything, and thank God he had decided to get out of her life.

If he had. There was no way she could go to sleep without being certain his horse was gone. She opened the door, staring out into the rain-shrouded night. She could just see the shape of the barn looming in the darkness.

Grabbing the lantern, she sprinted across the yard, ducking into the pitch-black stable and shaking the rain from her hair. She could see Molly and Ben, Jacob's horses, standing there in the shadows. She set the lantern on a nail, moving into the stable. She could see another shape . . .

An arm snaked around her waist, a hand clamped over her mouth, and a moment later she was lying face down in the straw. But it wasn't Maddox on top of her, pulling at her skirts, breathing whiskey fumes in her ear. It wasn't Maddox crooning at her, filthy words, as she fought to free herself from his crushing weight.

"You sure are a little fighter," the stranger breathed. "I shoulda known Maddox would pick a lively one. Where is he, little lady? Did you already tire him out? I'll tell you what—you won't tire me. I can keep you busy from sunset to dawn. I got something between my legs that never says die, and I can make you forget all about Maddox. But first of all, tell me where he is."

He'd stopped pulling at her skirts, but she could feel him against her, his erection pressing against her buttocks, and she knew he hadn't stopped for long. "I don't know what you're talking about," she said in a furious voice.

He caught her loose hair in his fist and yanked it back. "Sure you do, honey. I'm talking about Maddox. Where the hell is he?"

"He's gone," she said flatly.

"Then how come there are three horses here? You gotta do better than that, little missy. Though I know how to make you talk." He started clawing at her skirts again, his fingernails raking her legs. "Where is he?"

"Right behind you, Johnny."

The man on top of her froze in the midst of his gropings. It took Sara a moment to realize that his erection had vanished as well. "You gonna shoot me in the back, Angel?" he said, not moving. "You might want to reconsider the notion. The bullet might pass through me and hit the little lady, and that would be a powerful waste of womanhood, now wouldn't it?"

"It might be worth it," Maddox drawled. "Get off her. Now."

"Angel, if I do that then you'll shoot me sure as you're born," the man whined.

"I'll shoot you if you don't. In the head. And you know I'm a good enough shot to splatter your brains all over this stable and not touch her."

"Yeah, you're that good a shot. Almost as good as me." He climbed off her, scrambling away from her, and for a moment Sara couldn't move.

"What the hell are you doing here, Johnny? Did Ike send you out here? Or Stark?"

"Hell, it weren't neither of them," the man named Johnny said, and Sara allowed herself a furtive glance at him. He was dirty, belligerent, and surprisingly young. Some might almost term him handsome. Sara felt sick to her stomach.

"I just thought I'd see whether the little lady you've been shacking up with was anything I might be interested in. You never were a man for settling down, so I figured this one might be special."

"I'm not settling down with her, Johnny," Maddox said flatly. "I've been trying to kick her out of her house and she won't go. So I'm getting the hell out instead. If I were you I'd leave too. Stark's not a man you can trust—he'd gut shoot you if he thought it would save him two bits."

Johnny smiled, exposing stained teeth. "You were trying to kick her out and she wouldn't go?" he echoed. "Hell, Angel, you know how to deal with that. I've seen you do it before—you just blow her brains out."

"I wasn't in the mood." There was a deceptively calm

air to Will Maddox. Like a snake coiled in the bright
sunshine, seemingly too somnolent to be a danger. Sara
wasn't fooled, and she doubted Johnny was either, from
the way his feral eyes glittered and focused on the rifle in
Maddox's hands.

"Oh, that's right," Johnny said. "You don't take to killing women, now do you? As a matter of fact, you're right
squeamish about it. Well, since she's not your woman,
then she's free for the taking. Maybe I'll have a taste of
what you've been missing . . ." He was reaching for her,
and Sara tried to scramble out of the way.

The click of the rifle as he cocked it filled the stable.
"I'm not squeamish about killing you, Johnny," Maddox
drawled. "I might even deem it a pleasure."

Johnny dropped his outstretched hand, turning to grin
at Maddox. "You sure are possessive for a man who says
he's not interested."

"Yeah," said Maddox.

"Tell you what, Angel. I'll give you a choice. You can
try to kill me right now. I'd say you have maybe a fifty-
fifty chance—the rifle's not your weapon and you're not
even likely to slow me down much. And after I kill you I'll
enjoy myself with your lady friend.

"Or you can come to town tomorrow. Ike and me'll be
waiting for you at the saloon. You come alone, and we'll
talk about things." His grin was wide and evil.

"Yeah," said Maddox. "We'll talk."

"Unless you want to discuss it now," Johnny pushed it.
"Without my big brother to keep things gentleman-like."

"Tomorrow," Maddox said. "I've got things to do tonight."

Johnny turned to leer at Sara. "Yeah," he said. "I guess
you do. Do her once for me." He sauntered to the door,
and Maddox's rifle never strayed from its target. And
then he paused in the entrance, looking back, and Sara
saw true madness in his eyes.

"On second thought," he said, "I'll take care of her
myself. After I finish with you." And he disappeared into
the pitch-black night.

SEVEN

If Sara weren't watching him he would have gone after Johnny Walters and shot him in the back. He wouldn't worry about a fair fight or honor when it came to a mad dog like Johnny. You put a rabid dog down before he could take anyone with him. And that's what he needed to do with Johnny. What he should have done years ago, and would have, if it hadn't been for Ike.

He had no choice in the matter. He'd ride to town tomorrow and find Ike and Johnny at the saloon, like Johnny promised. And he'd do his damnedest to kill one brother and not the other.

But he knew Ike. Ike wouldn't let him get away with that. Disease was eating away at him, he looked like he was in pain, and he wanted to finish things up, all neat and tidy. And he wanted his old friend Maddox to be the one to do it.

No matter how hard he tried to avoid it he knew he'd have to. And he knew why.

Any other time he could just ride away. Into the night, into the sun, and never even think about it. But he couldn't this time. Because of the woman in the straw, her thick hair tangled around her pale face as she looked up at him. He stared at her, all innocence and unconscious need, and he hated her.

"The rain's stopped," he said. "You gonna spend all night rolling around in the hay?" he drawled in his most cutting voice, "or are you going to come back to the house?"

Her pale face flushed, and she scrambled to her feet. He resisted the impulse to reach out and help her. He was going to touch her. Things had moved past the point of rescue, past the point of keeping things sane. He was going to touch her, he was going to take her to bed, and then he was going to ride away from her. There just wasn't any other choice.

"I thought you'd already left," she said, and her voice was husky. "I just came out to see if your horse was gone, and he . . . and he . . ."

"Lucky for you I was waiting for him," Maddox drawled. "He's not what you might call a considerate lover."

"Are you?" she whispered, half to herself.

She wouldn't look at him. Her hands were twisting in her skirt, her face was flushed, and suddenly he couldn't stand it any longer. He crossed the dimly lit stable, caught her by the arms and pulled her up against him. The rifle was caught between their bodies, and he used his hand to force her to face him, for her eyes to glitter into his in the shadows.

"I'm a man," he said harshly. "A man who wants you. I've wanted you since I walked into that goddamned store and saw you standing there looking like a scared mouse. But there's no room in my life for a good woman like you. No room in my life for any woman."

She didn't move. He wouldn't let her look away, and he could see the gleam of tears in her eyes. "All right," she said. "Go away."

It made sense to have the rifle between them. Pressing against his ribs. But sense had nothing to do with that spring night. "Yeah," he said, tossing the rifle away from him. "I will. Tomorrow." And he kissed her.

Her anger surprised him. Her struggles surprised him as well, as she pushed against him, trying to free her trapped arms, trying to free his hungry mouth from hers.

He let her go then, taking a step away from her in the darkness. "Maybe I'll go tonight."

She stared at him for a moment. She looked wild and reckless in the lamplight, her thick brown hair a tangled halo around her face. "The hell you will," she said in a low voice. And she threw herself against him, twining her arms around his neck, putting her mouth against his.

He hadn't forgotten what it felt like to kiss her. The softness of her lips, the awkward shock when he used his tongue, the hungry noise she made when her panic faded. Her body softened and flowed against his. Her small, strong hands were clutching his shoulders, holding on for dear life, and he decided he needed to give her a good reason to hold on tight. He lifted her off the ground, pulling her tightly against him and her little squeak of panic quickly turned into a purr of astonished response. Until he started for the door.

"No," she whispered against the side of his neck. "I don't want to go back there."

She was a lady, and he knew it. A girl-woman of his last youthful dreams, and she should be made love to properly, on a bed, wearing a high-necked white nightgown with him fumbling beneath the hem.

But he was no gentleman farmer. He set her down, pressing her against the rough wooden wall. She was still wearing that rough-spun, dyed black dress, and he reached up and ripped it open to her waist.

He half expected, half wanted her to run then. She stood frozen before him, and then she pulled the torn, ugly dress from her shoulders, so that she stood in front of him wearing the plain cotton shift she'd bathed in.

The lamplight was fitful, shadowing in the small stable. Beyond the wall he could hear the horses, inside he could hear the panicked beating of her heart, as she waited for him to touch her.

"Sara," he said, a wealth of pain and longing in his voice. And then he caught her face in his hands and kissed her.

* * *

The straw was scratchy against her back as he carried her down onto the floor of the stable. Sara didn't care. She didn't want to lie in Jacob's bed and have this man take her. She wanted it here and now, in the dirt, in the stable. She wanted to embrace life completely, with the glare of the oil lantern illuminating the man who knelt over her, his ice-blue eyes suddenly filled with heat, his pale hair like a halo in the oddly shifting shadows as he unbuttoned his white shirt and pulled it from his pants. The Angel of Death. Angel, Johnny Walters had called him. Mad Billy Maddox.

"Are you going to hurt me?" she asked, unable to keep the fear and the longing from her voice.

For a moment he froze. Then he pulled off his shirt, laying it down in the straw beside her. "No," he said. "Love doesn't have anything to do with hurting."

"But does this have anything to do with love?" she asked.

"Yes," he said. And he picked her up and moved her over to lie on top of his spread-out shirt, so that her skin was protected from the roughness of the old straw.

He leaned over her then, blotting out the fitful light, and she tensed, telling herself she wanted this, she'd asked for this. She expected a punishing kiss, but instead his lips feathered across her eyelids, her cheekbones, dancing across her tremulous mouth until she reached for him, trying to deepen the kiss, hungry for it.

His long, pale hair fell around them, a curtain that blocked out the moonlight. He seemed content to kiss her forever, exploring her mouth with leisurely pleasure, using his tongue, his teeth, his lips, coaxing her to kiss him back, to touch his tongue with hers, to kiss him until she was breathless, trembling, hot and cold all over.

He kissed the side of her neck, his tongue on her pulse, and she clutched at his shoulders. She could feel his hands on her waist, hands so big they could span her, and then they moved up to touch her breasts, To cup them with long fingers, as his thumbs brushed across the nipples and she made a strangled cry of pleasure and protest.

His mouth on her breast was even more of a revelation. He suckled her through the thin cotton shift, and she reached out to stop him, shocked. But instead she threaded her fingers through his long hair and held him there, lost in a storm of crazy sensations.

When he moved to her other breast she slid her hands down to his bare, smooth shoulders. He was hot and sleek and strong and the texture of his skin aroused her in ways she hadn't thought possible.

She moved her hands down his arms, her fingertips tracing the rough flesh of a scar that had to have been made by a bullet. She could feel his hips against her, feel the hardness of him, larger than anything she had ever expected. The knowledge of what that was, what was going to happen, hit her, and she froze, suddenly frightened.

He lifted his head to look at her, then rolled on his side. Moonlight was peeking in the window, silvering everything around them. "What's wrong?" he whispered, his hands not leaving her body.

"I'm afraid." The words came out before she could stop them, and her fear grew deeper. She wasn't afraid that he'd hurt her, punish her. But that he'd pull away from her.

He didn't move. "What are you afraid of, Sara? Me? Or my body?" He caught her small hand in his big one and brought it to his naked chest. "You've got every reason to fear me. But not my body. I'm human, Sara, just like you. Don't be afraid to touch me. I have a heart that beats. Skin, bone, and muscle. Blood. Blood that burns for you, Sara." He moved her hand down his chest, slowly, and she didn't try to pull away, mesmerized by the sound of his voice and the feel of his flesh. Even when he drew it past the unbuttoned waistband of his pants, even when he placed her hand over the hot, rigid length of him.

It was a sin to touch him, she knew that. But everything she'd done and thought was a sin, and she wouldn't go back. He kept his hand over hers, and when her fingers curled around the length of him he groaned, a sound of such fierce animal pleasure she almost fainted.

He moved her hand up and down, slowly, rhythmically, and he seemed to grow bigger, harder. When he released her she continued the touch he had taught her, reveling in the dark fevered joy of it.

Don't be afraid to touch me, he'd said. And she leaned down and pressed her mouth against his chest, against the flat brown nipple that puckered against her lips.

He jerked, and she would have pulled away from him in embarrassment and shame if he hadn't clamped an arm around her, holding her against him.

He tasted of salt and soap and skin. She moved her mouth down to his flat stomach, letting her tongue trace the faint golden line of hair. And he groaned, deep in his throat, and gently pulled her away from him, so that she fell back against the straw, staring up at his dark, enigmatic face.

"Don't look so worried," he murmured. "Sometimes things just feel too good."

"I don't understand."

His smile was wry. "I'll show you." And he reached down and caught the hem of her shift, pulling it over her head.

She was hot and cold, lying there beneath his gaze. She wanted to cover her breasts, but he'd already tasted them. There was no reason why he shouldn't see them as well.

She was unprepared for his hands at the waist of her pantalets, pulling them from her before she could protest, so that she was lying naked beneath him.

He put his mouth on her nipples, and the sensation against her bare skin was so powerful she cried out with it. He kissed her belly, and she squirmed, restless, shy, as he cupped her hips.

And then he put his mouth between her legs, and she arched off the pile of straw, too shocked to do anything but beat at his strong, sleek shoulders, trying to stop him.

He ignored her struggles, holding her still as he used his mouth on her, and she wanted to weep, to beg him.

Another dreadful sin, a sin of such monumental pleasure she thought she might die from it. Her nails dug into his shoulders and she held on to him for safety, no longer protesting. And as he slid his fingers inside her she screamed aloud as her body seemed to explode, and she was lost in some dark and dangerous place, a sweet hell that seemed more like heaven.

She'd barely caught her breath when he moved up, over her, pulling her legs apart. She started to brace herself for pain, but when he slid deep into her she was slick and ready for him.

He dropped his head on her shoulder, and she could feel the tension throb through his body as he struggled for control. Everything about him was iron hard, even his choked words in her ear.

"Don't move," he gasped. "I don't . . . think I could stand it if you moved. Just lie there for a minute."

She tried to do what she was told, obedient. But the incredible sensations of his body, sheathed so tightly in hers, sent ripples of reaction dancing through her sensitized body, and she wanted, needed to touch him.

Her arms encircled his waist. Her hands slid down his smooth back, to his flat, hard buttocks, and he said something, a curse, a prayer, a cry for mercy.

He caught her legs and wrapped them around his narrow hips, pulling her tighter against him. He buried his face in the side of her neck and began to move, slowly, with agonizing deliberation, thrusting deep inside her, then withdrawing, only to thrust again, a smooth, sleek thrust that caught her breath and tore it away.

For a few moments she lay utterly still, waiting for him to take his pleasure, waiting for the rush and flurry and abrupt end of it. But he seemed in no rush at all. His body was covered with a fine film of sweat, his hands covered her breasts as he moved, in and out, advance and retreat, all and then nothing, until the loss of him began to tear at her, and she clutched at him, pulling him deep inside her, as a strange torrent of feeling began to build within her.

She was so lost in her own maze of reactions that she barely noticed he shifted, increasing the pace to shorter, faster thrusts. She was vaguely aware that she was crying, though she wasn't sure why. His body was rigid in her arms, covering her, smothering her as he pounded against her body, and instead of escape she wanted more, she wanted something she'd barely glimpsed.

It started with a fierce trembling at the very center of her. She cried out, frightened, begging him to stop, but it was too late. Darkness and fire covered her, he put his hand between their joined bodies and touched her, hard, and she screamed as he flooded her with heat and life.

Reality returned slowly, in bits and pieces. She was lying in his arms, crying, her heart still pounding with the aftermath of its race with love and death, her body still trembling.

And the wonder of it was that Maddox was holding her. Stroking her, warming her shivering body with his burning one. And when she finally moved her tear-damp face to look into his, he smiled at her, a faint, almost wistful curve of his hard mouth. "Sara," he whispered, and he kissed her, a slow, deep kiss of such heartbreaking tenderness that she wanted to die.

He carried her into the house. She didn't weigh much, and if she were his woman he'd see that she got some extra padding on those delectable curves of hers.

But she wasn't his woman, and never would be. Only for one night.

The alcove bed was narrow, but they didn't need much room. He set her down there, naked, and then added a log to the fire as she watched him out of solemn eyes. He grew hard again, just thinking of her eyes.

He went outside, to the spot where he'd stashed his saddlebags, and a moment later he came back, setting his gun on the floor by the bed. Johnny Walters wasn't anywhere around, he trusted his senses. But the woman lying in the bed, watching him, had a habit of disrupting those senses. And when it came to guns and death he was a thorough man.

When it came to Sara Elder he was a thorough man as well. He didn't believe in love. He'd never known it in his life. And yet, when he looked down at her in the narrow bed, he knew he loved her.

He tossed the yards of lilac-sprigged calico over her body like the softest, prettiest blanket. She stared caught the folds of it in her hands, staring at it in shock and wonder. And then she looked at him and smiled, and he realized he'd never seen his Sara smile before. Not at him.

"I love you," she said, the most dangerous words in the English language. And he stripped off the pants he'd worn and climbed into the narrow bed with her, underneath the yards of lilac-sprigged calico.

It was bright daylight when Sara awoke. She didn't want to. She buried her face deeper into the pillow, pulling the soft, light blanket around her body.

She had no soft, light blankets. She also had no clothes on. She opened her eyes, and saw the mass of soft calico covering her. And memory came flooding back.

She sat up, pulling the cotton around her, as she remembered all the things Will Maddox had done to her last night. And all the things he had coaxed her into doing to him. She waited for the shame and regret to flood her, but she waited in vain. All she could feel was an aching, helpless longing for him.

She rose, dragging the material around her and opened the front door. It was late morning, and he was gone, she had no doubt of that this time. His horse wouldn't be in the stable as it had been last night. He wouldn't be waiting, watching out for her . . .

And then the rest of the night came back to her. More than the dark, mindless pleasure he'd shown her. She remembered what happened before. She remembered Johnny Walters.

She dropped the calico, standing in the doorway numb

with horror, oblivious to the cold or her own nakedness. If Will Maddox were really Mad Billy Maddox, the Angel of Death, then he would have ridden away this morning, as far from the town of Cedar Bluffs and the two killers waiting for him as he could.

But if he was the man he hid from the world, he would have saddled his horse and headed straight for Caldwell's Mercantile and Saloon. He'd be ready to kill his best friend, or be killed.

And he'd be doing it for her.

She didn't even hesitate. She threw on the first thing she could find, a faded cotton dress she'd planned to dye black for mourning. She didn't even waste time with her shoes and stockings, carrying them with her as she ran for the stable.

His shirt was still crumpled in the straw where they had lain together. She caught it up, holding it to her face and breathing in the scent of him. Of them. And then she grabbed Molly, the fastest and least reliable of the work horses, and headed out into the chill morning air.

She wasn't going to let Will Maddox die. And she wasn't going to let him leave without her.

EIGHT

The town of Cedar Bluffs was deserted when Will Maddox rode in that cool spring morning. It came as no surprise to him. When there was killing to be done, most of the good townspeople watched from behind their lace curtains, avid for blood.

There'd be blood today, that was certain. His blood, most likely. A gunfighter developed a second sight about such things, and he knew his life was going to end that day. No more roaming from town to town, hiring his killing skills to whoever could pay his price.

He'd kill Johnny Walters before he went, though. Ike as well, if he had to. And Harrison Stark for good measure. The homesteaders might stand a chance if he wasn't around to hire another killer. At any rate, it wouldn't matter to Maddox by then. He'd be long gone.

He wouldn't think about the woman he'd left behind. Sleeping in a heap of lilac calico, her face flushed, her hair tangled, her lips swollen and red from his mouth. She didn't need a man like him.

Would she mourn him? He hoped not. He didn't want her wearing those dusty black clothes. She needed to live, to find someone to love. A good man.

He glanced toward Caldwell's place. He didn't need to see the brothers to know they were watching for him. He'd never been a godly man—he'd spent too much time watching his father and mother to have much faith in the creator they worshipped in their spare time. He had no doubt he'd be heading straight for hell. He'd lost count of how many men he'd killed. It was a way of life, one coming to a close, and he wasn't a man for regrets.

Unbidden, the scent, the taste of Sara Elder came back to him. She was strong beneath that fragile exterior. She survived her husband; she'd survive him. She'd grow and be strong. He didn't have to worry about her.

But it wasn't worry. It was something deeper, more longing, and he knew it would be his last thought before he died.

Maybe it wasn't so bad, dying. He'd done everything he'd ever wanted to do, including the one thing he'd always avoided. He'd fallen in love. Hell, it was time to die.

The three of them were sitting in the saloon, playing poker. The air was thick with smoke and whiskey, and Ike was watching him out of gimlet eyes, a faint smile on his wasted face. "Knew you'd come, Will," he said softly.

Johnny turned in his chair. "Hey, old man, I thought you didn't have the cojones. Then again, you spent last night proving that you did, right? How was she? Think she could handle a man like me?"

"I'm going to kill you first, Johnny," Maddox said in a calm voice.

"Gentlemen, gentlemen," Harrison Stark protested, moving away from the table. "There's no need for violence here. We're all men of the world. I'm sure the three of you could work together . . ."

"Stay put, Stark," Ike said in his smoothest voice. He had already drawn his gun and was pointing it directly at the rancher's huge paunch. "This is between my little brother and Maddox. No interfering."

Johnny rose, slowly, carefully, keeping his hand clear of the gun at his hip. "You gonna try to kill me, Angel? You know you're no match for me. Especially after the night you had."

"Why'd you come here, Johnny?" Maddox asked softly. "What made you pick this little town to come to? You think it was an accident?"

For a moment Johnny looked uncertain. He turned to glance back at his brother. "It was Ike's idea."

"Why?"

"Hell, I don't know. Maybe he wanted to see you before he died. He ain't got long—any fool can tell that." His voice was cool and emotionless. "Maybe he wanted to make sure I killed you so that the two of you could be together throughout eternity, like a pair of goddamned pansies. How the hell should I know?"

"Not exactly, Johnny," Ike said, lighting a cigar with one hand while he kept his gun trained on Stark. "I figured the two of you had unfinished business."

"Well, you know how it's gonna be finished," Johnny sneered.

"Maybe. Maybe not."

Johnny stared at his brother incredulously. "You think he can take me?"

Ike smiled sweetly. "I hope so, little brother. Without me around there's no one to keep you from killing everything you set your sights on. You're the one I aim to take with me. And I'm counting on Maddox to see to it."

Johnny's mouth was hanging open. "Haven't got the stomach to do it yourself, brother?" he demanded.

"I can't kill my own flesh and blood," Ike said wearily.

"I can." Johnny moved so fast his gun hand was a blur. The bullet hole in Ike's chest was a splatter of blood before the sound of the shot pierced the morning air.

But Maddox could move fast. In the seconds that it took Johnny to whirl around Maddox had his gun drawn, and the bullets that pierced Johnny Walters' forehead, eye and jaw dropped him before he could fire more than once.

Maddox was scarcely aware of the raw burning in his side. He shoved his gun back in his holster with weary self-contempt when Harrison Stark loomed into view, a shotgun in his hands.

"Now ain't this tidy?" Stark said. "'Course I was counting on the Walters boys to finish up the job you started, but if I can hire three men I can certainly hire more. And

I really don't want you living nearby, Maddox. That piece of land has some powerful nice grazing. Not to mention the pretty little widow.''

"You going to shoot me, Stark?" Maddox asked calmly. The sting in his side hurt too damned much to be lethal, but the gun in the old man's hands could put a pretty big hole in him. Somehow the thought of dying at anyone but a gunfighter's hands didn't sit well with him.

"Yup. Guess I will." And he raised the gun.

Sara heard the gunshots by the time she reached the edge of town. She slipped off Molly's bare back, grabbing her shoes and not even noticing as the horse took off toward home. Her fingers were numb with cold, her feet icy, and her heart pounding as she raced up the rough wooden stairs to the saloon.

She saw the dead man, lying in a pool of blood, first. Another man lay sprawled in a chair, soaked in blood as well, and Harrison Stark stared at her, a rifle pointed in her direction. And then she realized it wasn't pointed at her at all.

She turned, and saw Maddox leaning against the wall. There was blood on his side as well, and his guns were sheathed. "Get the hell out of here, Sara," he said in a furious voice.

"Now, now, ain't this touching?" Stark chortled. "Looks like you got beneath the little widow's skirts just like Johnny said you did. Guess I'll have to try a piece of it too. You wanna watch, Maddox, or should I do you a favor and kill you first? Maybe I'll gut shoot you so you can watch while you're dying."

"Leave her out of this, Stark," Maddox said. "You aren't a crazy kid like Johnny Walters."

"I'm a man who likes the ladies," Stark said, licking his thick lips. "You teach her any good tricks, Maddox? I'm partial to . . ."

He stopped in midsentence, a look of faint surprise on his florid face. And then he toppled over, face forward onto the floor, the rifle sliding away from him.

The man in the chair wasn't dead after all. He'd dropped the tiny derringer he was holding onto the green baize table in front of him and reached for the glass of whiskey with a trembling hand. He fell back in the chair, unable to reach it.

Sara didn't hesitate. She crossed the room, picked up the glass of whiskey and held it to his lips. The man's eyes fluttered open for a moment, and she could see the cloudiness of imminent death. But he smiled at her. "You take good care of him, missy. He's got salvation in him. You can do it."

Maddox had crossed the room behind her, silent as always, and he reached out and pulled the dying man into his arms, oblivious to the blood that stained them both. "Goddamn it, Ike, don't you die," he said fiercely.

"Too late," Ike said with a wheezy laugh. "At least you didn't have to be the one to do it. Look at it this way, Will. I won't have to hurt any more."

"There's a doctor not ten miles away . . ." Sara said.

"No," Maddox said, holding him.

"Good man," Ike said. "I was telling her that. You take her to Montana, Will. There's a couple of hundred acres across the border, near Twin Pines. Got it registered under the name Thomas. You take her there, Angel. Name your first kid Ike."

"Damn it, Ike . . ." Maddox cursed.

"Don't be a fool, Will," Ike said, his voice no more than a whisper. "Look at Johnny. You don't want to end up like that." He reached up a bloody hand and tapped Maddox's face. "Take your chance before you lose it." And his hand dropped.

The silence that filled the room was deafening. Maddox's held his old friend for a moment longer, tight against him. And then he rose, letting the body fall back in the chair.

He walked past Sara, not even looking at her, moving slowly. He was covered with blood, and she couldn't tell where Ike's stopped and his own began. He was moving slowly, but he didn't seem badly hurt.

By the time she reached the swinging doors of the saloon he was already on his horse. He glanced up at her, squinting into the sunlight, and she waited for him to say something.

"I can't stay here, and you know it. You need a good man, Sara," he said. "Someone who'll take care of you, treat you right."

"I found one," she said, looking straight at him.

"You don't know what you're asking. You just saw a good man die—do you want to spend your life with death peering over your shoulder?"

"Isn't that what life is all about, anyway?"

The first glimmer of emotion swept across his bleak face. It was frustration, with her, but it was better than nothing.

"I don't know where the hell I'm going," he said.

"Montana sounds about right."

He closed his eyes for a moment, those weary blue eyes that had seen too much. When he opened them again they no longer seemed so lifeless. "Where the hell are your shoes, woman?"

Behind her was blood and death. Ahead of her was life. "You can buy me new ones." And she stepped up beside the horse, waiting.

He reached down, caught her arm, and hauled her up behind him. "You're going to regret this every day of your life."

She put her arms around him, carefully. The bleeding had slowed, and she could feel the graze beneath his dark shirt. She'd take care of it when he let her. She'd take care of him when he let her.

"You give me enough kids to keep me busy, Will Maddox," she said, "and I won't have time for regrets."

He turned to stare at her for a long moment, and a curious kind of peace crossed his face. "I'll do that," he said.

And she leaned her head against his back as he headed north.

THE FOLLOWING IS AN EXCERPT FROM BARBARA DAWSON SMITH'S STUNNING NEW HISTORICAL ROMANCE, *A GLIMPSE OF HEAVEN*.

PROLOGUE

Waterloo, 18 June 1815

True to form, Burke Grisham, the Earl of Thornwald, stood surrounded by beautiful women. But for once, he ignored them.

The brass ring of the spyglass pressed to his eye, he intently watched the battle that raged in the undulating landscape to the southeast. From a distance, the vast armies of England and France appeared as tin soldiers in mock combat. But with a horror that gripped his gut, Burke knew they were not toys.

They were men.

Men with wives and children and mothers and fathers. Men with flesh now torn by bullets and sabers. Men whose warm blood soaked the muddy earth.

Sunlight leaked through the clouds onto a scene of awesome carnage. Wave after wave of cavalry swept across the fields amid a thunder of hooves and the glitter of swords. Tiny stick-men lay crumpled in the dirt. Here and there, black smoke belched from the cannon and obscured the action. The rumble of the artillery mingled with the tattoo of rifle-fire, the faint roll of drums, the far-off screams of horses and men.

With the slowness of one submerged in a nightmare, Burke became aware of someone plucking at his sleeve. Someone speaking words whose meaning failed to penetrate his stupefied mind.

He tore his attention from the battlefield and frowned at the woman beside him. A parasol shaded her dainty straw bonnet with the pink ribbons dancing in the breeze. Her limpid blue eyes blinked in a face of girlish purity.

But Lady Pamela Seymour was far from pure. Her morals were as low as his. No one knew that better than Burke.

"Well, answer me," she said. "Have we routed old Boney?"

We. He hid his shame behind a tight smile. "Not yet."

He raised the spyglass again, but she caught his wrist. Her lips formed a Cupid's bow pout. "Selfish man. Do allow me a peek. After all, my husband is fighting down there."

Handing her parasol to Burke, she took the telescope and surveyed the conflict. In a pale gauze gown that hugged her breasts, she might have been watching a stage play.

Burke clenched the parasol handle until his knuckles turned white. Never in his misbegotten life had he felt more worthless. He tarried here in supreme arrogance, clad in white cravat and spotless morning suit, his black Hessians polished to a high sheen.

While Englishmen lay dying down there.

How bold he had felt just hours ago as he and a few friends had set out in their carriages to view the warfare. Brussels had been in a state of frenzy with civilians fleeing to Antwerp for fear of a French invasion. But Burke had not crossed the Channel to run at the first cannon shot; he craved the chance to flirt with danger.

His own naïveté mortified him now. Only a braggart would call himself brave to watch from the safety of this ridge behind the British lines. Oblivious to such moral dilemmas, his companions chattered and gossiped. Now and then the shrill laugh of a lady punctuated the distant gunfire.

He forced his gaze to the battlefield. No, those below were not tin soldiers, but men of honor. Men whose belief in liberty and justice gave them the courage to die in defense of England.

Stinking coward. His father's voice rang from the cold vault of memory. Aware of a familiar pressure on his temples, Burke descended into the darkness of his own private hell. The broken weeping of his mother. The brutal reproach of his father. The body of his elder brother sprawled by the roadside in a great red pool of blood. As Burke ran away and hid in terror.

There was no escaping the awful truth. Colin's death was his fault. His shame. His alone.

Ever since, Burke had striven to prove his derring-do. He had raced the fastest horses. He had out-drunk and out-gambled his cronies. He had seduced more wives than he could count, even wounding the husband of one in a duel. He had earned his reputation as the most daring rake in London.

But in the end his father was right.

Burke Grisham, second son and—by default—heir to the Marquis of Westhaven, was a stinking coward.

Pamela stamped her little foot. "Oh, bother. We're too far away to tell one regiment from the next."

Beside her, a lady flaunting an indecent bodice pressed a handkerchief to her rouged cheek. "Pray don't suggest we move closer."

Pamela shuddered. "Heavens, no. I wouldn't fancy seeing all those wounded men."

Burke heard their exchange as if through a fog. A fever spread through his cold limbs and upward, pounding in his skull. Sweat broke out on his brow, his chest, his back.

Men lying helpless. Crying out in agony. Bleeding to death.

As his brother had bled and bled and bled.

"How glad I am that you were not foolish enough to enlist, my lord." Pamela was leaning against Burke, her breasts pillowing against his arm as she whispered, "Just think, my stallion, after today your mare may be free at last."

Her pretty features suddenly looked hard and garish. He might have been gazing at a painted mask. Yet the loathing he felt was for himself.

Stinking coward.

The fever raged out of control. He knew only one way

to silence that taunting voice, to entomb it in the black reaches of forgetfulness.

Blindly he turned, but Pamela clung to him, uncertainty on her face. "Darling, you look so fierce. I did not mean to speak out so plainly. Do forgive me."

"Go to hell." He jerked his arm free and plunged through the throng of ladies.

They stepped back, twittering like magpies. Some put their heads together, no doubt savoring the delicious drama of watching a notorious lord spurn his married lover.

Stinking coward.

He fled toward the cluster of carriages, shouldered aside the lolling coachman, and leaped atop the driver's seat. Seizing reins and whip, he urged the matched team of blacks down the rutted road. Vaguely he grew aware of someone shouting his name.

The carriage rocked. From the corner of his eye, he saw the door swing open. A man clung there a moment, then clambered up alongside Burke.

Alfred Snow plunked himself down, panting, his breath exuding brandy fumes. "Christ, Thornwald, I might've known it was you. Where th' devil are you going so all-fired fast?"

"Down there." Slowing the carriage, Burke nodded toward the battlefield. "I forgot you were inside."

"What do you mean to do?"

"I'm joining our illustrious fighting men. Now get off with you."

Alfred raked his hand through his fair hair, his blue eyes bleary and his cravat askew. He took another long swallow from his silver flask. "I'm going with you."

"No!" Burke spoke through gritted teeth; he couldn't stomach the guilt of embroiling a friend in his own penance. "You're drunk. Besides, you've a wife waiting for you at home."

Alfred sat silent a moment. "Perhaps Catherine is better off without me," he said, his voice bitter as he twisted the gold ring on his finger.

Not for the first time, Burke blamed the mysterious Catherine Snow for the bouts of angry melancholy in Alfred that turned him to drink so often of late. Burke never had met the woman who caused his friend to brood so. She chose to stay at the Snow estate in Yorkshire rather than join her husband on his frequent sojourns to London.

"No woman is worth dying for," Burke said.

Alfred sent him a keen look. "On the contrary, I pray you'll someday know such love yourself."

A vast emptiness opened in Burke; then the rumble of artillery fire distracted him. "Let's not argue the merits of romance again. Get on with you now."

Alfred squared his shoulders. "No. Call it belated patriotic fever, but I want to fight, too."

"Suit yourself, then," Burke said with a shrug.

His own fever had little to do with patriotism and everything to do with subduing—at least for the moment—the demons inside him.

Stinking coward.

The frenzy in him resurfaced, compelling him onward. He snapped the reins and the carriage rolled at a fast clip down the rutted track. Almost immediately, they passed a straggly line of wounded soldiers trudging toward Brussels. Smoke from gunfire formed a pall over the scarred landscape, the farmland of trampled wheat and rye. Somewhere ahead, buglers sounded a rally in a series of staccato blasts. A dense column of red-coated infantrymen charged toward an unseen enemy over the next ridge. The bray of bagpipes from a Scottish regiment joined the cacophony of gunfire and shouting.

Bodies littered the field as far as the eye could see. Burke stopped the carriage and leaped down, snatching up a sword that lay on the ground. The blood beat hotly in his veins. He could not think beyond striking out against the enemy in the desperate hope of slaying the foe inside himself.

"'Elp me, guvnor," croaked a boyish voice.

Burke looked down to see an English recruit, his face

chalk-white, his leg cocked at an unnatural angle. The youth reached up his bloodied hand in supplication.

Burke hesitated, drawn by the lure of danger a few hundred yards ahead—the lure of morbid salvation. The boy's grotesque injury sickened him and made his own legs feel weak.

Then pity overtook his bloodlust and he threw down the sword. With Alfred's aid, he lifted the boy into the carriage. Other disabled soldiers cried out for mercy. The orderlies who carted off the wounded were woefully inadequate in number, and from that moment Burke found himself caught up in evacuating the injured to an open-air field hospital, where surgeons labored to save the overwhelming rows of wounded.

On through the afternoon, he loaded soldiers into the carriage. It was grim, filthy, wearisome work. Mud mired the wheels, forcing him or Alfred to clamber down and push. The air felt like a furnace, tainted by the stench of blood and smoke. From time to time, the ground trembled from the thunder of cavalry charges. Too often, a soldier expired of his injuries on the way to the hospital.

The voice inside Burke jeered his efforts. It whispered that cowardice, not compassion, kept him behind the lines. He continued doggedly, seeking the numbness of exhaustion. In London he would have gone to the pugilists' ring and fought until physical pain deadened his mind. But that, like this, was only a temporary respite. He knew he would never find peace.

As the fingers of sunset touched an earth consecrated by death, still the battle raged. Cannonballs whistled in the darkening sky as the English gained ground in a furious advance that left many more dead and wounded.

Returning from yet another trip to the hospital, Burke slumped wearily on the driver's seat. Patchy fog rolled in with the dusk, and the fire of musketry sounded hollow and distant.

As the carriage rattled up a rise, Alfred tilted his head back and drained his silver flask. He grinned suddenly, his teeth a smear of white in his begrimed face. "Christ, man, if the ladies could see you now, they'd call you a frigging hero."

Burke grimaced at his bloodied clothing, his boots caked with mud. His cravat had vanished, along with the coat he had used to staunch an infantryman's abdominal wound. "More likely they'd run screaming in the opposite direction."

"Bugger it. There's nothing a woman loves more than—"

A fusillade of pops drowned his words. As the vehicle crested the hill, grapeshot and shells rained like hail. A row of French artillery stood not ten yards away, firing at a British regiment of foot soldiers that surged out of the mist.

Cursing his misjudgment, Burke struggled to turn the horses. "Get down," he shouted to Alfred.

"Hell, no!" Alfred stood up, swaying as the carriage bumped along. "Let's grab some guns and charge th' devils. Tallyho!"

His body jerked suddenly. With nightmarish abruptness, he fell backward, clutching at his chest as he toppled from the carriage.

A shell whined past Burke's ear. He vaulted to the ground, landing ankle-deep in muck. The jolt half-dazed him.

He scrambled toward Alfred. In the twilight, a deadly patch of blood blossomed on his shirt. Horror pounded louder in Burke than the roar of the guns. "A doctor," he muttered. "You need a doctor."

Alfred didn't seem to have heard. He fumbled in his pocket, then pressed an object into Burke's hand. It was a cameo locket of a white-garbed angel reaching both hands toward a diamond star. Opening it, Burke stared at the miniature of a smiling woman with dark hair framing exquisite features, her eyes sparkling in a face so lovely it might have belonged to a goddess.

"Catherine." The din of battle almost drowned Alfred's agonized whisper. "You must take care of her . . . promise me."

Burke stuffed the locket back into his friend's pocket. "You'll care for her yourself, you fool."

Alfred clung to Burke's wrist as if summoning every fiber of his strength. "Watch over her. Swear it to me. You must."

His fingers were cold. Burke would do anything, say anything to ease his friend's pain. "All right, for God's sake. I promise. You aren't going to die, though. Damn it, I won't let you."

But Alfred's grip loosened and he slumped into a stupor. Burke scooped him up, staggering under the weight as he hastened toward the carriage, the mud sucking at his boots. Urgency throbbed with every beat of his heart. He couldn't fail again. Not as he had failed his brother.

Then Alfred shuddered once. The shallow rise and fall of his chest ceased.

Burke gripped him in a hard embrace. *"No!"*

In that instant something struck his upper body with violent force. White agony exploded outward, numbing his arms. He wheeled backward and fell into suffocating darkness.

Panic clawed at his throat. He couldn't breathe. An iron clamp squeezed his chest. Through it all, he felt an odd sense of surprise. He couldn't die yet. He was doomed to suffer on earth.

The battle sounds faded into blessed silence. Miraculously the pain slipped away like shed skin. He had a peculiar impression of detachment, of weightlessness, as if he floated high above the world. With startling clarity, he saw men fighting on the dusky field below. Beside the carriage, his still form lay near Alfred's.

The dream-like darkness became a river that carried him ever upward. As he strained to see into the pitch-black void, a bright star appeared on the horizon. The light streaked toward him and formed a shimmering tunnel.

Warmth washed him in glorious wonder. Unable to resist, he moved toward the light, drawn by its irresistible aura of . . . what?

Love, he realized in faint astonishment. *So this is love.*

Peace flooded him. Boundless and brilliant. The sensation was so extraordinary, he felt the urge to weep. All those years he had struggled, never dreaming such splendor existed, never guessing the magnitude of what was missing from his life.

The light flared brighter, dazzling him with the awareness of another presence. Alfred?

Even as Burke hesitated, a woman's voice called to him, not by name . . . and yet he knew her somehow. Her sweet entreaty rose from the shadows below and made him ache with yearning.

Don't leave me. Please don't leave me.

No woman had ever loved him. Not like that.

The voice lured him from the light, sucked him down, down, down. With jarring abruptness, the voice vanished into chaos. Pain burst inside him, as shocking as a plunge into icy water.

The radiance receded like the tide. Desperate, he strained to swim up toward it.

But the weight of his body doomed him to darkness.

ONE

Catherine Snow clung to the ladder and contemplated murder.

A bitter breeze yanked at the black merino shawl knotted around her shoulders and threatened to dislodge the white-ruffled mobcap that protected her hair. Shivering, she gripped the top rung with one hand and carefully leaned over to wash the arched window of the drawing room.

It was the chilliest summer in her memory, and Catherine had lived her entire twenty-two years here on the moors of Yorkshire. A week of unrelenting rain left mud puddles everywhere. Today, the sun peeked from behind the leaden clouds like a coy debutante peering past her fan.

The day had gone from bad to worse when Martha, the downstairs maid, had succumbed to a bout of the ague. Never industrious under the best of circumstances, Martha had neglected to beat the rugs in the library. As punishment, Lorena had ordered the servant to wash all the outside windows. Every diamond-shaped pane was to sparkle by the time Lorena and her twin daughters returned from their afternoon round of calls.

The minute the family carriage had vanished down the drive, Catherine sent a feverish, sniffling Martha up to bed with a pot of honeyed tea. Then Catherine herself had mounted the wooden ladder. Two hours later, her arms ached and her fingers smarted. The stench of vinegar water from the pail stung her nose. Worst of all, looking down made her wretchedly dizzy.

Yes, murder might be in order, Catherine thought darkly. She inched downward, the heavy bucket bumping her black skirt. Perhaps a dose of rat poison slipped into her mother-in-law's tea. Or a timely tumble down the grand staircase.

Even as her own feet touched solid earth, Catherine battled her spitefulness. When she and Alfred had returned from Gretna Green four years ago, Lorena had raged about her son's impetuous marriage. But then, ever mindful of what polite society would say, she had taken Catherine in hand and molded her into a lady. Lorena had opened her home—if not her heart—at a time when Catherine despaired of having a family of her own.

Sadness unrolled inside her like an endless tunnel. Setting down the pail, she slumped against the damp, ivy-covered wall and inhaled the scent of crushed leaves. It was so easy to blame her mother-in-law. But Lorena was not responsible for Alfred's death at Waterloo the previous year. Nor was it her fault that Catherine had failed to conceive again after a hideous miscarriage early in her marriage.

The loss of her unborn child was Catherine's own cross to bear, the result of her impetuous behavior.

She swallowed the lump in her throat. The truth ached like a never-healed wound. By her rash conduct, she had driven Alfred to drink. By her unruly tongue, she had marked herself as common. When Alfred told her to act like a lady, she'd thrown an inkpot at him, barely missing his head. And proving his point.

Over the three years of their marriage, he'd changed from a flirtatious charmer into a morose stranger. Because of her aversion to faro and piquet, he sought amusement in the gaming dens of London. Because of her inability to give him a family, he had fallen in deeper with ne'er-do-wells like Burke Grisham, the infamous Earl of Thornwald.

Resentment oozed over the wounds of the past. How dearly she'd love to give that scoundrel a dressing down, and the devil take any ladylike restraint. But she would never have the pleasure.

Catherine plucked an ivy leaf and twirled the stem between her fingertips. Life was no storybook where good always triumphed over bad, where tragedy drew husband and wife closer together. Now she was older and wiser than the dreamy country girl who had been swept off her feet by a dashing gentleman. Now she had a plan for her future, though it might take her another ten years to scrape together the funds—

A twig snapped in the underbrush. Straightening, she peered toward the woodland of oaks and wych elms that bordered the green lawn. Deep in the gloom, the pale oval of a face appeared past the trunk of a sycamore, then vanished again.

Someone was watching her. And she had a suspicion who.

Catherine marched onto the soggy grass. "Come out," she called.

Nothing moved. A pipit trilled its song into the silence. Sunlight flirted with the shadows in the forest, then ducked behind another cloud.

"Please show yourself," she cajoled. "I want to talk to you."

Someone stepped out from behind the thick trunk. A man.

"It's all right," Catherine said, hiding her irritation while motioning him closer. "Do come here."

With a hesitant, shuffling gait, he walked toward her, a small golden-haired dog trotting at his heels. He was a rather large man with sloping shoulders, dressed in country tweeds and muddy jackboots. A cravat wrapped his throat like an ill-tied bandage. Limp blond hair framed a face with a crooked nose and cheeks tinted pink with embarrassment. In one arm he cradled a long rifle; a red-stained sack dangled from his other hand.

Catherine curtsied with aplomb, as if Alfred's cousin

hadn't been lurking in the woods and spying on her from afar. "Good afternoon, Mr. Snow. How pleasant to see you today."

Fabian Snow's blush deepened. "H-hullo, M-Mrs. Snow."

"Thank goodness the rain has stopped at last. I see you've been taking advantage of the fair weather."

His pale blue eyes blinked guiltily, as if he were a poacher rather than master of the estate. He opened his mouth, then closed it. Abruptly he thrust the sack at her. "F-for you."

"Thank you, but you shouldn't have." Hiding a grimace, she took the bloody bag and held it at arm's length. "If I may ask, what is it?"

"R-rabbits. For d-dinner."

He looked so painfully proud of himself, squaring his shoulders for once, that she lacked the heart to refuse his gift. For all his dearth of social skills, Fabian Snow was a crack shot and an avid huntsman. It was the third time this fortnight that he had brought her wild game for the table, once a brace of pheasants, then a pair of mallard ducks. His gifts disconcerted her not because she was squeamish but because he acted as eager for praise as a dog laying its kill before an adored owner.

Catherine didn't know how to discourage Fabian's bashful admiration without hurting him. "This is very helpful of you," she said. "Perhaps Cook can make a pie and you can join us for dinner. I'll take this 'round to the kitchen straightaway."

"M-Mrs. Snow?"

His squeaky voice stopped her. "Yes?"

"Y-you shouldn't be c-climbing that ladder. Or washing windows l-like a servant."

"It's only for today. And I'm nearly finished."

"But Aunt L-Lorena w-will be angry." He cocked his head, his lank hair blowing in the cold breeze. "Is that her c-carriage now?"

Distant hoofbeats drummed on the drive. But the long row of oaks shielded the bend in the road.

"I don't hear carriage wheels," Catherine said. "But thank you for expressing concern. You're most thoughtful."

His cheeks flushed crimson. He slowly backed away, bobbing his head and clutching the gun, the barrel pointed at her. "Er . . . goodbye then."

A horseman rode into view. He shaded his eyes and peered toward them. Abruptly the canter of hoofbeats accelerated into a gallop. At breakneck speed, man and horse came thundering down the drive.

Catherine clutched the sack to her drab mourning gown. Mane and tail flying, the black horse plunged across the lawn, clods of earth spraying. The rider bent low as if he were on a racetrack.

He meant to run them down!

Gasping, she jumped backward. Fabian Snow swung around and uttered a squawk of fright. The horse rushed into the gap separating him and Catherine.

The rider leaped from the saddle and down onto Fabian, knocking the rifle out of his hand. Both men went tumbling over and over on the lawn. The riderless horse ran to the edge of the trees and then slowed, prancing in a circle. Fabian's dog, Lady, barked furiously at the newcomer.

The sack of rabbits dropped from Catherine's nerveless fingers. Paralyzed by disbelief, she watched the stranger shove Fabian face down on the muddy lawn, then yank his arm behind his back. Who was this madman?

She certainly intended to find out.

She darted forward and snatched up the rifle. Clutching the gun and willing her hands not to shake, she advanced on the two men. Fabian moaned pitifully.

"Move away," she ordered.

Without turning his dark head, the stranger crouched beside Fabian and held him in an armlock. "Not until I subdue this bastard."

"I-I . . . *owww!*" Fabian sputtered.

The plaintive cry roused Catherine to fury. Though she had never held a gun before, she sighted down the barrel and caressed the trigger. "Release him this instant or I'll shoot."

The man lifted his head. He took a long hard look at her, and she stared in return, unwilling to let him see the shock of recognition that reverberated inside her.

His black hair in rakish disarray, his bone structure boldly masculine, he had a face of startling distinction. His fierce glower changed to an expression of surprise. His eyes widened, their color the gray of ashes after a fire has gone out. Yet there was nothing lifeless about him. Ablaze with intensity, his gaze burned into her.

Despite the brisk air, her skin felt overly warm. Her legs threatened to melt like tapers of hot wax. It couldn't be him. But that satanically handsome face was branded into her memory. For as long as she lived, she would never forget him—or the tragic chain of events set into motion by his act of depravity.

Burke Grisham. The Earl of Thornwald.

"It's you," he said in an odd, gutteral tone. "God help me, it's you."

"Pardon?"

The earl continued to stare at her, his tanned face gone pale. His expression softened and his lips parted slightly. His eyes drank her in as if she were a person who mattered to him.

Catherine shook off the fancy. They had never met. On the one occasion she had seen Lord Thornwald from a distance, he had been too caught up in his own debauchery to notice her.

Why had he come here?

A muffled groan wafted from Fabian Snow, who lay sprawled in the wet grass.

"Move!" she told the earl again, gesturing with the rifle.

He blinked. The keen absorption on his face turned to stony blankness. After a moment's hesitation, he released Fabian, who sat up, gingerly rubbing his arm.

Mud coated the front of Fabian's clothing. His hair

stood out in wild blond spikes. Quickly he scooted back from his attacker. "W-why'd you h-hit me?"

Burke Grisham rose to his considerable height. His plum-hued riding coat and fawn breeches were immaculate, with only a few clods of dirt marring his shiny black top boots. As he straightened his cravat, he epitomized the wicked elegance of a London rake. "I should think that's obvious," he said. "You were threatening her with your gun."

"He most certainly was not!" Catherine objected, lowering the rifle. "Where did you get such a lack-witted notion?"

"I saw him point the weapon at you."

She subdued a fleeting thrill that the earl would ride to her rescue like a knight in shining armor. "From all the way down the drive, you drew this conclusion? Then without stopping to ascertain the truth, you attacked an innocent man?"

"I believed you to be in mortal danger—"

"You might have asked questions first."

"And see you killed?"

"The situation was entirely innocent. I wasn't in need of a savior. This is hardly a battleground, sir."

A dull red flush crept from beneath his starched collar. He rubbed his cheek and a crooked grin lent him a certain charm. "So it seems. Apparently I made a foolish blunder. Please accept my sincerest apologies."

She took pleasure in seeing him brought low. He deserved far worse for bullying Fabian. And for what he had done to Alfred. "Kindly direct your regrets to Mr. Snow. He owns this normally peaceful estate."

Lord Thornwald turned to Fabian and bowed. "Do forgive me."

Fabian scrambled to his feet. He brushed at the mud and only succeeded in smearing the mess over his baggy tweed suit. "Y-yes, of course."

"You'll want to clean up," Catherine said quietly, stepping to Fabian's side. "I shall deal with our visitor."

Hands grimy, he took the gun from her. "Are you q-quite certain?"

She nodded. "Yes. Go on home now."

He hunched his shoulders and trotted off with the dog at his heels, crossing the lawn and disappearing into the woods.

"I thought you said he owned this place."

Catherine turned to find the earl devouring her with alert, hungry eyes. A fluttery warmth took wing inside her, a sensation that appalled her. Curtly she replied, "He does."

"Then where is he going?"

"He lives in the dower house." Upon Alfred's death last year, his cousin had inherited the entailed estate. Fabian had voluntarily given up residence in the manor house rather than evict Lorena, her daughters, and Catherine. But she didn't owe this man any explanations. "Now that we've settled that, you can be on your way."

"But I came to see you, Catherine Snow."

He spoke her name with such confident familiarity that she wondered if he *had* noticed her peering at him all those years ago. The memory brought a sickening roll of nausea to her stomach.

She groped beneath her shawl and touched the delicate oval at her throat, warm from her skin. The locket. Of course, that explained why he'd recognized her. Alfred must have showed the earl her miniature.

"You claim to know me," she said coldly, "yet we have never met."

"Quite regrettably true." All of a sudden, the earl stepped closer and yanked the servant's cap from her head. Her hair came half undone with several tortoiseshell pins popping loose and tendrils spilling around her shoulders. He fingered one glossy brownish-black curl.

His unorthodox action stunned her momentarily. Did he treat all women with such callous familiarity? Yes, she had seen as much for herself.

She snatched back the cap. "You're a rude, arrogant, and insufferable man. I must ask you to leave."

"I shan't leave. Not until I find out *why* . . ." His voice deepened, enriched by mystery.

"Upon my word. State your business and be gone."

"First," he said, "allow me to introduce myself."

The sullen clouds parted. A sunbeam streaked down from the heavens to bathe him in golden light. All of a sudden his dark, wind-blown hair shimmered with life. Tiny green sparks glowed in his gray eyes. The forceful angles of his face took on a striking male beauty, the luster of a bronzed hero.

"The name is Grisham," he said. "Burke Grisham."

Any feeble hope that she might have been mistaken died a quick death. "The notorious Earl of Thornwald."

"At your service, ma'am."

He reached into his breast pocket and handed her his visiting card from a slim gold case. Anger and aversion swelling inside her, she stared down at his engraved name.

Dear God. She had imagined this moment a hundred times while lying alone in her bed and watching the play of shadows on the ceiling. She had savored the idea of heaping contempt on this scoundrel, then consigning him to the sewer where he belonged.

But now her mouth went dry. The oft-rehearsed lines fled her mind. She could only manage to say, "You were at Waterloo. When my husband died."

The ray of sunlight vanished, robbing Burke Grisham of that superhuman brilliance. He lowered his eyes, as if peering at painfully private memories. "Yes."

Wrath formed a great clot in her throat. She threw his card down into the mud and ground her heel into it. Then she snatched up the sack of dead rabbits and stalked toward the house.

Footsteps scraped on the pebbled path. The earl caught her arm, his grip gentle yet masterful. "Catherine, wait. I've come halfway across England to speak to you. At least hear me out—"

With all her might she swung the sack and smacked his

midsection, leaving bloody dots on his plum-colored coat. "I am Mrs. Snow to you."

He cautiously held up his hands, palms out. "As you wish, Mrs. Snow. I came to offer my condolences—"

"You're rather tardy, then. All my husband's other *friends* managed to do so last year."

"I was . . . otherwise occupied. But I hope you'll invite me inside. Your mother-in-law would want you to do so."

He confused her with the gleam of a smile, the sincerity in his eyes. No wonder the ladies of London found him so charming. In spite of her fury, she heeded his words. Lorena would be furious if Catherine dismissed the scion of one of England's first families.

Even if his lordship was the blackguard who had corrupted Alfred. And then lured him to his death.

Coming from St. Martin's Paperbacks in December 1995.